an intrigue *of*

MUNDANE PROPORTION

oring *boring* boring **boring**

oring *boring* boring b

rg *boring* **boring** bo

HE WAS TRYING TO IMAGINE HER IN A WAY THAT WOULD BREAK HIS HEART. IMAGINE HER AS SHE WOULD WANT TO BE IMAGINED.

HER ROOM WAS LIKE AN AQUARIUM. COMBINED WITH A PLANETARIUM. SACRED AND OLD. ROYAL PURPLE WALLPAPER. DARK WOODEN FIXTURES. HARDWOOD FLOORS, FURRY FISH FLOATING JUST ABOVE THE SURFACE, DARTING UNDER THE BED SUDDENLY, DUSK BUNNIES SCATTERING IN THEIR WAKE. THAT SMELL FOUND ONLY ON THE TOPS OF MOUNTAINS, OR THE BOTTOM OF DRAWERS. MUSKY, RICH, OLD, NONDESCRIPT. LIKE THE WORLD WHEN IT WAS STILL YOUNG.

HORSE-FEATHER ~~DRAPES~~ DRAPERIES. *DRAPES IS THE VERB* THE EVENING WINDOW, AN IMPRESSIONISTIC MASTERPIECE. SPARKLING POINTS OF JEWELED LIGHT, HANGING JUST OUTSIDE, WAITING LIKE TIRED OLD VAMPIRES WAITING FOR THE DARK WINE OF NIGHT TO FALL. WATER FLOATING DOWN THROUGH THE STRATA OF SMOKE. RAINING. A DRESSER FULL OF HAND MIRRORS, DETACHED FROM THE 24 CONTINENTS, IVORY PILLBOXES, INTRICATE JEWELRY BOXES, HIDDEN DRAWERS, LATCHES. CONTAINING MINIATURE KEYS AND SILVER SPOONS STICKY WITH FORGOTTEN COUGH SYRUP. SLEEPING OPAL, TIGER SHELLS AND SKULLS SMOOTHED OVER FROM THE SEA

SHE RECLINED ON A MADE BED. HEIRLOOM QUILT, ANTIQUE SHAWL. GENERATIONS SPENT, LOCKED AWAY IN HOPE CHESTS, WAITING TO RECEIVE HER. DIAMOND GRAY EYES. BRIGHT ENOUGH TO LIGHT THE INSIDE OF A WHALE'S BELLY. SOME UNREAL CAVE BREEZE BRAIDING ITSELF INTO THE WAVY BLACK HAIR. GENTLY, INSISTENTLY BRUSHING IT OFF SMOOTH SKIN, AS THOUGH BY BLOWING LONG AND SLOW, THE STEEP DUNES OF FINE PORCELAIN CHEEKBONES WOULD SHIFT.

~~STRAWBERRIES~~ RIPENING IN HER HAIR. *TOO MESSY.*

GRAPES. PLANETARY COOL GRAPES, HANGING FROM THE CEILING IN VELVET BUNCHES OF MYSTERY, STAINING HER THOUGHTS DRUNK.

LITTLE BATS, SOFT AND BLURRY, FLICKERING UP TO PLUCK THE GRAPES FROM THEIR STEMS. TOOTHLESS MOUTHS GENTLY GRASPING EACH BOON. LAZY SPIRALS DRIFTING DOWN TO THE COMFORTER SHORE. OFFERINGS FOR THE WARM COIL OF HER PRESENCE, STILL AGAINST A MAVIS BACKDROP.

AND IF SHE WAVES THEM AWAY WITH A LIMP WRIST, THEN THE BATS RETURN THE BRUISED FRUIT TO THE VINE, BLACK TEARS STREAKING AND MATTING THEIR FUR AS THEY ROCKET TOWARDS THE HEAVENS.

AND SHE DOES WAVE THEM AWAY. BECAUSE SHE IS SINKING. TO THE TOP OF THE SKY, THE BOTTOM OF THE SEA. SLEEP, SOFT AND SWEET. CAREFUL NOW, THESE ARE

ng *boring* boring bo

g *boring* boring *bor*

boring *boring* **boring** bo

boring BORING boring boring **boring** boring BORING boring

written & designed by

Zach blague

featherproof

BOOKS

bleached whale design

This is a work of fiction. All names, characters, places, artworks, and incidents are the product of the author's imagination. Any resemblance to real events or persons, living or dead, is the product of *your* imagination.

Cover Photo: Mary Sledd
Author Photo: Anna Knott

Published by
***f*eatherproo*f* books**
Chicago, Illinois
www.featherproof.com

First Edition

10 9 8 7 6 5 4 3 2 1

Library of Congress Control Number: 2007909319

ISBN: 0-9771992-5-8
ISBN 13: 978-0-9771992-5-9

Printed in the United States of America

boring boring
boring boring
boring boring
boring

written & *designed* by

zach plague

featherproof BOOKS

bleachedwhale
design

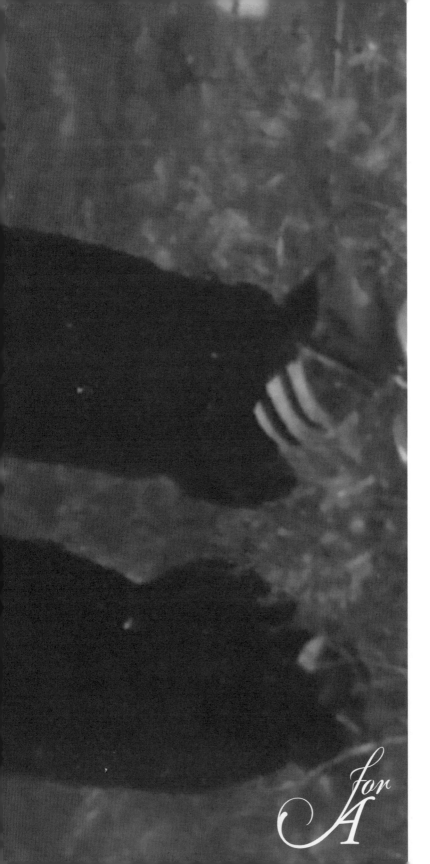

for
A

boring parts of this book have previously appeared in

BRUISER
review stories for the morning after

take the handle

SIX SENTENCES

The
Big Stupid
R E V I E W

THE2NDHAND

WEEKLY DISPATCH OF NEW WRITING

CHICAGO · BIRMINGHAM

thievesjargon

ASSEMBLAGE - BAGISM - HAPPENING

Review

ANNALEMMA

why vandalism?

ruined music

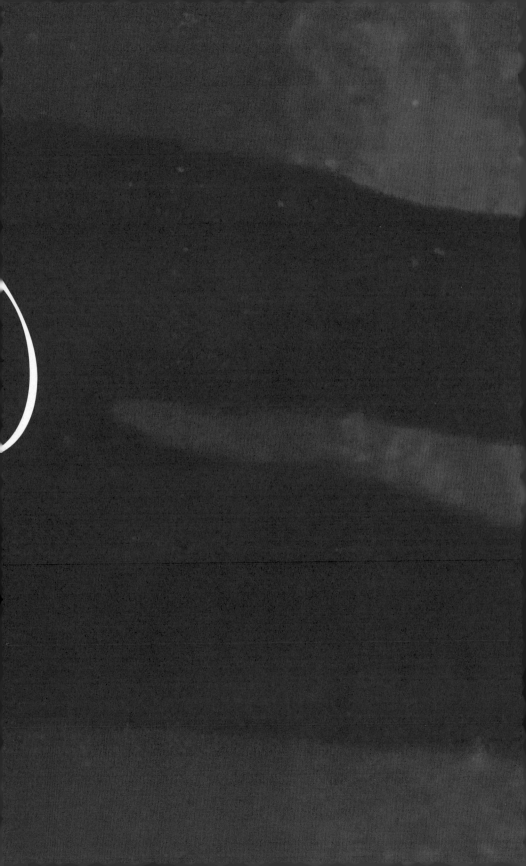

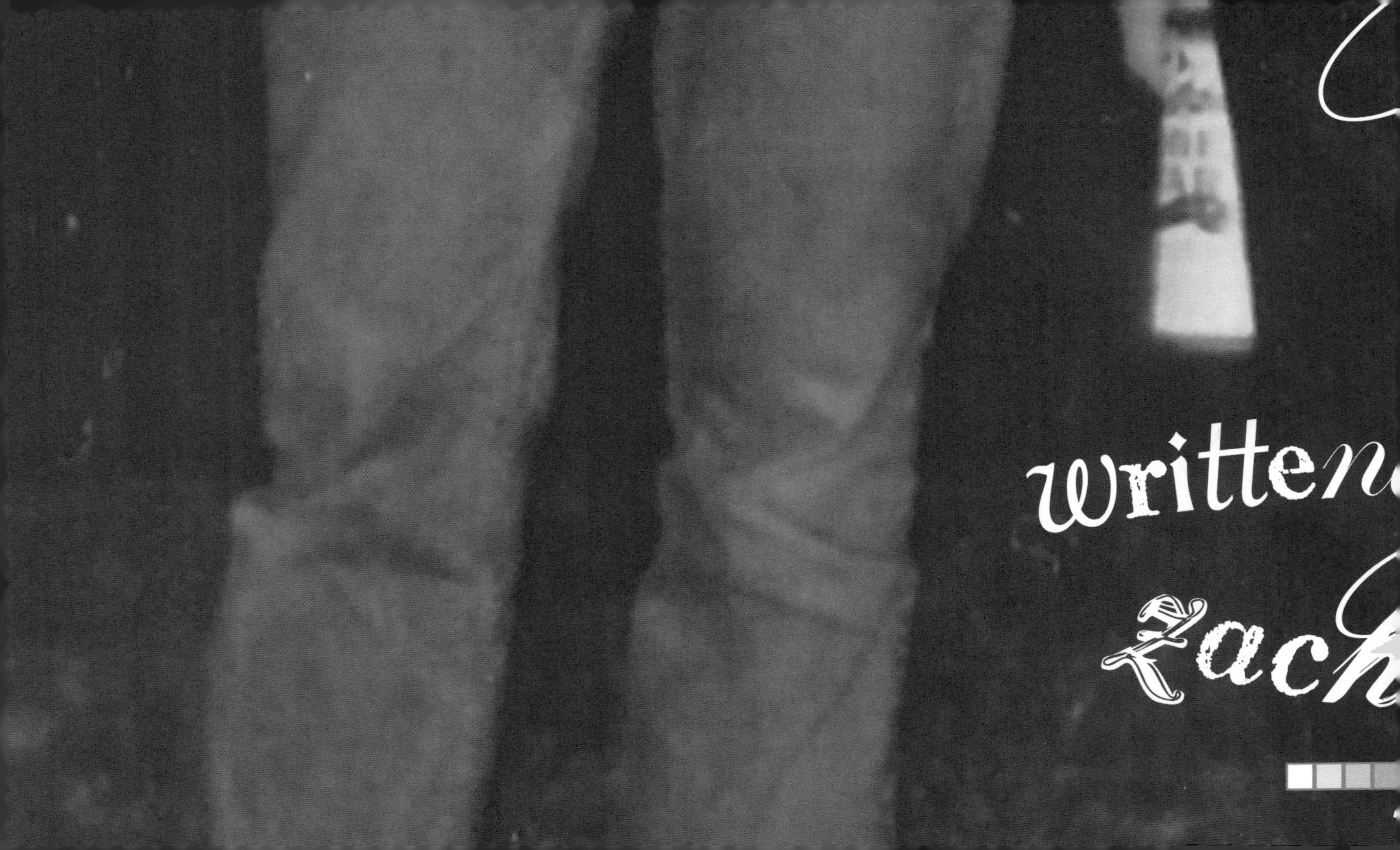
written
Zach

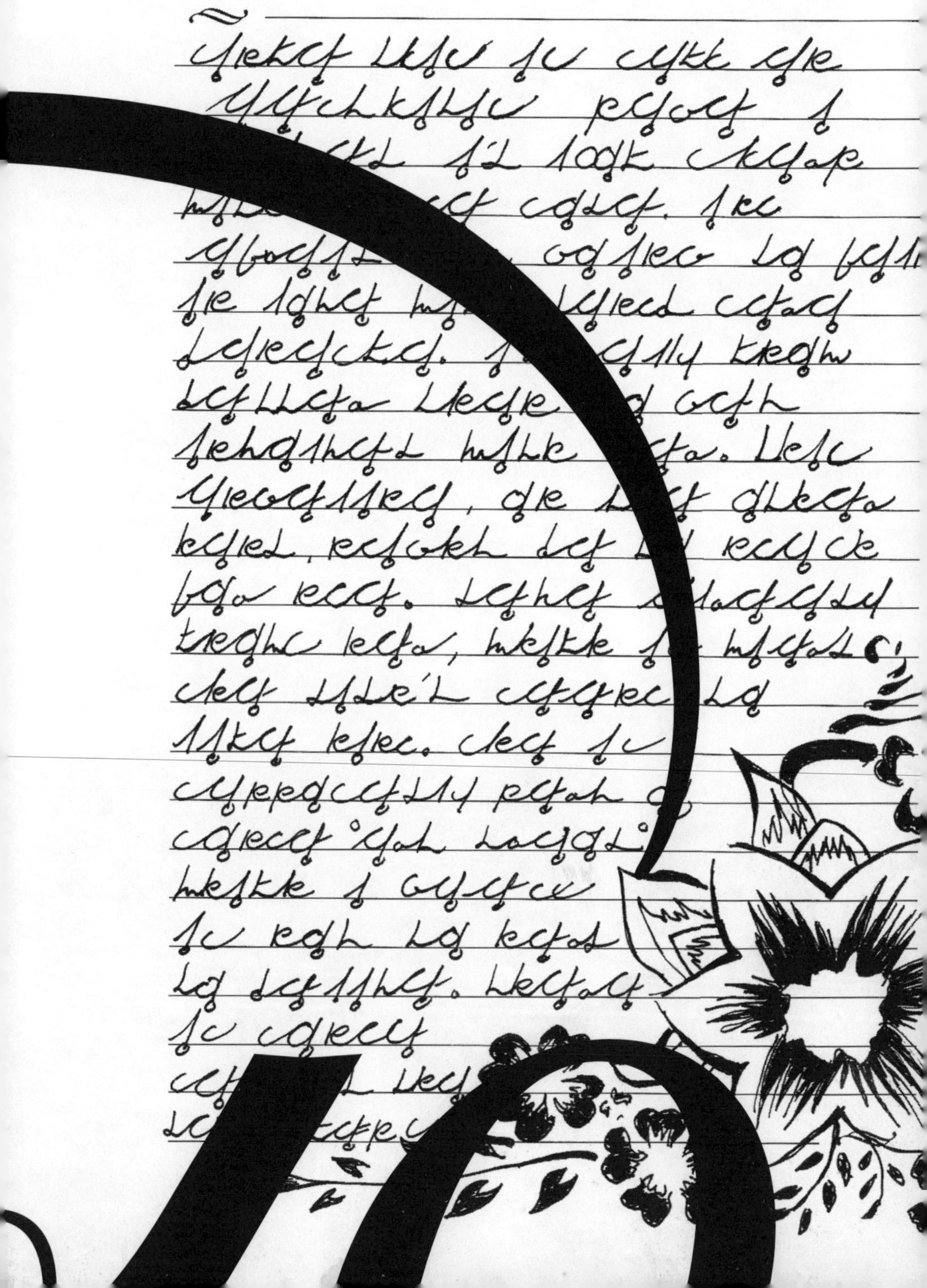

table *of* contents

The Art Kids

Ωllister, 19, *king of the scene*
His friends: Punk, 19, *a punk*

Adelaide, 19, *queen of the same*
Her friends: Theodora, Matilda, Zella, *all 19*

The Prep Kids

Graham, 19, in love with Miriam
Silas, 19, *in love with Miriam*
Miriam, 19, *daughter of Euphrates, in love with Graham*
Dolores, 19, *in love with Silas, friend to Miriam*

The Art Terrorists

Vance, Paul, Nick, Sebastian, Franc, Pete, all 19

The Adults

The Platypus, *Chair of the White Sodality*
Isadora, *his wife*
Euphrates, *father to Miriam, Dean of* The University of Fine Arts and Academia.

The Past

Is in the past.

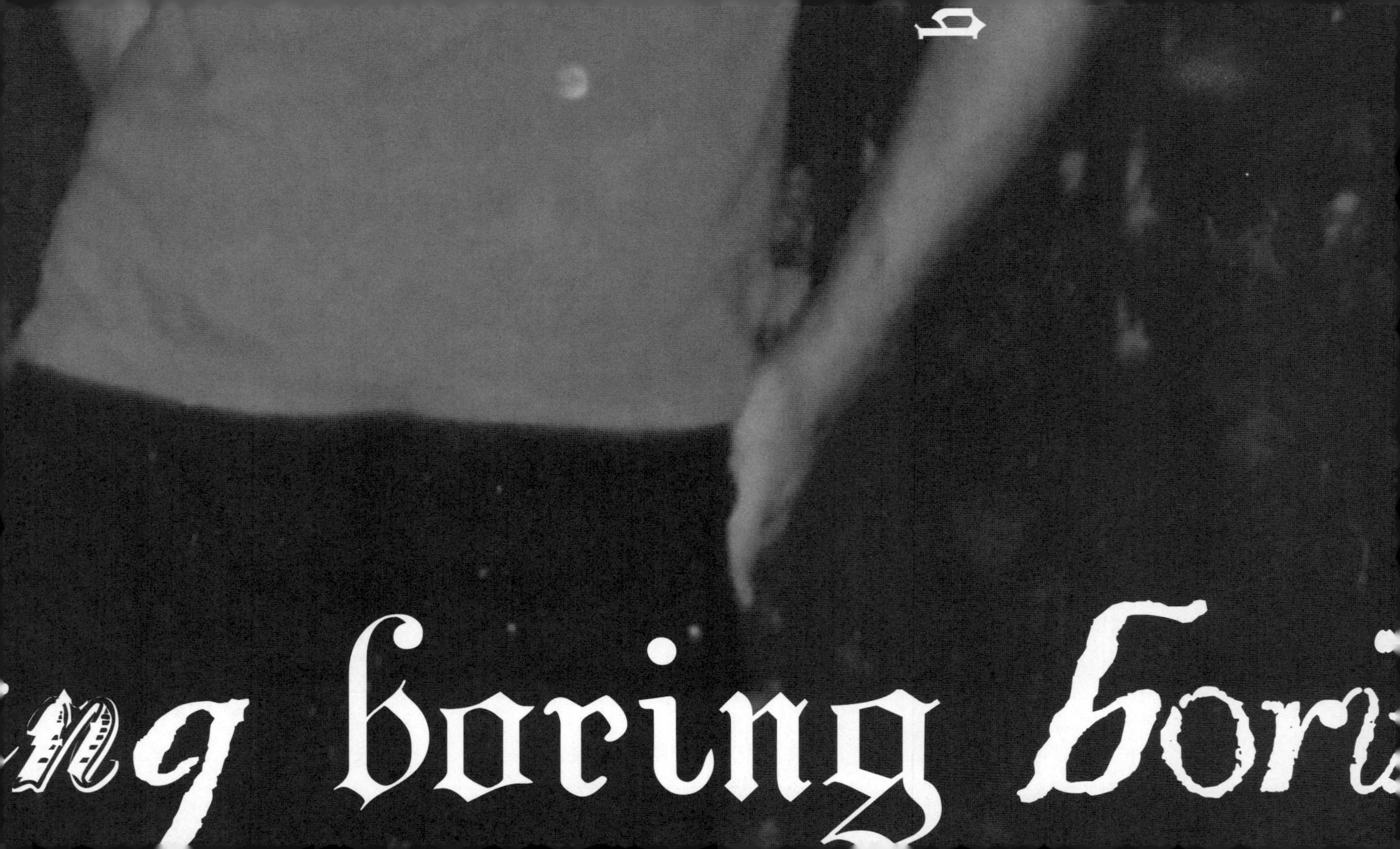
boring

boring boy

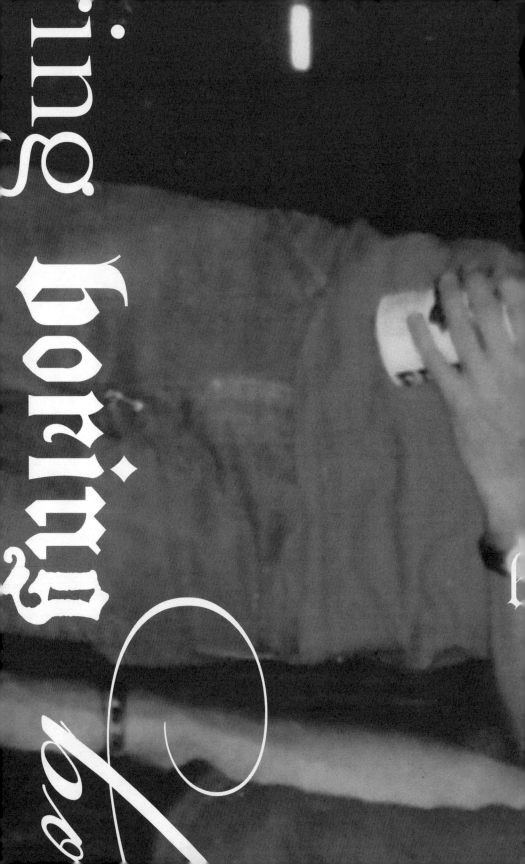

boring boring

ng

boring

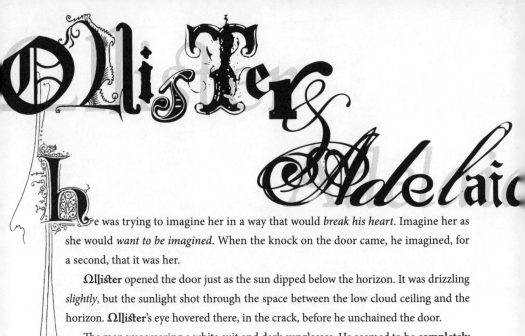

Ollister & Adelaide

He was trying to imagine her in a way that would *break his heart*. Imagine her as she would *want to be imagined*. When the knock on the door came, he imagined, for a second, that it was her.

Ollister opened the door just as the sun dipped below the horizon. It was drizzling *slightly*, but the sunlight shot through the space between the low cloud ceiling and the horizon. Ollister's eye hovered there, in the crack, before he unchained the door.

The man was wearing a white suit and dark sunglasses. He seemed to be **completely** dry despite the fact that the *only way* onto the porch was through the rain. He handed Ollister an envelope, also white and dry, turned *silently* and left.

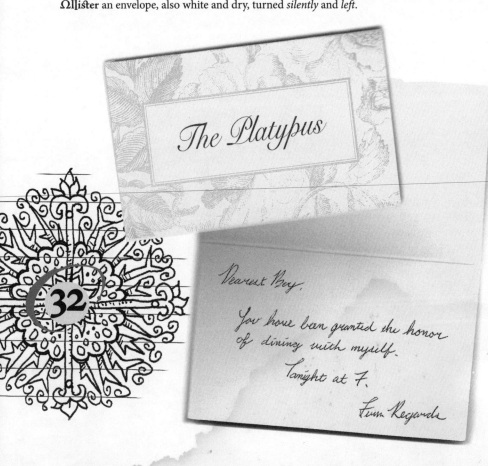

The Platypus

Dearest Boy,

You have been granted the honor of dining with myself.

Tonight at 7.

Firm Regards

32

Ωllister contemplated it for an hour. Made some phone calls, inspected his jawline in the mirror, and decided to go. It was an invitation from The Platypus himself. He hadn't seen the man in many years, but they knew *all about* each other.

The Platypus was the accepted **ruler** of the local art scene. He controlled the galleries, he controlled the artists, he controlled the patrons. He controlled **everyone**, except Ωllister, who had ideas of his own, ideas that made them *natural enemies*.

He was in a cavalier mood, having just booked two shows, and having ordered his henchman, PuNk, to **burn** someone's studio **to the ground**. So why not meet The Platypus face-to-face? The invitation was unexpected, certainly, but why couldn't they sit across from one another, at a table, like civilized men of leisure, and *converse*?

If he felt nervous, for his life or well-being, it didn't show on the outside, and he wasn't admitting it inside either. He took off his shirt and tie, and put on a T-shirt. He kept the dress slacks.

♃ ♉ ♌

Adelaide felt **nervous**, waiting at the table. It was a huge wooden slab, held at four corners by hunched suits of armor, each in the pose of Atlas shouldering the burdens of the world.

She had decided to respond to the sudden invitation, delivered to her door that evening. She knew Isadora was The Platypus's wife, and she had heard *plenty* about The Platypus. Though she couldn't think of anything specific about him at the moment. She pressed her finger into the **surprisingly sharp** prongs of one of the forks laid before her. Ωllister always used to say his name, as though he were some sort of *king* or *genius*, but she couldn't recall any details about what he was really like, or what he actually did.

The gilded candelabras slowly rotated, their flames **snapping** impatiently.

♃ ♉ ♌

After a number of white-clad servants had set the table with a *lavish* and medieval feast, Isadora appeared in the doorway to the grand dining hall, wearing a dress of **no color at all**.

"You aren't The Platypus." Ωllister. Sitting up **straight** now, in his chair.

"Neither, my boy, are you." She calmly sat down and gracefully swept her manicured hand over the table. "Eat."

There were boar heads, strips of dried anchovy, white pudding, roasted cranes, black trumpet mushrooms, black curry, smoked-lobster roll, pizza, fried peacocks, sablefish festooned with pineapple, quail egg, spiced pudding of pork, a small sautéed octopus, and rotten-looking fruit.

"Hmh," Ollister. "I would just love to get trapped in this fairy kingdom."

"Sarcasm is the lowest form of wit." Her eyes **pointed** at him.

"Then I suppose I'm at my wit's end." He stood. "Look, is he going to show or not? Because as much as I'm enjoying our date, cougars, such as yourself, really aren't my…"

"Look in the mirror." Isadora. Standing.

He looked to his left, at the giant mirror with a gilded gold frame. He'd glanced at it numerous times while the table was being set, to *inspect his cheekbones*. It was now a window, though it took a few blinks to figure that out. The room on the other side was an **exact replica** of the one he was in. The chair backs made of broadswords, the draperies hung **just so**, the table set in the same way.

The only *difference* was that where Isadora now stood was a man that could only be The Platypus. And seated across the long table from him, where Ollister had just been sitting, was Adelaide.

Adelaide!"

"She can't hear you. It's a one-way mirror. Of very thick glass." At her words it began to **darken** back to its original ɘɈɒɈꙅ ɘviɈɔɘ⌊ʇɘɿ.

He stared.

Her face was *early winter*, bathed in twilight. It was a clearing in a tangled forest canopy. Her choking labyrinth of **black strands**, all snake and false lead. Yet when one strand would arc up out of the *dark twisting sea*, it would catch the light and shift to cold, like some soft and lazy solar flare.

Her brows were small, and frayed at the ends. Her eyes were direct, piercing, curled like two small injured animals. They seemed to **suck in light** from around them. Earthen brown on eggshell white with a *sidereal glow*. Passing before them, one became immediately conscious of being observed, and a caricature, acting to please the critics bunkered in the balconies. The eyes made one feel watched. They *were* Adelaide.

Her nose was a snowy slope, which gave way to soft, thin lips. They had unusual vertical lines, which were raised rather than etched, lending them the cushioned feel of upholstery.

Lightly freckled, her skin was soft, but also taut. He remembered that her body felt **unnaturally hard**, like porcelain. Which made her hands and other appendages seem more delicate. Brittle. Her movements seemed *slow* and *lazy*, but precise. And executed with some old-world form of femininity, now lost. She smelled like *ox blood, cream rinse, pipe tobacco before being lit*, and *sleep*.

"Take me in there." Ollister.

"Relax. Sit."

34

The invitation had been from Isadora, so she was surprised when 𝕿𝖍𝖊 𝕻𝖑𝖆𝖙𝖞𝖕𝖚𝖘 arrived, bowing and formally introducing himself. The white-clad staff poured a noxious port, which she struggled to sip after breathing its fumes through 𝕿𝖍𝖊 𝕻𝖑𝖆𝖙𝖞𝖕𝖚𝖘's long and *inscrutable* toast.

"I've seen your art." 𝕿𝖍𝖊 𝕻𝖑𝖆𝖙𝖞𝖕𝖚𝖘. Pausing after some very boring small talk about the rain.

Adelaide tried to *force* the corners of her mouth upwards into a smile. She didn't like the way he was looking at her. She touched the **fork prongs** to her fingertips again, beneath the table.

"And I'd like to ask you to participate in this year's **White Ball**."

She was shocked. Her shows had been getting more attention lately, but that was the biggest event of the year. Those artists were *famous*.

"I'd… I'd love to…"

"Wonderful." 𝕿𝖍𝖊 𝕻𝖑𝖆𝖙𝖞𝖕𝖚𝖘. Raising his glass. "To a new friendship then."

She lifted her glass, a **bad taste** in the back of her throat.

Ωllister sat with his arms crossed. He refused to touch the food. He found food disgusting. Seeing others eat sickened him. Allowing others to see him eat made him feel like a **jackal**, edging out the rest of a hungry pack. Eating alone made him feel like a craven miser. So he didn't eat.

Isadora *drummed her fingers* on the thick slab of wood and waited for him to respond to her proposal.

"So, my friends often do me favors." 𝕿𝖍𝖊 𝕻𝖑𝖆𝖙𝖞𝖕𝖚𝖘. Tapping his fork on a cleaned plate. "That's how this little world goes round, I'm sure you're old enough to be aware of that?"

Adelaide raised an eyebrow. So he **wanted** something.

"Your friend Ωllister. I'm curious about him."

She waited. His mouth was fixed in a **false grin**.

"You know him?"

"We've grown apart."

"Yeah, I don't really see him much anymore myself." She shrugged her shoulders in apology.

"But you could."

"Yeah, I guess… I mean, he's not that hard to find. Why don't you go spy on him or something?"

"That I can do." The Platypus *flipped* his wrist to the right, and the mirror mounted on the opposite wall changed into another dining scene. Adelaide stared, confused.

She could see that it was some sort of **duplicate room**, with Ollister and Isadora staring at each other. It looked as though they'd just been in a fight. Suddenly Ollister turned and looked her right in the eye. She *jumped*.

"Don't worry. They can't see us. It's a one-way mirror." Adelaide felt sad, seeing him there like that. Handsome and stubborn. It looked like he wasn't eating. "So, my dear, I can look all I want. But what I need is to be inside his brain. And that's a place I have a feeling you can get. Am I right?"

She *shrugged*.

"Where are the **gray papers**, Adelaide?"

"I don't know what you're talking about."

"No? Is this something you recognize?" A small, weather-worn, **gray book** was suddenly in The Platypus's right hand.

"How did you…" Adelaide.

"Seems like you do have some idea of what I'm talking about. This one is blank." He opened it, and thumbed the white pages. "You don't have one filled with Ollister's hand, do you, my dear?"

She **did**. Her face flushed. Adelaide could barely hear what The Platypus was saying. Ollister kept *looking* at her, through the mirror. She felt watched, and guilty. In spite of the fact that he couldn't see her. She knew he was only checking his face in the mirror. His **arrogance** had never abated. She stared back, hardly breathing.

Ollister's face was a slippery slope. It was a walk through the backwoods alone, **at night**. It was the prow of a rich and merciless pirate ship. It was in shadow. More than any of this though, it was *surprising*.

She always noticed how everyone always noticed him. They marked him, remembered him. Surprising because it was one of those faces that looked different on different occasions. Like something had changed that was *impossible* to put a finger on. A new haircut maybe, a nose broken and reset. But it wasn't in the details, which, on closer inspection, never changed. It was in the face. It seemed the subtle morphing was *purposeful*.

However *ephemeral* the mood of the face, some things remained constant. It was long and thin. The cheekbones were **sharp**, the chin **strong**, the forehead **high and smooth** like a crystal ball. The bone structure blueprinted dignity and breeding. The brows were well groomed, and moved independently of one another. His eyes were ɘvitɔɘꞁɟɘɿ.

In looking at them, one could only feel them looking back and no additional information could be gleaned about their color, shape, size, or expression.

The nose was long and *perfect*. The lips were terse and precise. They shaped the most obscure and ancient lexicons of multiple languages, accents, and dialects effortlessly and with **almost no movement**.

It was anachronistic, perhaps slightly *otherworldly*. **It was a face she had loved.**

She couldn't stop staring. He had occupied her thoughts for so long.

"Ollister has them. Ollister has the **gray papers**." She finally turned back to The Platypus. She saw no other choice than to **lie**. He frowned.

♀ 𝕬 ♂

As the mirrored glass turned to smoke, Ollister had just caught a *glimpse* of the **gray book** in The Platypus's hand. At first he thought *Adelaide* had given him the **gray papers**. Which made him angry. But then he realized that she never would have done that – The Platypus must've **taken** them. And that made him livid.

He stood up. "This is fucked." It was one thing to fuck with him. But whatever The Platypus was doing or saying to *Adelaide* in the next room, he **could not tolerate**. The glimpse of the book had ignited him.

"Tell The Platypus he is fucked." Ollister. Fighting a loss of composure.

He thought of picking up a candlestick and hurling it through the mirror, but that seemed *dramatic*. He only ever seemed able to think of these things, and never act them out. Instead, he just walked out, lips pressed tight, Isadora's gaze on the back of his head.

♀ 𝕬 ♂

"Well, since you know where to find him, you'll take this blank one, and bring me back the real thing. I'll see you soon, my dear." The Platypus. Pushing his chair back from the table. Suddenly two men in white suits grabbed her upper arms forcefully. She hadn't even heard them behind her. One shoved the blank **gray book** in her hand.

"Ouch." *Adelaide*. Quietly, as they pressed her out of the room.

The Platyp...

Dearest Adelaide,

Looking forward to
your delivery.

Finn Rigard...

Adelaide

SHE WAS IN HER PAJAMAS. The rain *slathered gray* against the windows and tiptoed around the perimeter of the house, as if searching for a vulnerable point for forced entry. This day had been born **sans potential**.

She tried to wrestle her cat, Action, onto her lap, its claws *splaying out* like pitchforks raised from an angry little mob, **vicious** and **unwarranted**.

After dinner with 𝔗𝔥𝔢 𝔓latypus, she had been unable to get the image of Ωllister looking at her through the mirror out of her head. Had he *orchestrated* the entire thing? Were the two of them *playing* with her? Should she feel bad for sending the White Sodality after Ωllister? This **had** to come to an end. Maybe that should be the last look, she told herself. It was time to let go. She **couldn't** become involved with him again. Not even to give him up to 𝔗𝔥𝔢 𝔓latypus. Not even to get into the WHITE BALL.

Her **heart** felt like a dead starling, *cold* and *weightless*. It was an origami model of a **heart**.

She had found a thank you card, in a dry white envelope, taped to her door when she woke up.

Upon seeing it she became *frightened*. But then a plan occurred to her: she could throw 𝔗𝔥𝔢 𝔓latypus and the White Sodality off her and Ωllister's trail, by sending them after someone **much harder** to catch. She wrote "PuNk has the **gray papers**." on the back of the card, and taped it up where she had found it. It was still hanging there now.

Action had chosen her own place to curl and nap. Her face tucked inside the great pocket of **warmth** that a pelt provides. It would be nice to sleep like that, face tucked away, *turned inside*.

She wondered what time it was.

Ollister

His eyes slit open, *betraying sleep*. The gray
wash canceling all of the colors, erasing shadows,
making the world **dull** and **still**.

His movements were *underwater*. He watched, disinterested, as his hands made
him a cup of coffee. They gripped its warmth, not unlike the warmth just abandoned in
his bed, now **empty**. The phone rang, he answered. There was no one there. Shuffling
back and forth on the porch, half-dressed. The air was wet and stagnant. Some hipsters
on their bikes trailed through the drizzle.

He'd *tried* to go to a party last night. He thought it was going to be OK. Some
friends told him they were going, but when he showed up, there was **no one there**.
Save the girl who opened the door. The hostess. She was heavily made up and heavyset.
She wore a ball gown and a boa. The house was readied for a party, but dead empty.
She offered something to drink and beckoned him into the kitchen, but the situation
had already crossed his awkwardness threshold. He *certainly* didn't come to a party
to *talk*. Much less tête-à-tête with a garish clown. He made up some **boring boring**
about having to go home and check his messages, an unusually *ungraceful* lie, but he
was flatfooted. After closing the door, he found he was facing PuNk.

"You don't want to go in there."

PuNk, never having known Ollister to be anything but a **serious person**, took this
to heart. Wordlessly, he turned around and went back to unlock his bike.

Ollister sat outside for awhile after that. This was within the realm of the possible,
he thought. To throw a party that *never got started*. People arrived one by one, and each
seeing there was no one else there, promptly left; thus a party never accumulated. Or
maybe the girl just had no friends.

He walked to the **SNOOTY FOX** and proceeded to get **exceedingly inebriated**.

It had been a long time, but he thought of *Adelaide* everyday. He had been collecting
thoughts that belonged in the gray papers. **He wanted them back.** Whatever The
Platypus was trying to do with them, he could *not let happen*. He was using them to
manipulate her. It was time to make The Platypus **pay**.

Punk

Punk lay on the floor. *Waking*, it was the first thing he could feel. Carpet. Musky. He didn't know **where he was**. Some friend's apartment? If he had gone home with a *girl*, he would be in a *bed*. If it had been *Franc*, he would be on a *couch*. It was wide open then, his **location**. He was face down, and pulling his eyelids apart afforded him a view of the carpet and the leg of some abstract chunk of furniture, maybe a coffee table. He shut his eyes again.

He was trying to piece ***the night before*** together. It was all broken up, chunks of ice floating in an alcohol ocean. There was the **dragon**. That he remembered. Whatever party it was, they had rented one of those big, bouncy dragons that kids can get inside of and jump around.

The first party he had been to was **boring boring**. Some yupster-kids-cum-adults all standing in the kitchen talking about *cooking* and *whether or not to buy a house* on the East Side. He saw a girl he thought was hot, Matilda. Even though she was *obviously* on a **few handfuls** of pills, there was something motherly about her that excited him ***inexplicably***. He had tried to talk to her, but her eyes were like **clouds** and she didn't seem to be able to see. Frustrated, he stole a bottle of Scotch from the host's cabinet and rode on its *fiery wings* to a second party, the one with the dragon.

Bouncing in the dragon was **fun**. He had his shoes off. It was damp outside and a streetlamp, practically in these people's backyard, lit the scene *dramatically*. At first he was in the dragon with two Asian girls wearing **only their underwear**, their chests small and boyish.

Later, near the end of the party, after most of the people had left, and it had been raining for quite a while, he and Franc had *a go* at the dragon. They bounced in it spastically, **violently**, trying to pop it maybe. They discovered that by landing *simultaneously*, at a *certain angle*, they could make the whole thing *slide across the muddy ground* a few feet. This became the **thing to do**. And by their shouting and coordinated jumping the huge inflatable dragon, its head nodding sinister approval, slowly carried them across the backyard. Eventually, the dragon came belly up to the house, as if to **mate** with it. Having nowhere else to go momentarily destroyed the fun until the two gutter kids discovered that by jumping up they could catch a *fleeting glimpse* of what was in the window; one of the Asian girls being fucked in a wildly acrobatic way. This new **fun** was much **more fun** until, upside down on the bed, the girl opened her eyes and saw a dragon head, and two bobbing heads looking back at her.

Things get *fuzzy* here, but following was some **incident** starring a few largish gentlemen wearing white suits. Someone said they were looking for him, but that didn't make sense. A bunch of gutter punk kids had chased them off with baseball bats. He wasn't sure, but it might've involved the keg or the window-peeping. He was relatively positive no bats had been swung. Though his left knee felt **strange**.

He recalled ingesting marijuana that was being passed around in a circle of five or six fashion-plate UNI-ARTS girls in the backyard. He also could count *three* lines of coke on at least *two* different occasions. He had a vague recollection of spilling chili down his front, but he had *no idea* where he could've possibly gotten the hot dog.

He had tried to **scam out** with one of the Asian girls. To make up for the earlier rejection from MATILDA. They were in someone's bedroom, she was naked, and he was trying to convince her to bounce up and down on the bed, like she had done in the dragon, while he lay underneath, jacking off, and occasionally getting *stepped on*. She didn't seem to want to play that game and kept *weeping* and talking about her *daddy* in a shrill, confessional voice.

Somebody's band had played, or at least set up. Someone else was caught trying to light one of the trees in the backyard *on fire*, in the rain, no less. The cops probably came a few times, too, to lend the party legitimacy. He could recall nothing else.

He opened his dry mouth as if to ask a question, but instead rolled over. **Pain** shot through his left leg, turning his stomach over. He *winced* as the white ceiling above him *pulsed*. If he had broken his leg again he was going to *sue* that fucking dragon.

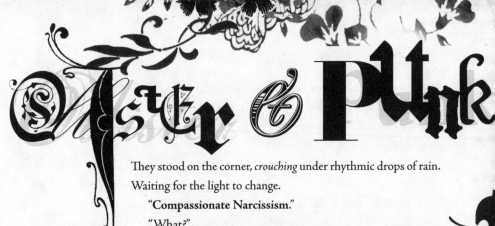

Mister & Punk

They stood on the corner, *crouching* under rhythmic drops of rain. Waiting for the light to change.

"**Compassionate Narcissism.**"

"What?"

"**Compassionate Narcissism.**"

PuNk shuffled his feet. "What's that supposed to mean?"

"It means I *forgive* you." Ωllister. Big insincere smile.

"For what?"

"For not being me."

PuNk's forehead creased. He squinted against the wind. "But I don't want to be you."

"If it were true, I would forgive you for that, too."

"Shut the fuck up, man, I don't need to hear any of this shit today." PuNk. Softly, with **seriousness**.

Ωllister stood like a patina'd statue in the downpour. It took the skies *thousands of years* to make solid stone droop, but Ωllister could be made into a softer, sopping version of himself in about ten minutes. A wet dog, *steaming* with purpose.

"Do you know that weird girl, Matilda?" PuNk.

"Yep. You're to stay away."

"Aw man, really? But she's hot. And… that's against my philosophy." PuNk. "Anarchy."

"Anarchy is not a philosophy."

"It's not just all about fucking shit up, man. It doesn't have to be chaos or whatever. Everybody is just, like, an individual. And you can do whatever you want. Even be nice or whatever. As long as, like, you're original, you know? An original individual."

"Everybody draws the anarchy symbol the same way." Ωllister. Using his eyes to *point* to the one stitched on PuNk's bag. "We need to create a little controlled chaos of our own. I've got some revenge to enact. We're going head-to-head with The Platypus. Mind-to-mind. You know Pete?"

PuNk nodded.

"He's in on it. He has *something* for you. Some **drugs**. I need you to go pick them up. Here's the address." He gingerly undid one of the many thousands of **safety pins** on PuNk's jacket and pinned the piece of paper to his front.

The light changed. Ωllister walked. PuNk **frowned**. ▬▬▬▬▬

Adelaide

She said she liked to think of the nighttime sky *in reverse*, as if the Earth were **enclosed** inside a *hard black cocoon*. Like an *exoskeleton*. With small holes, created perhaps by *meteorites* or maybe just *natural decay*. Like a **colander**. Holes revealing just a glimpse of the true sky beyond, *pure white light*. He told her that was **stupid**.

SPENT IN BED. A LIFE SPENT ON TOP OF A MOUNTAIN
IN A CABIN, LOOKING OUT FOR FIRES. A LIFE
SPENT ON A BEACH, AN ISLAND, A SUBMARINE.
A LIFE SPENT TEACHING THE SECRETS OF FENCING
TO YOUNG ITALIANS IN THE BASEMENT OF A HEALTH
CLUB IN FLORENCE. A LIFE SPENT IN A CAVE. A
LIFE SPENT BY THE POOL, BEHIND THE BAR,
CONSTRUCTING A TRANSCONTINENTAL FREEWAY.
A LIFE SPENT TOBACCO FARMING. A LIFE SPENT
IN THE HAY. A LIFE SPENT UNDERWATER WELDING
THE TRUSSES OF MAJOR AUTOMOBILE BRIDGES.

43

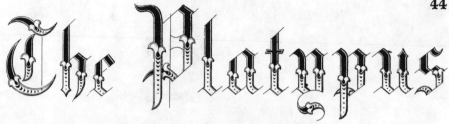

The Platypus

The Platypus sat in his armchair, in his study, stroking the stuffed osprey he kept *for that purpose*, looking out on the town (*See Appendix A. The Town*). Euphrates was *frantically* pacing in front of him. Little puffs of dust emerged as his feet padded back and forth across the ancient Oriental rug.

"Why don't you go away, Euphrates?" The Platypus. Not really asking for an answer.

"I think I will, it's just, you need… we need to decide how to deal with a few situations that have arisen."

"Hm." The Platypus picked at the osprey's **marble eyes**.

"Malet has finally decided to come out of the woodwork. You know his last auction, everything was over-estimated? Some by margins of $10,000? All because of this disappearance trick. All of a sudden he's not on the gallery scene anymore. It's rumored he's in Africa. A pygmy fetish or some such nonsense…"

"The child Ωllⅰſter. He's smart (*See Appendix C1. Ωllⅰſter at 16*). He has too much."

"…and his prices plummet. Now he's back. Will they return to previous levels or plummet even further? I'm of the mind to go change the prices in the book right now. But what should I change them to?"

"The Sodality wants him destroyed. Soon. He is a loose cannon. A variable that presents a risk. I have agreed to this. He cannot be allowed to continue in this manner. More and more of his 'projects,' set up with whatever puppet he chooses as 'artist,' are direct taunts, jeers, or joustings in the Sodality's direction."

"And what of Gerhardt? He failed us at the Biennale. The critics tore him apart like jackals. He was supposed to be curatorial director, instead he just sat, and smoked those awful long cigarettes of his, and the curators were allowed to make *their own decisions*. To exercise their *options*. It was a hellish nightmare."

"He should be reprimanded, don't you think? He can't be allowed to just go on smoking."

"And this boy, this usurper, has had his dirty little hands in cookie jars that he shouldn't have even seen. And if he thinks that I'm not well aware of everything that happens in this city, he's got another thing coming."

"And Stephen Kranmen, the interim chancellor, has appointed a new director to the art museum, Marta Kooling. She is driving the board batty. They just want the regular shows. As you know, there is no permanent collection, and she keeps turning up with all this contemporary lesbian garbage. I assure you there will be some seriously ruffled board members. You think they want conceptual art?"

"I must admit there is something in his more devious work that moves me. Stirs my heart from the dusty deathbed on which it was lain long ago. So few things bring me joy, nowadays. Nevertheless, neither emotion nor erection will stand in my way. What must be done will be done. I will have him. Him and that girl of his, *Adelaide*."

Euphrates stopped. "*Adelaide*? Oh, yes, let's get her. Her 'art school application' show? That threatened and mocked our finest institutions. My lawyers are fixing to make a blood bath out of that..."

"You will do no such thing. You will leave her alone."

Euphrates paced furiously, looking down, lips tight.

"She will bring him here. Bring him to me. Euphrates, once this boy is harnessed, there will be no more worries. We cannot risk being supplanted. If he could be convinced... Well, one way or the other he has to be neutralized. I will talk with him. We will talk. Euphrates, the girl told us that his minion has his plans, the gray papers. They are in a book. The boy is a punk, or some such thing. I want you to leave her alone. Find the punk, and bring me this book. It's important."

"A punk? Ok, I'll have him picked up. But can we deal with some of these other issues? Also, there's Mr. and Mrs. Kramer, who are upset because their foundation's grant was used to..."

"Euphrates." The Platypus. His voice rose as he did. "That is your one task."

"But..."

"I care about nothing else. Bring me the book."

"This weather's so nice, I just wanna... stick my dick in it." PuNk. **Small talk**.

PuNk was in some coke head's car. On Ωllister's **mission**. His destination was on the other side of town and he had needed a ride. This balding middle-aged man had asked him for drugs with such a *reasonable desperation* that he couldn't say no.

"It's raining."

"I know man, already wet... already wet..." PuNk fingered a white envelope he had found in his bag earlier that day. He had **no idea** how it could have gotten there, though he did spend last night in the squathouse, and fucked up things were *always* happening there. It looked like a fancy wedding invitation, but was all about somebody *messing up* the recipient if they didn't get some gray papers. PuNk kind of liked it.

The driver tapped impatiently on the steering wheel.

"Don't worry dude, we're almost at the coke factory." PuNk. Trying to sound cool. The man nodded.

There was **no factory**, and **no coke**. For 30 minutes PuNk had given the ailing business man *purposefully confusing* directions. They kept doubling back. PuNk said it was so he couldn't find his way back to the drug dealer's house, a **blindfold** precaution. In actuality he wasn't quite sure where he was going. He stared at the address still pinned to his jacket. 1024 1/2 W. STRAWDOG.

Finally, he spotted it on the left. A duplex, overgrown and broken down. He ordered his sweating chauffeur to go a few more blocks, a right here, a left there. In front of a **dismal** looking residence he shouted. "Stop!" The man violently kicked at the breaks. "Wait here."

PuNk got out and began to *run* in the opposite direction, back toward the house. He left the envelope in the sweating man's car. By the time he was ducking through the branches on the walkway to 1024 1/2 W. STRAWDOG, he was out of breath. And a little dizzy. For the thousandth time it occurred to him that he was most likely anemic.

The door was wide open. He knocked on the door frame and called out tentatively. His voice *echoed* inside the dark house. No answer. So he went in.

His step through the doorway met with a resounding *squish*. The floor was covered in about an inch of mud. PuNk was sickened by the green bog, and the **wet smell** that his footprint had shot up to his nostrils. Now he would have to bathe. Probably.

He slowly *squished* his way through the house. Water leaked from the sopping ceiling, and humid air pushed in from open windows. He felt **insane**.

Suddenly there was a *frenzied flapping* of wings and a piercing chirp. PuNk's left foot slipped out from under him and he sat down, **hard**, right in the muck. It was just a bird, and a small one at that. Now there was mud all over his pants, in his boots.

He stood up and sighed, his exhaled air harmonizing with the faint *HUM* of a television set, just now audible. Maybe there was someone here after all. He made his way through the **filth** toward the sounds, coalescing into voices.

In the main room a ***cavernous blackness*** was playing a spastic tug-of-war with the flicker of the television set. The windows were ~~blacked out~~. The changing colors spotlighted a figure, crouching as though to **attack** the glowing box. He was on the floor, in the **muck**. He was ***completely naked***, his hair long and muddy, full of leaves. He starred *intensely* at the television, chewing on a twig.

"Pete."

The kid jumped back, startled. He then smiled, as though to acknowledge PuNk's presence, and turned back to his television program. PuNk was unsure of what to do or say. Pete had always been *strange*. But, he hadn't been prepared for whatever kind of situation this was.

He walked around beside him to get a look at the television. It framed a car racing along a mountain road. He sat down behind Pete on the couch, taking off his *ruined shoes*. The **muck** was warm, actually comfortable. It felt nice when he curled his toes. He focused on the screen that had his naked friend so enraptured.

EEDING HABITS OF THE NORTH AMERICAN AUTO ARE QUITE REGULAR. AFTER TRAVERSED A CONSIDERABLE DISTANCE IT WILL STOP AT ONE OF MANY AL PETROL OASES. THERE IT WILL CONSUME AS MUCH PETROL AS IT DESIRES H A MOUTH, IF YOU WILL, IN THE REAR OF ITS BODY. MOST DOMESTIC AUTOS TROL, BUT THE LARGER RURAL LORRY PREFERS DIESEL. THIS MAMMOTH Y VARIETY CAN CONSUME MANY TIMES THE FOOD OF A NORMAL AUTO. IT S FUEL IN ITS BODY FOR ROUTINE MIGRATIONS ACROSS OPEN COUNTRY.

The Welsh baritone droned on, documentary style. Pete sat still, ***transfixed***.

"So, what's up man?" Silence. "How you been?"

PuNk felt like he was the only solid in a room full of gasses and liquids.

"Quite a set up, dude." No response. "I'm going to go find your john." PuNk got up and trudged into the hall. He noticed little plants, grass or weeds, growing at the edges of the walls, from the outlets.

At the end of the hallway he found the kitchen. Lush green foliage was growing out of the sink, the stove. Vines curled around the refrigerator. Water dripped down the walls. He *gulped* down the **hot, heavy air** of a greenhouse.

WATCH HERE AS THE CLEVER AUTO USES ITS WIPER-ANTENNAE, A
DEFENSE AGAINST THE RAIN. ITS HARD EXOSKELETON PROTECTS IT
INNARDS FROM MOISTURE, PREDATORS, OR OTHER ENVIRONMENTAL D

Walking into the bedroom he was struck by the *giant mess* of technology. All sorts of computer monitors had been stacked up, forming **new walls** inside the room, wires and circuit boards were everywhere. When he had last seen the kid, he was studying at UNI-ARTS, hitting the sciences hard, computer engineering, robotics, artificial intelligence. Also hitting the *drugs* hard. He supplied PuNK, as well as a good number of his friends, with a *wide variety* of illegal substances.

He was a smart kid. Aced all his classes, despite **constant struggle** with his instructors. PuNK was out of town on some hitchhiking misadventure when the *meltdown* happened. Apparently Pete had started holding his own "classes" after those of his instructors. He played *fast* and *furious* with fringe ideas: **String Theory, Psychodynamics, Hieroglyphics, Alchemy, Post-Modern Art**. He dressed like Akhenaton, the Egyptian Jesus according to one of his lectures. He recruited an *impressive* following among the usually apathetic student body. Mostly female freshmen.

Somehow he pilfered UNI-ARTS' cache of degrees, and started *passing them out* on the west lawn. This gave Dean Euphrates more than enough cause to **expel** him and have him **arrested** besides.

But Pete had gotten off with probation and community service and, last PuNK had heard, he was recovering in a new apartment on the East Side, working on a THERMODYNAMIC PERPETUAL MOTION MACHINE, or something like that. Not living like an ascetic monkey.

THE AUTO USUALLY RETURNS HOME TO SLEEP IN THE SAME DRIVEWAY OR C
SHELTER EACH NIGHT. IT RECEIVES ITS PRIMARY REST THERE BUT
KNOWN TO TAKE FREQUENT NAPS DURING THE DAY. THIS IS OFTEN DONE I
ENCAMPMENT LOTS WITH MANY OF ITS SPECIES NAPPING OR HIBERNATING

PuNK discovered the bathroom adjacent to the bedroom and *pushed* the door open, against the mud. An indescribably **foul** odor rose to meet him. His nostrils recoiled. He grabbed hold of them with his thumb and forefinger to steady himself, and stepped inside.

The bathtub was **blackened** and filled with **ash** and **burnt logs**. It certainly wasn't safe to light fires inside a wooden duplex, but he *supposed* that if it had to happen, the bathtub was the most **logical** place.

There was furniture disassembled in the corner. He picked up the toilet seat and immediately slammed it back down. **Bones**. Little skulls, tiny femurs. One glimpse was enough to tell him they were the leftovers of many small mammals, and also enough to *turn his stomach*.

Punk never minded a little binge and purge when he was piss drunk. Sometimes it was almost **fun** to throw up. He could drink more. But now he stifled the *volcanic urge* with all his strength.

He sloshed angrily out of the bathroom and back down the hall. He needed to get this *over with*. His **heart** was beating too quickly. The main room presented him with exactly the same tableau he had left a few moments ago.

"Pete, what the fuck man? I don't know what you think... Dude, Ωllister told me..."

"Braaawwkk." Pete barked at him. Loudly. He didn't want his show interrupted. Punk's anger quickly dissipated, then coalesced into **nervousness**. The slow monotony of the television narrator did not do much to soothe him.

ATING PATTERNS OF THE NORTH AMERICAN AUTO MAY SEEM STRANGE TO BUT IN FACT THEY ARE JUST UNUSUAL. WHEN IT IS AROUSED, ONE AUTO WILL NTO ANOTHER, PREFERABLY AT HIGH SPEED, AS TO CAUSE AS MUCH DAMAGE SSIBLE. THEN ONE, OR SOMETIMES BOTH AUTOS ARE MADE INTO SCRAP METAL IS THEN MELTED DOWN TO FORM NEW BABY CARS. THE MATING SEASON VARIES OLIDAYS AND LATE AT NIGHT ARE THE PREFERRED PROCREATION TIMES. THE MATING CALL OR DANCE OFTEN CONSISTS OF SEVERE SWERVING AND/OR YING OF SIGNALS AND SIGNS, WHICH THE URBAN AUTO HAS BEEN TRAINED TO OBEY.

Punk stood still for the rest of the program. He thought that if he didn't make it out of here, he might **never** see Matilda again. When the credits started rolling, he looked again at Pete, who was now holding a plastic bag in his teeth. Punk hadn't seen him move from his spot on the floor, all-fours. Pete was **staring** at him.

He approached very slowly, and *gingerly* plucked the bag from the naked boy's mouth. He was afraid he was going to get **bitten**.

"Careful with that stuff, Punk." Pete's voice was completely normal. And *unnerving*. He winked at Punk, his gaze fixed.

"Uh... OK." Punk turned and *ran*. He was still breathing hard when he hit the night air, caked in mud, plastic baggie full of a **strange drug** in his clenched fist.

Ollister

HE DIDN'T KNOW it was going to be such an **awfully stupid party.**

Ollister was *worried*. He hadn't heard from PuNk since he sent him to fetch Pete's **magic drug**. Franc also hadn't been heard from. Ollister had decided, as long as PuNk was in, he might as well recruit his friend Franc, the French thug. The guy wasn't very sharp, but he could provide **muscle**, if any was needed. But shortly after these arrangements were made, Franc *disappeared*. Word on the street was that he was **kidnapped** by THE WHITE SUITS. He needed information, so he came to listen to the gossip circles.

It wasn't an art party, but he was still *'in'* with the *'ins.'* The main **benefit** of this unspoken membership was some coke off the *courtesy tray* in the back bedroom. An assortment of pills. But somehow, tonight, the speed *wasn't enough*.

It had *rained* outside, and the dirt lawn was a mud pit. Everyone was inside, doing his or her **best** to grind the autumn muck into the threadbare carpeting. Ollister had been elbowing his way around talking to *this and that*. A room this full of people brought on a unique, *desperate* sort of **boredom** in him. He had already convinced two *mindless* hipsters that he was an actor, in town reading scripts for a new Generation-X daytime soap about *bestiality* and *snowmobiling*. They were more **fucked up** than he was, and the game quickly lost its novelty.

He found himself talking to some girl in a '60s mini-skirt, color coordinated to her plastic hoop earrings, lip gloss and apple-green hair. He had convinced her, two parties ago, that he was an aspiring movie star in town to read for a choice bit in a quirky indie film about the **lighter side** of heroin. He had been in a *decidedly* better mood then.

She had no information. He let his mind wander back to his *plot*. Tonight he was preoccupied with THE WHITE BALL. He had decided that this was the event where he should *make his move*. To strike at The Platypus in the **heart** of his den. He knew his old professor was after him. And the only way around it was to *strike first*. He tuned back to the dim-witted flirtations of the grating girl in front of him.

"And I just think, like, you know, it's too early for an '80s retro revival, you know?" As she spoke he would hum just under his breath, *soft* and *low*, but unmistakably imitative of her sing-songy voice. Once in a while it would get too loud and she would stop, mid-sentence, her mouth agape, as if she heard him say something. An inquisitive raise of his eyebrow would set her back on track.

Just as he was growing **weary** of his humming game, a new one occurred to him. What would be the *exact* force and angle his lips would have to assume to **propel an ice cube** through her left hoop earring?

He sucked some ammunition out of his empty tumbler and tried to *intuit* the physics necessary to create the desired arch.

It was a **masterful** shot. The ice hurtled through the dead center of the earring, *spackling* her face with only a minimal amount of spittle. Its downward trajectory planted it in the hair of a kid lying on the ground some ten feet behind her. A small crowd had gathered earlier in the evening to bear witness to his *uncanny ability* to projectile **vomit** on command. After filling various vessels offered for his autograph, he was spent, and still lying where he had collapsed.

A sharp sucking sound directed Ollister's attention back to the face in front of him. It turned a **bright red**, which rather complemented the pale green outfit. The impending outburst was preempted by a more forceful explosion from near the front door.

Punk had rammed his way into the room, **soaked** to the bone and **caked** in a thick crust of soil, which did not look unlike actual **cake.**

"Please! Help!" He screamed, *hysterical.* "Does anyone here know how to drive a backhoe?"

51

Adelaide

THE MORNING *wanted* her to stay in bed. She could feel the mattress and the dirty sheets sheath her against a **conspiracy of ache**. She hadn't had *that much* to drink the night before. It felt more like she had **overslept**. She rolled around in the bedclothes, on the periphery of sleep all morning. She nestled her head under her pillow and dug between the blankets. Today she would *not* think of Ωllister.

Soon she feared her muscles might atrophy. So she lifted herself up and out, carried like a cub in its mother's mouth.

The slippers. The hair tie. The toilet. The toothbrush. The shower. The lotions and potions. Back into the pajamas.

As she was blow-drying, the phone rang. She put the dryer down, *almost* into the full sink of water. (The authorities, after talking to friends and family, would not have ruled it accidental.) She rushed to her bedroom, *irritated*. Picked it up. There was **no one** on the other end.

The blow-dryer again. The coffee maker. The toaster. The fridge. The computer. Some important e-mails. RE: Velveteen Gallery. FWD: Art Garage Sale. RE: Your Framing Order. She didn't feel like thinking about *any of it*. She uncapped last night's diminished bottle of brandy and poured a **bit** into her morning coffee.

Adelaide had a reserve of spite for these lazy days. Even those ducking around in the **underground** couldn't escape the overarching American tics. The *collective neurosis*. This particular one: wasting time. There were *acute* pangs of **guilt** when she was unproductive. Hours applying nail polish and taking it right back off again. Afternoons spent *staring* at her walls, out the window, at her feet. All of these made her **furious**.

The drive that prodded her forward, also hindered. It was hard to relax. Have a cheap beer in the sun with her friends, curl up on the sofa with a novel. There was a miserly accountant pressed against his oak desk in the back of her mind, tabulating, keeping track of the stray minutes, *documenting* the time that couldn't be had again. Ollister *never* wasted any time. He always… She stopped her thought. She needed a distraction. And almost in answer to the idea itself, the phone rang. She picked it up.

"Yeah?"

"Hey dude! What's up?" Zella. She called girls 'dude.'

"Oh… nothing. Nothing much, how are you?" Adelaide poured another **healthy** shot into her coffee.

"Oh shit. You'll never guess who got kidnapped."

"Someone got kidnapped?"

"Yep, that exchange student, who hangs out with the gutter punks? French, is that his name?

"I don't know."

"Yeah, totally kidnapped. His friends think it was the F.B.I., or the ILLUMINATI, or some shit. A bunch of guys in white suits, they said. But those gutter kids are all high as fuck, paranoia, or whatever. It was probably just like, some immigration officer or something."

Adelaide **stared** out the window. The ground was wet and the sky was an innocent gray, as though rain was not its fault.

"I've gotta go Zella…"

"Call me soon, yeah?"

"Yeah. I will."

The receiver sank back into its cradle with a *sigh*. And then Adelaide did something she rarely did. Something that likely would require penance of some sort later on. Something that only ever made it **worse**.

She went back to bed.

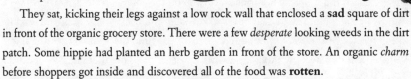

"You get Pete's stuff?"

"Uh… yup." PuNK. He was *manically* huffing and puffing on his bony hands trying to get them to **warm up**.

"Stop that."

They sat, kicking their legs against a low rock wall that enclosed a **sad** square of dirt in front of the organic grocery store. There were a few *desperate* looking weeds in the dirt patch. Some hippie had planted an herb garden in front of the store. An organic *charm* before shoppers got inside and discovered all of the food was **rotten**.

"I'm gonna go get a cup of coffee." PuNK.

Ollister looked across the street to the record store and the clothes shop, travel agency, coffee shop, noodle house. All of the GUIDE BOOKS let their readers in on *'the little secret'* of this *'hip pedestrian district.' 'Quirky and artsy,'* it was an *'out of the way'* bohemian mecca. Ollister wished he could get out of its way. The books didn't say how to **get out** of this area.

People, in *ridiculous* variety, poured out of shops and down the street. The crisp seasonal hustle and bustle juxtaposed sharply with the variety of **youth costumes** on display. The clouds overhead were getting lower by the hour. He watched a gaggle of 'English'-style punks across the street as they *affected* various slouches and harassed the occasional elderly passer-by. They **sucked** down cigarettes and **spat** on each other, their technicolor mohawks unfolding like peacock tails. Puffs of steam rose from their mouths like cartoon bubbles.

"What?" PuNK was back.

"Nothing."

"Motherfuck. It's cold…" PuNK gripped his recycled coffee cup for warmth. He brought it to his cracked lips but didn't drink.

"Now you're blowing on your coffee?" Ollister.

"To cool it down."

"Weren't you just blowing on your hands to warm them up?"

"Uh…"

"How do I trust someone who blows hot and cold with the same breath?"

"Whatever, man." And then, quickly directed at someone walking in front of them: "'Sup?" Ollister looked up. Some fat guy, *girdled* in tattoos, with a **disk** in his lip and ear holes large enough to stick a hand through. Even before all that he must have been *ugly*.

"You know him?" Ωllister.

"Yeah. Sort of." And laying a finger aside of his nose he punctuated this ambiguity with a **snot rocket**. The fat guy was all in black, with dreads. A *gutter punk*. Filth. Closer to PuNk's kith and kin than those fashion plates across the street. The *'newer,'* more *'hard-core'* punks hated the ones that looked like London in the '70s. Even though that's where it supposedly started. According to PuNk, they were *'trust-fund faggies'* and deserved to be **beat up** when the energy could be mustered. Ωllister didn't like to get involved in the punk world. It was *grotesque*, and held little interest. Like a minor train wreck.

"Why does he do that to his face?"

"I dunno." PuNk had once had his lobes stretched a little and a few rings in his face.

"Because he looks..." Ωllister began.

"Body modification is an art man, it..."

"I wouldn't use *that* word..."

"Well, whatever, it's rad, man. You know, like making a project out of your body. Pushing it to the limits and shit. Those motherfucks are crazy, man. Cutting, burning, you know... scarification. They've all got their tongues split, some of them their pricks..."

"Can you even do that?"

"Totally fucking serious. Surgically inserted horns into your forehead. Elf ears or Spock ears or whatever you want to call 'em. Tattoos and piercings aren't enough anymore man. You gotta get your lips sewn together..."

"That one actually sounds like it would be a good..."

"Ritual scarification, breathing fire, hanging from meat hooks. You know, by your piercings or whatever. It's spiritual..."

"Do any of them ever, say, cut an arm off? That would be rebellious."

"Shut up, man."

"Seriously... what is the next generation of kids going to do to rebel against their nipple-pierced parents? It's going to have to become more extreme. They're going to elongate their legs and fingers. Or maybe erase their faces..."

"Shut the fuck up, man."

"Don't tell me to shut up. Ever again. Did you get the stuff?" Ωllister.

"Yes. I already told you. Yes. You wouldn't believe the shit I went through to..."

"I don't care about that. Let's see it..."

"What? Right now, in the street?"

"Yep."

"But..."

"I don't give a fuck. Do you?"

"I guess not..." PuNk started digging through the **ratty** patch-covered messenger bag that accompanied him everywhere. He produced a small plastic sandwich bag filled with what looked like *wet leaves*, and unceremoniously presented it to Ωllister.

"That's it?"

"Mhmm."

Ωllister opened the bag and stuck his nose inside. It was surprisingly *pungent* and his face **recoiled**. Citrus. Lemons. It smelled of *lemons*.

"How are you supposed to smoke it when it's all wet?" Ωllister.

"I don't think you smoke it. It's the wetness that does the magic, man."

"Oh yeah?"

"Yeah. Just squeeze some of that juice into any old orifice. At least that's how I got it to work best for me."

"You tried it on yourself? For fuck's sake, PuNk..."

"Dude. No. I'm not stupid. I tested it on a dog first. And then me."

"What the fuck...?"

"My friend, he got this dog and..."

"All right, all right... so what happened to the dog?"

"I don't know. I never saw him again..."

"OK, then what fucking happened to you?"

"Man, it was intense..."

"Details. Not abstractions."

"I jacked off for like 24 hours straight. Like, until I fucking bled."

"Don't tell me that sort of thing. Ever. That's not the drug, that's your own disgusting habit."

PuNk launched another **snot rocket** toward the sidewalk, a *sneer* on his face.

"Well... as long as it significantly alters your consciousness or distorts reality..."

"Oh, it totally does that, man. I'm going to give some of it to that girl, Matilda, and then maybe..." PuNk.

"You absolutely will not. You are staying away from her. She is one of *Adelaide's* little friends. In any case, we are going to need it for THE WHITE BALL."

"Um... OK."

"This is serious, PuNk. Get that through the thick layer of filth that encrusts your skull. Your friend Franc? They kidnapped him."

"Who did?"

"The Platypus. He's after you."

"Why?"

"Because he's after me. He has the gray book."

"What's that?"

"It's, uh... my plans. Look, here's what you need to do. Listen to me. We need more people. To do things."

"Uh, Pete's pretty whacked out, man. He would do anything."

"Great. I'll talk to him. In the meantime, you know that kid Silas we saw at January's party? If you want to try this thing out on someone besides your perverted self, give it to him. As encouragement."

"Are you serious?"

"When was the last time you heard me make a joke?"

"Fuck." The bag rifling began again. For Ωllister, the temptation to peer inside was easily resisted. He *didn't* want to know. "I don't have anything to put it in." Shuffle. "Except this maybe." He dangled an identical plastic baggie high up in the air, this one full of pot.

"That'll work. Dump it out." Ωllister.

"But..."

"Just dump it out, Puɴk. It's only fucking pot."

"Dude..." Ωllister's face settled it. "Fine." Puɴk angrily started shaking the contents onto the ground in front of him. The green flakes lightly speckled his little hills of **snot**. "You're kinda pissing me off today, man..."

"Save it." Ωllister dropped a *dripping pinch* into the now empty baggie. He put his own baggie back into his coat pocket and walked off, into the ***mist*** that was just beginning to mature into ***precipitation***.

"Motherfuck." Puɴk. Remarked to the **empty space** now beside him. He pulled on his hood and lit a damp **cigarette**.

A prickish-looking guy in a **black turtleneck** was coming out of the organic grocery store with his recycled sack full of organic food.

"Spare change?" Puɴk called out. Just to say something. He didn't *need* it. Ωllister gave him more than enough money to support his various **vices**. But this, too, was an *old habit*.

"Change comes from within." The turtleneck quipped.

Puɴk promptly *kicked his ass.*

57

Adelaide

The breeze was *chilled* from the drops of water trickling through it, like a swamp cooler. Adelaide sat by the open window, where she could smell the air, and taste the rain.

She felt **guilty**. The French gutterpunk had been kidnapped *because* of what she told The Platypus. Had they actually **messed** with Punk, she wouldn't feel so bad, but she *hardly knew* this Franc kid. She didn't know what to do about it. **Maybe** she should tell Ollister that she had the gray papers. **Maybe** she should give them to The Platypus.

She had just gotten off the phone with her mother, who had been calling a couple of times a day for the past few weeks. Adelaide's irritation at this was **justified**. She found herself *longing* for those stretches when she wouldn't hear from her mother for months. This happened often enough, especially during the first years that Adelaide was away (*See Appendix C2. Adelaide at 14*). Then, the **neglect** made her feel *scared* and *alone*. Now she would give *anything* for a little peace and quiet.

She hadn't been able to *really* produce for years. Everything that she was giving galleries was **old**, or from school. She had *half-heartedly* started a few projects. Cookies in the shape of all 192 countries, interlocking into a giant, edible map. Paintings made from the ashes of other paintings that she had set on fire. A photographic essay about spayed dog genitalia. But none of it was **worth anything**. None of it *felt* like *her*.

When the time came, the decision was made that she would go to Uni-Arts, and board there, also. Her *mother's* decision. Which was quickly followed by her *mother's decision* to divorce her father and her *mother's decision* to move to a small, rural village in the Azores. Adelaide felt **abandoned**, and rightfully so. Her mother made it clear that she was on **her own**. Money came in small disbursements. Instructions, *cloaked as advice*, came even more randomly. Chaotic, nonsensical orders, *murmured* through the phone. She felt she had to follow them **to the letter**, or concoct clever enough ploys to make it appear as though she were.

She never had *created* like she did when Ollister was around. It wasn't that he gave her ideas, or feedback. Those were reserved for everyone else. For her art, thoughtful nods were the extent of it. But just his **presence**, *vibrating* and *pulsing* in the next room. She could feel it. It *electrified* her brain. Without this high frequency wavelength she felt **dull** and **stupid**, unable to create. Unable to make her fortune, her living, her **art**.

About a year ago, she went to her mother's bank, after the *typical* financial fight they had: *Adelaide*'s abject poverty and growing indebtedness to any number of parties in light of her mother's *disgusting* fortune and **gross misuse** thereof. So she had decided to close the account her mother had set up for her. As a small act of **protest**. But when she expressed this wish to the ponytailed, horse-faced teller the response she received was, "Which account? There are 24." *Adelaide* was able to smooth away what little *reaction* had escaped onto her face and ask for a printout. It was true. 23 identical accounts in her name that she was unaware of. Each containing **exactly** $24,000 dollars. She left the bank and the baffled teller. Her mother's money was a constant source of *suspicion*, and as a child she remembered late night phone calls from accountants and lawyers. **Serious as death**. She was to bring her mother the phone *immediately* if one of these wispy-voiced pedantic men should call. She knew all of their names by age 10. Saw them more often than her own father. The bank printout made it **clear** that *Adelaide*'s name and social security number were caught up in it as well. No wonder she was never allowed to do, *much less see*, her own taxes.

She was on the *verge* of true, viable commercial success. She could feel that. Her curriculum vitae was **stellar**. She had graduated early, with honors. Her galleries *loved* her. People were buying the art. *Rich people*. It was exciting. But her excitement was tinged with *foreboding*. If she made it, if she became famous now, Ωllister would **never** love her again. If he even did now. And without him, her ability as an artist was *quickly* ebbing. She would be caught on the **pedestal** with *nothing* to show for it.

She could empty the bank accounts and *leave town*. It would be **dangerous**. Her mother would disown her. No, her mother would **hunt her down**, send people after her. Find her out. The money was clearly not to be *messed with*. Someone's head would likely roll if her mother knew *Adelaide* possessed the knowledge at all. Besides, if she waited, all her mother's *cigarettes* and *martinis* would catch up to her, one day sneak up behind her and press the **tired air** out of her shriveling lungs. And it had been *intimated* more than once that *Adelaide* was heir to the throne. There was no one else, really, and, to be fair, *Adelaide* had learned a great deal about money and what should be done with it from her mother. *Training*, in a way.

She thumbed the **gray papers**. The book was damp with *humidity* and *palm sweat*. It felt like **all she had**. It could be her ticket into THE WHITE BALL, and The Platypus's good graces. But what would Ωllister do? It could destroy him, expose him. It could uplift, *validate* them both. But only **together**. If it was over, why should she have the **gray papers**? She didn't *want* the book anymore. She couldn't decide who to give it to. She *wanted* to throw it out of the window. Into the **rain**. Into the **night**.

WALKING through the city alone, he felt like a *sleek* and *shimmering* **titan**. The prow edge of his jaw jutted out, **splitting** his future before him like a *soft ocean*.

He had a **plan**. A big one. He would recruit some more local miscreants, and stage a complete *take-down* of THE WHITE BALL. The Platypus would be *ruined*, and Adelaide would come to him. These thoughts made him feel **incredible**.

The people around him were *miniatures*, the buildings a faded backdrop. With extended arms, and a **sharp press** of the palms horizontally he could part the sea of damp automobiles and tractor-trailers. Even so, he waited patiently at each crosswalk, inhaling the puissant fumes given off by objects *existing*. Following his own ontological thumbnail blueprint, *slipping* down the sidewalk.

His collar crisp. The subtlety of his movement *betraying nothing*. Dirty locks of hair catching the breeze and sending the gusts shooting off again in new **fucked-out** directions. Out of the corner of his eye he could just detect the *sparkle* in his eye. His thoughts felt *diamond round*.

He did not care now, and he probably never would, but he knew with *bright certainty* that his only destination was *doom*. His **plan** was doom. And *yet* he walked only faster. He knew that one day these great minutes of majesty would be used up, would *diminish* and flow back into the gutters of the city. He knew that only now, and never again, would his **singularity** and his **foresight** imbue him with such a mighty **prowess**.

His thoughts were interrupted by a grunge guy with long stringy hair and paint-splattered overalls, setting up shop on the sidewalk. There were two plastic tables that he was placing a stool behind when Ωllister happened to walk by.

"I'll take *that* one." Ωllister pointing at a random spot on the empty table.

The guy looked up from the stacks of dirty canvases and chuckled mindlessly. "The invisible one is my best."

Nobody understood his jokes, even the *less difficult* ones. At least the kid recognized it was supposed to be humorous. Ωllister knew that the real jokes were soon to be on the table.

But the absence now made him think of **her**. He *hated* the way his brain reached for connections, **pounced** on the subtlest movement.

The brain was the **thing** after all, *the internal*. He was interested in the external: success, money, finagling, socializing, conquering, arting, posing, schmoozing, looking hot. But interested in these as a *manifestation* of the **internal**.

The *shallowness* of others baffled him. He had been privy to more **private thoughts** and **hidden places** than he would've liked. And, almost *unfailingly*, they were blank and benign. All of these kids were **conformist** underneath.

When he scratched most surfaces he got childhood trauma, repressed frustration, naïve dreams of lottery numbers adding up to yachts, confused desperation, perceived wrongings. **Bland** baggage. Few *really* had more than one corridor, a few different doors to try. Very few. One had a plan.

Her brain. It was a **behemoth**. *In her mind a* **palace**, *on a wind-swept oft-flooded* **plain**. *Its towers gilded gold. Its spires sighing silver. Her kingdom, its subjects, its serfs and foot soldiers, whispering forgetfulness. The halls, strewn with rich tapestry weaving in and out of thoughts half-remembered. The* **trees**, *gravity defying, shading even the mountains. Birds of prey with whetted beaks surfing carelessly through the air, dodging the giant leaves. The* monstrosities *morphing into fineries, on her bed-stand intricate candle snuffers of fair fortune.*

Unlike Ωllisˇter, she always returned from her mind *undamaged*. The drawers could be **shut** and **locked**. The doors would *sigh* closed. The drawbridge would press its lips together and everything would be **finished**. Toys in a chest.

It made Ωllisˇter envious. Of the *control*. Of its *closing*. But more than that it made him **want her back**.

He found himself standing still in the street, not fifty yards from the artist's table, now set up, hawking his gawk. He looked back and the kid gave him a look that might have triggered embarrassment in some. Ωllisˇter briefly thought about walking back and buying all of the *awful* splashes just to put them in the trash can adjacent to the kid's appropriated bit of sidewalk. To make the tables empty again. **Clean.**

Adelaide

Matilda had a sack of *really good* pot. She **accidentally** found it in that secret hiding place of her brother's where interesting things could often **accidentally** be found.

If the day hadn't been so **boring boring**, *Adelaide* never would've smoked pot. She gave it up years ago, months ago. But it was a drizzly day so… *whatever*. It might make her stop **thinking**.

Matilda had driven them from her dorm to the *ThriftWhopper* very slowly. Dream pop ratcheted to an *embarrassing* volume. *Adelaide* sat in the front playing with a paperclip, bending it back and forth, *annoyed* that the wipers wouldn't **keep time** to the music. She felt **weird**.

The *ThriftWhopper* was a bust, as usual. *Adelaide* **cursed** at each garment as she pulled it from the rack. Finding fault in size, material, or general existence. Matilda tried to keep to the *other* side of the store.

While driving back, Matilda fondled her purchase. *Adelaide* gnawed on a paperclip and **eyed** her friend's treasure *dubiously*: a broken sno-cone maker with some cartoon puppies on it. Matilda would be remorseful about this object once *clarity* returned to her mind. But she still would **not** throw it away.

"Maddy, I did something bad."

"What?"

"It's nothing like that. I just have something."

"What is it?"

"A book, with some writing in it. A gutter punk kid got fucked with because of it. I have to give it back. A lot of people think it's some sort of plan or plot of Ωlliſter's, but it's not."

"Oh."

They drove through the *drizzle*, just south of Uni-Arts. Backpacked students stood outside waiting for the bus, or **smoking** in the rain. A group of boys stared at them from inside a muddy game of yard football. She watched Matilda shift gears.

Adelaide **stared** out the window wishing Matilda would say *something*.

Toward the end of their relationship, she had a **hard time** being around Ollister. In spite of her constant *desire* to be around him. Something was *flat*. He went through the motions, saying that he *loved her*, holding her hand, sitting with her, being with her, making her beautiful things.

But something was *flat*, the way that he looked at her, at everything around them, his eyes **matte**. The way that he would *recite* his feelings, as though they should be **taken for granted**, as though they had discussed the very thing only ten minutes prior, as though he were soothing a *child* about some *imagined danger*.

It wasn't as though she didn't **believe** him, or **believe** that he didn't **believe** himself. It was *subtler* than that, smaller. It was as though he had *fixed the thought* and allowed his mind to move onto other things.

Which became a problem for her, because she wasn't able to *feel* it. She couldn't feel his **heart**, even though she knew it was there. He acted like it was, but she needed to be able to feel it.

And this was the thing that had *dulled* it all, had *grayed* everything, because his **sweet** nothings started to wash over her like **plain** nothings and she was reluctant to return them, fearing for her own **heart**. This retracted state *vacillated* with one where she **desperately** threw herself out there, laying herself on the line, *aching* for a response. She knew she wasn't **unstable**. The problem was that there never was a problem that ranked above *minor inconvenience*.

She couldn't give the gray papers back. Now that so much had *already* been **lost**.

"Let's go to the mall or something. Don't you want to?" Matilda.

"Not really. Just take me home…" *Adelaide*. Rolling her window down *despite* the **rain**.

# PUNK

Punk was at Matilda's. He had finally cornered her at a show last night. She seemed pilled to the gills, as usual, but it still took him a suspenseful 25 minutes to talk her into taking him home with her. By that point he was bursting.

But after he finally got her undressed, it was boring boring. All of a sudden he wasn't interested in having anything else to do with it. But he had to stay, and hide out from those guys in the white suits. He had been to the squathouse, and his friends there had confirmed the story. They were snatching gutter kids.

So he decided to have a little more of the drug. Just a little. Though he had injured himself, sort of, with his previous experiments, they were also really good, in a strange way. Also, he was really bored, and Matilda didn't turn him on. He had to do something, he had wasted all that time talking to her.

He had taken just a pinch, and not ten minutes later found himself masturbating while staring at his face in the bathroom mirror.

It looked like the dark side of the moon. Round, cloaked, unassailable, it reflected no light.

His black hair was thick, cropped at random, according to his most recent haircut. He only allowed friends who had never cut hair before to cut his, and only if they were drunk and it was dark. This resulted in plenty of faux-hawks, dried blood/hair clumps, and joke haircuts, but at least it was different. His eyebrows were big, and dark. They were so close to his hairline that from a distance it looked like they were part of his hairdo.

The eyebrows were also close to his eyes, which were also close together. They had the requisite street sadness, that pulled-over, yellowed look, like tarnished coins. The thoughts behind the eyes were well concealed, and if they seemed slow to track it was only a guise. It was hard to stare, but in this way an odd flash of mischief might be caught. But on the whole they kept up appearances: turned off, lights out, no one home.

His nose had been broken so many times that it looked like it had never been broken at all, or rather that it had stopped growing when he was about 7-years-old. It was small and squat, and the interior was regularly exposed to view. A viscous cache of hair and bloody mucous that required a constant sniffling, just to keep the stuff from trickling down his face. Even so, there was usually something unrecognizable hanging out of it, or around it. Although this nose was not without its seasons, often it was shiny pink, cracked and peeling, bloodied from a coke binge or scuffle.

But his mouth, the *seat* of perverse human pleasure, was by far his *least attractive* feature. He watched it slowly open, as he **manipulated** himself. It looked **painful** to possess. It was small and tight, and had to force itself into *impossible contortions* to make **words**, or allow sustenance inside. He used only the left side of it. This looked *cool* and *nonchalant* when sucking on a **cigarette** or **whiskey bottle**, but otherwise it was tic-ish, *palsied*. The right side had been scarred into asymmetry. He had made up so many stories about "What happened to your face, man?" that he had *long forgotten* the **truth**. He did remember how he had chipped his tooth, however. His *SNAGGLE* had been earned in an *attempt* to ride **two** skateboards at once—one for each foot. He flashed it proudly through the manhole of his lips now, to inspect it. The accompanying *smell* made him retch *involuntarily*. The vomit in the back of his throat **only adding** to the halitosis.

His cheeks were **battlefields** of exploded landmine zits, pocks, scars, and fresh pimples. They were forever red, forever raw. The occasional cyst, rising like the *grandfather peak* in an already majestic range, was not an uncommon sight. These grisly skin conditions made shaving akin to **butchery**, but this was never much of an issue as he only could cultivate about nine thick black hairs on his chin at a time. He *let* them grow and curl, plucking only if he caught one in his peripheral vision.

It was, however, clear that he was **extremely attractive**. Almost everyone thought he was **hot**, almost *always*. Even now, looking at himself in his bathroom mirror, he couldn't help but to be astonished at how **hot** he was.

———

"You look really hot." Matilda. Walking into the bathroom, *forcing* her eyes on the mirror, away from Punk's **furious** hand.

He grunted in assent. "Uh, but you can't tell Ωllister about this, OK?"

"You can do whatever you want with your own hands."

"No, I mean about us."

"I don't even talk to that guy. After he broke up with *Addy*. But I don't want her to know about us either, OK?"

"No, it's cool man, I'll probably never tell anyone about this, ever. Anyway, I think I'm not allowed to talk to her either." Letting himself go.

"She's been acting all weird. She's worried about some gray thing."

"A **gray book**?"

"Yeah."

"She has it?"

"Yeah."

"Rad. Let's fuck."

Zella & Matilda

Zella and Matilda were late to school again. (*See Appendix B. The School*)

Zella never *cared* when this was the case. She sauntered into **Portfolio** class waving to various friends, trying to make sure her entry was **marked**. Matilda shuffled behind her, *embarrassed* at the attention. Most of the desks were full; it was the beginning of the year. They found two together in the back. Almost **immediately** after they sat down, Nick, with the *greasy* hair and *lascivious* grin, leaned over to breathe in Zella's ear; "Hey... uh... did I ever tell you about the time I... uh... invented the... uh... knife fight?"

"Uh... shut the... uh... fuck up?" Zella retorted loudly. She pushed her desk over three feet, toward Matilda, away from Nick. The metal legs *screeched* like a trapped owl.

Portfolio was a required class. Its purpose, from an administrative perspective, was to make sure that seniors had an art portfolio of *sufficient* quality to secure their admission into prestigious galleries or graduate schools. And if they graduated from UNI-ARTS they were *expected* to secure an offer of admission at one of the **top three** masters programs in the country, or become rich on their own, very quickly.

Ms. Man taught the class. She was **serious** and **strict**. Her parents had emigrated from Korea and *instilled* in her utilitarianism and a **neurotic** work ethic. She applied these to art, which made her *perfect* for this class, in the eyes of Dean Euphrates. She whipped the kids into shape: every year producing custom-made applicants for each of the big art programs. She **knew** what grad schools were looking for, and she **knew** how to produce it. She also had an *unfortunate* penchant for pant suits, which made jokes built around her name frequent and easy.

Zella and Matilda slouched in their chairs as Ms. Man **barked** the class requirements like marching orders. **Portfolio** was the only class held in the auditorium. Ms. Man looked small and dictatorial on the large stage. A scattershot of kids splayed randomly among the rows made the room feel *empty*. There would be no talking, laughing, or gum chewing. No absences allowed. During the first part of the year each class would be dedicated to a *single student*. On that student's day, he or she would haul in all of the **crappy art** that they had managed to produce, set it up on stage, and **present** it to the class and to Ms. Man, who would conduct the interview.

After all of the presentations were finished, the *rumor* was that Ms. Man made everyone do everything over, though she did not mention that now. At the end of the program, a professional photographer would come in, and take photos of everyone's completed portfolio, so they had slides for their applications, or for galleries. There was another class **just** for filling out these applications. It was *assumed* that every student would make **money** with their art, usually after grad school.

The school boasted an **impressive** placement rate, especially when it came to the top three grad programs. Those universities in turn boasted about admitting students from UNI-ARTS. It didn't seem to matter that a commercially, or critically, successful artist *had not* been produced by this system in more than 25 years.

Zella was still *wiggling* around in her chair, trying to get used to the idea of being in class. "What'd you do last night?"

"Um... I don't know." Matilda never got asked things like that. "Addy's all upset about Ollister or something."

"That's not news."

"Or, yeah, about his book or something."

"Whose book?"

"Ollister's. It's called a gray book or..." Matilda looked up. Ms. Man was giving them a **stern** eye. The girls *grudgingly* tugged notebooks and writing utensils from their bags and tuned into the lecture.

"...the art work is to be perused vicariously. In doing so, a picture emerges of the way Jack Mackerel reinterpreted performance pseudo-sculpture. When convoluting one's personal grid of perception, we risk a pedestrian mix of bake-sale ingredients coalescing into a multi-omniscient theory of art orientation, ad nauseum. The mutable, inchoate historical context belies a murky avant-garde, buoyed by no small dearth of imagination. The pre- and post-distopian confusion created an almost tragicomic contextual self-dramatization. Therefore, it's easy to see why most iconoclastic, unformed statements of the zeitgeist, albeit ensconced in artworks unrecognizable to the larger cultural milieu, were nevertheless created by Mackerel, probably. Redefining 'anti-art' by pointing at what it was not, allowed him to successfully skirt any sort of showy un-involvement with the shaky notion of an 'art community.' The neo-irrelevantists of the day were hostile to dialogues with 'danger boy' Mackerel.

The seasons of output following his early-mid-late period afforded a disciplined rejection of sophistication doctrine and a platonic macro-perception, uninhibited by any kind of cohesive, self-flatulating juxtaposition of disconsolate sentiment, and jubilant belligerence. Mackerel's pervasive and carefully orchestrated social mock-disregard incited a group of..."

"Are you getting this down?" Matilda. Whispering, panicked.

"Don't worry." There wasn't a pen anywhere near Zella's paper. "This class is easy." The *droning* from the front of the room continued, Ms. Man's nasal voice creating modal tones that harmonized with the steady *HUM* of the slide projector.

"...in the contemporaneous lifeworld. His disciples could achieve no empathy with the wider aesthetic agnosticism. The null-and-void framing device, definitively a post-modern anarchistic stratagem, discouraged would-be imitators from filching, referencing, or indeed even knowing about their work. The implied ideological bias was folded in to the larger thought-form of radically sensitive misanthropy. Mackerel's unified anti-manifesto, while never directly stated, unregardless whipped his constituents into a frenzy of converging artistic and mock-conscience thought streams. They operated on the subtext that 'art' does not equal 'art,' and thus, what we find when a revisionist subjective doctrine rears its ugly head is that..."

"It doesn't sound easy to me." Matilda. Whispering again.

Zella replied loudly. "Listen, on the test just answer that every question is impossible to answer because of cultural bias and, you know, shifting context or some shit like that. Then, at the end, complain about how much better arts-funding is in other developed countries. You'll get an A every time. I had one in this class last year until I stopped coming..."

"You stopped because of the pregnancy, right?" A *concerned* whisper.

"Shut the fuck up, Matilda. Don't think that because we're in class right now, I won't scratch your beady little eyes out."

"Jeez. Sorry. I was just kidding."

"Oh. I mean... so was I. Let's go get lunch. You're gonna tell me about Ollister's book." Zella stood and put her things in her bag, *oblivious* to the continuing lecture. Matilda was too **embarrassed** to follow her out.

MANIACAL STRETCHES OF TIME HALF GONE. THE
THOUSAND CRUELTIES THAT HOLD THE WORLD
THER. THE BATTLE FOR THE UNDERWORLD.
BOTTOM INCH OF DRINK LEFT IN EVERY CUP
E EVER USED, AN OCEAN OF BACKWASH.
WAY EACH MOMENT BEGINS AND ENDS, THE
I LAGGING BEHIND. THE BATTLE, INTO THE
I. THE PITFALLS OF PROVIDENCE. THE
RAIN SMELLS IN THE DESERT. THE
LION OF THE COTTON GIN, IN A DREAM, OR IN

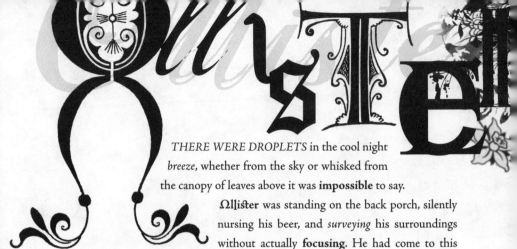

THERE WERE DROPLETS in the cool night *breeze*, whether from the sky or whisked from the canopy of leaves above it was **impossible** to say.

Ωllister was standing on the back porch, silently nursing his beer, and *surveying* his surroundings without actually **focusing**. He had come to this party to scout for willing **participants** to populate his machinations. To truly disrupt THE WHITE BALL he would need more than his usual staff, which only consisted of PuNk, really. Franc had been snatched, Pete was not to be found at his old dilapidated address, and there the list of *motivated* and *ruthless* individuals **ended**. He was **loath** to start an open casting call, but it seemed he had *no choice*.

Ωllister had a way of making himself **unnoticed**, if he wished to. It wasn't *physical*. He was there, unhidden, but there was something he could do with his manner that *eluded* awareness. People saw him, but **forgot** that they had a moment later.

The party was getting full of kids he knew. This made *invisibility* considerably more difficult, but he had somehow managed it, getting away with only a few knowing nods to select guests. He wanted to **observe** candidates without approaching anyone just yet.

The **beer** came from the keg, which they had inexplicably just begun to charge for. They being Virginia and January, whose porch this was. Whose *party* this was.

It was billed as an 'opening reception' for their **art** and that of a number of their *less-lazy* friends. They had also talked some local rock-n-roll 'it-kids' into contributing their crappy sketches to up the profile of the *party*. A few important people had come in the early evening. People with **money**, gallery owners. Despite the fact that it was at their house, it was well publicized, and the attempt was at *something* legitimate. For the eyes of **money**. The **money** quickly recognized the show for what it was: *dirty kids, bad art,* and *cheap alcohol.*

Virginia expressed **disappointment** to Ωllister early in the evening. He didn't understand what she *expected* to happen. Things were now as they should be: all of the same *stupid* people at the same *stupid party*. It even had a lingering air of the intended **pretension**.

This air was also a fun-killer and people were dropping out early. Throughout the last ten minutes, he had observed the *zenith* of the *party*. Not in any visual way, but it could be felt. There were a few minutes; **70** an **upswing** where it felt as though something was about to happen, some *event* to define the **party**. An epileptic fit, the cops, anything really. Instead the moment passed quietly.

And now people began to *dissipate*, Ωllister nodding slowly at a couple of hipsters as they made their way around the side of the house and out through the front. Not **ruthless** enough.

Punk had come with him. Unwillingly. Ωllister declared it a 'mandatory event'. Punk had *responded* by dropping **six hits** of acid. Earlier in the evening he had caught Punk trying to set the plastic siding of the house *on fire* with his *lighter*. He had put a stop to it, but Punk's current project, which was trying to **flip off** every single person at the party, individually, without actually *getting in a physical altercation*, was fine with him. Most people **ignored** him, but amusement was provided by the occasional **drunk** guy that needed *serious* calming down. It was **juvenile** (*see Appendix C3*. Punk *at 12*). But Ωllister also felt this activity gave him a fine insight into people's characters, and their **potential** for *subversive action*.

He looked out at the sea of ironic haircuts with a mix of weariness, affection, and disgust. He knew **everyone** here. Not just that, he knew **everything about them**, as well. He weighed the potential of each candidate in turn.

Virginia Downing *once* slept with her cousin, an older one, from Boston. She had been young and *off her medication*, but she didn't **regret** it. She had a *genuine* fear of werewolves and could only sleep with lots of bright lights on. Boyfriends *continually* disappointed her. But she found that lots of things **don't matter so much** if one has a lot of money.

Art Mortimer *always* wore his pressed peach-colored suit, no matter the day, no matter the weather. He was **obsessed** with Grover Cleveland and sent pitches daily to *Nouveau* magazine for stories concerning the ex-president. He wanted to *revive* Cleveland's celebrity. He could no longer eat cheese, as over-consumption of it, and little else, had given him **kidney stones**.

Margo Decaraux was editrix of the local feminist rag, though she would object to it being called that, **doubly**. She had survived a childhood with an absent father, and *nearly always* topless mother, and had come out the other end **swinging**. She liked motor sports but not dykes, *lace* but not dresses, and **death** but not weapons.

Zero was bartender at the **SNOOTY FOX**, as well as lighting technician for the low-end rock club **SNOT BLOCKER**. His line of work once got him slobber-knockered so **hard** he fainted. But it *also* got him laid once. He had a gas mask collection to **rival** even the most fanatic Nazi memorabilia collectors. And he had been writing a gutter punk mystery novel *in his head* for years. **Years.**

Jolene Bakersfield wrote things on her hands **all day** while working at the *VELVETEEN GALLERY*. She used those same hands to *masturbate violently* and paint pictures of her cat, Puppy Surprise. One time her boyfriend took her car to pick up a friend and **crashed** it, **killing** both himself and, in a way, the car. Jolene was more upset about the car because it never *cheated* on her, *farted* under the covers, or *laughed* at her brand new shoes.

BRODY FRANKEN was a **child prodigy** until the age of 13 when, having been caught shoplifting in Saudi Arabia while vacationing there with his parents, an overzealous shopkeeper had cut both his thumbs off, *ending* his precocious thieving career. The **incident** also destroyed his dreams of becoming a photographer. However, thumbs were not necessary to squeeze tubes of *frosting*, and he had since become one of the **top cake decorators** in the region. He also liked camping.

JANUARY was into *romance*: distilled, plasticized, or sparkly. She *obsessively* collected gemmed or bedazzled clothing, snow globes from around the globe, and used glow sticks from Halloweens long gone by. She played xylophone in an experimental all-metal, new-thrash art band called **Tar the Shitfucker**. Her grandfather had an old WWII tattoo of tits on his bicep, *pale* and *lonely green*. She *loved* him but **hated** all his children. One of them gave her that *awful name*.

PAOLO MERCEDES' house was empty. It wasn't that he was *too cheap* to buy furniture or that he had some strictly minimalist aesthetic. It had just **never** happened. It was clean, though, and that encouraged his girlfriend to stay over more, even if his mattress was *saggy* and they spent all *sweaty* night long pressed together by gravity. He called her **"Trucker"** in private, and she did not know what *exactly* he did at work all day. She knew he was an 'assistant nurse' at the Munsing Hospital just down the road. But the **secret** was that he was on the elderly ward. Rooms full of impacted feces, bowel evaluations, diarrhea, constipation, phosphate enemas, bloody stool and occasionally vomit. He spent his 12-hour shifts *gently* wiping down wrinkled old **thighs** and **buttocks**.

VIVICA RICHARDSON was a darling sock collector. Both the socks and herself, *darling*. She would tone it down a bit to go watch **underground street fighting** matches, or spy on **porno casting call** lines. She worked at a coffee shop and *didn't much care for anyone*.

JULY GREENBACK was a reformed prima donna. No fewer than **three** indie rock records had been dedicated to/used to *seduce* her. After an accident at the cookie bakery where she worked **singed** her eyebrows off, she began her studies in *humility* and *selflessness*. Her girlfriends *blanched* as she threw out clothes, make-up, phone numbers. She stopped shaving her armpits and began eating fast food on public transportation. She felt *mostly bored* these days.

All of these **fucked-up** kids, and not one of them **fucked-up enough** to accomplish Ωllister's end. The party was a **big boring** *disappointment*. Clearly, he would have to look elsewhere. Time was short.

Adelaide

Adelaide was at UNI-ARTS standing in the hall outside of Ms. Man's office. Fighting off *clingy memories*. She **hated** this place. It was a tomb, but one which *actively* suppressed her. Imposed its monolithic **stupidity** on her. Having graduated recently, and ahead of her class, she wanted *very much* to no longer think about her years spent here.

An irritating **necessity** had brought her to this stank waiting room. Certain lawyers were getting *serious*. The calls had mostly stopped and ominous-looking paperwork had begun to arrive in the mail. Clownish words; *slander, libel, reputation-damaging,* something about *disclosure of admission policy*. As far as she could tell, the lawyers were sent by Dean Euphrates, who never liked her much. Apparently he was *seriously* ruffled, a fact that was making her *extremely nervous* to be in his school building, in the same wing as his office. But she **needed** to tell Ms. Man about what had happened.

About six months ago, *Adelaide* had a show at the *VELVETEEN GALLERY*. First, she had assembled a rather *shoddy* portfolio of 'artwork.' Some reindeer her 6-year-old niece drew in marker. A Polaroid of the Mona Lisa. A few lines on paper, an empty Kool-Aid packet, spilled paint, the ugliest piece of art she could find at the THRIFTWHOPPER by her house, a sketch of a jeep by her friend, poorly plagiarized versions of some well-known contemporary work. A bunch of *crap*, really. In slide form, these images constituted the *centerpiece* of her applications to **25 MASTER OF ARTS** programs across the country. She filled out all of the forms. Her statement of intent was a finely crafted missive of **aesthetic ignorance**, well-placed **typos**, and **sub-par grammar**. *Every single* institution sent her back a warm, yet professional, letter of acceptance.

She framed these letters and hung them alongside the various pieces that made up the **portfolio**. They were up at *VELVETEEN* for a month. *Adelaide* pulled on her hair bitterly. The whole thing was a **bust**. It was *funny* and it was *fun*. But she had spent $60-100 in fees on each application. So far only a few of the pieces had sold. Critically it was a *success*. Especially if success was measured in *criticism*. Most everyone who had received an art degree from one of these institutions was **insulted**. The deans, and heads of departments, and professors, who represented these stalwarts of American Art Education were *outraged*.

And that's when the legalese started arriving in the post. She had tried to make the problem go away by *ignoring* it, but it seemed like she was going to be in some very real **trouble** soon.

Ms. Man was about the **only** one who might be able to advise her. Artists in general, and *especially* those affiliated with 'lesser' universities had been, for the most part, **highly amused**. Ms. Man had made a name for herself back in the '60s by wrangling with the legal system. Her project involved an *extraordinary* amount of horseshit and a little bit of government property. She was highly political and stubborn, and *Adelaide* hoped that she would pick up the banner and go to **battle** for her. Rumor had it she was tight with Jack Mackerel, before he died. *Adelaide* hated controversy. It was **boring boring**.

She could hear Ms. Man and someone else talking in *hushed voices* inside. So she waited. Ms. Man made her a little nervous. Not only because she **disliked** people who stared at her face, but also because she was aware that Ms. Man was currently involved in a suit Ωlliꟃer was bringing against this school. It alleged that his Uni-Arts diploma was **completely worthless** and he was *demanding* his money back minus the printing costs of the actual diploma. The fact that he never **actually graduated**, and didn't even have the diploma in question, nobody seemed to have noticed yet. This was the *last thing* she wanted to talk about.

She did need to go in soon. She was *desperately* afraid of seeing Dean Euphrates, or, for that matter, **anyone** she knew, in the halls. A steady stream of students *glided* by and she kept her eyes glued to the notice board as a camouflage technique.

Tacked to it were various flyers. **EBOLA PARTY.** *For sale: school books, laptops, a broken car, keys to my parents' house, 50 pound bag of rabbit food.* 'WE'LL MAKE YOU GAY' PARTY. No condoms scam-out scavenger hunt! *Zella* was on the list, of course. *Tetherball team: Meet after school by the flagpole. Double down. No take-backs.* The only thing that seemed **interesting** to her was a '*Coping with Death*' seminar. She was about to take down the date and time when someone grabbed her hand and **jerkily** pulled her into the *flow* of students.

Zella. Her mouth moving. "Omigod. I can't believe you're here. What are you doing? Did I tell you what happened to me last night? It was like the weirdest scam-out of my life. Weirder than that dad thing even. Omigod, you see her…?"

Adelaide felt like an embarrassed spy, just **apprehended**. She was *terrified* that *Zella* would bring her to the center of unwanted attention.

"At the Dirty Moss show last weekend all her friends found her passed out in a stall in the girls' bathroom. Toilet papered."

"*Zella*." Interruption was futile.

"No, I'm serious. Like someone's tree. Like a mummy. Like a yard full of mummies. Except maybe ones that had been knocked over because she was on the floor, well, half on the toilet. Supposedly she had gone in there to puke, and after barfing had passed out on the pot. And then someone came in and like, totally wrapped her in TP. Rumor has it that **Pu**n**k** did it."

"That's…"

"Oh. You see him?" Fierce stage whispers. Loud enough to disturb *Adelaide's* balance. Loud enough for a hallway six times this size. "Hemophiliac and cutter. How does he do it? He told Margo who told Brody who told Virginia who told me. At this party Thursday – why weren't you there? It was at January's. **Ωllister** was there. A friend of a friend of Paolo's brought her 7-year-old daughter. Can you imagine? And it was in the backyard. So I was staying in the house, with the band, cause you know how I feel about that. Until Matilda grabbed me to see, apparently January wouldn't let it play with her bangles. And it grabbed her by the hair and pulled her to the ground and kicked her in the face. Can you imagine? She got her ass kicked by a kid. I mean she was drunk, but shit…"

"Zella, I have something to do." *Adelaide.*

"What? Is it about the **gray book**?"

"The **gray papers**? How do you know about that?"

"Matilda told me."

Adelaide was silent. She stared over Zella's shoulder.

"Whatever. Don't be pissed. Who cares? Listen, I need a ride home. Let's go."

"I can't give you a ride home." The kids streamed past them in the hall. The occasional mohawk stuck up like a *shark fin* in the bobbing sea of heads.

"What the fuck are you doing here anyway?"

"I have to see Ms. Man."

"What the fuck do you want… oh that girl right there." Stage whisper again. "She gives hand jobs with green paint. Fifty bucks. I kind of like her." Zella paused to stare. Then back. "What the fuck do you want to see Man-boob for?"

"Look, I don't want to talk about it. I have to go."

"Ooooh. I get it. It's about **Ωllister**. Well, well."

"Actually, it's not."

"You know who I heard he scammed out with?"

Adelaide stuck her fingers in her ears and proceeded back in the other direction, up the hall. Ms. Man's door was open and she looked up, **offended**, as *Adelaide* walked through her door, *fingers in her ears*.

Art Terrorism

All of the underclassmen had to attend UNI-ARTS Lecture Day. They would bring in some visiting artist or alumni, and the entire student body would have to sit and yawn and fidget through whatever drab thing this person chose to drone on about. Dean Euphrates wanted the student body to know that some kids did actually make it through to the end of the program, and made them witness this every year in the auditorium.

Ollister would normally have nothing to do with the school anymore. He patently despised being anywhere near it. But his goal of recruiting a wrecking crew for The Platypus's White Ball was far from being met. He was desperate. They had to be the most fucked up art kids he could find. He had chosen to hide among some adults, dressed sharply and looking casual, when some dirty hipster jumped out of the crowd, and grabbed the live microphone, before the show had even begun. The student body was assembled, but the authorities were nowhere in sight.

"The art at this school sucks. All the students, artists, whatever you want to call them, actually I wouldn't call them artists, they all suck." He shouted at the students, now quiet and rapt on the old wooden bleachers.

"The teachers suck too, that's part of the problem. They're too scared to have a viewpoint, they're all touchy-feely, roly-poly, wishy-washy. There is no consensus. They're so naively eager to embrace everything, so that they're perceived as open-minded, so that they are hip, so that they're never fucking wrong, basically, that, that, that any kind of value judgment is just unthinkable. I mean, the fact that they don't even give out grades here. That right there should tell you something. 'Oh, but how can you grade a work of art?' they ask. I'll tell you how: with an 'F.'" He glanced around, nervously looking for faculty or staff.

"All a student needs to do here is say, 'Look I made this, it's part of me.' And that's good enough. If they've got a 'concept,' or, god forbid, a 'style,' well then they must be a genius. Well, all you fucking geniuses out there are all subject and no form, just a bundle of shitty soap-box ideas. A bunch of fucking TV screens is what I'm looking at right now, a bunch of fucking bullhorns. Bullshit-horns.

"Right, right, I know all about your veganism, and your uncle with the wandering hands, and your Third World covered in flies, and your reverse reverse subjugation of women, but fucking come on. Do you really need to be doing *this* about *that*? Art should have no more message than the light falling across a clearing, than... than...

than the fucking wind. It is aesthetic, immediate, and communicates nothing outside of exactly what it communicates.

"All you kids make me sick. Revolutionary, my ass. Nobody likes to be preached to, and that's what you're doing with your fucking 'concept.' Preaching through painting, bullying us into your boring boring worldview by telling us what we know. You give no aesthetic value, no beautiful alternative to the shit you are whining about, be it your own banal shit, or the insolvable shit of the world. You are cowards. If you want to change things, change them, if you want to change the world, I don't know, go fucking change it. Stop fucking around with art. Because this is not the tool that makes that happen. And, also, you suck at it. And your bullshit 'cause,' your piddling 'concept,' is poor cover for that.

"It's also poor cover for your pitiful lottery rags-to-riches champagne-on-the-yacht greedy desperation for success and what that really is, which is money. How does that idea fit in? What's your plan? To make something that is unique aesthetically, something very personal and anti-social, revolutionary, with the goal of having it institutionalized, subject to a waddling mass of tourists on the walls of a mausoleum, excuse me, museum? Or worse, in a gallery, sold like candy at the movie theatre, undersized portions in oversized boxes, candy sold to teenagers who are more interested in scamming out in the back row than in the movie itself.

"Congratulations, students of UNI-ARTS, you just learned to make products to fill the walls of the shopping-mall galleries. You might as well have been making fucking herbal shampoo or something. How can we make this hairbrush more marketable?

"I'll tell you how: call it art! I mean, do you know how long ago Mackerel's toilet was 'art?' Look it up. That's a one trick pony, you know? Once it's been said, how many times do we have to say it again? It's not only boring boring, it's self-defeating. This crap art can't be judged aesthetically. It's a mockery. Of whoever's looking at it, and, at this point, whichever of you choose to pull that tired old stunt. Not to mention that, when all is said and done, a toilet is a fucking toilet. And that's it.

"There's no seriousness left. It's mundane. It's what you hang above the sofa. It's what's printed on your tote bag from the museum. Art is the same as everything. And everything sucks.

"Art is useless. It used to speak to like this, this, this aesthetic idea, and appeal to an enlightened few. In the hands of the tourist masses, it's useless. It's a circus. It's theatre. Cheap sideshow showmanship. It's marketed as entertainment.

'Let me tell you the back-story of this ugly looking piece of crap.' There shouldn't have to be a story. A painting should explain itself, on its own terms. Marketing, entertainment, it's all the same crap now, you might as well go to the movies. It's a sitcom, a space-filler, and it's no revelation.

"And this, *this*, should be the escape from that. Making stuff is the only way you have to escape, to break, to shape the fucking mundanity of the universe into something else. Something useful. Useful for nothing maybe, but useful, you know what I mean? The very fucking center of your being. I'm not getting metaphysical or spiritual here, believe me, that would be worse. I'm not saying you are supposed to be answering some primal urge to create, or let your inner-whatever shine, or any of that horseshit. Just because art shows emotion doesn't mean that it can explain it.

"I mean, looking at art, the artist's mind should be inescapable. It may not show you who they are, but it damn well better show you who you are. It's like watching someone else's movie while thinking about your own problems or, no, it's like... It's like remembering a movie someone else made in a dream you had when you were a kid. I mean, it's like..."

And while he fumbled to get his simile right, Euphrates followed by a phalanx of guards in white suits arrived to drag him away. "I'm subject to all this shit too, I mean, I'm so fucking idealistic I don't even have any ideas..." He tried to continue, keeping a nervous eye on their hasty entrance. But it was over. They grabbed him roughly and hauled him out the door, to jeers and a smattering of applause from the student body.

While he was waiting on the sidewalk for Dean Euphrates to come out and lecture him, Ωllｉｓｔｅｒ appeared, as if from nowhere.

"You don't have to wait." In a low, conspiratorial voice.

"Uh, yeah, I guess you're right, but..."

"Come with me."

"Why?"

"I have something for you to do. A project for you to be inspired by."

"What kind of project? I only work alone, because..."

"It's... uh... an Art Terrorism project."

"Art Terrorism?"

"Yep, Art Terrorism."

"And I'm in charge?"

"Yes, whatever, come on, we've got to leave before Euphrates shows up."

"All right... sounds cool I guess."

Ωllｉｓｔｅｒ placed a bony hand on Vance's shoulder, and quickly led him around the corner and out, away from the school.

Adelaide

She was **mad**. Owed an *explanation*. Some sort of *capitulation*. An *apology*. A *reason*. She would even be happy to hear a *lie*.

The bath water was dirty and cold. She had been sitting in it for well over an **hour**. She had brought her book, a field guide to the trees and shrubbery of southern Spain, *in Spanish*, with her, but hadn't touched it. Her hands were wet anyways, her fingertips gooey, and *sickeningly* white. Her eyes were **closed** and her hair stuck to the pale plain of her face like rivulets of **muddy rivers** as seen from a helicopter.

She was **mad**. The **gray book** was *missing*. She had gone to look at it earlier in the morning, and found it **missing** from its usual spot. Which meant someone from The White Sodality had broken in and *taken* it from her. They **knew**. She had only told Matilda. Who must've blabbed. Why couldn't she just lie? She **hated** her friends.

And none of this would be happening if it weren't for Ωllister. She **hated** him. She **hated** him for *existing*.

Revenge fantasies bubbled up in her mind, as she lay still in the tub. She couldn't stop them. She became *rich* and *famous*. The first artist in 20 years that anybody **truly** cared about, that was **truly** celebrated by people everywhere, outside the incestuous *backbiting* circles of critics, gallery hucksters, wanna-bes, and blind patrons. He was *failed*, *miserable*, living on the *street*, *poor*, *ugly*, and **alone** above all else. She would slide past, with her **entourage**, drop a knowing look in the plastic cup gripped in his *emaciated* hand.

Or he **died**. And she was at the **funeral**. Stoic, *unmoving* but not *unmoved*. Everyone knew of their history. She gave the final eulogy. **Tears** over the soft hills of patent leather toes. Some *final* dramatic action, and then it would be over, and *memory* could shape him to suit her.

Or she called him up, and he came to the door, *disheveled* and *wet* from the storm, eyes besieged and recessed into **dark sockets**. She fucked him *passionately*, *beautifully*. And then kicked him out. Without his pants. At the weather's **mercy**.

Or he mentally **collapsed**. Preferably in public. Was admitted to some *horribly debasing* treatment program for a year, after which he had to live with elderly relatives, who spoon-fed him in his generic back bedroom with no sharp edges, from which he refused to emerge.

Her head was *slowly sinking* below the water. Her nose created two little ripple rings on the oily surface, in tandem.

When she put her head under, the dull thud of her **heartbeat** echoing in her water-filled ears made the thoughts stop. She could only hold her **breath** *for so long*.

79

THE PAST

The first time Ollister lived in the East Slope dorms was a tribulation. Stress presided and the events themselves glided in and out of a fog, as if we were looking back remembering it many years later. Which is what he was doing now.

He had been living over there for just a few months, having abandoned most of his homework, personal art, or any kind of structured existence, to fully experiment with altered states. Theodora told him, one foggy afternoon, that Adelaide and Zella were moving to the East Slope. To the floor below him. He was fine with that at the time. Not that it mattered, because come they did. In broken cars, with sushi and perfume.

The details of their arrival were lost. It marked the start of the chaos that would forever mark him, and, indeed, the entire East Slope.

The girls got drunk. He got drunk. It occurred to him within these first weeks of their stay that Adelaide was, in fact, beautiful. And, yes, he was attracted to her. However, it did not escape him that she was very dangerous. Long black strands of hair, like tree branches backlit in winter. Eyes like drills, chatoyant. He sensed doom. He knew not to get involved. He heard stories. Of other boys, turned to columns of smoke, piles of dust, pillars of saltpeter. He had terrible forebodings.

He flirted nonetheless. Brave, pushed by wine and friends who could highlight his cleverness. And they flirted oh-so-subtly, as only Ollister and Adelaide could have, glances from under dark brows, asides, and thoughts unfinished. One night was clear, star-lit. He sat across from her at his kitchen table, Scrabble board between them, passed-out friends at their feet. The stares were longer tonight, and her laughter was easily teased forth with his barbs, his faux-posturing. She was poison, soft and sleepy. She was beautiful.

"Marry" was on the Scrabble board, 16 points, although neither would later claim this play as their own.

"Will you marry me?" Ollister. Flatly.

She called him drunk and unserious. He gently protested, asserting that he was indeed quite serious. She said that, fine, in that case, she would marry him. He declared she didn't mean it. She said she did. A grotesque and abasing flirtation.

He further proposed that they take her car, a sedan which smelled of turn-of-the-century brothels, potporroui, old rugs, and pot. Take it and ride it all of the way to Vegas, to be married in the Vegas way. They could be there the next day. These declarations were not a wind-up. His tone was mocking, but it masked an absolute seriousness.

It was all-or-nothing. Any other way seemed impossible to him. All avenues in his mind led to him dumped, on the side of all roads, abandoned for all nights. The only avenue by which he could get what he wanted was the one proposed. He was young and he wanted to be married.

Looking behind him, he missed this presence of mind. Not that he did now, but then, at that age, there wasn't even the possibility of him making a mistake. He never, before or since, asked anyone to marry him.

They ended up in his bed that night. A mattress on the floor. They didn't kiss, although he wanted to. They just stared for awhile. Wine finally took her under. But he could not rest. His mind was electric, and he was awake all night, sometimes looking at her, sometimes lying on his back, listening to her breath, heavy with alcohol. She had nightmares, tracing them out in arching kicks and violent twitches. By morning he knew her every look, smell, and shape.

The next day was bright, the details burned out in his memory. She woke up, got out of bed, and left the room without so much as looking at him. Sobriety can play tricks.

Alcohol returned with evening, and the drunken tableau was reset. Now he was crawling across the floor, trying to kiss her. She put up appropriate resistance, before finally giving herself over to his whims. They scammed-out, like anybody. She put her hands over his eyes and asked him to describe her face, a challenge. He described it exactly, painstakingly, beautifully. A small feat after his long study of the night before. But she didn't know this, and kissed him more. He tried to unbutton her shirt. She would not let him. So they lay there, languid, with lips burning from over-use. Nearing sleep, she asked him to tell her a story, which he did. He felt sure that she had asked this of others before, asked all her lovers maybe, all her fathers. But he obliged whole-heartedly.

The next night was lost now. Something bad happened. He ignored her, sulking for attention. He stayed in, alone, miserable, sitting at his table. Mundanity blew in, up through the floorboards. Theodora came to fetch him out and deliver him into her presence. He sat on Theodora's bed. *Adelaide* sat on a chair, holding a half-empty wine glass. She wanted to know 'What's going on?' and other things besides. She wanted to discuss it in sobriety. Meaning hers. He didn't know her then, and thought she might be the sort that allowed her drunk self to do what her sober self had no real interest in. Only later did he learn that drunk, she could allow herself to be as she was. It was sobriety that was a hindrance, a muddler, and a shirker.

On that night she insisted she was no different drunk or sober. And she liked him. She wanted something. He replied that marriage would be fine by him. He had already proposed. This was stupid, and he wasn't being serious. He made it clear that, no, he was – deadly. She wasn't ready for marriage, but she did want to be with him. Full of pride, and weary, he agreed to consider this. She disappeared into Theodora's bathroom, slamming the door behind her, not without the wine.

Later that night, he went outside to have a cigarette, and found her passed out in the dormitory yard, soggy from the night's rain. A wine glass toppled next to her; she had been spent. He walked out, and squatted beside her. She stirred, and he held out his hand, an offer. She looked at him for a long moment and then closed her black eyes again. He stayed, hand outstretched, for a long time, fear growing in his heart, stubbornness and pride fixing his haunches. She finally put her limp hand in his, and he helped her up and into his bed.

He had called other feelings love before, and since, but this was the only feeling that he felt truly deserved the name. The others were something else, something less.

Now his recollections fully fell apart. Emotions override details. Sometimes it seems only one wisp can remain, and that feeling is the true stuff of memory, rather than fact. He remembered the day, as though it didn't even happen to him, a picture. The feeling flooded his heart, and he didn't know what made it beat so fast, what made it toss and turn while he slept.

Maybe he went to bed the next night, and left the door to the third floor ajar, whispers and rain leaking in, and she never came.

So maybe then he chained his door. Perhaps because of some imagined slight, perhaps against the absence of the night before. And that night, she came, and he turned her away, and made his floor a silent library of regrets.

When he awoke the next morning, there was a large horsefly in his room, buzzing loudly. There was no way it could've crept in during the night. His windows were shut, the door bolted and chained. He was certain that if it had been there all night, he would've woken. Unless it had been sleeping itself.

He went outside for a morning cigarette. She was there, but not for him. All of their friends had gone to get day-drunk at various city monuments, in the hopes of causing a civic stir. He apologized for the night before, and said things meant to facilitate their reconciliation. He found himself making a full and unforced confession of his feelings, of his slayed sense of self, of his dedication to her in spite of his pride. She had no interest. He threw a veritable fit. There was yelling. He dug deep for barbs, personal attacks, open wounds, nasty things. Accusations of teen angst and over-dramatization. Things that would have fit his behavior more accurately.

She wouldn't hear much of it, and made for her car. He was so confused, angry, and frustrated. He felt the hot pressure of tears against the back of his eyes and in his throat. The first time since he was a boy.

Zella & Matilda

Ωllister sat in the back row. He had been coming to **Portfolio** class, incognito, to scout for *participants*. After successfully whisking Vance away, directly after his outburst on lecture day, he had decided that the school was *the place* to **recruit**. Besides Vance was anxious to get started on some **terrorism** plans, and meet the crew Ωllister had promised him. So he had to find a crew.

Today was *obviously* not going to be fruitful. It seemed Matilda was presenting. Ωllister sighed dramatically and crossed his arms.

She wasn't exactly well-liked at school. There were **rumors** that she let Punk stay in her room. **Rumors** that she crashed her luxury pink automobile, giving herself *significant* brain damage. **Rumors** that she had not produced *one piece* of art since coming to Uni-Arts. **Rumors** that she was pretending not to be as rich as she was. Everyone knew she was raised by nannies. And nobody liked *spoiled nanny brats*. Ms. Man included, which meant that this was a portfolio review the class had looked forward to. Many sat in the front row to watch the show go down. She was sure to **cry** or **freak out** in some way before the hour was up.

Zella was also in the front row, in a **supposed** show of support. Matilda was the only one kind to her about her **art** (*See Appendix Z1. Zella's art*). Because she knew Matilda would be nervous, Zella had brought her a variety of *pills* procured from her grandmother's medicine cabinet. In the last hour she had given her muscle relaxers, handfuls of anti-anxiety pills, Beta-Blockers, and a half-bottle of gin, *just to be safe*.

Zella watched Matilda clamor onto the stage, banging a medium-sized canvas against its edge while *simultaneously* flashing the backs of her thighs. She looked like something **primordial** struggling out of the **ocean**.

"Hello. My name is Matilda, I'm a painter. I like to paint. I must have something in my teeth. Do I have something in my teeth, Zella?" She looked down at the first row. "No? Zella says I'm cool. Uh... my boyfriend, I mean... uh, my day was good. I uh...I went to my psychologist for the first time. She's really interesting. We had deep talks... We're all wonderful, interesting people, I do believe. Placed on this earth to do wonderful interesting things. Like make art. Sorry, I'm getting 'presentation funny' now. And, uh... we're gonna talk about my painting today. Sounds like a commercial. Life is one big commercial. Let's get all eggs-istential. I'm trying to be funny again. I'm a comic. Most people wouldn't say that about me. But they don't know me." At this point she put on a pair of dark sunglasses and affected a deep voice. "I was hanging out. There was all this coke there. It was so not cool. Do you know who I am? I'm not the coke dealer. Y'all can leave me with your stuff. I don't do coke. Coke is a crime." Her normal voice returned. "Did you ever watch metal bands?"

It was going to be a **long** presentation full of *self-reference*, *tangents*, and *third person* remarks. Ms. Man already looked **agitated**.

"We're here to talk about your work, Matilda. If that's the only painting you have, set it on that easel there, and let's get started."

The painting was made of blobs, scribbles, junk on a canvas. It looked like a 5-year-old had done it in about five minutes. Zella shot Matilda a look. She had seen more of her **art** than anyone, probably, and yet each new piece *stunned* her.

"Uh... OK... yes ma'am... I will proceed to give you the verbal... estimate on my painting. Basically it starts out with this cat. This cat right here." She touched the painting in a seemingly random place. "You can see it if you're up close. His tail is going behind this root thing. But you step back and get other dimensions, like cooler levels. Objects like this here. You see, that's a volcano with a star and a sun facing each other. They're creating a different level through the light." She touched more amorphous blobs of paint. "This is a basketball player. He's got a world, like, a basketball... player right there. Here's like this womanly form who's traipsing her hair up, like draipsing it up. That's like the sexual area. It's erotic." It was a large green smear. "If you take it back there's like... holy shit... there's a..." She began snapping her fingers as if to remember. "A... guy. He's like, doing a secret. Next to my boyfriend, I mean, uh... this punk guy, who's like leaning. And then, you see this little corridor. There's like this little star, and it's kind of like an island, and that's another central point, you gotta look up close." She demonstrated this by turning her back to the class and putting her nose right up to the painting. "Uh... we'll do that after class. There's also this huge kind of cat figure right here. He's got like two noses. Like, these ears coming up. You can do lots of stuff with the painting. Loads of fun. Anyways so... oh yeah, and an alien. I was painting and an alien totally showed up in my painting and I was like 'Dope, I'll take him.'"

"Matilda, I'm not seeing this stuff." Ms. Man. **Frowning** at the mess on stage.

"You gotta get close... the horse, also. Right there, see? He's got a green nose, and the little leather thing, the bite. It's like a horse... with no horns! This is all lava, like kind of a forest scene. And then if you take it on a whole nother other level, and take it as a whole, you've got this area, and that area, and you can find all the little fun uh... stuff in it. There's some really dope stuff. Like a gypsy woman with her skirt pulled up."

"I don't see the woman."

"Wait, what? You just have to focus on this part of the painting, like you can see the face right there. That's why I love color so much."

"All right, Matilda. Let's move on. What did you use to make this?"

"Or it could be a mermaid. Oh... uh... I made this right after I got my White Sodality badge, and I thought, 'What a career he's had!'"

Zella shot Matilda a surprised look. Ollister coughed in the back row. Ms. Man didn't blink. "So you made it for him?"

"Yes. I don't know if he's ever gonna get it. I'm probably just gonna give it to him one of these days. Like, 'Hey Platypus man, you inspired me to do... this.'" She motioned toward the painting with both arms like she was a spokesmodel on Gameshow Surprise.

"What do you think he'll do with it?"

"I hope he looks at it. I'm hoping his family looks at it. I believe in art therapy, as an energy, too, not just as... everything is like, dimensional. And I think art, energy, and art should be science too. It's cool. So, I painted this for them. It mused in me."

Ollister got up quietly from his seat and *slipped out* the back door.

Ms. Man sighed. "OK Matilda. Next question. Are there artists that inspire you?"

"Yes, all of them. Oh, I tagged it, right there. If you look really hard you can, like, find an astronaut there. It's tight like that."

Ms. Man put her pen down.

"I see a punk." Some kid shouted form the crowd. Snickers.

"Huh, that's the first thing I've actually seen." Zella. Whispering.

Matilda was unfazed. "I see someone kicking it in their room. And that's his face and he's got the clicker. He's watching T.V. Hey, uh... this should be a glass table painting. It would be better on a glass room table." She picked up the canvas, and threw it down flat on the stage to get a bird's eye view. "I think I might do it." She nodded her head slowly as the class stared on in **silence**.

Ms. Man stood and clasped her hands in front of her plaid pantsuit. "Matilda, that's enough. See me after class. The rest of you are dismissed."

Punk used one of the *last* of the crumpled dollar bills stolen from Matilda's dresser. He had gone by last night, against even his **impaired judgment**, and had attempted to have ~~terrible~~ sex with her. But he could *barely* remember. He needed to leave the new **drug** alone. If he kept this up, there wouldn't be any left for THE WHITE BALL. He thought that he probably did it because he felt guilty. After Matilda told him about the gray book in her friend's apartment, he went over there. He broke in, pet her cat for awhile, and *took* the book. It was easy enough to find. Just like this money from Matilda's dresser.

The dollar slid, with the same ~~lewd~~ mechanical glide, into the slot that had swallowed almost the *entire* wad. A slot inside a video booth inside Bunny's, out on the East Side.

He had been in the sticky black booth for well over an hour trying to coax his ~~half~~ erection into maturity. He had been *unsuccessful* from the start. The regular video fare of the **old in-and-out** just wasn't doing it, so he had been flipping channels, hastily turning the dial in search of some new and inspiring perverseness. Three-way, anal fisting, leather, Japanese cum bath, pseudo-rape, ~~gay twink sex~~, electrocution, ~~foot jobs~~, midget ménàge a trois, ~~blacks-on-blondes~~, tranny spring break, nothing seemed to satisfy his member's *laconic disinterest*. At a dollar every 90 seconds, this self-solicited activity was becoming a **very** expensive proposition.

He had finally settled on one channel, some over-dyed, dried-up old redhead, who looked like she had *no idea* where she was or what species she belonged to, and tried to get down to business. Spitting on his palms, switching hands, using both hands, ~~one finger in his asshole~~, he just couldn't make it happen. He became *increasingly distracted* by the string of **disappearing** dollars. This was all of the money he had. And he was hungry besides being horny. There was lunch to think of.

Just as he was about to *resign* himself to this small failure, ~~this little death,~~ a man's face popped on the screen. It was old, pink, and mustachioed. "Hello, Pᴜɴᴋ." It said.

His eyes **widened**. He turned the dial frantically. The channel wouldn't change.

"I know you have the gray papers. I need those. I'm going to send some nice men for you to give them to, OK? You'll recognize the white suits."

Pᴜɴᴋ *bolted* out of the sweaty seat, his **heart** racing. He quickly walked back through the rows of glossy covers painted with acrobatic contortions, impossible configurations of flesh. His hair was on end. ~~Did that actually just happen?~~ Who was this guy? How could he know what he had? He made the obligatory non-eye-contact nod to the proprietor, Rageena, and was about to *push* his way out of the glass door when he **stopped short**.

The Platypus

The back of a head he recognized. A **black** baseball cap with metal lighter covers clipped along every available edge. *Chainsaw*. He deftly slipped back into the racks of videocassettes.

He pretended to browse, ~~while surveying the scene outside~~. They were all there. **Chainsaw, Fag-ass, Knees**, and... **Crystal**, that was the last one. She looked shorter somehow. Perhaps due to her namesake. **Street kids**. Wanna-be ~~fucking~~ gutter punk *posers*. Pᴜɴᴋ once had to pretend to be tight with them—his other meth connection had skipped town, and he was in a bad way for a while. But even under the blanket of sense-dampening **drugs** his nerves were raked over by their particular brand of *idiocy*. And he would hang out with anybody, ~~really~~. But these kids were too **fucked** to handle.

He knew they all had nice homes to go to in the ~~fucking~~ suburbs. It was raining now and he would bet all those dollar bills that *not one of them* could be found sleeping on the **streets** down in the square tonight. That's how he always knew an *oogle*. Everyone was poor as shit, homeless, ~~whatever~~, until it rained and then half of them **disappeared**. Pᴜɴᴋ knew, he was out there rain or shine.

They were always *harassing* people, or making up stories about stomp-downs in train yards, giving themselves **bruises** and **scrapes** as proof. They were the ones pissing all over each other for kicks, talking to local reporters ~~to propagate the stereotype in the media~~, mugging elderly couples, creating false homelessness statistics, and generally giving the streets a *bad name*.

He knew they were all **pissed** at him right now. The ~~rumor was the~~ guys in white suits had been looking for Pυɴκ, and picked up Franc by accident. He thought it was all *bullshit*. Until just a few minutes ago.

The **last thing** he wanted to do was go outside, but he knew they would be camped there for a while. It was one of their favorite places to **spange**, right in front of the porn palace. This backdrop tended to reduce a night's change intake, but they didn't care ~~much~~. Chainsaw preferred this *scenery* for his come-ons. Plus, it was one of the only places on the strip that still had a canopy—in case it started raining again.

He had to find Ωllister and unload the ~~stupid~~ **book** before this *crazy* old guy and his White Suits found him. He didn't want to, because Ωllister would want to know where he got it, ~~and he wasn't good at lying~~, and then Ωllister would know about him and Mατildα. But he was **scared** now, and time felt short.

"Hey!" Rageena. "This ain't the forkin' homeless shelter."

Rageena recognized Pυɴκ as one of them. And the **gutter punks** were, ~~most~~ definitely, no longer allowed in Bunny's. He would be *thrown out* if he didn't leave.

He put his hand on the glass door's bar, looked in the direction of his half-erection, which now **refused** to retreat at all, preferring to remain in stubborn, aching limbo. He sucked in a deep breath and *pushed* his way out into the wet ~~ignorance~~.

He was looking down, with his hoodie up over his face, *hoping* that they wouldn't notice him. But they were always on the lookout for other **squatter kids**. It would be impossible to escape notice. And sure enough, as he walked quickly down the sidewalk, the cries of 'Oy, you!' and 'Hey faggot!' were raised. Knees ~~chased him down and~~ peered under the hood.

"It's Pυɴκ!" He shouted back to his gang.

"He's in with them!" Chainsaw.

"He sent ~~FBI~~ agents after us!" Fag-ass.

"He fucked me once!" Crystal. Never mind she was *willing*.

Pυɴκ knew what came next. He ran. As fast as he ~~possibly~~ could with half a boner, *slipping* and *sliding* on the oily wet concrete. The **gutter punks** followed in ~~half-hearted~~ pursuit.

THE ✤ PAST

He could remember the first time that he saw _Adelaide_. He was hanging out at Theodora's place. It was a converted firehouse, and Theodora was fond of entering the living room by sliding down the pole that came from her bedroom. Theodora had just been kicked out of UNI-ARTS a few months from graduation, and was living with a catholic rollerblading champion in the first of what would be a long string of identical apartments. There was a portrait of a mouse hanging from the ceiling, and some ripped posters of various rock starlets infamous for heavy drug use.

He had just moved back from the East Side, where he had been bumming around with friends, living in an abandoned house, selling found appliances, and trying to scam out with some blond rich girl who didn't wear underwear. He had discovered cool and felt flash with new jargon and _THRIFTWHOPPER_ fashion. He was wearing a gold lam   shirt, some ripped jeans, and fuzzy red hospital booties, years ahead of a time that would never be.

He and Theodora were sitting on the floor, chatting, when _Adelaide_ showed up with some guy. He didn't remember being acknowledged in any way. He didn't remember if he said anything to either of them.

The two of them, interlocked, came right in and sat down on the couch to his right. He was taken by this girl wearing an awful 'funky' hat and smoking out of a glass bong. Even high, she was more serious and rad than any girl he had ever met. Being impressionable, he was impressed. And embarrassed for his immediately apparent mantle of immaturity and awkwardness. For the first time, but certainly not the last, in her presence.

Either they left or he did. Nothing extraordinary happened. He didn't know anything about love that day. If a seed was planted he never noticed it. If anything was clear, it was that she didn't have anything to do with him. Nothing really occurred to him until later. But it was a point. Where something was.

89

89

It was nowhere *near* Christmas but Matilda's dorm room was draped in Christmas lights. There were **typical** art posters on the wall, Jack Mackerel ones that could be bought at the downtown art museum, or at *any* art museum. A glance at the bookshelf proved **disappointing**. Nothing but text books and novels that belonged to one syllabus or another. A picture of Matilda and some ex-boyfriend, *obviously a homosexual*, smiling falsely at one another. The frame was a pewter representation of Noah's Ark. Apparently for baby photos, it had big-eyed giraffes and elephants, ears swaying gently in the sea breeze as the animals rode the frame around the hopeless couple. Perhaps the frame signified that they were two of a kind, or that they were somehow capable of repopulating the earth. *Adelaide* **felt ill.**

"Hey, where were you last night?"

"Nowhere. I mean, here."

"Are you lying?" *Adelaide*.

"No." It was easy to tell when Matilda was lying. "Did you want something to drink?" Matilda. Scooting a sock under the chair with her foot. It looked *curiously* like the kind of sock PuNk used to wear.

"Mm-hm." She did.

"We've got cranberry juice, ginseng tea, slim-fast…"

"What about some wine?" That would help things. *Adelaide* felt **uncomfortable**. They didn't *used to* lie to each other.

"Well, um… It's my dormmate's and…"

"That'll be fine." Her mind wandered back to one of their first days at UNI-ARTS, when Zella had somehow gotten a hold of a couple of bottles of **wine**. And three hits of **acid**. One for her, one for *Adelaide*, and one for their new roomie, Matilda. Matilda had *freaked out*. Freshman year is a bad time for a bad trip. She sat in the corner most of the night, fixated on a candle that emitted rivulets of burning **black wax** down the fresh pink of her knuckles. When Zella had taken *Adelaide*, and the wine, out to explore the nearby fields and *possibly more*, Matilda finished her candle and proceeded downstairs to throw herself *violently* against Dean Euphrates's door. **Convinced** that they were already found out, she had decided, at 3 AM, to turn herself in. The janitor contained her until morning. Zella was **promptly** suspended from UNI-ARTS, for **administering L.S.D.** to a classmate against her will. Matilda was kicked out three months later for **self-inflicted cutting**. But they let her come back. To think of those happier days now made her sad.

"Here you go."

"Thanks." She took a sour mouthful straight from the bottle. It had been open for a while. *Adelaide* decided to *come out* with what she wanted to say. "Listen Matilda, that thing I was telling you about? Ollister's **papers**? They're gone."

"What?"

"Yeah, they're gone. And you're the only person I told." Matilda's eyes and mouth opened at the same time, in protest. "Wait. I'm not accusing you or anything. It's just that there's some people out there who really want them, and they could've manipulated you into…"

"I told Zella."

"What?"

"I'm sorry *Addy*, it just slipped out."

"Matilda! She's the biggest snoop of anyone! You know that firsthand. Oh god, well no wonder they're missing. She took them when she was at my house."

"I'm really sorry." She looked it.

"No, it's not your fault, I mean, it is, but you know what I mean… You didn't have to lie about it…"

"I'm… so… sorry." Now she looked as though she were going to cry.

"Jeez, Maddy, it's OK. I didn't tell you it was a secret. And we're both friends with Zella. I mean, we're supposed to be friends. When I see her, I'll get them back. She's in big trouble. Let's just go to the stupid show."

They were waiting to go to an art opening at the *VELVETEEN GALLERY*. *Adelaide*'s art opening. Matilda had a car, so she would be free to be as **wasted** as she knew she needed to be. This prompted her to come here first and grace Matilda with the *privilege* of giving her a ride to and from the opening.

"OK." There was **guilty** silence. "Well, so, like what work are you showing?"

"Don't call it work. It's not work. The show is called Exs."

"Like Xs and Os?"

"Like ex-boyfriends."

"Oh. Rad."

"You'll like it. Just wait." She was **confident** that Matilda wouldn't like it. The project was the result of eight years of *meticulous* collection. In the gallery she had set up ten stalls, each a shrine to some **stupid boy** or another. They all had *secret* videotaped footage, most often of them having sex with her. There were many pictures, paintings, portraits of the boys. Anything she had written about them, either during or after the affair, was bound in a volume on a podium for the viewers' perusal. Each station had earphones with a looped track of the corresponding boy's voice, recorded *secretly*, phone conversations, or pillow talk. There were artifacts that each had given her. Tokens of **imagined affection**. Love letters. Also, artifacts that she had **stolen**. Locks of hair, stray socks, semen samples, all surprisingly *easy* to procure. The semen she had taken to Pete, at the university lab, to have the DNA *sequenced*. Pete had a computer program that hypothetically combined it with her own DNA and then produced an approximation, a prediction, of their **future child**. These images were combined with *age-enhanced* portraits of the boys and morphed together to produce **mall photo studio** images of a happy family. Pete was a *genius*. This part was by far her *favorite* of each stall.

She had no idea why she had done all this. She didn't really **like** any of these boys. Most of them *weren't* particularly interesting. And as far as she was concerned they said absolutely **nothing** about her.

She couldn't include Ollister. Though in pitching the show to the gallery, she *intimated* that a show called 'Ex-boyfriends' would include **him**. But she had never **promised** anything outright. She simply couldn't. Their relationship wasn't codifiable in this way. Besides, she *wasn't* thinking about him anymore. She had to *stop* thinking about him.

"Ex-boyfriends. Rad, I remember all of yours!"

"Not like this… But you'll like it. You will. It will be a good party anyways. The Velveteen is about the only place in town where the free wine isn't also cheap wine. And it's big time stuff, you know, important 'art' people will be there, or whatever. This guy, The Platypus, maybe. If he is, I'm introducing him to Zella, and they can sort this whole thing out." *Sighing*, she turned the wine upside down.

"A platypus?"

Matilda & Zella

Portfolio. Zella and Matilda arrived just as Sebastian was setting up four or five small pieces of art on the lecture hall stage. They sat quietly in the back, hungover, *barely awake*. And in a **fight**.

"I can't believe you took *Addy*'s thing." Matilda.

"I didn't. I already told you. And now she's all pissed at me because of whatever you told her. And why didn't you call me back last night?" Zella.

"I was busy, and it's none of your beeswax."

Permutations of these sentences had been traded back and forth for the past 20 minutes, while they waited for class to begin. Zella didn't notice ꙮllister sitting in the **dark**, directly behind them, because she was pre-occupied with Matilda. She wouldn't have known to keep quiet either, because she didn't know what the fuck it was all about, only that everyone was *pissed* at her. And being that she didn't really do *anything* other than be told things, she felt **resentful** about being on the outs. She crossed her arms, and all three of them watched the stage.

Ms. Man seemed all business today, her pantsuit professional. "All right Sebastian, let's get started. Introduce yourself to the class, please."

Sebastian smoothed the front of his skin-tight suit. "Well, I have a few names. Some are from rapping, some are from Berlin, some are from, well, not really art, but another reality or life of mine called 'Black Cat Schlingensief' (*See Appendix D3. Sebastian*). Schlingensief is my last name and I added the 'Black Cat,' making it a little more witchy, a little more like a fuck-up. My rapping crew's name was "Slime Time," but a lot of weirdos took it, and said it too much, so I don't like it anymore. It's a good one, but it's not good anymore. I like that dead rapper. What's his name? His stuff sucks. But he's cool. Being dead and all that."

"Let's get to the art, Sebastian." Ms. Man.

"This is one of my art. Pieces. Can you see it?"

"Yes. We can see it. Why don't you tell us about it?"

"Oh, there's nothing to tell about it. But, what it is, is a cat. It could be a dog, though I'm pretty sure it's a cat. An X-ray on Solar Graphics paper. Solar Graphics. Like the sun. And there are various screws and wires in its legs, which I found entertaining. It's an actual cat's x-ray from the animal hospital on Clark. I suppose it got ran over or something. It's probably dead. Now. One of my big-breasted friends gave me a box full of cat and dog X-rays. And in the corner is, I think a shadow of a music box."

"Was music a part of this piece? Something you like?"

"No. I don't like musicians, that's for sure. And this one here. I don't remember which, some other student was making a collage for this class, and I got these two pieces and was just fiddling. Like I do, and tipped it upside down. And the lines matched really well. I really like Jews, and this is a picture of a Jew, at the wall, western wall, prayer wall that I'm trying to purchase, actually, at the moment, but I'm having a hard time. Apparently it's some sort of sacred monument, but I really like this piece. It's probably my favorite because, you know, the lines and the black, and the beard. The sorrow. It looks a lot better than the other ones. I don't know if it means anything. Better."

"So, what were you thinking when you painted this, Sebastian?"

"I like it. Or this piece will be damn expensive. And once again, there's only a couple real things in this. It doesn't mean anything. I mean, if I turned it into my psychologist he might interpret what it means, and it's probably true. There are crows. You see how they're crows? There's the beaks and the black is black like a crow. And this down here, this is water. It's pretty. Really pretty. Here's a bone. It's a little bloodied, and it's buried. In the water. For some reason the water's edge is bloody. Like it's alive or something. What my psychologist would probably say is that, I'm looking toward hell. I like to swim and..." Here he pointed at the bone. "...I have some pent up sex. Energy. He's probably right. Oh, this is another blood splatter. Again, doesn't mean anything."

Zella, thinking about Matilda's painting, and the way it got tossed and turned, raised her hand. "Have you ever tried turning it upside down?"

"Yes and it looks like shit. It's painted the *right* way." Sebastian. Looking rather **offended**.

Ms. Man brought it back around. "Do you have any favorite artists?"

"Nope. I like some a little. I really don't care about other artists. It's important, I know, but I'm no good with names, and I just trash anything that doesn't hit me right in the gut. There's a lot of horseshit. I mean this one someone wanted to buy, and I didn't want to sell it, really, and when I told her how much, I mean, I don't know if she thinks I'm doing her a favor by making her a piece of art, but, is your doctor doing you a favor and you don't pay him? A lot of people in my social circle are all, 'Make me a piece, make me a piece.' And they don't want to pay for it. Like they're complimenting me. I could care less if they like it. I mean some of the amounts I've been offered, you can't even get a decent-sized sack of drugs."

"So why do you do this, Sebastian?" Ms. Man was about done.

"Well, it kills the boring boring. I really like it when I like something, and I also like the fact that I don't care if other people will like it. That's fun. It's just something good to look at. It's not like, 'Oh, this is my father and this is my mother. And this screw in this cat's hip is my problems in elementary school. It's a cat with screws. In its leg. And if you need explanation about that, whatever, it's like Judaism. I had my Bar Mitzvah about three weeks ago. I'm still a little sore. But it was fun. My circumcision stitch. It turned purple."

"That's enough." Ms. Man dismissed the class with a *weary resignation*. She didn't even ask Sebastian to stay. That probably meant that he **passed**.

Ollister was standing in the back. He had tuned out the girls quickly after deciding that PuNk should pursue Zella instead of Matilda. She seemed to have the most information. He had missed the girls' conversation about the gray papers, because his focus had turned to his true purpose here. He didn't even bother waiting till Sebastian was outside. He made **directly** for the stage, confident in this new and *perfect* recruit.

Adelaide

"You ever get this weird foreboding thing?"

"What are you talking about?" It sounded like Zella was chewing gum over the phone. Or eating noisily, at the very least. A habit that **disgusted** Adelaide.

She held the receiver away from her ear and continued.

"Well last night I was at this party, at January's? And it was fine, fun, I mean…"

"Was PuNk there?"

"I don't know. I was leaning against…"

"What about Sebastian?"

"I don't know, Zella. I wasn't paying that much attention. Can you just listen for a second?"

"Jesus. Sorry."

"So I'm there, and actually having a nice time, talking to Virginia about some clothing line she wants to do for cats. And the music is good, and everyone is there and I've had a few to drink, and I swear it, I know it's weird, but I was having a perfectly nice time. But then it hit me."

"What did?"

"That feeling. I just had to leave, to get out of there."

"To be by yourself?"

"No. I mean, on the way home I was regretting it. I didn't really want to leave."

"Well, what was it then?"

Adelaide let the other end of the phone receiver fall away from her face.

"Addy?"

"Zella, I need the gray papers back."

"Mattie was already freaking out on me about that. I don't even fucking know what that is…"

"They're just really important, OK?"

"I didn't steal them." Zella sounded serious. And a little pissed. Adelaide considered her tone for a long moment, and decided to believe her.

"Fine. Someone did. Matilda swore she didn't tell anyone else. Maybe the White Sodality broke into my house."

"I have no idea what any of this is about. But I have real gossip for you. Can we talk about that now?"

"Listen, Zella, I have to go." She **hung up** the phone, and stared at it for a long time.

Mister

He stood outside **smoking**. It was a *golden-gray dusk* and the rain drops were few and far between. He could see the trees bending, but there was no breeze on his own skin. In the tree above him the **sparrows** were having their monotone conversations about what to eat or where to sleep or how to *get inside a human being*.

He wished a **ghost** would come from the **future**. With a requisite *otherworldly glow* and *flowing robe* about her. Hair riding over the breeze he couldn't feel. He wished that she would come and **whisper** all that was *yet to come*. His triumphs. And his defeats. And he would be comforted. Comforted *especially* by the defeats.

But knowing would likely cause **problems**. He had stopped reading the book on his toilet tank because of this. He had casually leafed through it for months as an *addendum* to more serious reading. But during his last few extended bowel movements he had noticed the characters and events contained within its pages began to **resemble his own life** more and more closely. To an almost *eerie* degree. One particularly constipated day, when the book began to describe him sitting there, reading the very book, it became **too much**. He ripped out the pages and *flushed them* down, one by one.

He had performed this exercise with his current journal only the week before. The characters and events contained within that book no longer came **even close** to resembling his own life. He only felt *impatience* as each entry was sucked into the pipes beneath his feet.

Every so often he would imagine himself, **fifty years on**, the wrinkles of his grandfather superimposed on the *not-dissimilar* topography of his own face. He would look back through those deteriorating eyes and *smile*, with an understanding comprised of respect and pity, upon his *former selves*. He would laugh at his old thoughts and ideas, so far off the mark. He would laugh at his old daydreams. *Especially* the one in which he imagined an older version of himself looking back, **laughing**.

Today, though, he was **looking forward** to the future. Which is why he had invited PuNk here. He had a few recruits, and he certainly needed a few more. He thought he would send PuNk in search of some.

He had watched his friend *wander* around the park for a better part of a half hour, waiting for him, before he finally decided to emerge from the **shadows** to address him.

"Punk!"

"Shit!" Jumping about a foot in the air.

"Come over here."

"Fuck, man, you scared the shit..."

"You've been sleeping with Matilda."

"Uh... um... man... I... uh... I'm sorry."

"Hm. Here's what you're going to do..."

"I found this." Punk held the **gray book** out to Ωllister. Maybe it would be like an apology, and Ωllister would let him be.

Ωllister slowly shut his mouth. The trees stopped dripping, and the wind died down to **nothing**.

"I... uh... took it from your girlfriend's apartment. I... found the key somewhere, so yeah, it seems like people want this..."

Ωllister grabbed it. He opened it up. It was **blank**. He flipped *wildly* through it. It was all **blank**.

"It's a dummy. Fuck. Punk, where did you get this?"

"I told you, I got it..."

"No matter. We can use this. This, we can use. Ok, let me think." He sat down in the wet grass, and gripped his forehead with *long fingers*. Punk, not knowing what else to do, sat down with him. "OK, change of plans, this is what I want you to do. Take this book, break into The Platypus's mansion, I'll write the address down for you. Find the book that looks exactly like this. The only difference is it'll have my handwriting inside. You know my handwriting?"

"Well, kinda, I guess..."

"Of course you do. Wherever that book is, take it, replace it with this one, and bring me the real one. Bring me the **gray papers**!" He was really getting **worked up**.

"Uh, OK, but aren't mansions usually pretty, like, heavily guarded, or whatever?"

"Also, stop sleeping with Matilda. I need you to sleep with the other one, Zella."

"Aw man, I don't..."

"Go!"

So Punk leapt off into the night, **gray book** in hand.

Adelaide

There were *so many things* that made her want to **cry**. When Action had gotten lost, and she found her camped out on the porch one *chilly fall morning*, her ribs **showing**. *Adelaide* gave her food and water. The thankful cat spent the day in her lap, as she read some *awful* book about leather daddies. That time by the pool, the summer before 7th grade when Meredith Lerner had pulled one of her pigtails **so hard** half of it came out in her little hand, and she had thought Meredith Lerner was her *friend*. That older woman, on Gameshow Surprise, who began to **tear up** when she won the jackpot. The time her father called to wish her a happy birthday on the 17th, not the 19th. That day she was so sick, in pain, in her dorm *alone all day*, too **weak** to pick up the phone. That joke Vance would tell about the pirate, the peanut, and the wide-mouthed frog. That day she found out that Theodora had an ulcer, even though it was *about time*. That jeweler's ad, with the big diamond ring. The only **reason** that the one ex-boyfriend kept falling back on, 'I just fell out of love with you…' That pop song on the radio, with some *terrible* shrill girl whining about **lost love** in *unthinking trills*. That old thought of herself, alone, and elderly, without a blanket to cover her knees, her cold feet. That **expression** the blond girl was wearing in the cheap clothing catalog. That way her mother would stroke her cheek, as if she were a *house pet*. That *Zella* was **raped**, that it always fucked up her relationships with boys, that she remained *blindly optimistic*. That time the airplane dropped about 3,000 feet at once, everyone **screamed**, and the stewardesses hit their heads. That last day as a waitress even though she **hated** the job and everyone that worked there. That sun, finally peaking through wet leaves, its rays piercing the falling droplets. That *warm contentedness* that half a bottle of codeine cough syrup produced.

And this morning, when she picked up the **gray papers**, and even though she knew it was the blank version that The Platypus had given her, she started flipping through the book, and the pages **weren't blank**. They were the **gray papers**. The *real thing*. Safe in her apartment. That too, made her **cry**.

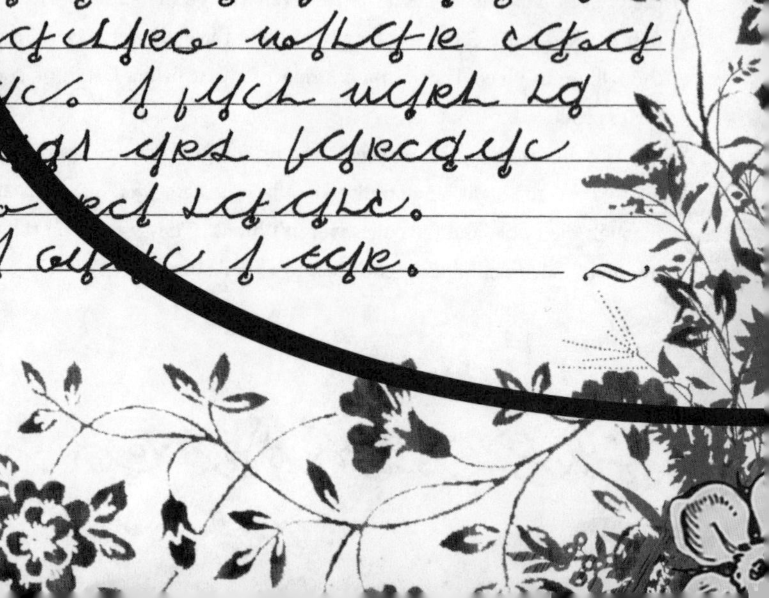

THE RUMOR had been going around for weeks. Paul was *living* in the small art museum downtown. Ωℓℓіꜱꜩᴇʀ believed this **rumor**. He *liked* to believe **rumors**. And, if it were true, then he knew Paul would come in handy in his plot to ruin THE WHITE BALL. Paul **hated** 𝕿𝖍𝖊 𝕻𝖑𝖆𝖙𝖞𝖕𝖚𝖘.

He checked his damp coat and scarf at the cloakroom and paid for his ticket. "Suggested admission: $15?" They weren't fooling *anyone* with that. He tucked the politely informative brochure into his back pocket and proceeded into the *near-empty* galleries. He wandered lazily through "American Folk Art" and "The Impressionists" because he knew if Paul were here, he could only be found in **one** place: "Antiquities" (*See Appendix D2. Paul*). Despite the rumors, he wasn't entirely sure if Paul was still **alive**. So he had to find out for himself.

The museum was *completely silent*. Ωℓℓіꜱꜩᴇʀ walked softly between the glass cases filled with ancient armor or earthenware. As he bent over to examine a particularly *striking* ivory inlaid comb, he felt a **presence** beside him.

"Paul!" Ωℓℓіꜱꜩᴇʀ. Trying to affect the tone of happy coincidence. "Hey, how've you been?"

A slow, unnatural **chuckle** pulsed from Paul's unshaven face. He turned, and began to *lope* toward the sculpture section. Ωℓℓіꜱꜩᴇʀ, not knowing what else to do, followed. As they walked, he furtively glanced into the **shadowy** corners. Supposedly Paul had found a way in between the walls, into the *substructure* of the museum. This allowed him to hide from the guards, and sleep safely at night. Ωℓℓіꜱꜩᴇʀ didn't feel terribly *serious* about **art theft**. However, the potential here was in the **millions**.

The ancient sculptures were kept in a large, airy gallery. Gray squares of skylight gave the room an *underwater, slow-motion* light. The toga'd Greeks stood stock-still, like they were attending Hades' frozen frat party.

"So… um, I heard about Mitchell. I'm really sorry Paul…" Ωℓℓіꜱꜩᴇʀ. An offering.

"You need to watch out." Came the **whisper**. Paul was caressing the face of a dead emperor.

"What? Who?"

"The White Sodality. They want you."

This brought a lump of **panic** to Ωℓℓіꜱꜩᴇʀ's throat. He couldn't stage a pre-emptive strike if 𝕿𝖍𝖊 𝕻𝖑𝖆𝖙𝖞𝖕𝖚𝖘 staged one *first*. But this was what he had come to talk about.

"Paul, help me. Come with me. I've got some kids together. We're really going to fuck everything up."

"The Art Terrorists?"

"Yeah… how did you know that…"

"Sure. I'll join. But you'd better watch that Vance. He's after your girl."

"My girl? You mean… Adelaide? What the fuck are you talking about?"

Ωℓℓіꜱꜩᴇʀ spent the next **four hours** trying to get Paul to tell him *more*. Begging, pleading, threatening, bargaining. But his old friend had assumed a motionless pose, his face, in line with the other busts, **would not crack**.

Zella & Matilda

Portfolio class again. This time, a *much-despised* student dragged his **dirty self** and his **dirty art** up onto center stage. Zella elbowed Matilda, her eyes rolling. Ωllister watched from the back row. He *actually* didn't think having Punk sleep with either of these girls was particularly useful. Also, he was quite sure Punk couldn't infiltrate The Platypus's mansion. He had sent him as a decoy, a **dummy**. Punk could be the distraction. If The Platypus thought that that was the best man he could send for the job, then he would be in good shape for when the *real* infiltration began. And for that, he needed one more **Art Terrorist**. Since Paul seemed trapped in the museum, he was back here.

Vance assured him that Nick was a *perfect* candidate, and had come along to watch the deal go down. They gazed up at the stage in **silence**.

"Uh. Totally." Opening remarks. "My name is Nick." He was short, rangy, with a black faux-hawkish haircut and pencil thin pubescent mustache. "Rad." He leaned his piece against the back wall. It was painted on a door, the type that might go to anyone's **bathroom**. "Uh, do you want me to unpack it for you, there's a lot of different layers. Do you want me to just talk about its surface, or sort of in an art historical context, or, or a symbolic context, or, I mean, you know?"

"Well, Nick," Ms. Man. "You can talk about whatever you like. Anything that you have to say about it, I'm sure will be relevant. That's what the class is for."

"Uh. Rad. This guy," He grabbed the door forcefully. "Is called '**ALL I WANT to DO TODAY IS FUCK**.'" He pulled a black marker out of his hoodie pocket, probably the *same one* that had been used to create the piece, and ran it underneath this exact sentence, **scrawled** across the bottom half of the door, as he read it **loudly**. "Huhuh. I thought that would be pretty funny, if it was called '**ALL I WANT to DO TODAY IS FUCK**.' Basically, uh, OK, basically, I'm, uh, trying to do a lot of different things on this one. I think mainly, uh, OK, so you have the naked girl here OK, right? And she's like a real traditional, like, porn-style figure. And I'm trying to, it's sort of like this cartoony thing, that sort of evokes, you know, the Sunday comics, y'know?" He tapped on the crude drawing of a girl, who was lowering her panties. She had no head. "But then you also have all these different layers of, like, flesh tones, y'know? And she's really sensual, you really just want to touch her." He was actually **doing so** at the moment. "She's kind of, like, irresistible, and at the same time, I'm really trying to evoke, you know, like it's fuckin', uh, uh, I want to make erotic, like, uh, like this whole no head thing. OK, like, she's a sex object, like, you know? Do you get it?"

"I'm not sure, Nick. Is this meant to be shocking, or offensive?"

"No, uh, fuck. I mean, do you find this offensive?"

"No, Nick, I don't." Ms. Man had been teaching at UNI-ARTS for *too long*.

"So then you've got this guy, this is me." He banged on the other figure sketched out on the door, kneeling across from the girl, wearing the same jeans and black band T-shirt that he currently was on stage. "It's interesting because, you know, I'm gonna have this whole, you know, well, the gallery that I'm showing it at, I'm gonna have this whole self-referential thing. I'm gonna be wearing this same outfit, and then I'm also, I was thinking about hiring..."

"You have a gallery?" Unable to mask the **incredulousness** in her voice.

This stopped the rant momentarily. "No, well, no, but whatever, I mean, I'm gonna show it at some point because I'm not one of these self-effacing artists who are like 'I don't know if I'm good enough.' I'm just saying, 'Hey, this is my fuckin' art, I know that you guys are gonna like it. And I know that it's gonna be seen, because, like, not because of the like 'myth of the solo genius,' because, it's out there, you know? It's out there.

"OK, so this is me, and I was thinking about when I show this painting, I'm gonna hire an escort. And bring her to the opening with me. You know, so it's gonna be this figure, which is me, and there's this other figure, which is, you know, this escort that I'm gonna hire."

"Is she gonna be that naked?" Nick's only friend shouted from the first row, which caused some mild *tittering* through the auditorium. Ωllister thought that this was shaping up to be a **boring boring** presentation.

Nick looked at Ms. Man nervously. "I, uh, haven't figured that out yet, but the important thing is, she is being hired for money, and me, as the artist, I am commodified in the same way. Do you guys know what I mean?" Silence had regained the auditorium. He was tapping on the very top of the piece, where there was a giant dollar sign in a thought bubble emanating simultaneously from both of the headless figures. "I mean, what's on both of their minds?" He dropped his marker and coughing, bent over to retrieve it. "OK, so like, she's getting paid to, like, look a certain way, and do certain things, like, she's not getting paid to be herself, she's getting paid to work as like a meta-symbol of sexual desire. You know? 'All I WANT to Do Today IS Fuck.' I'm trying to separate the signified from the signifier, you know what I mean? OK, so here's me, I'm like on my knees, in the same position that she is, because I feel like, as an artist, I might as well be sucking dicks too…"

"Nick." A **warning** voice. More *titters*.

"I mean, should I make money playing the stock market, or should I make money being an artist? I want to make money doing art. She wants to make money fucking."

"So then, Nick, what do you think the monetary value of your work is?"

"Well, clearly it's gonna go for at least $5,000." Again, **violent** coughing. "But probably much more, cause it's a pretty large piece. And I put a lot of thought and effort into it. If you'll notice here, and I haven't really finished it, I kind of want to do it a little darker."

He pulled the cap off of his marker. "As you see here I have these Corinthian columns." He began to draw them out, under the figures, adding to the work as it leaned against the back wall. "Can you guys see them?" He scribbled *furiously* to make them **darker**. "Like, what is the value, what is the artist's value? And for me, uh, I'll say $10,000 dollars. You know what I mean? If they are gonna put me on a pedestal, fuck, I mean, I don't mind being put on a pedestal, because, like at the end of the day, I'm just like this guy, and I do my craft, which happens to be art, and I end up with a commodity, and if I get put on a pedestal…" A protracted coughing fit, he put his hands on his knees to bark out a few big ones. "Hence, making me an object, I mean, I know about that, and I'm referencing it, so, I don't know, maybe $20,000 dollars."

"All right Nick, I won't haggle with you on the price, how about you tell us if there's anyone out there who influences your work."

"Well, not really, yeah, you know, I could talk about this and that artist who I think is making a difference, but it's not really about that. It's about... Hold on."

He leapt down into the front row, and grabbed a small boom box out of his backpack. He climbed back on stage coughing, and turned it on, as **loud** as it would go. "Do you know this album? Have you ever heard this album?" Ms. Man shook her head. "See, that's what I'm fuckin' talking about." He had to *shout* above the static thump coming out of the stereo, which made him seem even more **angry** and **rude**. "That's Goldtoothwa, you know, Goldtoothwa, the hip-hop artist? You know, she reaches more people, you know, than any fuckin' fine artist is gonna do. So, you know, she talks a lot about experiences that I haven't had, so to speak, you know, about ghetto livin' or rough ridin', or whatever but at the same time I feel like I can appreciate it. But, you know, I can have an ironic distance from it at the same time. And I think it's really important to keep that ironic distance because, uh, it's fuckin' pop music. And, uh, I need to fuckin' be able to critique it. But you know, artists like that will be gone in two years, and my painting, my painting?" Banging on it **loudly**. "Will fuckin' stay. You know, how do you have the visceral impact of you know, ghetto livin', and rough ridin', with lasting effect? That's gonna be this." He pounded some more, while coughing. "You know what I mean?"

"Can you please turn the music off, Nick?" He did so. "I wasn't really asking about pop influences, I was more looking for other artists."

"Well, uh, Jack Mackerel, he was an influence on me, I mean, not in an aesthetic way, I mean, I sort of see myself as what Jack Mackerel would've done, if he were more connected to pop culture, and more connected to you know, fuckin' life. Cause, you know, I like what he did in terms of like you know, uh, 'this is my expression, this is my expression!' but, you know, my expression is 'All I WANT to Do TODAY IS FUCK,' you know? All I want to do is fuck, but at the same time, having ironic distance because, I, uh, forgot the question..."

"OK, Nick, what did you use to make this?"

"Uh, it's oil. I, uh, work in oil, to again, reference the, uh, art historical process. What's that fuckin' asshole who did the uh, ladies, lounging naked lady, uh, I think that's what this is. It's fine fucking art. You don't have to draw a line between higher and lower, because they've both been commodified, they're both in fuckin' *Nouveau*. Like Mackerel, you know, they take pictures of it, it shows up in *Nouveau*. You know, same with the naked chicks who send in their photos to *JailBiscuits*. I uh, wanna point something out to you."

He hopped off the stage, taking the boom box with him, and exchanging it in his bag for a creased, rolled up magazine. "This is *JailBiscuits*." He began to *leaf through the pages* as he spoke. "Again, I don't take this seriously, I don't think there's redeeming value in it. But at the same time, you know, I want to find the unredeemable, I want to see what keeps you, what keeps you going, I mean, how do cultural products like this exist?" His eyes were not looking up from the pages. "Like what's going on here? Like this girl, this girl here." He held up the magazine. "Sent in pictures of her and her boyfriend fuckin', I guess. Well, you know, what's going on here? It's sort of this unredeemable cultural product, and that's what I'm interested in exploiting."

Ωllister turned to Vance in the back row. "We absolutely can not take this kid. He's an ass."

"Aw, come on man, he's good, he's my friend." Vance. Protesting wildly.

"Absolutely not. I've got to go. This is a waste of time." Ωllister stood, and **walked out** the auditorium door.

"OK, Nick, what kind of reaction do you want that audience to have?"

"Uh, I mean, I don't know." He threw the magazine back toward his seat. It fluttered spastically like a wounded bird. He had seen someone walk out. "I fuckin' work my ass off, all day, doing shit like this. But when it comes down to it, you know, I don't give a fuck. You know, I'm gonna make money for it, so I don't care what you think about it." At this point he delivered a lazy kick to the bottom of the painting, and the whole door began to fall forward. He half caught it, though it looked like it clipped him hard on the ear. He stood there coughing, and struggling to right it again.

"All right Nick, I think that's enough, you can take it down. I'll need to see you after class." She turned to face the rest of the auditorium. "Class dismissed."

Although he didn't expect to, Nick also met Vance after class, who had *far more interesting* things to say than Ms. Man. About something called **Art Terrorism**. Something he asked Nick to **join**.

THE PAST

After the incident, the East Slope Dorm was hell for Ollister. He didn't see *Adelaide* much, but because they were mutual, close friends of Theodora's, it happened often enough.

Theodora despised the situation. She was forced to flit between the two of them, a weary, ego-soothing shuttlecock. The fact that neither of them would fully open up about it, preferring to ignore the existence of the other, only made it more annoying.

Adelaide found her own place not far from Uni-Arts, a rented room in a dilapidated mansion, raccoons in the ceiling, door frames all askew. She got a cat, mostly out of fear of the raccoons. It was a kitten, actually, so it probably would have been eaten had it actually encountered those monsters in the attic. The cat's name was Action.

They shared a small gray room with wooden shutters.

Ollister came over only once. Dragged by Theodora, with no choice but to cross the threshold. He was there and bristling, rude and sarcastic, trying his hardest to look down on her life. Action was an easy target. Ugly, with a squashed hairless face, and mean. Even as a kitten it was fat, full of claws and screech. Ollister hated the thing. The cat had done nothing to him, but it was impossible to stop thinking about stepping on it, or tying its tail to a raccoon's.

Ollister couldn't stand to be in her house, or in her presence. Not so much because of what had transpired between them, but rather due to his own inability to detangle himself from her web. Just when he was discovering his true prowess, and his mind's mastery over other people and things of the art world, she had dealt a crippling blow. His burgeoning confidence was forever deformed and swelled into ego, now meant to conceal rather than conquer. His introversion intensified.

He was grateful when Hal showed up. Hal was a girl with a boy's name. She came to a party at Theodora's, wearing a tight T-shirt with two large owls, stretched to maximum size, on her chest. She was simple to seduce and stupid enough to really get under *Adelaide*'s skin, who sat on a couch ten feet away, watching as Ollister made an awful fool of himself, Hal, and *Adelaide* by extension. Her lips were tight. But she did nothing, and said nothing.

He tried this for a few weeks, but got no real rise out of *Adelaide*. Eventually, the East Slope became overrun with trash, drugs, and other couch surfers. He was stewing in hatred. He decided to leave Uni-Arts, and everyone in it. There was a vague hope, like always, that she would protest his going, but when she did not, he truly had no other option left, and he moved to the other side of town.

"Pete, I'm glad you're out of there."

"I know, that house was a mess."

"It was a forest. I didn't know where you were for months. What happened?" *Adelaide* had been *concerned*. She was actually a little relieved to see him across the diner table from her now, fiddling manically with his silverware, on his **seventh** cup of coffee.

"I don't know… I thought technology was against me or something… There was lots of chemical experimentation."

Not generally **unpleasant** to be around and plain enough to the eye, Pete was nevertheless *cracked up* as he was *cracked up* to be. There was an irritating *enthusiasm* about him. An ugly, shabby, *desperate* sort of hopefulness. She could see it in the way he snorted **coke** or nursed his life-threatening **crush** on the next-door lesbian. He was unable to grasp the easy realization that *nothing is fair, nothing is good,* which lead to an unfounded **bitterness**. She could see it flash out from under his brow when he was **angry, drunk, ranting,** which was *often*. Smoking the length of a **cigarette** in three or four long pulls, stubbing them out with punctuated **violence** as he would snarl and yelp at *perceived* injustices. The outbursts were seemingly saved for *Adelaide*, and in public, or around unfamiliar situations, he was painfully *shy* and *soft-spoken*.

There were times when his manic-depressive **mood swings** were so comically predictable that she wanted to take out a bet. Gamble and win somehow. Make *something* of it. Only listening to his rants, she heard her voice take on modulations of **condescension**, almost against her will. In the end he always did it to himself. **Humiliated, defeated** and **down**. No viable target in sight.

Just watching his self-inflicted *ordeal* she felt better about her own life. His *endless defeat* coupled with a *baseless optimism* brightened her own prospects.

But there were other reasons for hanging out with him, as well. He listened to bad music at a volume that made listening to bad music **essential**. He would suddenly desire a drive, and they would get in the car and go for *long loops* around the *pointless city*. He was a real whiz at anything technical or electronic. The talking computer he built was **amazing**. She was quite sure he was *sexually attracted* to her. Yet she had used the word 'friend' frequently and consistently enough near the beginning to know that nothing would ever come of it. He played ping-pong as though channeling the devil himself.

In the end there was no real choice. Pete was an **obligation**. Like a family member. Someone she could never be rid of because she pitied and respected him for the same reasons: his **shitty life**, his **shitty self**. Treading water inside a *dull* and *dirty mind*.

"Wait, what?" She had zoned out for most of his current monologue, but something **pricked** her ears now.

"The Art Terrorists. I've joined them. I mean... I don't know exactly what it is, exactly... but it's going to be rad."

"Art Terrorism? What's that?"

"I don't know... something rad?"

"Pete..."

"It's... uh... Ωllister."

Adelaide's face went blank.

"I know, I'm sorry. And I might've given him some drugs. I was on a lot of drugs. But it's finally something interesting. And I'm telling you, right?"

"Tell me more."

"I don't really know anything. He's gunning for The Platypus. He wants some book or something like that."

"The gray papers?"

"Something like that..."

"Pete, you should stay away." Adelaide. More to herself. He was after the book. She had to be realistic. He didn't want her back. He never would. He only wanted the book back. She wouldn't give it to him. She bit her cheek, hard.

Punk couldn't believe he still had this **stupid book**. Even though it was **blank**. He wanted to get rid of it. He wanted everyone to *leave him alone*.

He strode purposefully down the main drag, fists **clenched**, soaked in rain. He knew he had to obey Ⲟⲗⲗⲓⲋⲧⲉⲅ. But maybe that was OK. Whatever happened when he went to 𝕿𝖍𝖊 𝕻𝖑𝖆𝖙𝖞𝖕𝖚𝖘's, whether he got caught or not, he would still be rid of the **book**, and it would be over. He looked up in time to realize he was walking past Bunny's. The **gutter kids** weren't out front anymore. It was too early for that. They were probably out in the suburbs, having dinner with their *grandparents* in chain *restaurants*. For no reason at all he turned, and went inside the porno store.

Rageena didn't seem to care. It was off-hours. And a glance around, at all of the lewd positions on the shelves, was enough to convince him that he *needed* to relieve himself before he carried out his mission. So into the **black booth** he went.

Ⲟⲗⲗⲓⲋⲧⲉⲅ had given him some **money**, and he slid all of it into the slot. He wasn't going to *mess around* this time.

When the screen snapped on, he saw *three seconds* of thigh before it turned into 𝕿𝖍𝖊 𝕻𝖑𝖆𝖙𝖞𝖕𝖚𝖘's pink face. He **jumped**. He had forgotten. 𝕿𝖍𝖊 𝕻𝖑𝖆𝖙𝖞𝖕𝖚𝖘 smiled.

"Coming to see me?"

"Man, what, are you fucking following me?"

"Of course I'm following you. I don't talk to just anyone who walks into these things. Listen my little friend, I need that **book** from you, OK?"

"Uh... I thought you had the real... I mean, the **book**..."

"Just turn it over, and we'll stop following you, and leave you alone. How does that sound?"

"No, man, fuck this. I'm tired of this shit."

"I don't want to turn my men loose, I've heard they can be awfully nasty."

"Dude, I don't give a shit about your threats. You're gonna get terrorized anyway."

"What ever can you mean?"

"Ωllister's gonna fuck you up man, he's got all these guys, these terrorists, and a plan, and they're gonna..." PuNk suddenly realized that he shouldn't be talking about Ωllister's **plans**.

"Hmm. Sounds interesting. Want to come over, and tell me more?"

PuNk bolted out of the booth. He was going to be in so much **trouble** with Ωllister now. He should've just done what he was *supposed to*.

"That was quick." Rageena half smiled at him as he pushed his way out of the door. Once again, there was a gang waiting for him. But this time they were all **grown men**, dressed in immaculate white suits. He started to *run*.

But they were ready for him. A small, burly guy in sunglasses tackled him, and they dragged him around the corner, into the alley behind the store. He struggled, kicking and spitting, but the little one held him down, while another went through his pockets.

"I don't have the fuckin' **book** man!" PuNk. Desperate.

"Quiet." The White Suit. The one standing still. He sounded smart. The other one, who was searching him, finally put his hand down the back of PuNk's pants, where he was hiding the **book**. He **yanked** it out, and handed it to the smart one.

The White Suit held it gingerly with one hand, *disgusted*. He turned it upside down, so the pages flapped open. Everyone could see it was **blank**.

"Where's the **book**? Where's Ωllister?"

"Um... uh.. *Adelaide*, this girl..."

"She has it?"

"Uh, yeah..." PuNk. Clawing at the floor, trying to get up.

"Let's go." The smart one. Giving orders. The other guys dropped him, and the suits disappeared quickly around the corner.

PuNk sat up. He was amazed they *believed* his lie. He touched his ass. It was bleeding. The guy had **yanked** it out of there so *violently*.

"Fuck!" Shouting at no one.

Mister Adelaide

The Annual Uni-Arts Exposition. It felt more and more like a **circus** every year. Aided by the fact that it was held at the convention center which also hosted monster truck shows, ice charades, various costumed children's shows, mini-rodeos, and the *actual* circus.

It functioned both as a Uni-Arts Senior Show, and as a city-wide Art Fair. The convention center was divided in half. Floor paneling was brought in, and partitions were set up. On one side, graduating seniors, faculty, and a few *poorly chosen* alumni from Uni-Arts had their personal artworks displayed. On the other, various galleries, museums, and local artists rented small cubicles to sit in, their pieces **crowding** the walls. A few sat in the stadium seating, sipping white wine from plastic cups. The murmur drifted upwards into the rafters to compete with the pattering footfalls of *ominous* roof rain.

Adelaide elected **not** to have her own stall this year. It was *expensive*. And two different galleries here already represented her. They both had exorbitant commission rates, but luckily their pricing was exorbitant **as well**.

She sat in the *VELVETEEN GALLERY* cubicle, **not** chatting with Jolene, the artist's assistant, who sat *pretending* to read some new French novel. Jolene had most of the requisites for her position. She was thin, attractive in a birdy sort of way. She wore a black mock turtleneck with thick black framed glasses under dyed-black hair. Her family was *wealthy*. She would perform fellatio on the gallery owner, **never** intercourse. Her apartment was so minimalist as to be empty. Her tone was just condescending enough to sell **art**. She did not, however, have a foreign accent. This was her only *clear* disadvantage.

Adelaide was contemplating asking her if she thought perhaps one could be borrowed from a book, when someone caught her eye. From between all of the dealers and critics, the bald old collectors and the students, desperately trying to look poor. *A familiar stride.*

Compelled by hopelessness, she got up to follow **him**. She didn't know why. Pushing through the sea of black outfits. She caught up to him, and slowed her stride to match his. Shoulder to shoulder. He *inhaled* sharply.

"Hello, *Adelaide*."

He continued to glance in every booth, not meeting her eye, but grabbing her hand and **pulling** her along though the aisles. Somewhere in the steel rafters way above their heads, the *chirp* of a trapped **swallow** echoed.

"So much boring boring this year." Ωllister. To no one. He *paced* up and down the aisles **menacingly**. Ωllister had always looked at art quickly. Besides, she thought, he's probably *behind* half this crap.

Then the **tirade** began. Never looking at her, or the work at which his rather **loud** offhand comments were directed, he proceeded to make his *opinions* known.

"No more pictures of your friends."

"No more giant cartoon icons engaged in lewd acts."

"No more paint drips, on canvas, peeled from cellophane, on top of famous works. Absolutely none."

"No more old photographs of amputees or circus freaks."

They passed a tattooed lady redone in pastel watercolors. People nodded to Ωllister as he walked by. Those who knew him **steered clear.** Adelaide smiled weakly at mutual acquaintances.

"No more inflatable cellophane creatures."

"No more statues of men in dresses."

"No more glorified etch-a-sketch, doodle pen, geometrical crap."

"No more fine oil paintings of beer cans, or boxer-briefs."

"No more art executed by animals, the impoverished, the mentally disturbed, handicapped, or the underaged."

When he came to the monochromatic canvases, just a black square, just a red square, he **stopped**. A scowl fixed on his face, and the older lady at the booth *fussed nervously* with her clipboard. Adelaide stopped too. She turned just in time to see some liquored-up prick, who was talking on his cell phone, walk through a sand circle laid out on the floor, *supposedly* a piece of **art**. The man glanced back apprehensively but **kept walking**.

Adelaide snorted in amusement. Ωllister glanced in her direction. She didn't meet his eye. He took off again, in his *long stride*. As she followed, the **rant** continued.

"No more dead swans or decomposing doves."

"No more videos of people wearing flippers, or naked women covered in fake blood."

"No more collections of found receipts. No more pages ripped from books."

"No more breasts on men or penises on girls."

"No more white trash children or jungle gyms."

"No more art you can get inside of, or on top of. No more art you have to walk around to see 'another side of.'"

"No more trash taped together."

Adelaide looked at the balls of candy wrappers, straws, soda cans, and used tissue. "At least it's honest." Under her breath.

"No more naïve drawings of prepubescent children with their eyes too far apart."

"No more sheets of metal with bullet holes or piss stains. No more ceramic shit. No more piss on anything."

"No more mutilated horror show dolls. No more hastily executed organs."

"No more thugs, ghettos, or graffiti."

"No more shadowboxes or dioramas."

A blind man with a white cane had to be circumnavigated. He was wearing an *Official Critic* name badge. "That's right!" Ollister. **Triumphantly.** Adelaide wondered whether any of her pieces had sold.

"No more photographs of poor people."

"No more shit glued on canvases, including, but not limited to: rocks, puzzle pieces, polaroids, string, and more canvas."

"No more take-offs, interpretations, or mockeries of paintings already in existence."

"No more oversized art. Big canvases only make bad art bigger."

Ollister stopped at an **empty booth**. Nick was inside. Only his name on the otherwise **blank** walls.

"What's going on?" Ollister demanded.

"Oh, I rented this space, but I couldn't really be, like, bothered to make anything for it. Well, I mean I had this one thing, but I didn't like it. And I, like, had to come, this space was so expensive…" He shrugged.

"Interesting." Ollister. Looking over his shoulder.

"Uh look man, I'm excited about the terrorist organization and all…"

"I don't know what the hell you're talking about."

"But I got this…" He handed Ollister a white envelope. Ollister rotated away from Adelaide and opened it up. It read:

The Platy

Darling 'Art Terrorist',

I know about you, and your cute little plot. Give Allister my best.

I'll be seeing you soon, I hope…

Fun Regards

Ollister handed the envelope back to him, **pinching** his temples with his fingers. "This is why you weren't invited."

An older, clearly moneyed, couple shuffled up to the booth. The man wore a pink turtleneck. He asked, "Did all of your things sell, young man?" Nick quickly moved over to them. "No…um… I haven't painted anything yet. But I could if you want?" A disbelieving pause. "Like, I could paint your wife or something. Five thousand bucks." The couple pressed their lips into lines and shuffled away, his frail pink limbs **gripping** her shoulders.

Adelaide failed to suppress a burst of laughter. Nick shrugged. Ollister strode away, more quickly now, *eyeing* the exit door.

Adelaide sat down on a bench near the mobbed espresso stand. She folded her hands in her lap. After an eternal minute, Ollister came and sat down next to her. For the **first time** he let his eyes *fix* on hers.

"All this stuff. Nothing new." Ollister. Calm, now.

"New?" Adelaide.

"It doesn't have to be new. There's nothing new under the sun. But can't it at least be nice? Why doesn't anyone make something beautiful?"

They allowed many minutes of **silence** to pass.

"This isn't art." Ollister.

"Anything that sells here today is art."

She looked at his eyes.

Adelaide. Did you talk to The Platypus?"

She didn't answer.

"What's this Art Terrorism?" Adelaide.

"Have you been hanging out with Vance?"

"No."

Adelaide…" Ollister. Softly, measured, like he could barely control his voice. It was hard to tell what he was about to say.

"I have the **gray papers**, Ollister. And I'm never giving them back to you."

They were both quiet for a long minute.

He stood up, *expressionless*, and walked back into the crowd.

When Adelaide returned to the VELVETEEN booth late that day, and Jolene described the young man that had purchased her painting, Adelaide realized where Ollister had run off to. She imagined how her **art** would look in various states of *destruction*. On fire. Torn to bits. At the bottom of a lake.

"He was hot." Jolene. Flatly. Still looking down at her book.

Miriam &

They sat on a bench outside the Goldenplate Girl's dormitory. It was the most expensive at UNI-ARTS.

"Don't cry, Miriam. I mean, it bums me out when you cry."

Hearing this, Miriam only cried louder. Graham ran his fingers through his uneven crew cut. Lacrosse practice was in twenty minutes. He should be in the boys' locker room by now.

"Come on babe, stop crying."

"My dad is such an… a-hole!" Squealing protest. With the volume of a walrus, at the pitch of a dog whistle, from the lungs of an infant.

"Uh… So what did he say?"

"That I can't see you anymore."

"We'll just go away."

"And that I need to find someone in my own… league."

He ran his hands over the back of his skull again. "My aunt, she's got this place, it's like a whole mansion."

"And that I have to take my pills or he'll have me committed…" Sucking snot back into her tiny nose.

"It's across the freeway, on the East Side, where all those artist fags live."

"And rapists." Looking at him directly. "And my stupid cat needs stupid 3,000 dollar surgery."

"I mean, it's weird, she's got all this shit in there, my aunt, but she'd totally let us stay, 'cause…"

"And Silas won't stop calling."

"What?"

"Silas. He calls all the time. If I'm not at the dorm, he'll talk to Dolores. If I'm not at home, he'll talk to my father. About politics or school or whatever, 'cause he's the Dean, and then my father calls me and tells me I need someone in my social milieu."

GRAHAM

"I'm gonna kick that dude's fucking ass. Hole."

"Graham, don't." Voice flattened.

"Nah, nah, I told that slimy bitch."

"He hasn't done anything weird. He just calls."

"Nah. Un-uh. That guy is a freakin' pervert."

"I talk to him. I mean, he's nice but…"

"He's into all this porn shit. Seriously. OK, like, the other day me and Davy were over at his frat house, right? It's that huge colonial one. And out in the back there's all these birds, being all loud."

Miriam started to cry again.

"And Davy was gonna go get his air rifle, you know? But I was like, 'Nah bro, just get rid of that birdhouse, and they'll go away.' They had a… like a… mock replica of the house, as a birdhouse, you know?"

She pulled a scented pink tissue from her leather clutch and dabbed at her nose.

"It's Silas's house, and it's his freakin' birdhouse, right? He's all slimy and faggoty, I'm gonna kick his ass…"

"Graham."

"Davy found porn in the birdhouse. Like pinned up to the walls inside. Really small porn."

"Porn?"

"Yeah."

"Pinned inside the birdhouse?"

"Yeah."

"Was it of naked girls or naked blue jays?"

"Uh… he didn't say, actually."

"That's an important difference."

Graham kicked his toe against the hard ground. "We're going to my aunt's."

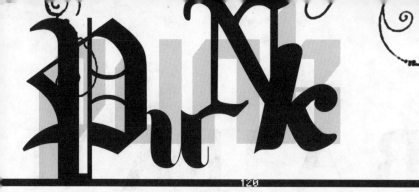

Punk and Franc were sitting out behind the doughnut shop. Punk wouldn't be there if it weren't for the doughnuts. Franc had fished them out of the **dumpster**. Every night the shop threw a bunch out—in black plastic trash bags—to make way for the fresh ones. They weren't *half-bad*, if retrieved before the **squirrels** and **rats** got to them. Sometimes that's all of there was to eat. Franc, in his combat boots and cutoff black T-shirt, had jumped right in and pulled out the haul, like some *Viking fisherman*.

"Man, were those White Suits scary?" Punk. Eyeing the doughnuts.

"Yeah, kind of."

"I think I got a thing from them. Like a note, calling me a terrorist or something. It was signed 'The Platypus.'"

"Yeah, that's them. It was freaky. I think I'm going to make a movie about it, man." Franc. Announcing. "I been writing the script for a while now. I mean, a lot of it's in my head. But I know it pretty well."

"I don't even know what that terrorism thing is about, but Ollister called it off."

"Why are you always doing whatever that guy tells you to? That's why they're after you."

"Whoa. You think they're after me?"

"Yeah. Probably. I mean, you got a note. They snatched me as soon as I said OK to Ollister about whatever that thing is. I thought we were just gonna rob galleries or something." Punk looked scared. "Stop hanging out with that dude."

"I'm not. Anymore. You're right. That's it, man. I'm not doing the terrorism thing. And I'm not sleeping with Zella."

"Who?"

"Zella, it's this girl he wanted me to sleep with so he could get gossip about this guy Vance, or who knows what, cause they're friends, and she likes to gossip, or whatever. But I'm done. I'm a free agent now."

"What did you tell Ollister?"

"Nothing. I mean, I haven't seen him. Not even at the **SNOOTY FOX**."

"There's this guy, my friend, who bartends at the **SNOOTY FOX**, Zero, you know him?"

"Mmm-hmm." PuNk. Mouthful of pink frosting.

"Well, he says there's this guy that always comes in there, this rich dude, and he leaves big tips or whatever." He paused to scratch a skull-headed wrench tattoo on his arm. "And my friend, he's like a film kid, and he was telling this guy about, you know, our project, and the guy, well, Zero said he was drunk, but he seemed into it. So I said..."

"Mm." PuNk. Alarmed. "Mm. Dere's a roush, roush ona donuh."

Franc tossed the *offending bite* over his shoulder and fished around in the garbage sack for a new one, his train of thought un-interrupted.

"These guys like this. Twenty grand is nothing to them. That's like twenty bucks to you or me. So I'm supposed to go to the **SNOOTY FOX** some night this week and me and my buddy are gonna talk him into it."

"Mm."

"I'm real excited. This could be my big break, man."

"Mm. Wha's it abood?" PuNk. Spraying powdered sugar like a snow blower.

"It's loosely based on, uh... my life, you know? (***See Appendix D1. Franc***) Leading up to the kidnapping. It's just about this kid, in his teens, who works, you know? Doing something, his dad's dead, you know, real life stuff."

"Mm." Franc had bad B.O. All of PuNk's **gutter** friends did. It was requisite. But there was something *sickeningly sweet* about Franc's. He wondered if he wore perfume because he was French. On top of the sugary donuts it was beginning to make PuNk a little *nauseous*.

"I mean, movies these days. It's like spoon-fed to you. These corporate guys are like 'What do kids want?' And then they try and write something for them, like aimed at them. It's bullshit. I'm not writing for an audience man, I'm writing for me."

PuNk **threw up** a little in the back of his throat. He put the chocolate éclair he was holding down on the sidewalk.

"And I'm not moving to L.A. either. They can fuck themselves. It's gonna be filmed right here where I'm from. In real fucking spots man, like this corner right here."

A corner that was *shortly* covered in **rainbow sprinkle vomit**.

Miriam & Dolores

Miriam was packing. As she pulled out the fourth suitcase, Dolores sighed and let droop the Nouveau magazine that had heretofore blocked her view of the ridiculous, frenzied spectacle.

"Don't you think that's a little much for an overnighter at Graham's? You've got a ton of crap over there already."

Miriam continued to cram crumpled panties into the zebra-striped suitcase.

"Or did he auction all your underwear off on the Internet?"

"Have you seen my vanilla cake lip gloss? Life blows without it…"

"All right. Fine. Where the freak are you going?"

Miriam embarked on an archeological hunt through strata of clothes, shoes, magazines and crap spread all over the floor of their large sleeping quarters. If this weren't the most expensive dormitory on campus, her room wouldn't be so big, and she could find what she was looking for. Dolores waited, slack-jawed, for a minute for some response before returning to her magazine charticle with a snort of nonchalance.

Like many rich girls, Miriam was piggish. Dolores wasn't going to pick up someone else's crap. But wading through it every time she wanted to get in and out of bed grossed her out. A Fire-Hot CheeseDoodle in last fall's hottest stiletto pump. Mascara marrying magazines to panty hose. Countless empty bags of giant marshmallows. Slim cigarette butts fused onto CDs. She even found a diamond once, in an old diet shake can. She kept that.

If only the boys who were constantly breaking like waves against Miriam's pristine façade could see this trove of trashiness. The face Miriam presented to the world was polished, brushed, sprayed, plucked, made-up, and completely made up. Her hair was done every other day by a sculpture student from East Slope, who had yet to convince Miriam to let her enter it into the student exhibition show. Her clothes were fresh off the hanger, or right out of the box. "Thank God for catalogues!" She would scream. In short, she looked like every other rich girl in the dorm, only hotter. Dolores wanted to send out a memo or put up a banner, disclosing Miriam's rotten, putrid insides. She especially wanted to notify Silas.

"Silas called." Dolores. Still pretending to read.

"Why would I care about that?" Trying to find a top for any one of sixteen topless tubes of lipstick arrayed on the sink counter before her.

"Um… because he has the hots for you?"

"He's a pervert."

"So? They're all perverts. Get realistic. He's gonna be so rich."

"Graham is not a pervert."

"And he's the head of UNI-ARTS Lacrosse and you're queen of the Cheerbleaters, and that means…"

"And what the freak would I need money for?"

"Because Graham is a loaf of flippin' white bread, that's why. And if you ever expect to be even somewhat respected…"

"I love Graham." Miriam. In her big-screen voice. "He is everything to me and I would kill myself for him. We're eloping."

Dolores began to chew on an interesting thumbnail. "That's cute. Don't forget your curler set." Pointing to the never-used plastic bubble by the sink.

"Drat!" She began trying to stuff it into an overfull shopping bag.

"Well, I guess that explains the packing. Where are you going?"

"The Mousy Inn. For now."

"Classy. Your dad is gonna freaking love that."

"Look, I don't give a flip, OK? You can all go to heck." She began to drop various bags into the hall, in preparation for what was sure to be a grand exit. "Bye, Dolores. Good luck with your crush on Silas." Fake smile.

"Screw you."

Miriam slammed the door. Dolores could hear her best friend dragging bags down the hall, away from the door, for the next half hour, as she leafed idly through '15 Ways to Get It On in a Pond." Each issue of *Nouveau* was better than the last.

It would be a relief to have her out of the picture. She was sure that if Miriam was absent from the next dance, and she were wearing that green low-cut top, Silas would turn his sights on her. She had been practicing her blowjob technique on members of the freshman dorm next door. As long as he didn't find out that Miriam had eloped with Graham, he would probably just forget about the whole thing and then Dolores could bag him.

The phone rang. She pressed the button and put the receiver to her ear. There was no one on the other end. She hung up. It rang again.

"Hi, Silas. Um… did you just call?"

"Is Miriam there?"

"Um… She eloped. With Graham. They're at the Mousy Inn."

He was *despondent*.
His **plan** had to be called off,
the whole thing. He wouldn't
go to THE WHITE BALL.

But that didn't even seem to *matter* now.
It seemed to him that he would feel the same **void**
whether he had plans or not. It was all a wash. Like he was
floating in an isolation tank, **senseless**.

Above all, he did not want to see *Adelaide*. **Ever again.**

There was no escape. His friends, THE WHITE BALL, PUNK, The Platypus, all
distractions from the pure flat plaster *nothingness* that the universe is, and **demands**.
Consciousness could not more clearly be a *curse*. He envied the birds, *lighter than air*,
flickering in and out of the trees, letting air from their tiny beaks in *lilting staccatos*. Air that
was no more than they were.   Songs gone as soon as they were sung.

How he longed for a mind   that could adhere to the **task of the present**. But
memory and *forethought*, in their big dumb wrestling match, managed to entirely **blot out**
the here and now. Not that he particularly wanted to be
conscious of that either. He wanted air, bright and clean.
Nothing, rather than the absence of something. If only self-
destruction didn't look so
abominably stupid.

People didn't make sense to *Adelaide*. They were *unalike* and *unrelated* to her. She found their actions **perplexing**, their motives **indiscernible**. People made her **uncomfortable** because she had no idea how they thought, and no idea what they thought of her.

She sat outside, under her small porch awning. It was raining, *steadily*. Small drops were finding their way to her shoulders, her hair.

There was a pair of **sparrows** tucked up under the awning. They were nuzzling, talking about the weather. Action watched them from the sill behind the window screen, eyes wide, alert to their movements and to the *thunder*. The sky was **darkening** and the lightning came regularly, rhythmically. Inside the muted television flashed *cryptic answers* against the wall.

She should've given him the **gray papers**. She would give them to him now, if he were here. They *represented* something. An understanding that only he had reached. She couldn't fathom why she would **reject** that. She felt *ashamed* and *embarrassed*. She didn't want to leave her house.

People **misunderstood** her, they thought she was flighty, spastic, they thought she was rich, spoiled, self-centered. She had no talent for small talk and this made people think she was **rude**, closed-off.

People seemed to *want something* from her. They made her **wary** and **strange**.

He was the only one she had believed, trusted. Being in the UNI-ARTS Exhibition, surrounded by throngs of people, she was only able to see Ωllister, and that was because he was **different**. *He wasn't people.*

125

Ωllister & Adelaide & punk & Zella & Matilda

It was one of *those things* that everyone else was going to, everyone he knew. There was *considerable* hype, for an **art kid party**, and the vague feeling around it was that if you didn't go, you would *miss something*.

Ωllister wanted to miss it all. He didn't want to talk to anyone at the **party**, so he decided to *lurk*, stick to the margins.

After cutting through the rain, climbing the three flights of stairs to the top floor of the warehouse, and walking in to the hot thrashing **party mob**, he was sure he wasn't missing *anything* at all.

He wasn't in the **mood** for this. Things were weighing heavily on his mind. He felt *melancholy* and *groundless*. His usual wells of sarcasm and invention had been **dry** lately, and he felt a stretch, a tightness, in his mind. There was *paranoia,* too. It would be hard to escape The Platypus's reach, now that his **plot** had been exposed. He hadn't been taking enough **pills** or **liquor** lately, and **shadows** were beginning to *coalesce* into shapes. He feared it was The White Sodality, or some whacked-out **art terrorist** he'd abandoned desperate to strike back. To *expose* him.

He scanned the crowd quickly, looking for faces he knew, or rather, skipping faces he knew, and looking for ones that he **didn't**. He doubted she would come to something **stupid** like this, but he couldn't help thinking about seeing Adelaide. He was *desperate* not to see her.

It was late in the festivities and the room was full of empty **beer cans** and **cigarette smoke**. It was the usual mix, kids from UNI-ARTS, art gallery fucks, the anarchists, a few enclaves of punk rock dweebs, hipsters, clueless yups, the mods, half-breeds, and some girl in nothing but body paint. The **party** was nearing its *apex*. It was so hot and crowded inside that anyone still hanging out had to be *significantly* wasted. The drunkest kids bounced next to the DJ table, singing along to Goldtoothwa's latest hip-hop hit. There was palpable mania, and that sort of *desperate playing at fun* that characterized the young modern mind. Most of the **art** that was hung on the walls, as an excuse to gather in the first place, had been torn down, or mutilated with **cigarette** butts and **beer** spray. Ωllister walked a quick perimeter. There would be *nothing* new or good here. But he always had to check.

There were psychedelic computer-generated landscapes, palm trees made of trash, photos of the sun, a taxidermied tiger to which someone had done *unspeakable* things involving spray paint and cocktail umbrellas, installations of

sand dioramas and childhood bedrooms (complete with hipsters **scamming out** on the beds), a fetus ice sculpture with a kiddie pool below it to catch the drippings (and a fair amount of vomit), some foam tubing, a beer-amid: clearly an impromptu sculpture of this evening's making (*See Appendix E. The Beer-amid*), a rather clever installation where they had knocked a hole in the wall and peering through it one could just make out a pair of naked girls *dining on duck* under hot stage lights. Drawings of bears and medieval peasants, and a giant 'pussy piñata' that was hung high enough that it hadn't been destroyed yet. One could only **guess** what it was filled with. But all in all, **boring boring** stuff. Just as Ωllisder had expected. Then his **heart** skipped a beat. There was the back of ᴄAdelaide's head, it was her, *unmistakable*, standing in a circle of friends. **She was here.**

PuNk, he didn't see. This was because PuNk was up on the roof, braving the inconsequential *dribble* to talk to a grad school couple that Zella had told him were **swingers**. The girl was *banging on* about her thesis, something bland about museum funding. When PuNk could stand to listen he would try to insert some *sexual innuendo*, so they might pick up on the fact that he was open to **swinging**, and would be delighted to accompany the two of them **to bed**, but it was proving difficult, given the subject matter. "I'd like to see those 'figures' some time." was the best he'd managed to do, but she didn't really seem to be *getting it*. Mostly he was thinking about his bowels. They were grumbling, moving. He hadn't taken a shit in **days**, and now his mental energy had to be focused on keeping his rectum tightly closed. He kept shooting *pained* glances at the boyfriend, who was lazily peering over the edge of the roof, trying to figure out if his girlfriend's hotness justified dealing with this guy's assuredly small cock.

Suddenly, with the force and stink of an exhaled **cigarette**, Zella wafted up to them. She was wearing something ridiculous (*See Appendix Z2. Zella's **outfit***).

"I thought you said these dudes were swingers." PuNk. Forgetting the girlfriend was three inches from him. The couple looked at each other and then back at Zella. The girl started **screaming**.

"If you don't fucking stop spreading shit about us, I'm gonna kick your ass, you freaky bitch." Her boyfriend locked his arms around the *hysterical* girl and proceeded to carry her downstairs. Zella watched them with an expression meant to indicate she had absolutely **no idea** what they were talking about. The girl yelled from the stairway, "You're dead, bitch." And then they were gone. Merged back in the *teeming mass* of the **party**.

Zella turned back to PuNk. "Thanks a lot, genius."

"Oh…" PuNk shifted his weight *uncomfortably*, trying to escape the **dull ache** of his sphincter. He didn't want to be alone with her. He wasn't following orders anymore. "Yeah… sure…"

"What's the deal, anyways? Are you really that hard up?"

"I just…"

"Are you horny, PuNk?"

"What?"

"Right now. Are you horny?"

PuNk just stared back at her *vacantly*, squeezing his cheeks together as hard as he could. His viscero-motor skills required his full **concentration**. He wondered where Matilda was. He couldn't **scam out** with Zella. It was strange that she was even *talking to him*. She never had before. Maybe Adelaide had sent her to do the same thing Ollister had wanted him to do. And she was in with The Platypus, for sure. He had to get away from her.

Staring into his eyes Zella *flicked* the front of his jeans, making a dull **thud**, which confirmed his erection. She couldn't have known that the shits always gave him a boner. She grabbed his face and began **furiously scamming out** with it. She smashed her mouth into his, painting a beard on him using the slut-red lipstick she was wearing. Her breath tasted like *rum* and *perfume*, hot and sickly sweet. His tasted like pot smoke and old french fries.

With dramatic stage timing, Adelaide opened the door to the roof, framing the **grotesque tableaux**. Zella pushed herself off the **untouchable**. PuNk, out of surprise, or muscle fatigue, let his bowels go. *Diarrhea*. A major blow-out. He *involuntarily* doubled over at the waist, and with a loud flapping sound, the wetness quickly ran down the backs of his legs, soaking into his pants, running into his shoes, and all over the ground. The smell was **immediate**, and **horrifying**.

Adelaide, with a blank face, shut the door calmly and went back downstairs.

She rejoined her friends, standing in a corner by a number of porno star cardboard cutouts. If PuNk was here, Ollister might be, too. She *needed* to **talk** to him.

"I thought you were going to find your cigarettes?" Matilda. Always concerned.

"I was."

"Did Zella have them?"

"I assume so." Zella was in the recent habit of stealing Adelaide's **cigarettes** from her purse and then pretending they were her own.

"What's wrong?"

"The usual. Everything." Adelaide.

"Is it the lawsuit?"

"Yeah. It sucks." Adelaide. Lying. "I think if the Velveteen finds out about it I might lose my deal there."

The only thing that would *really* make her lose her deal was upsetting 𝕿𝖍𝖊 𝕻𝖑𝖆𝖙𝖞𝖕𝖚𝖘. Which seemed **easy enough** to do. Men in white suits had been leaving **envelopes** on her doorstep. She didn't open them. But she knew what they were about. He wanted Ωllister. Just like she did.

Adelaide had come up with an ingenious **solution** to all of their problems. They could work together, like they had before. She could *pretend* to turn him in to 𝕿𝖍𝖊 𝕻𝖑𝖆𝖙𝖞𝖕𝖚𝖘, or feed him false information. Ωllister would be smart enough to find a way to *manipulate* the situation to his **advantage**. It would make a fantastic chapter in the **gray papers**. She could have him back and have art up at THE WHITE BALL. Now all she had to do was tell him what 𝕿𝖍𝖊 𝕻𝖑𝖆𝖙𝖞𝖕𝖚𝖘 had offered her across the dinner table, and he would know how to take advantage of it. Her eyes scanned the **party** for his profile.

"That would be awful." Matilda placed a sympathetic hand on her shoulder. She could be so **annoying** sometimes.

"Is Vance still staring at me?" Adelaide. *Sighing*. Matilda looked around quickly and spotted him, sitting on the defaced tiger.

"Yeah. Gross. How long has he been doing that?"

"All night." Adelaide waved away the **joint** that was being passed around. Matilda did the same, imitating the style and duration of the wave. "I just caught Zella scamming out with PuNk on the roof."

"Oh my god." Matilda's face fell. "Why does she always have to do that? I thought she hated his guts." She seemed upset.

"Apparently not enough to keep her tongue out of them."

"Well… I bet PuNk really catches it from Ωllister." Matilda. Crossing her arms.

At the thought of this a *slow smile* crept onto Adelaide's face. It vanished a moment later when she saw the back of Ωllister's head drift out the front door. She was on the other side of the room, the throng between them. He was **here**, but *leaving*. She could run out into the rain after him, but that might look **stupid**. She quickly grabbed the **joint** out of some orange-haired kid's hand and took a **long pull**. The moment had *passed*. He would be at the next **party**. He always came to these things even if he slinked around and pretended not to.

Matilda didn't notice. "Why would PuNk do that?" She carried on with her strange pout. "Doesn't he give a shit?"

And suddenly, with perfect comic timing, PuNk came *barreling* through the room, pushing **drunk kids** out of his way, right and left, head bowed, dripping *copiously* from his ass and legs, stinking something **awful**. Once the path to the exit was clear, he ran, peels of laughter trailing out behind him, down the stairs, and into the **night**.

Dolores & Silas

The phone rang. Dolores picked it up. There was no one on the other line. She set it down in the cradle, her hand still resting on it as she gazed at the blur the rain was making of her window. When it rang again she started, and answered it too quickly.

"It's me. I'm downstairs. Hurry up." Silas.

Chaos enveloped her mind. So much to do in the next thirty seconds. Pick out an outfit, change clothes, change shoes, do her hair, do her nails, do her make-up. She lurched around the dorm room like a cat tied to a lightning rod.

There was still a ton of Miriam's stuff coating the floor. Her mess had not eloped with her. Dolores cut her foot on something. In multiple places. She pulled on a crumpled green sweater belonging to her former roommate, hoop earrings, and was now peering fearfully into the mirror.

In her panic, she had coated her eyes in a thick black sludge of mascara and eyeliner. Attempts to wipe some of it off had created gray raccoon bags under her eyes. These served to highlight the already skull-like appearance of her face. She was trying desperately to color the rest of it in when the phone rang again. That would be him. She abandoned the paint job and crammed her feet, one still bleeding, into a tiny pair of Miriam's pink slippers.

He was pacing impatiently in the lobby. The plump housemother behind the desk, with the chin hair, singular, eyed him suspiciously. Boys weren't allowed upstairs in the Goldenplate dormitory.

Silas looked much the same as always. Handsome-boy tailored suits. Polished shoes. A touch of anachronism. His hair slicked back, unguinous. It was greased completely to prevent any stray locks from escaping. The black shimmer of his crown contrasted with his natural dull eyebrows. It gave the unsettling impression of borrowed hair. His eyes were dark, and small. They bugged out so that even when his eyelids were closed the roundness of his eyeballs could still be seen. His hook nose was broken and swept out, slightly to the right. Combined with the lift of his left eyebrow it gave him a comically quizzical look. Spanish Inquisitor, maybe. His lips were small, thin and over-moist. But the thing that tied these disparate features into a rather handsome and determined face was his jaw. It was like a support beam for a railroad bridge. It was often stuck out, violently. Dolores thought he would make a wonderful rapist.

He motioned her into the main sitting hall, right off the reception room. They sat in giant, and pungent, antique armchairs. A girl played the grand piano in the corner. Smashing out some cartoon mermaid theme song.

"Where is she?" Silas.

"Um... At the Mousy Inn. I told you that, like, days ago."

"Who'd she go with?"

"Graham. Duh. What's with you...?"

"I'll kill him."

She opened her mouth, as if to speak, and instead paused, running her tongue over her teeth, her brow furrowed in consternation.

"What?"

"There was something on the tip of my tongue."

"Well, spit it out."

"No, I wasn't going to say anything, there was actually, like, a thing, on the tip of my tongue."

"I know. That's what I'm saying. Spit it out." He turned his face, still frozen in annoyance, toward the pianist, now into the second verse of "Fish for Friends."

"There's nothing Miriam can do that I can't. I've seen your website."

"Fascinating."

She visited it frequently. It was a porn site. He never starred in the movies, but the voice of the director/cinematographer was clearly his. He slick-talked drunk socialite girls into getting 'natural' on camera, in the middle of a kegger, at the mall bathroom, in a rented van. He, or whichever of his friends wanted to 'star,' would promise money. If she was in a bathroom, they would steal her clothes and leave her stranded at the mall. The van videos always ended with them dropping her off in some ghetto, or out on the freeway, waving her promised money, or sometimes even her purse, out the window taunting, as they drove away.

Videos of this van variety were especially popular, and so he and his friends had created VirginVan.com. It had many paying customers. Silas was promoted to demi-god status by his perverse kindred. Somehow, no one who would've disapproved of this activity, no one of authority who could have brought consequences crashing down around his ears, ever found out about it.

"I'll re-enact episode 13 for you." She batted her blackened eyelids. The first bars of 'Chariots of Conch' tinkled in from across the room.

He looked at her blankly then stood and pointed at the girl on the piano bench.

"Stop that. Now." Forcefully, loudly, across the length of the sitting hall. The girl, clearly offended, and more than a little scared, scampered backward from the room. He turned back to face Dolores, still standing.

"My black book is full. I know plenty of girls exactly like you. What I need is a trophy wife." Calm and even. "If you tell Miriam about the website, I'll kill your face."

"Jeez, Silas. She freakin' eloped, all right?"

"Your slipper is bleeding." By the time she looked up, he was gone.

He would go away. The **only** thing to do was to start over. Somewhere *else*. A fresh palette. Things here were *fucked up* beyond repair.

Ωllister decided to leave town. He had **nothing left.** Especially after he sold most of his possessions. His extended family had a summer home in a small town *far away.* He would go and stay there, and figure out what to do next. He didn't want to see these *people*, or this *town,* or any *art*, **ever again.**

The gallery was **small** and **dank**. It had been converted from an industrial garage, or storage unit maybe. It was owned by an over-the-hipster-hill guy who made his living by throwing **parties** in this space and then *pick-pocketing* the teenage guests.

Adelaide, Matilda, and *Zella* stood in a tight circle **clutching** their bags. It was **crowded** inside, it was **loud**, and it was much **hotter** than outside. The floor was **wet**. *Adelaide* had gotten new shoes at the *ThriftWhopper* that day. The heels were *insane*. They were painful, but *potent* in some sort of witchy, bitchy way.

The **party** was an opening for *Beaches and Cream*, the stage name of some Uni-Arts girl. *Adelaide* couldn't remember her real name, but had met her numerous times. She was the *type* who pretended she had never met you before, *every time* she met you. She was currently at the front of the room trying **desperately** to call attention to herself. She stood in a pile of white beach sand and mouse bones, wearing a white thong bikini. She had a *myriad* of paint cans, full of creams, milks, half and halfs, whipping creams, buttermilks. Of varying color and consistency, she was **vigorously slopping** them onto the first of a dozen or so canvases hung on the wall. The idea was '**live art**,' she would continue painting, splashing, until someone *completed* the current work by buying it. Then she would move onto the next canvas. She had been on the first one for an **hour and fifteen minutes**. Almost everyone in the room *happened* to be facing the other direction, save two or three lonely oglers, who stood right at the edge of the sand watching the droplets of **sweat** and **cream** combine on her *bare ass*.

There was also *supposed* to be some art dork with a showing of **robots that broke things** or did some other anti-productive robot work. But all it turned out to be was a lame little box in the center of the room that *dirtied dishes*. Someone had knocked into it and **broken** it ten minutes before their arrival. ⟨Adelaide stared idly at its exposed wires and coils and thought about the gathering puddles of *rainwater* and *milk* on the floor.

She was *sure* Ωllïſter would be here tonight. He had propped both these artists up. Booked the show. She was **dying** to talk to him. She wanted to tell him her new plan, wanted to give him the gray papers back, *more than anything* wanted to see him.

The girls passed around a tear-drop bottle that held just a few fingers of **black liquor.** The rest of its contents could be found in the **pits** of their stomachs, Matilda included. Some friend of Zella's had brought it from Prague. It had been *full* at the beginning of the **night**, when the sky was still just a threat. They had begun at the **anarchists' commune**, then to some show with a band that used **barking dogs** chained to the drums for their *vocal section*. This seemed to be the after party. '*Opening*' was an idea lost on this crowd.

So was *conversation*. When Matilda was inebriated in any way she became very **confused** or **weepy**. At the moment she was the former. Zella had been speaking non-stop since about 6 PM. ⟨Adelaide suspected her of *furtive pill-popping*, and hadn't tuned in to the monologue in about an hour. Her friends were starting to **grate**. She squinted, looking around for Ωllïſter, the **party guests** overlapping in *blurry* duplicate.

"…because I knew them, you know. Jill tried to borrow my oils in class one time. I didn't let her, of course, but…"

"Wait, who?" ⟨Adelaide. Trying to **focus** on Zella's face.

"Jill and Darren. You know, the suicide artists?"

⟨Adelaide looked down at her **witch shoes**. She felt like the **house** on top of them.

"You remember?" Zella. Carrying on. "It was like two years ago. They made a giant stretch canvas and put it on the sidewalk below the ceramics room on the ninth floor, and jumped onto it. It was a huge deal. They had that big manifesto written about how they wanted the canvas displayed, or whatever, and how they would be famous, starting 'suicide art.' They had even signed the corner of the canvas before the whole stunt, isn't that hilarious? Of course, the authorities took the whole thing away, as evidence, or some bullshit, and there were all those 'concerned' parents who pulled kids out of UNI-ARTS right and left, and Dean Euphrates was all trying to cover it up. I don't know… I mean, I thought it was one of the better ideas I had heard in a while. I mean how are you supposed to get famous nowadays, anyways?" She took a punctuating drag of her cigarette and chased it with a swig of the black Prague liquor. She tried to pass it to Matilda, who didn't seem to be able to sense it in any way, so ⟨Adelaide took it instead. Zella coughed, drew a wheezing breath, and began again, looking over Matilda's head.

"I hate that girl." Arm raised, pointing right at the girl she was talking about, from all of three feet away. "She wears so much makeup. Light won't even reflect off her face. It's like a black hole face. It's like I can't even see it. And her clothes…"

"It looks like she found them in a dumpster behind a French circus." *Adelaide. Quietly slurring.*

"You are so right, *Addy*. That observation is so… right-on." The **cigarette** again, then: "Omigod, it's Sebastian." She rotated away from the surprise of his presence.

"Didn't you fuck him already?" *Adelaide. Gently trying to pry the* **bottle** *out of Matilda's* **unconscious fingers.**

"Yeah, so?"

"That guy looks gay." *Matilda. Whispering.*

"Who?" *Adelaide. Squinting again.*

"Are you drunk? What's your deal tonight?"

"I… I miss Ollister." *Zella and Matilda turned to* **stare.** *Adelaide looked* **drunk.**

"Oh." *Zella, at a loss.* "Um… I thought you were over that. I mean, just at last night's party, I was telling Vance…"

"What?"

"…that you were available. Or, like single or whatever."

"Why would you do that?" Her friend stared back at her, and shrugged. "No, *Zella*, that sucks. That'd be like me… like me telling PuNk that he made the right choice by picking Mattie over you."

"What?" Now it was *Zella's* turn to be **pissed.** She looked from a defiant *Adelaide* to a sheepish Matilda and back again, her mouth agape. They were all so *drunk.* "Is Mattie…? How come you didn't tell me? I liked him…"

"Whatever, *Zella*, the only reason you want boys to fuck you is so that you have someone's undivided attention for ten minutes."

Zella's shoulders went limp. Her eyeliner *narrowed* and *darkened.* "You know what? Fuck you." She flicked her **cigarette** into *Adelaide's* torso before stomping off. It bounced *harmlessly* off of her overcoat and **hissed** when it met the liquid on the floor. *Adelaide* hadn't meant to be **mean**, she was just being… **factual.** *Zella* would be waiting by the car at the end of the night.

Adelaide looked at Matilda, perhaps for some sort of *justification,* or at least *agreement,* but Matilda had begun to **cry.**

"There were so many different kinds." *Matilda sniffling.*

Adelaide could *barely* hear her. "What?" Annoyed.

"The dinosaurs. They were so cute. And now they're all… so… dead."

Adelaide turned away. Right in time to see *Beaches and Cream* smack some guy in the **face** with a **paint can.**

Miriam & Graham

Before she even woke, Miriam felt herself rolling over, the sheets sticking to her back. She cracked open her left eye to confirm it was light in the room. Seeing it was, her eye involuntarily squeezed closed again. She could've done without the visual verification; she could feel the light, the heat. She sighed in that way only rich girls really can. The heavy hotel curtains added to the hot and stifling stagnation. Graham must've not switched on the air conditioner when they arrived at room 182 last night. Dolores always kept it completely frigid in their dorm room. Graham hated that.

She could feel his sweating hulk next to her, emitting a toaster warmth, and the stench of humidity. She cracked her eyes again to check his. Closed. He was still naked, and now she saw that she was too. Save for a green stiletto still on her right foot. It felt heavy and she attempted to dislodge it from her foot by digging the heel into the mattress. When this proved difficult she lifted her head to peer down and this made her immediately aware of something stuck to her cheek. She batted it away, startled with revulsion. It was a condom. Last night.

Graham had driven her here. She had been pissed in the car, on the way to the East Side. Pissed at Graham for taking her to a cheap hotel like the Mousy Inn. Like a hooker or something. His aunt could not be reached, and her house was, surprisingly, locked-up. They'd had to come here. So she hadn't said a word, her lips thin, her arms crossed tight across her chest. The green stiletto tapping furiously. When this show didn't do much to catch Graham's attention she switched to loud stage sighs and exaggerated slouches. Sitting in a convenience store parking lot for 40 minutes was not her idea of eloping.

Graham must have had some inkling of her state of duress because he bought a bottle of champagne at the convenience store. He was trying. The gift didn't appease Miriam until 3/4ths of it was gone.

And then they'd had sex. Despite being quite drunk she remembered the details. The parade of positions lined up in her mind, like on the pages of *Nouveau* Magazine. He always fucked her so hard when they were somewhere new, or when they weren't getting along. She idly wondered what was wrong with her bed back in the dorm room. She had removed the stuffed animals from it. But a new place, the outdoors, a bathroom, and he was like a jackhammer.

Reliving Graham's night moves was lulling her back to sleep when the phone rang. She picked up the dirty plastic handset and tried to say hello, but the first word of the day caught in her dry throat, and it was a minute before she could croak an approximation out. No one was on the other end anyway.

She sat up in bed, fully awake in a strange place. The phone had roused Graham and he groaned wearily. She could hear the rain on the aluminum car coverings in the parking lot.

"Graham… are you awake?"

He groaned.

"I had a weird dream." (*See Appendix F: A Midsummer Night's Longueur*).

He rolled over. The phone rang again. Miriam picked it up. This time she didn't even have a chance to say hello.

"This is the front desk. Check out was at 10:00."

PRIME TIME. THE SUN GOING DOWN OVER THE HORIZON OF HER WINDOW LEDGE. A RECORD SPINNING IN LAZY LOOPS, TRACING OUT SOFT TRUMPETS. LYING ON THE BED, IN OLD PAJAMAS, THE RERUNS AND FAVORITES WOULD COME. BEER BOTTLES CASTING SEPIA SHADOWS ON THE SIDEWALK. HER BROTHER LAUGHING. THE IDEA OF RUNNING HER FINGERS THROUGH HER LOVER'S BEARD, AS THEY SAT ON LAWN CHAIRS AROUND A SLOW-MOTION BONFIRE. HER WEDDING, ON AN ICELANDIC CLIFF, HER TRAIN RISING IN THE WIND LIKE A PLUME OF SMOKE. A DESIRE TO EXPERIENCE

THE PAST

His summer after East Slope felt strange. He had rented a room in the house of a friend, one with thick walls and no furniture. It was outside of the city, or far enough away from Uni-Arrs that it didn't feel much like the city. He kept himself to the bare minimum: alcohol, cigarettes, sometimes food. When the electricity went out he used candles to light joints, or read his books.

Adelaide remained in his thoughts. Isolation guaranteed that. He wanted his heart to settle. It wouldn't happen. Some of the anger slowly leaked away. His pride was slowly restored. He daydreamed often of kind, forgiving reunions. Or sometimes revenge. It depended on the weather.

After a season had turned, he was again restless for culture; dark holes full of loudness, punks, and art. The **SNOOTY FOX.** He moved back to the city, under the cover of night and rain. He found a wooden house, with trees that filled in the windows, and light that swept out the hard floors each morning.

He could not make contact with *Adelaide.* Nor, by extension, with Theodora. He knew where she was, but refused to find her. It wasn't easy in such a small town. But he had decided to forget, and there were all sorts of good reasons. He made new friends, and

started to gather a new clique about himself, instructing them in his tastes and preferences. Not students this time, but older kids. Building art with other hands, as he was wont to do.

The reason he couldn't see her was that he knew himself to be in love with her, still. She was dangerous, and to be avoided. Daydreams notwithstanding, it was not possible that they would be together. He hated her for loving her. He reproached his mind, his heart, for absolute failure to unfocus.

Her presence permeated the sidewalks, the grass lined curbs of that season. He saw her in passing cars, smoking cigarettes, he heard her talking around corners, from other rooms, he woke up in the night, and checked the pillow next to him. He was sure that she was going to walk over the horizon and into his sight at any minute. The paranoia was excruciating. He couldn't sleep.

And then she was there. He had no idea how it happened. The city was too small, the circles began to overlap. He began sleeping with other girls and his guard came down. He was hanging out with Theodora. And there she was. Asking questions.

His birthday came, and he threw a party. Friends, artists, gutter kids, his current lover, Ren, serving as a buffer. And *Adelaide.* She brought her entourage, her buffers. And didn't stay long. His birthdays were always shit.

Dolores hated her miserable life.

Silas had gone off to track down Miriam, who was with that tool-head Graham. And she was alone. Again.

She was worried because things could fall apart so easily if Graham got sick of Miriam. Dolores knew that Miriam didn't have the brains to resist Silas's charms. Or his grating, wear-you-down-find-you-out persistence. He would talk her into it. It was as simple as that.

Dolores wouldn't need to be coerced, and Silas probably could tell. She felt transparent. She worried that everyone knew what she was thinking all of the time. She listened to herself talking to people, stumbling along, making it up, blending words that didn't belong together, and would see their eyes squint in confusion at inconsistencies, left-out details, a shabbily constructed self-esteem. No one bought it.

She had had three anxiety attacks alone this month. Horrible, hour-long ordeals where her stomach turned inside out, and her eyes darkened over. Air came in gasps few and far between. She felt dead inside. Unable to think or feel. Unable to cry.

She was worried that she'd never find a job after school, worried that she wouldn't finish school. Worried that she'd never find someone who didn't cheat or lie, who made enough money, and could stand her. She worried that she was malnourished, that she was eating too much. She worried that her car required some sort of preventative maintenance that she could not think of, or name. She worried that she was crazy, annoying, that the anxiety attacks were a certifiable, diagnosable long-named something she did not want to have. Thinking about them gave her another one last Tuesday. She was worried that Miriam would never be her friend again. Worried that she had no friends. Worried that her mother knew how many boys she had slept with. Worried that the whole school thought she was a whore.

Suicide made her nervous. She was pretty sure she didn't have the wherewithal to go through with it. She was thankful for fatalism. It is *never* too late for fatalism.

Adelaide

The **three girls** sat out on the back porch, despite Zella's **restlessness**. Adelaide eyed the rain dripping from the awnings and fidgeted with an empty canister of **carbon dioxide**. She felt *despondent*.

Her opening at the *VELVETEEN* hadn't gone well. The Platypus hadn't come. Ollister hadn't come. Hardly *anyone* had come. She had gotten really **drunk**. Which seemed to ease her depression for a *while*. This led to experiments with a *variety of substances* over the course of the last week, to see which would best **quiet her thoughts**. Tonight they were doing whip-its.

"Zella, I wish you hadn't talked to Vance about me. He's practically stalking me now." Adelaide.

"Let's do another." Zella. She had been *ignoring* this conversation for a while.

"Don't you think we should wait at least a minute between them?" Matilda. Cautious even when **high**.

"What difference does that make?"

"I don't know."

The girls were **snapping** at each other. Zella had wanted to do her *favorite* **carbon-dioxide** stunt. It involved driving to Mt. Botch and stopping the car at the **precipice** of the road atop the big hill. She would then shift into *neutral*, suck all of the CO_2 out of her balloon and let the car *careen* down the steep pavement, her hands thrown up, shrieking on her **self-made roller coaster**.

But it was *raining* and the only available vehicle was Matilda's, and not even **peer pressure** could convince her to yield to the *recklessness* of this plan. They sat on the porch, deflated balloons in hand, listening to the **groaning thunder**.

"What if every time you killed a brain cell it made a popping sound? Like loud enough for you and everyone around you to hear?" Matilda.

Adelaide smiled.

"I mean, sucking down these balloons, our brains would totally sound like bowls of rice krispies."

"I don't know…" Zella. "I think that would make it even more addicting. Like bubble wrap. Who can stop popping that stuff?"

"Yeah, but you're addicted to everything, so whatever."

"Punk has a drug." Adelaide and Zella turned to look at Matilda.

"What do you mean, Mattie?"

"That's why I'm not going to see him anymore. He takes it, and gets all… sexual."

"What drug is it?" Zella. Fascinated.

"I don't know."

The rain *popped* against the tin roof sheltering the girls from the hours-old **storm**.

"I don't like it." Matilda. She looked sad. "You remember that first dorm we lived in, Addy? The first day we were there?"

"Do sprinklers work in the rain?" Zella. Interrupting. She was annoyed that her *other* question wasn't answered.

Adelaide nodded at Matilda.

"It was so scary."

"All right, fine." Zella. "What happened?"

"Well, we were baking pot brownies, to celebrate, you know, like a dorm-warming, and we put them in, and kind of forgot about them cause we were smoking pot. And we were just looking out the windows, at the neighborhood across the east lawn, and it was all sketchy, at least we thought so then—remember, Adelaide? I mean later, we felt OK there, even though it was sketch cause we met those gangster kids down the road…"

"The pot brownies."

"Oh yeah, so suddenly, we hear this gunshot from across the street, like it was so loud, a gun might as well have gone off, and we freaked out, cause, you know, we didn't know if it was a gangster or a robbery or what, so we ran out the front door and there's more gunshots as we ran, and we're screaming our heads off."

"So we get outside, and I call the cops on my cell, cause we're like alone on campus, right next to gang land. And the fire department comes, though they had a hell of a time getting through the front gates, and we're like 'oh shit,' because they want to go in the dorm, but we've got these pot brownies baking, so I'm like 'I can't believe we

141

called the cops on ourselves.' And *Addy* is like, 'It's cool. They're firemen, let them in, they won't know what's going on in the oven.' So we all go inside, and there is smoke everywhere, cause the brownies are starting to burn, but it's actually a good thing because it doesn't smell like pot smoke, just like… burnt smell… you know? But of course, them being firemen, they go straight to the source of the smoke, and run in the kitchen and open the oven, and this one fireman grabs the tray and pulls it out, the smoking brownies looking like meteors or something. And he says 'What's this?' and points his finger at one of them, and we all lean in close, us and the other firemen, and my heart is thudding in my chest cause I'm sure he's pointing to a bud or whatever. But he's not. He's pointing to a bullet."

"A what?" *Zella*. Looking up, *yawning*.

"A bullet, yeah, like a real one, lodged in the pot brownie. And so then he looks in the oven again and sees all these bullets like sitting on the bottom, and he's like 'Oh shit.' And slams the door shut and right then, I swear, one goes off, and we all jump, it is so unbelievably loud. And the head fire guy is like, 'Are those your bullets? Is this a prank?' and so then I'm freaked out we're gonna get busted for bullets *and* drugs now. But *Addy* is all calm and cool, remember?"

"I was scared shitless."

"Anyways, she's acting cool and explains it to the cop, I mean the fireman, explains we just moved in, it was our first time using the oven, whatever. And like, 'They must've been put there by whatever weird art kid lived here before,' and the guy seems satisfied, but is like, 'Well, don't open the door and stay out of the kitchen until the oven cools down tomorrow, and then just take them out and throw them away.' And this one fat fireman is like 'Well, there's a lot of brownies that don't look that burnt, and maybe these hungry firemen need a little reward for saving your lives.' And they all laugh, but he seems serious, and what were we supposed to say?"

"So you gave them brownies?"

"Yeah, all of them, we had, like, no choice."

"Did they get high?" *Zella*. **Sarcastically**.

"I don't know, they didn't eat them there. The one guy who asked for them was biting into his as they drove off, and…"

"Can *we* get high?" *Zella*. **Seriously**.

"What?"

"I'm tired of the story." She started to *fill* another balloon.

"Boring boring. I'm tired of all the drugs I know about. I want to hear about *Punk's*."

142

Miriam & Graham

"What the fuck, dude?" Graham. Under his breath.

Miriam followed his gaze across the hotel lobby. She squinted against the fresh light flooding the windows. Silas's seated silhouette, legs crossed, one foot bobbing slowly, was unmistakable. She turned back around calmly and continued settling up with the scruffy guy behind the front desk of the Mousy Inn, clearly at the end of his night shift.

"What the fuck is he doing here?"

"He followed me." Miriam, tucking her father's credit card into her purse.

"But how the fuck did he…"

"Dolores told him. And can you please stop cussing? It's 11 AM."

They had woken up early that morning. Or Miriam had, rather. She was afraid of having another dream, and this caused her to sleep restlessly. She had been awake for hours. She lay still on her back and thought about the backyard, no, the garden, she would call it a garden, of her daydream estate. A long manicured lawn, fenced in on two sides by a hedge maze, the bushes tall and stock straight. Lawn chairs, lemonade, croquet, chardonnay. Peacocks roaming about freely. Miniature cats, if she could get them. She wondered if they made miniature cats. A picnic, replete with basket and 'picnic silver' out on the long flat steps that led to the push-off for the rowboat. She couldn't decide if she should have a lazy stream or a small lake for the rowboat. She debated herself while Graham groaned and farted under the sheets. A lake was finally decided upon, because there would be a gazebo in the middle of it. Swans would be sleeping at its foot, or eating grass…

"Nice place." Silas. Still sitting in the armchair. He said it more loudly than was necessary. His shoes shined. They weren't getting away without a confrontation.

"Fuck off, man. We're going to my…"

"Don't." Miriam. "Don't tell him where we're going."

"You must be going to your aunt's?" Silas. Addressing Graham, but continuing to stare at Miriam. "I hope it's as charming as this quaint little getaway."

"I'm gonna beat him up."

"No… Graham…" Sigh.

"Yeah, I think I am." With that he walked over to the chair. Silas's eyes widened in confusion. The bigger boy grabbed him by the front of his expensive shirt and hoisted him up out of the chair. Silas put his palms up to show that physical confrontation was not really the kind he was after.

Then Graham began to shake him. Back and forth. Roughly, but not in an overtly violent way. Silas's head rolled around on his neck, and his carefully slicked hair came all undone. Graham continued to shake him, emitting a low rumbling sound from the back of his throat.

This went on for a significant period of time. As Miriam watched, the scene began to look surreal to her: Silas, a tuxedoed sock monkey, Graham, a disgruntled polar bear playing with his prey. To tell them to stop didn't really occur to her, as things weren't escalating. They seemed to be slowing down, actually, just this repetitive shaking, shaking of Silas.

When he finally let him go, Silas crumpled to the floor, dizzy. Graham punctuated this action with a final "Cool."

He walked back to where Miriam was standing and picked up her bag. "Come on, let's get the fu…"

"Enh! Not in the morning." She looked down at Silas, all disheveled, whatever high he had come in here with probably destroyed, and wondered if this was what she looked like after one of her dreams.

"Your father…" He managed to cough out. "…would not… approve."

THE PAST

Ollister lived across town from *Adelaide* for a while. Winter had thawed, and they were friends, albeit shaky ones. In her absence, his feelings had not subsided. They had only grown. He couldn't let on.

She had scammed out with a few guys, all inappropriate. He smoldered at the thought of their hands, their shirtless torsos. During the summer something much more dangerous happened. She got a boyfriend.

He wasn't really around to see how it happened. He heard about it through friends, and by the time he returned to the East Side, *Adelaide* and this new kid were pretty solid.

The kid's name was James, a helicopter mechanic, who had graduated Uni-Arts a few years earlier. He built single-person prototype helicopters in his backyard, where unused blades hung a drunken whirl once. But she had done the same to any number of lesser boys. And it couldn't be that she was harboring some secret crush, as he had begun to do. *Adelaide* had her secrets, but this couldn't be among them. She wouldn't contain something like this. Especially feelings that were the magnitude of his. She had plenty of opportunity to explore those feelings if they were there. He was practically at her beck and call.

The scenario that played itself out in his head, endlessly, was one where he told her. Confessing, getting down on his knees, getting up on a mountain, and making his declaration. Something big and grand, something moving. This was where the plan veered into daydream.

She would be surprised. There was no way of her knowing. He had told no one. Or, he had told few, and they were ones unlikely, or unable, to spill the beans. So she wouldn't have known vis-à-vis the grapevine. Sometimes he stared too long, or got too drunk, and said something telling, but for the most part he was a master of his emotions, giving away nothing, saying nothing, acting against his every impulse.

Her surprise would quickly subside. She would feel alienated, the friendship would be ruined. Her constitution was not one that tolerated unspoken tension. He would be unable to be around her. James would find out. He would be angry, and his rag-tag-fag

from ropes tied to branches high up in the tall trees. There was one he welded together from parts of a dozen wrecks, Frankenstein was its imaginative name. He was tough and smart in his own bad boy way. His art was crude, welded sculpture. Mostly leftover helicopter parts. He couldn't see beauty, and the fact that he drew her away from it, and into this base existence of jump suits, rotors, and keg parties, disgusted Ollister.

She said she loved James, and plainly, it was true. When she spoke of little cracks in their relationship Ollister exaggerated them in his mind, always ready for the fallout. But it was nothing out of the ordinary, never anything nearing a crisis. James loved her, or at least he did initially. Not in the way that Ollister imagined himself doing. But in his own stifled, **boring boring,** unemotional way, it seemed as though he really did. It was hard to blame him for this.

Ollister was not jealous of him. His superiority here, as elsewhere, was clear. He sometimes wanted to be in his place, when he lifted off into the after-party dawn, on one of the contraptions, with *Adelaide* clutching tightly at his waist. But mostly he wanted his own place. With *Adelaide*. Away from this kid and everything else in the insipid, humid city.

James was never the problem. The problem was, heli-boyfriend or no, *Adelaide* did not want him. They were friends. She gave him

THE PRESENT

Outside the city, lying in bed at night, listening to the rain leak through the roof, he would think. Maybe he liked this state of affairs. Maybe he chose this. Maybe he preferred the furtive desire, the unreachable plateau, the radiant muse. It allowed for no deleterious confrontations, it saved him from having to live up to his potential, and provided plenty of daydream fodder besides. His plight was easy to romanticize, and allowed for many variations on self-pity and self-recrimination. In its own way it was preferable to the alternative.

Finally, he had to admit that he couldn't completely presuppose rejection. His hope was alive. It was all he could think about that empty season.

He was out of the city again, but this time hope had to be stifled. Vance was a different story. He was worse. And an artist. Which was also worse. Vance had blown the cover of the Art Terrorism operation. This was unforgivable. How could he have been so short-sighted as to take that idiot kid under his wing? There would be revenge, if he went back.

But the deed was already done. And there was The Platypus. She had been changed, for him. He wasn't going back.

helicopter gang would come after Ollister, and throw sand in his eyes. The strain on the relationship would be too much. The secrecy of it would creep her out. The inevitable rejection would crush him.

Sometimes he thought she must know, he had given it away, it was obvious, his subtlety was nothing against her perception. But in the clear light of day, this looked like paranoia, and their friendship continued in a perfectly normal manner.

She would frequently take up the task of finding him a girlfriend. This was both strange and difficult. She pointed out other girls. She would lavish praise upon him, extolling his worthiness, his suitability, his artistry, his deservedness, nay, inalienable right, to an equivalent mate. He looked at her plainly, and said nothing. He didn't need encouragement, or confidence-building praise — his ego was hardy. She wasn't trying to build him up either; it was simply kindness. The frustration of it boiled his brain. He did not want

Adelaide finding him a girlfriend.

He remembered, when they both lived on the East Side, and she was getting into her car, and he made his last stand, declaring all or nothing. When the word 'love' came out of his mouth, she looked at him as though he had just ejected a rotting fish from between his lips and onto the wet sidewalk. If he told her now she would make that face, crinkle her nose, again. And that would be more than he could bear.

Miriam & Graham

As they approached the house, the cats began to wander out to meet them. At first there were only two or three that had been sitting in the yard, but they were quickly joined by more who slipped out of the shadows under the porch or the bushes, willing to brave the rain for the possibility of cat food.

"Awww." Miriam. Genuinely.

"Yeah, my aunt's got lots of cats." Graham. "I guess you could say she's sort of a cat lady, you know, like one of those cat ladies?"

"Yeah, that's really sweet." Miriam bent down to stroke the back of a skinny tabby. Clumps of fur came off in her hand. She sneezed.

"Probably doesn't have time to brush them all." They creaked up the stairs. The screen door was leaning on the porch, blocking a window. Graham set down the five giant suitcases he had been saddlebagged with. The night before, in the dark, the door had been locked. But it was cracked open now, so they went in.

Miriam stood in a vast and dusty living room. There were boxes piled to the ceiling, an old lopsided piano was shoved against one wall, quilts piled on its bench. There was little light coming in, despite the many windows. Most were obscured with dirty lace curtains, stained-glass baubles, or stacks of stuff. Miriam coughed as she squinted into a dust-covered mirror, barely able to make out her reflection.

"Uh... I'll go look for her." Graham. His voice sounded loud and dull in the quiet air. Miriam stayed behind and circumscribed the room. There were old boxes of photos, cartons of witchy-looking boots, cat toys, and candles. She could tell it smelled weird, but the stagnant air brought no scent to her nostrils. She crept over an old canister vacuum cleaner to peer though the doorway into the kitchen. It was an even bigger mess in there. The scent hit her, and she quickly spun back around and nearly got poked in the eye by what she thought was a bird. After a bit of arm flailing it turned out to be a unicorn. A wooden one, hanging from the ceiling. She looked up and around, and saw that there were many mobiles, and dreamcatchers, and all sorts of hideous doodads hanging from the ceiling. This particular unicorn was purple, and it was designed to be held up with two pieces of string, one of which was missing. This gave it a pessimistic slant, as though it were running downhill, its sparkly horn aimed straight for the ground.

She touched her fingertip to the point of the horn, gently, to stop its neurotic rocking.

"I don't think she's here…" Graham. Confused.

"Well, where are we supposed to sleep, in one of these boxes?"

"No. No! Jeez, there's a room upstairs."

"OK, can we go there?"

"Uh, yeah." He started up the stairs.

"Don't you think you should get my bags first?"

"Oh yeah." Graham sheepishly picked up the large bags. Miriam led him up the stairs, past all of the old portraits of relatives, all of which looked like they'd been taken and hung a hundred years ago.

The guest bedroom looked just as ancient. There was a moldy futon, and stacks of romance novels. Everything was blanketed by a snowy layer of cat hair.

"Are you serious?" Miriam. Turning to Graham, hand thrust into hip.

"That futon folds out."

"Why would I care? I'm not even going to sit on that thing, much less sleep on it."

"Don't be a priss. It's just a futon." Graham plunked down violently, as if to prove his point. Cat hair curled up into the air around him.

"Well, can we at least clean up?"

"I guess." Graham reached over and turned on a small black and white television set perched atop a wobbly TV dinner tray. "The semis are on." Little half-helmeted men leapt back and forth across the tiny lacrosse field. In black and white, millimeters high, the teams were indistinguishable.

"You didn't have to shake Silas like that." No response. Miriam turned with a snort, and stomped downstairs. She kicked through some boxes as she made her way to the kitchen. Walking through the doorway she swatted the unicorn with an open palm. Its remaining string broke, and it went crashing to the ground, scattering three kittens hidden near a plant holder. She felt only fleeting remorse as she pinned her nose with two sharp fingernails and retrieved a broom and dustpan from the kitchen.

When she walked back into the bedroom, Graham was cutting his toenails, his face inches away from the television box.

"That's disgusting." She started to sweep. The surfaces first; tops of boxes, chairs, the rest of the futon where Graham wasn't sitting, cutting his toenails.

"Gross." At the sound of the clip, dull and painless. It sounded as though his toenails were wet. There was no sharp pop, just this dull sound of severance.

"I'm trying to sweep here." Miriam. Loudly.

"I'm trying to watch the stupid game…" Graham. Mumbling, especially toward the end of the sentence, when he began to regret beginning it. "What?"

"Nothing."

"I'm trying to sweep this nasty rat-hole and you're clipping your gross wet toenails right onto the floor. What the heck is that?"

"Wet?"

"You know what, Graham? Screw you. You bring me to this place and then I'm trying to clean it and you're all clipping your toenails."

"I just…"

"Get out."

"Of my aunt's house?"

"No dumbo, of this room. I'm going to clean it, and you aren't going to be here to re-dirty it, because I'm sleeping in it alone tonight, and you can just go downstairs with the stinky cats and the piano and tickle the ivories or whatever."

"God! Sometimes you're such a bitch… babe." The affectionate name was an afterthought, meant to dull the harshness of the cuss word.

She closed the door in his face and started sweeping violently, flinging mounds of cat hair into the air. Sneezing then overtook her so violently that she collapsed on the futon, sinuses draining onto its fur-coated fabric. She began crying. Through the tears she took out her pink cell phone and called her dorm room number. Dolores picked up on the first ring.

"It's… unh… it's gross!" Miriam. Through choking sobs.

"Well, what did you expect?" Dolores. Gloatingly. But, then: "Listen, you've got to hang in there. He's the love of your life."

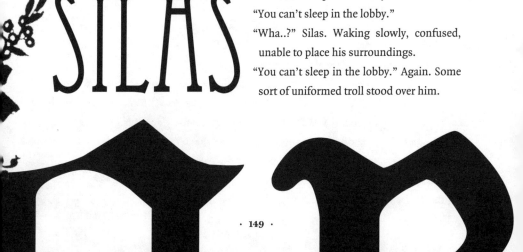

SILAS

"You can't sleep in the lobby."

"You can't sleep in the lobby."

"Wha..?" Silas. Waking slowly, confused, unable to place his surroundings.

"You can't sleep in the lobby." Again. Some sort of uniformed troll stood over him.

Adelaide

Ωllister was **gone**. She couldn't find him. No one had heard from him or seen him.

She was in a *mood*. A nameless one. Foundationless, it had swept over her like some terrible cyclone of **night-come-too-soon**. She was choked and confused but *without* foreboding or dread.

Violently enlightening, it felt like the universe, *infinite* and *changeless*, expanded before her. An **emptiness** that was not an absence of anything else, a **true** vacuum. The great **caverns** in her mind expanded so rapidly, the ceiling recessing upwards and outwards, so fast and far that soon she could not see *anything*. No clue as to the dimensions of her chamber.

Although this episode was about *nothing else* except **being alone**, she wanted someone to tell. She had been thumbing through yet another self-help book on *coping with death*. *Adelaide* didn't know anyone who had died, anyone close to her. But the books were good reads. Not *uplifting* exactly, more like *satisfying*. This particular one, however, was subpar. It focused on some plodding doctor's conversations with terminally ill patients. Old women whose **wallpaper** had peeled back, revealing that everyone was indeed their beloved second husband, or first son lost to the meat-packing plant. *Adelaide* found these long drawn-out discussions, which skirted too carefully around the **topic** on the book's cover, *ridiculous* and somewhat *disgusting*. She wasn't coping well.

There was a message on the answering machine from her mother, *threatening* to cut off her funds. Which normally wouldn't have been a cause for concern, it was her mother's favorite threat. But when she had gone to the bank later, she found her accounts **frozen**. She had really done it.

She needed to sell some **art**. She needed some money. If she was in The White Ball, she would sell a lot of **art**. At this point, it seemed like she was *disinvited* once again. She couldn't deliver Ωllister to The Platypus anymore than anyone else could. He probably knew about his **disappearance** before she did.

There was another letter from Vance. "*Addy*, you are the most amazing…" was as far as she got. One a week, if not more. Always with *poor grammar* and *lewd diagrams*. The boy barely knew her.

She needed to talk to another person, **live**, in front of her. Misery loves company, whether the company is made miserable or not. She didn't want to *inflict* her **bad mood** upon someone else, although sometimes that could be enjoyable. She just wanted to **sit**, chin propped on hands, and listen to someone else rant about their *imagined dramas*. It wasn't comforting, but it would at least be mildly *distracting*.

Her **moping** was *always* theatrical. Careful never to reveal the source of it, she was *vague* and *inconsolable*. After hearing her **breathy sighs** through someone else's ear for awhile, she came to believe that it was all an *act*, and once alone again, she could come back into possession of herself, and feel much better.

It was hard to decide who to call. Theodora had the advantage of **distance**, which often made her a target for *extended* complaint. It was easier to talk to someone she didn't have to face. But it was **difficult** to listen to Theodora bend and shape the facts of her life into what she *believed* comprised a *convincing episode*. Wracked by **manic-depression**, the report was either all good or all bad, *equal exaggerations*. The cheerful forecasts were **harder** to listen to. They seemed more filled with **falseness**. She would paint her life, as she had for so many years, in terms of *potential*. All of these wonderful dreams *about to come true*. She would rationalize her **sex** or **alcohol abuse** before ⨽Adelaide could criticize, a practice ⨽Adelaide refrained from anyway. Theodora was *forever* saying something about how it was good for her, that she didn't **drink before noon**, or that he made her take it **up the ass**. Her stories of nearing happiness were often couched in *vague criticisms* of ⨽Adelaide's life. Attacks on her city, or profession, or preoccupation. They were always so wildly off the mark that ⨽Adelaide just agreed right along, smiling at the safe end of the phone receiver. On the whole, listening to this *showboat monologue* was exhausting. And expressing *surprise, incredulity*, or *encouragement* at any number of obvious spins was more than she could manage at the moment.

She could always go to Matilda's dorm room, but inhabiting that place invited **loneliness** to inhabit one's self. The things carefully arranged, pulpy books, and THRIFTWHOPPER knick-knacks, meant to display a sense of humor and playfulness Matilda did not possess. The things unarranged, bras on doorknobs, macaroni stuck to pans. All of these things spoke of *sadness*, so that even as she sat there, facing her, propped on *excessive pillows*, she felt as though she were a **ghost** watching Matilda shuffle about the empty dorm, late at night, in bunny slippers, crying softly to herself, as not to wake the other boarders.

Zella didn't have much to say when ⨽Adelaide was down. She could **curse** her life for hours, and assuredly Zella would take it all in. Inserting a probably sincere, but still *false-sounding*, "that sucks," or "shitty," at the appropriate intervals. She couldn't really speak to **sadness**, unless it was a third party's, and then only with *glee*.

So she spoke to no one.

A LONG FLIRTATION. A GUARDED ONE, GLANCES FROM UNDER THE BROW, THE SUBTLEST INCLINATION OF THE HEAD, THE SHOULDERS, ANGLED FORWARD AS IF TO RECEIVE A MEDAL, OR OFFSET A GUST OF WIND.

THOSE CONVERSATIONS WERE ALSO LIES. THE PRETENSE OF THE DESIRE FOR INNOCENCE. THE REALITY: A SHARPNESS TOO ACUTE TO IGNORE. WIZENED OLD MANIPULATIONS. THE FAMILIARITY OF THE DEVICE, ITS PATHWAYS AND PITFALLS, UNAVOIDABLE BUT ALSO, MAYBE UNTRUSTABLE THIS TIME. SOME PLATITUDES STILL HAVE MEANING. SOME CLICHÉS SUM UP PERFECTLY

AND BODIES, SILVER-LINED WITH MOONSHINE HUMMING, ABATING IN STILLNESS. THE SOFTEST BRUSH SETTING OFF EVERY LAST NERVE ENDING, EVERY CORPUSCLE AFLOAT IN THE PRIMORDIAL SEA. BODIES IN LINE.

Silas & Miriam

Silas had placed a phone call to Pete and had him hunt down Graham's aunt's address. The Jag was still in the shop—he had wrecked it last month during a coke binge—so he had to take the van. The VirginVan.

It was the dead of night. He parked two houses down from the place that could only belong to a member of that slob Graham's family. He grabbed the ladder off the luggage rack (the VirginVan was equipped with everything, and then some) and proceeded to drag it across two lawns, and slam it against the side of the house. He grunted with its weight.

Halfway up to the window he had to pause, still dizzy from the shaking Graham had given him in the hotel lobby. But more angry than dizzy, that was sure. At the top of the ladder he tried to peer through the darkened window. But it was curtained, from the inside.

"Fuck." Silas. Cursing loudly. He pulled on the crumbling wooden window, twice losing his grip and skinning his knuckle. "Fuck!" When he finally got it open a few inches he pushed the dusty curtains aside only to see a wall of cardboard boxes pressed against the window. "Fuck!" Really screaming this time.

He stomped down the ladder, and scooted it over to align with the next second story window, scraping the side of the house with its top.

The second window was open a crack and he crawled in, almost losing his balance. Miriam was there, on top of the bed, fully clothed, her mouth open and drooling a bit on the old afghan she had bunched up for a pillow. It didn't occur to him to wonder where Graham was. He crawled over to the bed. He briefly considered disrobing, himself and her, but thought better of it, and reached down to gently shake her arm.

She roused, confused, with one eye lidded.

"All dreams are pink and perfect." Silas. In a soft lilting voice.

"Wha? Silas? What are you... This isn't a dream..."

"Mushrooms made of gophers, over the hills, we must go."

"Oh." Understanding now, she rose, and he steered her by her elbows to the window.

"It feels so real..." Miriam. Yawning. Her hair was plastered to the side of her face.

"Tomorrow, it won't. Now, down the lady's ladder."

She climbed down, slowly, as Silas impatiently twitched above, waiting his turn. Once on the ground he grabbed the ladder, and her hand with his other, and dragged them both across the dew-dappled yard, streetlamp lighting the scene like a movie set.

The answering machine picked up. The outgoing message was so **loud** *Adelaide* had to hold the phone *away from her ear*. It sounded like a **phonograph**, eking out some old jazz band made up of **seals being eaten**.

"Hey Teddy. I wish you were there. I was just thinking about that one night. Last summer. That time we four all got smashed on that plum wine you stole from your grandmother's. And we went to the 24-hour supermarket and ended up stealing a whole cartful of crap because *Zella* saw a midget in there and got all freaked out like she does, and ran out with the cart and no one noticed… And we went to the park and it was raining and we skinny-dipped in the fountain, and you and *Zella* were trying to pin Mattie down to joke-fuck her with the carrot or the whip cream from the store, but you couldn't because she was truly terrified. But she forgave you instantly, of course, and we all went back to her dorm. Remember that was during the time she was crying every night and had an endless supply of boxed wine. We were so drunk by then that we puffy painted all her walls. I remember when Mattie woke me up in the morning, you couldn't even tell what any of it was, except this one unicorn you started and my handprints everywhere. You and *Zella* were passed out on the floor covered in paint, *Zella* was lying next to the tiniest puddle of wine vomit and mustard. I had to move you guys into the car and then cover all of the painted spots on the wall with Mattie's posters. Because her mom was coming over later that morning. So the posters were in fucked-up places. Like three of them right next to each other on the bottom corner of a wall, to cover up that unicorn. It was all so obvious, but when her mom finally got there she didn't even notice that because the thing that…"

154

Here the machine beeped. **Abruptly** cutting off *Adelaide's crescendo*.

She set the phone down and softly scratched the back of her neck. She really did want to **talk to someone**. So she called Pete…

"Hey."

"Hey, what are you doing?"

"Nothing. Working on a laptop." Pete had come a long way since coming out of hiding.

"You remember that time you and I played badminton at…"

"Ωllister left town, *Addy*."

"Yeah, I guess I knew that."

"The Art Terrorists are going ahead with our mission."

"What! Pete, what are you doing? What is this?"

"Vance said he fired Ωllister, and he's the new leader. He also told me later that he's your boyfriend. Is that true?"

"Of course not, this is ridiculous. Pete, I don't want you hanging around him, or whoever he's with…"

"Sorry, *Adelaide*, it's too late. I have to. It's them or The White Sodality. I was forced to choose a side."

"Pete, I have no idea what you are talking about…"

"Sorry, can't talk about it. Gotta go…" **The line went dead.**

155

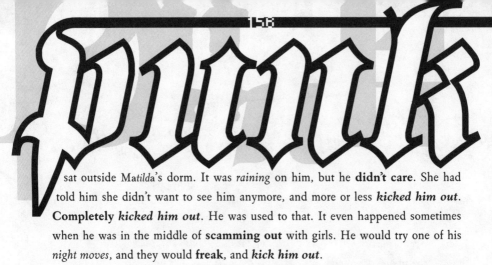

punk

sat outside Matilda's dorm. It was *raining* on him, but he **didn't care**. She had told him she didn't want to see him anymore, and more or less **kicked him out**. **Completely** *kicked him out*. He was used to that. It even happened sometimes when he was in the middle of **scamming out** with girls. He would try one of his *night moves*, and they would **freak**, and *kick him out*.

But he had pulled almost all of his *moves* on Matilda, since he started staying over in her dorm room. And she had been surprisingly **tolerant**. Almost enough for him to imagine that she *enjoyed* the **things** he was doing to her. Either way, it couldn't be the reason that he'd been **kicked out**.

She wouldn't give a reason, and that made him **suspicious**. He got up, and started to walk. He felt **paranoid**. What if *someone* knew he was there? What if *someone* had gotten to her?

He slipped into the alley behind the dorm. **Wet rats** shot behind trash cans. He walked quickly, his cold hands shoved into his pockets. He **knew** The White Sodality got Ωllister. He hadn't seen him in *forever*. He had spent the last four nights wandering around to all of the usual spots, and Ωllister never appeared. He had never gone **this long** without seeing him.

It meant they were *coming for him*, **next**. Without Ωllister, he had no idea how to escape. He knew that ᴄAdelaide was in with them, maybe she had gotten to Matilda. Maybe Matilda was trying to protect him. He had to **hide**.

Stashed behind one of the trash cans, he found an old tattered camping tent. It was neon green and orange. Which wasn't the most **concealing**. But he knew a thicket behind this lawn ornament place. It used to be a **gutter punk** spot, where they would all *smoke out*. The fat owner had called the cops a few times, and since then it had been **abandoned**. But if he took the tent back there and *hid* it under some branches, nobody would see him. And he could *come and go* in the **night**, and be *safe* there.

He dragged the tent down the alley and through the park, the vinyl *squelching* on the **wet grass**. His face was *sopping*.

THE IRRESPONSIBILITY OF LOVE. THE SKEWERING
OF ANOTHER. THE THINGS YOU DIDN'T MEAN TO SAY
BUT DID. WHEN YOU WERE CRUEL BUT DIDN'T
WANT TO BE, COMPELLED BY SOME DESTRUCTIVE
URGE. WHEN YOU SAID KIND THINGS, LOVING
THINGS OUT OF LAZINESS, OBLIGATION, PURE DUMB
HABIT. WHEN YOU SAID NOTHING. WHEN YOU WOKE
IN THE MIDDLE OF THE NIGHT WITH THAT SCRAPED
OUT FEELING, SICKENINGLY HOLLOW, THAT DEAD
OF THE NIGHT WHERE THERE IS NO FUTURE OR
PAST OR PRESENT, AND YOU FEEL SUSPENDED ON
SOME INESCAPABLE PLAIN, TIME STRETCHING IN
BOTH DIRECTIONS, THE WEIGHT OF LIFE TERRIBLE
AND DULL. THE INFINITE IS THE WORST NIGHTMARE,
SITTING THERE ON THE EDGE OF THE BED. YOUR
LOVE, KICKING IN THEIR SLEEP, IMAGINED LOVERS
LICKING. THE
OF HER, HER. THE INABILI
OF THE IMPOSSIBILITY.

Dolores

had taken at least half a bottle of mini-thins trying to stay awake long enough to get her paper done. She hadn't even started. It was 3:46 AM.

She had every intention of writing this paper. She figured she needed to write at least one if begging for a pass from her teacher was going to have any chance of working at all. But so far all she had done was drag Miriam's laptop out from under her empty bed, place the required reading in a pile on the bed, consume six cans of diet soda, swallow an exponentially increasing dosage of mini-thins, and shop for a new purse online.

She sniffed the backs of her hands. They didn't smell much like anything. She was getting bored and more than a little antsy. It was too late to go out and trawl the SNOOTY FOX for boys, or ones that were sober enough to do any good anyway. She wondered how drunk Silas was at this very moment. And where he was. And who he was with. And that's what led her to log onto VirginVan.com.

Not that it was the first time. In fact, she had an account. She didn't really mind watching porn, but that wasn't what held her interest. Silas was in all of the movies. Well, not in them, technically. He was the filmmaker, the cinematographer. And, most importantly, the director.

His face was never shown, it was glued to the hand-cam permanently as he hunted down dumb girls with his driver, and whatever UNI-ARTS dude was lucky enough to get to ride on the VirginVan this week. He would spot them across the road, or waiting at a bus stop, and the van would pull up and he would start smooth-talking whatever tube-topped bimbo appeared through the lens. He offered a ride to get them to come inside, and then proceeded to tease them or sweet-talk them out of their clothes. Sometimes this required an offer of money, sometimes not. 'Show me your tits' quickly led to other things, especially with a drooling boy in the back seat, chomping at the bit.

She didn't like the girls, or the ugly guys. But she could listen to his voice all night long. His sarcastic come-ons, his wheedling put-downs. She liked his camera angles. He came up with some really creative shots, especially the past few episodes. Often times the live web cam, mounted on the ceiling, that showed what was happening in the Van at that very moment, was off. She suspected that the little scheme failed as often as it worked, and the boys were not inclined to broadcast the girls who slapped their advances away.

But sometimes it was on, and tonight was one of those times. Nothing exciting was happening, except that it was clearly the back of Silas's head, leaning over some passed-out girl. Whom she recognized. Miriam.

"Miriam!"

As though he heard her, Silas suddenly reached up and switched off the camera, clearly upset for not having thought of it sooner.

"That whore-bitch!" Dolores. Really screaming now. She swept the laptop off the bed, and it broke into two pieces when it hit the floor. She grabbed the bottle of mini-thins and the can of diet soda from her night stand and leapt up, tipping the former down her throat and the latter all over Miriam's perfectly made bed. She then found Miriam's large box of photos under the bed, and proceeded, with a thumbtack, to poke thousands of tiny holes in thousands of photographs. First in Miriam's eyes, or teeth, and then all over everything, for hours, until the pills wore off and she dropped from exhaustion.

Night Falls

(See Appendix G. A Particular Night, Well Advanced)

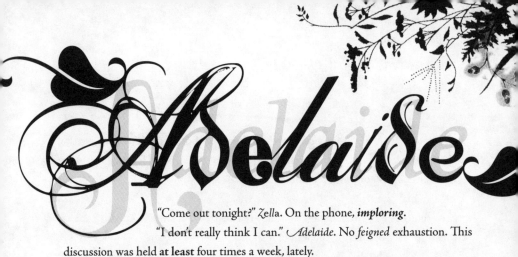

Adelaide

"Come out tonight?" Zella. On the phone, *imploring*.

"I don't really think I can." Adelaide. No *feigned* exhaustion. This discussion was held **at least** four times a week, lately.

"Come on, it'll be so fun. Zero and Brody built this thing out by the train tracks. They've been working on it for weeks and tonight they're gonna take a bunch of us there." She paused to wait for the requisite question.

So Adelaide asked. "What is the thing?"

"Oh, I don't know, some art-palace-shack-thing they built out of junk they found on the tracks, they've got it filled with birthday cake and this old Jacuzzi shell that they use for bubble baths. It's supposed to be a commentary on consumerism or, you know, create a dialogue between art and space, or how a space defines art or something, you know, all that business."

"Well…"

"There'll be drugs."

"As fascinating as it sounds, I don't think I feel like doing anything."

"I bet Punk will be there. I need a good scam."

"Well… Matilda kicked him out, I guess."

"Rad. Scam city. Your boyfriend Vance will be there, too."

"Vance is involved in some sort of bomb plot, Zella, and he's not my boyfriend."

"Bomb? It's probably just some brilliant art, he's a brilliant artist."

"You would think so…"

"God, you're such a bore whore. Snap out of it."

"It's depression, Zella, not pajamas, you can't just snap in and out of it."

"Depression?"

"Yeah, depression, when there's a gray film over everything, and absolutely nothing is interesting including reading, watching TV, talking to people, eating, sleeping, or going to your friends' art shacks where some dude pretending to be your boyfriend is, and your restlessness is unsolvable, and your despair is baseless and you feel stupid and hateful and boring boring."

"Well, I'm going out."

Miriam & Silas

Miriam woke to bumps. She was in something moving. It was the van, the van in her dream last night. It smelled funny.

"Stop." Miriam. Forcefully to the back of Silas's head, which swiveled from the driver seat, aghast. The dream hadn't been a dream.

"I'm sorry... the Jag is in the shop, and..."

"Stop the van." He slowed it.

"Listen, Graham is an idiot and I think you're so hot and so cool, and not like all those other girls, can't we just..." Silas.

"I'm getting out. Stop the van." Anger.

He sheepishly pulled up to the nearest curb, a park where children were chasing each other with muddy sticks in the mid-morning light.

"Please, Miriam. I love you."

She emerged from the Virgin Van, perhaps the first girl to do so with her dignity mostly intact. He got out to follow her.

"Give me the keys." Miriam. A demand.

"What? Why?"

She turned to look at Silas's face, black rings around his eyes, locks of gelled hair rebelling against their intended direction.

"Because I want you to walk home in the rain."

He handed them over.

"Now get back in the van." He did as he was asked. She felt a twinge of sympathy as she slammed the door in his face.

She stomped through the muddy drizzle, upset to be wearing last night's clothes, to have been abducted, to have stolen Silas's keys, to have her heels ruined by this filth.

Some hipsters were standing around a trashcan out on the baseball diamond. She approached them.

"Hey, what direction is Goldenplate?"

"Oooo... Someone had a fun night." The tallest one. Taunting.

"Shut up jerkface and tell me where the dorm is." The tone in her voice was not to be messed with. One with a round face pointed in the direction she had come. She glanced down at the gray trashcan they were huddled around.

"Is that a keg?"

"Uh, yeah, you want a beer?" The taller one. Genuinely hopeful.

"Uh, no. Where did that come from?"

"Well, it wasn't finished at the party we had last night." The round one. "So we thought it'd be nice, you know, to drink it in the park."

"You guys are going to get arrested." Their eyes widened. "That's the biggest open container you could possibly have. It's totally illegal. There are children right over there." They glanced at each other, concerned. No one had thought of this before bringing the keg to the park.

"Jeez." Miriam. She turned and headed for the Goldenplate Girls' Dormitory. "Who doesn't finish a keg at a party anyway?"

She didn't want to work on her **art**. She didn't want to *not* work on her **art**. She didn't want to lie around, watch TV, or call her *friends*. She didn't want to go to a **party** or eat dinner at a **restaurant**. She didn't want to *masturbate*, have *sex*, or 'meet' *someone new*. She didn't want to talk **or** sit in silence. She didn't want to *think*, or *feel*. She certainly didn't feel like sleeping, **much less dying**. She didn't want it to **stop raining** so she could go outside. She didn't want to be cooped up in this *room* anymore. She didn't want to go to school **or** work. She didn't want to *do nothing*. But as much as any of these things, she didn't want to be *restless* anymore.

The Platypus

The Platypus sat with his cigar lodged between two stubby fingers and his head *cupped* by two stubby hands. He was slowly opening and closing his jaw, stretching it. Something he did when he felt a **headache** coming on. Ice cracked *lazily* in the glass of Scotch on his desk.

They were going to **string him up**. Ring his neck. Things were on the **brink**. The situation was *out of control*. He had lost track of Ωllister. His **idiot** men had. They uncovered the whole ART TERRORISM plot, and now it was clear that it was a bunch of stupid kids, with *no plan*, and Ωllister was gone. Which made him think the whole thing was a ruse, a clever decoy. And now he didn't know where Ωllister's next move was going to come from. Which made every *nerve* ending in his body **constrict**. The White Sodality would be *furious* if they knew the extent of it. The Platypus would find himself on the chopping block, all sticky **tar** and tickling **feather**. Isadora would leave him without so much as a glance. He would end up on the streets, of New Orleans perhaps, eating only grapes and cheese, selling small reliefs in the French Quarter, just to get a goddamned drink.

He would stay after the punk kid. He had a feeling the girlfriend was about to **come around**. They were still out looking for the **gray papers**. But without Ωllister, all of these things were **pointless**.

The glass crackled again, and the ice shifted position, cubes bobbing to the top like *stricken whales*. The Platypus stared at the glass, at the amber snakes of light it drew on his polished desktop. He wondered what a **photon** was.

He needed *distraction*. He picked up the phone, grimacing. He had to **fire** the designer of his latest yacht. The man was *intolerable*, and devoid of imagination. If he wanted a fencing salle, stripper's pole, and miniature greenhouse on his latest ship, he could find **someone** to tell him **yes**.

He put the phone down softly. He opened and closed his jaw. The **headache** was not going away.

Miriam & Dolores

Dolores opened her eyes slowly. Rain pounded against the plastic dorm window. She felt Graham's body next to hers. It had been a long time since someone had stayed the night with her. She snuggled down under the comforter, pressing against his warmth. He stirred and draped a bicep over her.

"I really do love you, Dolores, I'm not joking." Graham. With his eyes closed, grinning like a child.

"Mmm." Last night she had argued against this sentiment. But, by morning, he had said it so many times, and with such insistence, that she was beginning to accept it. It felt nice.

Then she heard a key turn in the lock. Graham's eyes shot wide open and she pulled the blanket over his head just as the door opened

Miriam's hair and clothes were wet. Dolores peered at her through a slit eye. She flopped on her bed and pulled out her shiny pink cell phone.

"Are you awake yet, Dolores?" Miriam. Asking softly. "I had a rough night."

"Unh…" Dolores. A murmur from pretended deep sleep.

Miriam dialed a number and waited, picking polish off her pink toe.

"Graham, are you there? Where are you?" Her voice was suddenly choked, panicked. "I really need you, I don't know where I am, I got… Silas… He came in the window and… I'm in this van… I don't know where I am…" She started to sob, but quickly hung up the phone. Her composure returned immediately, and she resumed picking at the offending toe.

Then, as though it were a giant surprise birthday cake, Graham sprang straight up out of Dolores's bed, flinging the covers behind him. Miriam gave a short yelp of surprise. Dolores winced. He stood there, naked, breathing rapidly, pointing an accusatory finger at Miriam.

"Liar! You went in the VirginVan!"

She looked confused. "Virgin? I don't know what you're talking about. I was kidnapped. Silas came with a ladder and tied me up, and carried me out the window."

"You've got the keys in your hand!" Miriam looked down at the large set of keys that were clearly not hers, denoted by the miniature purple dildo key chain.

"I had to steal them to escape! I didn't want to go in his van."

"Oh yes you did. You wanted to be… to be… Virginized!"

"That doesn't make any sense. Put some pants on." He angrily kicked clothes and photos around the floor, looking for them. He inadvertently caught his foot on one half of the broken laptop, sending it flying in Miriam's direction.

"Great. My laptop. And besides why… wait. What are you doing here, even?"

"I came looking for you." Graham. Mad, pulling on his khaki shorts.

"Oh… well… I see… I see you found someone else!" Miriam's voice escalating.

Graham paused and looked at Dolores, her nakedness tucked under the sheet. She froze at his gaze, a lighter held in midair, beneath her unlit cigarette.

"What the hell are you doing naked in bed… with her? Huh, Graham? Answer me that! Is she naked too?" They both looked at Dolores, who exhaled nonchalantly.

"You were in the VirginVan." Graham. Meekly, looking down.

"I was kidnapped! Flipping kidnapped! Go look in your aunt's yard, I bet there are ladder tracks right through the middle of it! You weren't kidnapped. You came right over here and slept with my best friend the second I disappeared." Dolores coughed.

"But I don't… I mean… I love you…"

"Hey guys…" Dolores. Attempting an injection.

"Shut up!" They both yelled in unison. She rolled her eyes.

Miriam turned her finger back on Graham "I am so sick of your… of your garbage!" She began flinging things. "Get out. Boys aren't allowed at Goldenplate!"

He quickly grabbed his shirt and ball cap and made for the door, ducking as he waded through all of the stuff on the floor.

"Wait!" She demanded. He stopped. "Fix my laptop that you broke."

He opened his mouth as if to say it hadn't been him, but then closed it again, realizing that this task meant he could see Miriam again. He picked up one piece in each of his big hairy hands and gave Dolores a pleading look before lumbering out into the hall, where the door was slammed in his down turned face.

"What a jerk!" Miriam. Screaming to no one.

"Yeah…" Dolores. Offering.

"You be quiet. I can't believe you slept with my boyfriend."

"Sorry, but it was all him."

"Yeah right, whatever." Miriam plopped down on her bed, and screwed up her face. It looked like she was trying to make herself cry. Silence was winning. She bent down to the floor.

"My pictures…?"

"That's what I mean." Dolores. "He's over you. He poked them. Graham did."

Dolores & Silas

Miriam curled up on her defiled bed, desperately clutching the pocked photographs, and wept herself to sleep. Thankfully the process only took about an hour. When she was out, tears and snot puddling on the ruined glossies, Dolores took the key chain with the miniature dildo and left.

She was now driving the VirginVan down the main drag by UNI-ARTS, kids lingering outside coffee shops and records stores on the weekend, spending their parents' money. She felt high. She had wished to see the VirginVan pull up at her front door so many times. And now, here she was, steering the thing.

She had already stopped at the convenience store and bought a bottle of red wine and cigarettes. She had also stopped at Bunny's, a strippers' clothing boutique.

Her friend Rageena had told her about it sometime ago. Rageena was a stripper, or at least used to be. Now she worked at the topless carwash. For a hundred bucks a few illegal immigrants would scrub the hell out of some sports car or SUV or whatever, and the pervert owner would drive under this giant pink tent where six topless blondes would giggle and bounce around, pretending to dry the car. It was pretty lame, but Rageena had been in two rap videos, and the VirginVan always stopped by after a shoot. It regularly needed cleaning from the inside out.

So, on Rageena's recommendation, she had gone to Bunny's to get a sexy outfit. She wanted to make her intentions clear to Silas. And to show off certain assets. She had originally intended to get the classic bunny costume: a G-string, some fishnets, some cute bunny ears, and a cottontail. But the woman at Bunny's, Bunny, had convinced her that the bunny was passé, out of style. "Men have been there, done that, honey. Your costume needs to be cutting edge." She flipped through similar get-ups on the rack: cats, maids, all sorts of dominatrix leather things. "Our newest is the Horny Toad." Dolores didn't like it at first, it was prickly and brownish-yellow, but Bunny talked it up. "If the horny toad loses a limb, it regenerates. Like, all night long." The ear ridges were 'cute,' the claws were 'sexy,' and it was, after all, the latest in sex fashion. She bought it, and wore it out of the store.

She pulled up in front of Silas's dorm house, and leaned hard into the horn. Some kid passed out on the porch lifted his head drunkenly. "Hey!" Shouting inside. "Hey, the VirginVan is back." A couple more guys came out to look, but no one approached the van. She honked again. "What the fuck is driving that thing?" she thought she heard one kid say. Finally, Silas emerged, shirt unbuttoned, hair flying, walking fiercely across the wide lawn.

He approached the window with a pointing finger, ready for confrontation. When she rolled down the window and leaned out, he stopped, a good six feet from the vehicle.

"Dolores?"

"Hey baby, wanna go for a ride?"

"Uh... That's my van." Anger sliding into confusion "Where's Miriam?"

"God, is that all you think about?"

"Give me the keys."

"Get in the van."

"All the boys are watching." Silas. His voice lower, pleading.

"If you ever want to see the fricking VirginVan again, Silas, get inside now."

He did. And she crawled into the carpeted rear, arching her back and purring like she imagined a horny toad would. "Ready to make the episode of your life?"

"Uh, look Dolores, I really don't... I don't have my camera, and..."

"There's one on the ceiling."

"I'm hungover, and you're wearing... I don't use the VirginVan, I just film..."

"The same camera that filmed you and Miriam."

"What?"

"That's right, it was on the Internet. You crouching over her, with your hands down your pants." Dolores. Still using her come-on voice. She had thought this scenario out three steps ahead.

"Did she see it?"

"Maybe."

"Did you tell her about it?"

"Maybe."

"Please don't."

"Well, what would stop me?"

"Please, I'll do whatever you want."

Dolores sat back on her thighs, and eyed the ceiling of the VirginVan. "OK."

"OK?"

"Yeah, OK."

"Well... What do you want?"

"I'm dressed like a fucking horny toad, Silas."

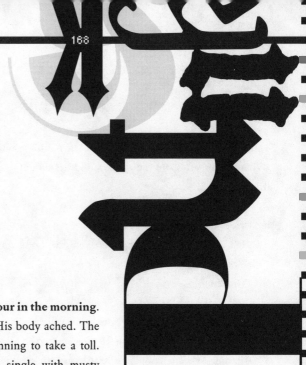

The phone. *Ringing*. It was **four in the morning**. Puɴk squinted and stirred. His body ached. The **drug runs** were really beginning to take a toll. He was in Matilda's bed, a single with musty old blankets. He kicked her *lightly*, and rather uselessly, as she was under the sleeping spell of a ***handful*** of Valium.

He had spent **one miserable night** in the tent. It leaked everywhere, and he was *cold* and *wet*, and *couldn't sleep*. The next day he went back to Matilda's and told her all about it, and about 𝛺llister getting kidnapped by The White Sodality, and about how he got the *note* from 𝕿𝖍𝖊 𝕻𝖑𝖆𝖙𝖞𝖕𝖚𝖘, and how Franc said **he** would probably be **next**. She felt sorry for him, and took him back in, and they *slept together*, this time without **drugs**. Or without the **one drug,** anyway.

The phone kept *ringing*. So he got up. "Fuck, dude," under his breath, "annoying things are so annoying."

He surveyed the *blurred shapes* on Matilda's dirty carpet for something that looked like pants. The convex view afforded to him by a head *filled* with **cotton** and **throbbing light** was confusing. What **drug** had he taken? Come downs were always really *harsh*. "Dude." He chided himself. He always referred to himself as 'dude.' ***In the dude.*** As if it were some disgusting pet name his brain had for itself.

The Phone. *Ringing*.

"Fuck's sake." He grabbed Matilda's smeared *floral panties* and pulled them up over his hairy legs and tender entrail. Not by choice, his pants were not in the vicinity. It seemed as though he were the **only one** who could fling accurately in the heat of the moment. No one gave a shit about *romance* anymore.

He picked up the phone as it began its next *screech*.

"What?" Trying to sound *sleepy* and *belligerent* rather than just **drunk**.

"Omigod Mattie. It's Zella. I'm totally freaking. We were at January's and..."

"Who?"

"Mattie, is that you?"

"She's dead, I mean dying."

"This is serious. There's a fucking emergency. Put her on the goddamned phone." Zella's voice was **hysterical**, affected or not. She didn't recognize his voice. PuNk creased his brow at the wafting **odors** of his own **breath**. He had better not say anything else. He didn't need her knowing that he was here. She'd tell *Adelaide*, then The White Suits would come. **Nobody** could know. Zella continued.

"Paolo was there. And you know how he thought that Brody was fucking his girlfriend in the butt, that whore Nadine, even though they only fucked once, and not in the butt, in an alley, behind the Pizza Pit? So Brody's just sitting there, and Paolo comes up to him and he's like 'Suck on this, bitch!' and then he whips out one of those little pepper spray canister thingies, you know, like the kind... the kind... the kind a fucking soccer mom keeps on her key chain, right? And sprays him right in the face. Like right now. He's totally fucking choking, OK? And I need someone to tell me whether or not to call the cops and the ambulance, and that whole fucking 911 business, because there's fucking heroin involved, but he hasn't, like, taken a breath in five minutes and he's turning fucking blue, I swear to..." PuNk pulled the phone away from his ear, *gently* pressed the 'END' button, and *tossed it* onto the sofa.

Without Ωllister around he didn't know **what to do** with himself. At first he had been glad that he disappeared. He felt *free*. But now he was **worried** about Ωllister. And about The White Sodality.

He had to dodge looming **corners** and jutting **walls** in his attempt to float toward the bathroom. He was in a *sea of dark*, and ache. His body was dangling from his bowed head, an **appendage**.

He stared in the mirror, his mouth *loose*. **Dark dictatorial eyes** flickered back at him. He was simultaneously attempting a vigorous *dig* (which he found the panties didn't allow adequate room for) and sticking out his tongue, when he became **alarmed**.

Green bumps or moles or *something* covered the back of his tongue. He removed his fingers from various orifices to grasp his tongue **firmly** with both sets of pinchers and stretch it out over his chin. "Fug!" With real *feeling* now.

He **lunged** back out of the bathroom, **vomiting** a little in the back of his throat as his heel squeaked on the tile. "Fug Fug Fug" He knew it would be the *death of him*.

Crawling around on the floor of Matilda's darkened dorm room he found what they had both been seriously debating, the night before: THE PILL BOOK, ninth edition.

And although the larger, pill identification section was the *oft-used* and *more useful*, there was a set of pink pages in the back for self-diagnosis. A publisher who knew **hypochondriacs**. PuNk squinted *frantically* from page to page. Writhing on the floor in **agony** of anticipation, he inadvertently kicked over Matilda's bookcase. The cascade finished its last crash as he found what he was looking for. Matilda mumbled a bit of *incoherence* as some of the **book fallout** bounced off her. PuNk wanted to wake her, but the page had to be read *immediately*.

He rushed back into the bathroom, **careening** off the walls and furniture he had so judiciously avoided before, to discover in the fluorescent light what his **fatal ailment** would finally be. The Latin name was indecipherable, but the layman's below it said: "WOMAN'S GOUT, C. 1860"

"Fug! I Fugging knew id!" PuNk. Shouting now. He *slammed* the book into the open toilet, spraying stale urine everywhere. He turned his attention to Matilda's medicine cabinet. Knocking aside *anti-depressants, anti-anxiety pills, appetite suppressants,* he found her plastic ringlet of **birth control pills**. Women's gout. He took **twelve**. His tongue was *burning*. It must be swelling. **Athlete's foot spray!** He vaulted horizontally, and with eyes *wide* and *tearing* he sprayed **five full seconds** into the back of his throat. Even though his **retching convulsions** sent him doubling back into a bathtub that *might shortly* be filled with his **vomit**, he managed to hold on to the aerosol can. Fetal, in the tub, he gave himself **another long spray**, for good measure.

While *belatedly* trying to breathe, his brain rapidly mapped out his **last moments on earth**. Trying to think of what was important. **Sex. Procreation**. His genes would survive. He'd better get back in there and **give it** to Matilda's still body before she got whatever it was that would bring about his own *unsightly end*. One last time. **Jungle style**. Like a *fucking panther* fucking a *fucking snake*.

SILAS & Dolores

He attacked her, more or less. Flinging off bits of the horny toad costume in every direction. She was surprised by the ferocity of his passion, by his mouth slobbering over hers. Especially given that he had been so indifferent in the past. At first she thought it was just a show for the VirginVan cameras. But then they were in the back, behind the bench seat, where the camera couldn't see, and he was still going at it.

"I'm gonna tie you up." Silas. Growling, strands of black hair hanging in his flushed face.

"Unh..." Dolores. By way of assent. Or at least submission.

He reached under the seat then, and began to pull out all sorts of sex toys: dildos, leather, lube, whips, nipple clamps, chains, it was like there was a dungeon beneath the van.

He strapped her ankles and wrists together, roughly. She was really getting turned on. Then the ball gag. At first she objected, shaking her head back and forth to get away from his strong hands, but they finally forced the ball in, and when he tied the strap behind her head, she thought that this, too, felt pretty kinky.

But then he did something she did not expect. He covered the ceiling camera with a T-shirt, and opened the rear door of the van. Not as some voyeuristic gesture, but to get out, which he did, slamming the door behind him. He walked around to the front of the van, and turned the ignition.

She groaned and screamed through her gag, but it was not very loud. He turned up the radio, a metal station, got out of the running van, and walked back toward his frat house.

171

Adelaide

Her gray eyes took the color of the sky as their own. They reflected, *in miniature*, each swelling cloud streaking the lightscape. If a stray raindrop fell into one of her mud-puddle eyes it would have found them to be the familiar consistency of **water**, the rings of ripple distorting the clouds' silhouettes and momentarily blurring her vision before the silt settled back down to clarity, *lucidity*.

Matilda fed the parking meter as *Adelaide* gripped her left mitten **tightly**. They stood outside the **SNOOTY FOX**. To see *some kid* play guitar.

"Do I have to?" *Adelaide*.

"He's my friend. And he's cute. You'll see."

They pushed the heavy doors open and de-scarved, de-mittened and de-muffed before receiving the requisite stamp on the back of their hands. *Adelaide* sucked on her lower lip.

Their friends were easily spotted, and had luckily snagged a table before the place had been full. There was *Zella*, Vance, Sebastian, and various *hangers-on*. The girls hung their pea coats and went to join the table.

"What's up?" *Zella* got up to give hugs. *Adelaide* was **irked** by her manner of greeting. She was in a *mood* tonight. She didn't want to sit next to her, so she wedged in on the other side of the table, a move she *instantly regretted*. She was sitting next to Vance. He smelled like he had **jerked off** in a bath of **beer**, with his too-cool clothes on, before coming here tonight.

"Hey girl, you're looking hot…"

"Shut up, Vance."

"I'm just saying, because, you know… I know."

"You know what?"

"I know what's hot."

"Oh really? Then what are you doing at this show?" He didn't have an answer ready for that. The bands that played at the **SNOOTY FOX** were much too psychedelic, too hippy, to reaffirm his *supposed* cynicism. He stuck out like a **bruised thumb**, all in black, practically the only hipster there.

Adelaide interrupted the jabbering ping-pong of *Zella* and Matilda. "You promised to get me drunk."

"Oh, OK..." Matilda got up for the bar.

"Liquor..." *Adelaide*. Calling after her. She turned back to a **leering grin**, much too close to her face.

"Yeah, girl. Let's get trolleyed together..." Vance wasn't going to let up.

"Yeah... OK."

"Yeah, then we can go scam out."

"Mm." There was *no amount* of alcohol that would allow that to happen.

"You know you want to girl. I mean, shit. Look at me. I'm a fucking genius. I'm a hot genius. What most girls don't understand..."

Adelaide already wished she hadn't left the house. She couldn't *believe* this guy was going around telling everyone they were together. She thought about confronting him, but decided that **any** conversation with him was too high a price to pay. When Matilda returned with her **whiskey** she grabbed *Zella* and the three of them moved to an empty couch.

"Mattie, what guy was at your house?" *Zella*.

"What?"

"I called your house the other night. Some guy answered. Was it Pu**N**k?" She was being **confrontational**.

"I thought you kicked him out." *Adelaide*. Half interested.

"Um, yeah I did, of course..." Matilda bit her lip. Even she knew that her answer seemed **unconvincing**. But Pu**N**k had to be a **secret** again. It was too *embarrassing*. Besides she might just have a new boyfriend after tonight. "Here he is, guys." Matilda tried to direct attention toward the front of the room. The jukebox cut out and the opening act was coming up on the small stage with an acoustic guitar. This was her friend. *Zella* couldn't **care less** about other people's friends.

"Did you see that thing that January is prancing around with?" Shot at *Adelaide*.

"Yeah. He looks like he was born from a pod. Like his head was in a rock tumbler for about 20 years." Maybe she could come down to *Zella*'s level.

Anything was better than *being herself* right now.

"He sure does. Woke up on the wrong side of the tracks."

"Speaking of tracks. Nick's arms…"

"Oh yeah. I know. He's back on. But pretending he's not. What a stupid fucking…"

"Guys! He's starting! Look how nervous he is. Isn't it so cute?" Matilda.

"What about Paolo?" Adelaide. Had to know.

"Oh, not him. No, he got into grad school, a good one…"

"That's rad. He's real smart…"

"…but he doesn't know if he's gonna go. He doesn't want to leave town because of the girlfriend."

"Seriously? She's a crazed slut."

"Yep."

"Probably giving her psychiatrist blowjobs on the couch…"

"Guys! Are you watching? That song was adorable…"

"Oh shit. Did you hear about Bart?" Zella. A grave mirth in her voice.

"What, the kid who did those Mackerel knock-offs?"

"Yep. He died."

"What! How?"

"Well, you know how he had those big seizures?"

"Yeah. I saw him go off at one of his openings. THE TRIPLEKITTY GALLERY, no less… I assumed it was just publicity."

"No. He really had 'em. This last one while he was driving that old Mustang of his."

"So he wrecked it?"

"Into a tree. Eighty miles per hour. His guts everywhere."

"So he ended up painting the windshield, Mackerel-style."

"Heh. Yeah. It was probably his best work yet." Poorly concealed laughter.

"Guys! Cut it out!" Matilda. Agitated.

"Oh fine." Zella. Concession. "I'm going back to the bar."

This time she turned back to Matilda's **glare**. Adelaide quickly focused her attention on the mop-headed blond boy on stage cradling his guitar. He was mumbling into the microphone: "…for sale in the back. If anyone wants one. Which probably no one does… I mean, I'm not trying to sell anything, I just… they're only five bucks. Anyway… um… this next song, uh… I wrote it for a 12-string guitar. But… I… only have a 6-sting guitar, so… I, uh… I…" He produced a small object from his pocket. "I taped two picks together… so… you know… each string would be hit twice and then it, uh… sounds like I'm playing a 12-string." Someone in the audience chuckled as he produced something else from his guitar case.

"And then... I thought... well, I could tape these three... picks together and... Um... that would be like a... like an... 18-string guitar." Laughter as he reached again into the bag of tricks. "And then I taped these... um... 9 picks together which... makes a... um... 54-sting guitar... I think..." he strummed, for effect. It didn't sound like any guitar ⟨Adelaide⟩ had ever heard.

"Boring boring." ⟨Adelaide⟩'s face was a **plaster cast** of itself.

"Isn't he so funny?" Matilda.

"Mm. Let's move back by the group. You could probably see better over there." Matilda agreed and they nudged their way through the standing crowd, and slipped back into the booth by the wall. Zella's hand was on Sebastian's knee and she was *whispering* rapidly into his ear. ⟨Adelaide⟩ wanted to give up.

"Vance. Buy me a whiskey."

"Really? That's more like it girl... all right..."

"Just hurry up..."

Matilda's golden boy was dragging his chair offstage to a lukewarm smattering of applause. **Much of it** coming from Matilda. The headliners were supposed to be some psychedelic slowcore band from two towns over. They had a *pet snake*, which they brought out on stage to sing all of their songs. It was mostly silent. But there was *plenty* of hissing from the audience.

"There you go." Vance shoved a **double-whiskey** at her. "Get your palate all wet."

"It's a drink, Vance. I'm not scamming out with you. That goes for all of eternity." She turned away. He slid closer and blew his **hot breath** right in her ear.

"Awww... ⟨Addy⟩, I'm sorry, really girl. Listen. You're just such a rad girl. And I'm like, a rad guy, you know I'd be perfect. I got this thing going on, with some guys from around. We're really gonna make a splash. All that jerky stuff, it's just a front, you know that. We'd be like, the hottest couple in town..."

"Vance. Shut up. You're grossing me out." She tossed back the drink in **one go**, pushed past him and lurched to her feet.

"I want to get to know you, you know, like..."

"I have to go home." She started elbowing her way toward the door. Matilda was there in a *sympathetic second*.

"⟨Addy⟩, are you OK? Honey, what's wrong?"

"Let's go."

They pulled on their mittens and pushed back out the big doors that separated the smoke from the rain. *An exhalation.* ⟨Adelaide⟩'s eyes rolled upwards. Perhaps in **disgust** and **ridicule** at the last hour and a half. Perhaps in *praise* of the worsening weather. Or perhaps as a *prelude* to **fainting**.

Miriam 8

Silas was sitting on the sofa in the frat house telling a few of the guys about Dolores's ridiculous outfit, which was turning out to be very hard to describe, when the knock came at the door.

He nearly swallowed his tongue when he saw Miriam. "Hey, I'm sorry I..."

"If I'm going to be accused of something, well... I might as well do it." Miriam. Matter-of-fact.

"What?"

"You want me? Here I am. Let's do this." A gaggle of boys peered nervously from afar. The silence droned.

"Uh, yeah, OK, I'll get a ring, and..."

"Not that. I mean... Don't you want to try the milk before you buy the cow?" She lowered her eyelids to a sexy half-mast.

"Oh, yeah. No, I know. Yeah." His voice louder now. "Let's go upstairs."

"Actually, what about the VirginVan?"

"Oh. No... No, it's not here."

"It's parked out front, Silas."

"Oh, I mean, I wouldn't take a girl like you, I mean, you, into the VirginVan, I mean, that stuff is just a joke."

"I've already been in it, if you'll remember, and I want to go back. That's what I got accused of, and that's what I'm going to do."

"No, really, it's not..." But she started walking back down the walkway to the van, idling on the curb. He had no choice but to follow. The boys gathered in the doorway, snickering. He turned and tried to give a hip thrust in midair, to show them what he intended to do.

"Can you turn off the music?" Miriam. Asking, once they got inside.

"Sure thing." As soon as he switched it off, a low groan emerged from the behind the backseat. "Uh, actually, what if I just change it?" Quickly turning the dial back on.

"Fine, but no rap, and no country." He found a smooth jazz station. They sat and listened to it, for a minute, neither of them looking at the other.

Silas

"I thought you were this big ladies' man." Miriam. He looked up. "So why don't you come over here and kiss me?" She glanced up, and seeing the ceiling camera, pulled the T-shirt off of its lens.

He followed her instructions, elated to be with the girl he had dreamed about, the only one he thought would make a suitable trophy, but uncomfortable at the circumstance and timing.

"You really like me?" Silas. In a small voice, pulling away from the kiss.

"Now I do." Miriam. Pulling down his fly. This was moving quickly.

When he was fully exposed they both looked down at his member. It was limp, and shriveled, like an over-cooked tomato that fell off a slice of pizza and into his lap.

She set her jaw, and began trying to massage it to life gently with her hand. They both stared. The smooth jazz announcer came on and started naming song titles.

Suddenly, Silas started to cry. Big choking gasps.

"I... I just love you and..." He looked like shit. She felt sorry for him. She put down his penis, and cradled him in her arms. He started talking, words like blubber coming out of his mouth.

"Shhh... It's OK, I love you, too." Miriam. Cooing, as if to a baby pigeon. She didn't know why she felt it in that mollifying moment. She just knew that this was what he wanted. And she wanted to give it to him. He was calming down, his head against her chest.

"I... I want... I just want to be with you."

She heard a muffled screaming, rising above the smooth jazz saxophone.

"What the hay was that?" Miriam. More than a little concerned. Silas's eyes reflected fear. She rose to a crouching stand and shuffled back to peer over the rear bench of the van. Where Dolores was tied up.

Silas thought that he would never see such a lovely, feminine gasp again. "What is your deal?" She spun to face him, furious. "Why does everyone... have... have a woody for that little... tart?"

She gave his lap one last disgusted look before slamming the door of the VirginVan on them both.

GRAHAM

Pete hated his job. He took the laptop into the back room and snapped the monitor back on. When the Art Terrorists took over he wouldn't have to do this shit work anymore.

Graham leaned over the computer repair counter, rubbing his palms nervously together. When Pete came out of the back room, with Miriam's laptop intact, he sighed with relief.

"Actually they just snap back together, it doesn't really damage this kind of laptop. By now the manufacturers expect you to snap it in half at least a few times. Everybody does."

"Awesome, dude. It's my girlfriend's, and she's all pissed at me right now."

"No problem." He flipped it open. "In fact it restores itself to the exact place you left off."

Graham watched as the web browser popped up and a webcam flickered on, small and choppy. He squinted at the screen. It was unmistakable. Miriam in the back of a van with Silas's deflated dream in her hand.

THE PAST

He recalled when she made it clear to him, with no certain words or gestures, that he was no longer welcome. Maybe the revelation was his alone. Maybe this was what they called insecurity. Maybe she never batted an eyelash.

He took it personally. He always did. He overreacted. He almost never did that. But, he had been young.

A few weeks holed up in his room. Burning through cigarette and coffee filters. No showers. Jars of peanut butter.

He created a travel book, a guide to the different parts of his mind. Scenic daydreams, photographic thoughts. Local finds, hidden spots. Five-star reviews by travel writers embedded in these far-off regions of his brain. Maps. Grids. Conversion tables. A short section with translations for common phrases (this part was actually useful). The coverage was exhaustive. The book was immaculate. When his hibernation was over, he gave it to her.

She hadn't realized anything was wrong. She had barely noticed his protracted absence. The book puzzled her. She understood what it was, but not what it was for. And it was nothing compared to the gray papers, which came later.

How much of her disaffection was put on he never could decide. They carried on as before, exactly as before. But, for him at least, the juncture marked something. Something had changed.

SILAS & Dolores

"That's it!" Silas. Yelling, unusual for his cool and collected person.

He was doubled over the back seat of the VirginVan, his finger in Dolores' face, yelling. Miriam had just slammed the door, and Dolores was going into convulsing fits so he had removed her ball gag. She burst out laughing.

"You... couldn't... get it up!" She screamed between gasps for air. Her laughter was becoming hysterical. He reinserted the ball gag, she didn't even resist, like she had before. There were tears streaming down her cheeks, and the grin would not leave the corners of her mouth, even with the gag in.

"Fuck you." Silas. Teeth clenched. He leapt out of the van, walking with angry purpose back to the frat house. A lot of the other boys were still on the porch watching. There was silence, respect for their disgraced leader.

"Mike, I want the number of your drug guy. And could someone go and get my fucking Jag. I can't drive around in the goddamn VirginVan for the rest of my life." Some of the boys slinked back inside the house.

"Uh, actually, he doesn't have a phone, I just call this kid, who calls this other kid, who knows where he is, and then he just kind of shows up, but he always acts like it..."

"I don't give a shit about all that. Make him appear, whatever you do..."

The guy flipped open his cell phone and started making calls. Silas sat down on one of the plastic chairs strewn about the front porch. Everything was screwed. Miriam would never be with him now. And she had wanted to, even. The tragedy was unspeakable. He bit his lip and stared at the van, which was rocking, slightly. The whole VirginVan was ruined too. Two webcasts had gone out, both with the same girl, neither ending in the promised payoff for the website's subscribers. It was over, and his reputation had been ruined. He took a warm can of beer from the porch railing and downed its contents. It was disgusting. He wanted to die. Or get really fucked up. He sat out there with that thought for a long time.

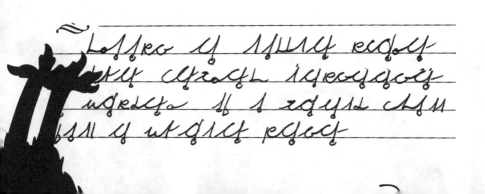

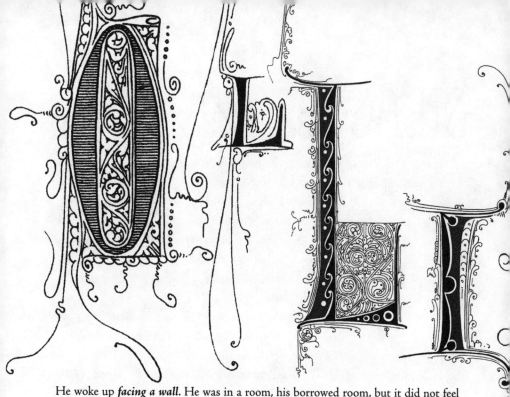

He woke up *facing a wall*. He was in a room, his borrowed room, but it did not feel *familiar*. He couldn't place it, had forgotten the details, clouds of gray floated in front of his eyes.

He lay still on his back, and tried to imagine the layout of the house around him. The other rooms. Doors. And he **couldn't**. Was he facing north? East? Was most of the house next to him? Behind him?

He got out of bed. *Semi-panicked*. It was cold. He crossed his arms in front of his chest and leaned through the door that had **appeared** on his left.

The rooms were becoming familiar, but he couldn't seem to find his way around them. The floors were **uneven**. And all of the doors were **unexpected**. Was that a closet? The living room? The way out?

He was *upset* with himself for not knowing these rooms, this house he was in. It was right there, in his frontal lobe, the information he needed. He just **couldn't** grasp it. It was as if he'd been studying for a test for weeks and choked, or momentarily forgotten how old he was. Except this was something he *knew*.

Once he was fully awake, he went out onto the porch and looked out at the *air*.

He had begun to think of the *air* as a *physicality*. Not the absence of space, or a blankness. But as a soup that we float around in.

THE AIR

Much as he imagined the bottom of the ocean to be. The sea life never stops to consider the water. For them it is everything, or maybe **nothing**. And if birds and insects can flit through the *air*, using movements *not unlike* those of sea creatures, then the *air* must be like water. Full of stuff, things floating around. Animals **laboring** through it. Great winds sweeping everything along, like tides, *undercurrents*.

He watched with a careful eye, the speed at which smoke floated from his **cigarette**, the way the *sheets of rain* would drift slowly toward the ground.

Gravity was certainly stronger in this *upper ocean*, bodies so **heavy**, so packed with **guts** that they are confined to crawling along the floor, *leaning* against the currents. The jet engines **fail** and bodies *sink like handfuls of gravel*.

These thoughts of *air* made the space around him **rich** and **fretful**. Gave him something to hold, something to touch. The *air*, hot or cool. The *air*, running its fingers through his hair. The *air*, sickly sweet, all of the *flavors* of oxygen, carbon dioxide, nitrogen.

The *air* is not the **vacuum of space**, and to treat it as such, to ignore it, is denial of this *immediate* and *intimate* surrounding. The pulpy stuff that animals must suck in and out constantly. **Or else.** The way *air* must taste on the gills of a fish, **hot and dry**, like fire.

These thoughts made him feel so **heavy**, suddenly aware of the mass of substance, of *air pressing down* on his body, his heart, at every moment. He was sure that the *air* would squash him, suffocate him. The *air*.

The exiled air.

PUNK & Silas

Silas **started** when he saw PuNK. *Under one of the bushes* by the front porch. He looked **paranoid**, frightened, and barely concealed by the thinning bush that had lived on **beer dregs** for too long. He motioned Silas to *come over*.

"But don't look at me! Act casual!" PuNK. A *hiss*. Silas stared out at the road.

"You Silas?" PuNK. Suspiciously.

"Yeah."

"Drop your I.D. under the bush."

Silas rolled his eyes, pulled his driver's license out of his wallet and dropped it under the bush for the crazy **druggy kid** to inspect.

PuNK stood up, satisfied that identities matched up, person and card. "You're licensed to drive commercial vehicles?"

"Uh, yeah, for the van." He indicated the VirginVan, white against the dimming drizzle of evening.

"That looks like a fucking surveillance van to me, man." PuNK. "You sure?"

"Nope, not a cop."

"Cause if you are you have to tell me."

"I'm not."

"Cause that's entrappingment."

"All right," Silas, finally **exasperated**. "You want me to prove it? Come here." PuNK followed him across the wide lawn, ducking as he walked. Silas threw open the back door of the van, to reveal Dolores, half-costumed, *tied up* and *groaning*. "Does that look like a cop to you?"

PuNK fixed his dumb stare on Dolores's **angry** eyes. "Uh... yeah... I guess not."

"All right then. Did you bring the drugs?"

"Shh, man. Shit. Don't just say it like that."

Silas slammed the door without looking at the **writhing toad**.

"We gotta go get them."

"Are you serious?" Silas. Becoming irritated.

"What, dude, you think I just run around with drugs all over me?"

"Well, they're certainly inside you."

"Safest place for 'em."

"Come on, they just brought my Jag back." Silas started to walk toward the back of the building, where their garage entrance was hidden, one level down. PuNk followed, looking **back** every few steps at the gleaming white van.

Night fell, as they pulled out of the garage in the black Jag. The raindrops gathering on the windshield each reflected tiny streetlights, kaleidoscoping the **cityscape** like the eyes of some *sleek* and *evil* fly.

PuNk would **only** give directions one turn at a time, no specific final destination was mentioned. He would indicate a right or a left just by pointing with his hand. His *smell* filled the small interior of the car. Silas tried to breath shallowly.

"So, whaddya want?" PuNk. He peered out the window **anxiously**.

"What do you have?"

"That's not how it works, man."

"Uh... OK, then, I don't care... some pills? Some weed? I just want to get fucked up. Really fucked up."

"OK, dude. Right on. I'm down with that. I got just the thing for you."

"Great." Silas. Fiddling with the wiper speed. It was either *too fast*, and squeaking against the glass, or *too slow*, allowing the rain to obscure his vision. Seven settings, and **not one** to match the speed of the rain.

They stopped at a light, by a gas station. A bum lurched out of the **dark**, and toward the passenger side of the car. He held a cardboard sign that said something about 'pardon my appearance.' PuNk *quickly* hit the lock on the door and *slouched down* in his seat. He caught a **half-grin** on Silas's oily face.

"What?" PuNk. Somewhat violently.

"Oh, I just wouldn't have thought you'd be the type to be frightened of bums."

"I know that guy."

"Oh."

"You want him in your car, man? He uses a toothbrush to wipe his ass. You leave it open, he'll get in the fucking car man, I've seen him do it."

"No, no I don't want him in my car."

"Then shut up and drive, man."

They drove past burger joints, and strip malls. Lights from titty bars and gas stations blurred together, slipping over the body of the car, jumping off the chrome.

"You see that white car?"

"What? Where?"

"No, man. Don't look." PuNK. Sitting **stock-still**. "It's been following us for four blocks."

Silas checked his mirrors. No white car in sight. "I don't see any..." And then a white car pulled up to the light opposite them and sat, *menacing*, in the rain.

"Put your left blinker on, but go straight."

Silas did as he was told. It was impossible to tell if the **paranoia** was justified. He had no idea *how deep* into **drugs** this kid was. Mike said that this kid always delivered to the house. He wondered if anyone else had been out with him. This could be a *dangerous* situation. He wasn't about to go down on drug charges with this mangy clown. He had had too many narrow scrapes with the law during his own hijinks to get nabbed for **someone else's** stupidity.

"What are you all tense about?" PuNK. Shifting moods.

"Um... I don't know. Well, there is this girl, and..."

"She's mad at you?"

"Yeah."

"Yeah, well not all of them like to be tied up, man."

"No, not that girl. Another one."

"Oh. Yeah, they're all the same, man."

"That's not really..."

"Speed up, speed up!" PuNK. Now orchestrating a **getaway** from the floor of the car. He had collapsed completely out of sight.

Silas followed the instructions, checking his mirrors *frantically* for any sign of a white car, gripping the wheel tight at the top, spine straight.

As they drove around the city, making ***random turns*** according to PuNK's directives, his grip slowly loosened. There was no white car. Nobody could have followed them through all that anyway. PuNK popped his head up.

"That's it! Go, go, go!" Screaming at some white car or another. But it was not the first one they had seen. In fact, it was a different one every time. Silas hit the gas anyway, to appease PuNK and, well, just in case. But soon he *tired* of the game.

"That's not the same white car, you know." Silas. Finally.

"You don't think they have more than one white car? This is the fucking Sodality we're talking about, man."

"Look, are there drugs or not? I can't drive around all night acting like..."

"I know, I know. Look man, pull over right there." PuNK. Pointing to a corner about a block down the side street they were on. Silas pulled up in front of a storage lot for lawn ceramics. Birdbaths, hippos, and gnomes all sat stupidly in the dark.

"Uh, I thought we were going to someone's place."

"My place." PuNK. "I got my tent back there. Dude, you see any white cars?" His head wildly rotated right and left.

"No, no white cars." PuNK leapt from the car, leaving the door hanging open. He scrambled up and over the fence that enclosed the ceramics lot, and went streaking into the **dark**, dodging fake roman plinths and bird fountains.

Silas leaned across and closed the passenger door. And then he sat. And sat. He saw a few white cars pass on the street up ahead, but it didn't seem like anything outside of the normal number of white cars in normal traffic. He still felt a *little* nervous, though. It was taking a **long time**.

Finally there was a knock on his car door, which made him jump, because there was no one standing at the window. He rolled down the window and looked around. Still no one. He opened the door completely.

"Don't get out." PuNK. His *disembodied voice* coming from beneath the car.

"For fuck's sake." Silas, looking down at the wet pavement. PuNK's head slid into view, as though he were some sort of undercover agent posing as a dirty car mechanic.

"Here's the junk. Gimme the money, quick." He tossed a wet plastic bag up and into Silas's lap.

"Is this the good stuff that you...?"

"Yeah, gimme the fucking money, man."

"OK, OK." Silas. Handing him a small roll of bills.

PuNK's hand reached up to grab it, and then head and hand were **gone**.

"You were never here." This *disembodied voice* said again.

Silas closed his car door, and started it back up. For a second he was worried about driving off, on the chance that the **dirty kid** was still lying under his car. But then he realized he didn't much *care*, and peeled out, back into the **night**.

Almost every single car he saw on his way back was white.

Loneliness. Not the *romantic* kind. Not the **mad genius** concocting in his basement. Not the bloodthirsty **highwayman**, plotting in the brush, a **lone wolf**. Not the ancient **tyrant**, in his old gilded tower, hovering over the terrasphere, unequalled in stature, might, or wealth. No, the **loneliness** that *asks pity*. That looks away from creased brows, concerned eyes.

He was in a diner, waiting *long* and *alone* to be served. He was waking himself up in the morning. He was at some bar that wasn't the SNOOTY FOX, surrounded by someone else's **empty friends** and their **empty bottles**, his face a mask, the *eyes missing*. He was sitting on a park bench in some neighborhood he didn't know, watching a bag lady or a bulldozer. He was in the express checkout line, putting a divider between his **bottle of bourbon** and *not-his* stack of frozen gourmet dinners. He was saying hello, into his phone, *no one* at the other end.

It was a *mundane* **loneliness**. Deeply, personally *embarrassing*, moreso because there was no one around to see it. It made him feel out of place, out of character. He wanted his life to be a **legend**, a stylized **work of art**, with clean sharp lines. He wanted to read his life in a book, listening to the pages as they described beautiful tableaus, his **silhouette central**. He never had asked to witness the entire thing, **first hand, close up**, *minute* by *excruciating minute*. From this vantage point it was too difficult, or even **impossible**, to edit out the incongruities. They **displeased** him.

He would not allow himself to think of *returning*. Or to think of her. Naïveté and stupid dreams. The only dream now was to dream. Sit back on the porch. Watch the leaves blow across the dark. Drag his tongue across the ground.

The Platypus

His desk phone rang. He watched the ancient gold-encrusted receiver *dance around* on its cradle. He'd been meaning to get rid of the thing for this very reason. He couldn't **stand** for his thoughts to be interrupted. They were getting **more important** as each moment passed.

After the caller had failed to ring off, despite being ignored for fifteen minutes, The Platypus decided he might as well act. He placed his pipe in its holder and picked up the phone instead, *hacking into it* by way of greeting.

"Sir, it's Euphrates. Sorry... I don't want to bother... I wouldn't call if it weren't..."

"What is it? Be quick."

"Certainly. It's... the retrospective show, I mean, Redcote specifically. He's out of control. We hadn't heard from him for weeks, because, well, he says he ate a spoiled duck, but I have it on good authority that he was at the bathhouse last Thursday,..."

"What's the problem?"

"Yes. I was just coming to that. He's refusing to curate the show. He called the entire show... cat shit. He threw his cell phone at one of the artists' assistants. He put all the works outside in the empty lot next door, where some were rained on... And the Johansson piece suffered what seems to be a cigarette burn. As you know it's worth 250. I have no idea what to..." Euphrates paused. He thought he'd heard a **snort** on the other end. The silence *ballooned*. He decided to carry on. "He's filled the gallery with cat litter. 150 bags, shipped in by truck. My phone is ringing off the hook; the artists that know are livid. And it is spreading to the others quickly. They're calling him incompetent, pretentious, and..."

"Pretension is the brother of all invention."

"Oh... well, yes... certainly, I mean, I see your point, it's just that, well, the show opens tomorrow night..."

"Listen we've got real problems. Surveillance on Ωllister's associates continues to turn up nothing. He's still nowhere to be found."

"Well, sir, if I may say so, I've always thought we should just bring the girl in. You know how I felt about the show she put on with the art school applications, and all the..."

"Here's what we're going to do. Get her an invitation to THE WHITE BALL. We'll invite her after all. If she comes, he'll come too. We'll bring him out of hiding. It worked the first time. He went crazy with her behind that mirror." The Platypus suddenly felt **better**. This was **right**.

"Ok, well, what should I do about the show then? I mean, this ludicrous fop is the appointed curator, and I don't... I don't know what to do..."

"Fuck him."

"I agree completely, sir. His behavior warrants immediate removal. We all know you are the only one with the clout to oust him, and I'm so glad that you see the..."

"No. I mean fuck him. It's an order." The Platypus dropped the phone back in its cradle and looked up. Isadora's eyes met his as she looked up over her *star chart*. She was perched in her usual corner of the study, completely nude, *soaking* in purple lamplight.

"He is an intolerable curator when he doesn't get laid."

Isadora blinked assent and returned to her private divinations.

"What are you thinking about?" Some girl traced an *idle figure eight* on Ollister's chest. He picked up her hand and moved it to her own naked chest.

"Can't you think of a more annoying question?" He was staring at the ceiling. Her bed smelt **strange**, musty. He thought maybe *sleeping with someone else* was what he should do.

"What's wrong?" She flipped over and affected a clownish pout.

"There you go. Well done."

She **snorted** and her fake pout took on the wrinkles of a real one.

"I have to go." Ollister. Wearily.

"But why?"

"Have you seen my other sock?" He peered over the ledge of the mattress.

"Why would you go? Like right after? How do you think that makes me feel?"

"Slutty, probably."

"Why won't you sleep over?"

"Seriously, I have to go." He was upside down, squinting into the **darkness** underneath her bed trying to discern if this or that shape *constituted* a dress sock.

"I won't be taken advantage of."

"Is that right?"

"We spend all night together, we hang out, we sleep together. What else do you want in a girlfriend?"

"My other sock?" He was on the floor now. Pants on, shoulder shoved in the gap between floor and box springs, fingers blindly dancing over dust bunnies and debris.

"Like at the movie tonight. I felt like we really connected."

"We were sitting in the dark, three seats apart, staring at a screen,"

"We laughed at all the same parts."

"They were the only two funny parts in the movie." Ollister. Into the floor. "Ah, there it is." He removed the sock and brushed it clean.

"Can't we talk?" She was *really* whining.

"We are talking." He tugged on the sock. And slipped on his **shiny black shoes.**

"No, I mean really talk. I think I'm falling in love with you. And it's getting all serious. I think about you all the time. And I just want to talk. And hang out and get to know you. I want to know what you're thinking. And it seems like you never..." She went on like this for a while. She hadn't seen Ollister get up and walk toward the door, buttoning his shirt as he *left.*

SHE HAD BEEN OUT WALKING AGAIN, TRACING HER FINGERS THROUGH THE NIGHT SKY, IMAGINING SLOW RIPPLES FEATHERING OUTWARD INTO THE DEEP BLACK POND.

THE THING THAT OCCURED TO HER TONIGHT, WHEN THE SURFACE RECLAIMED ITS TAUT VENEER, WAS THAT, IN FACT, THE NIGHT SKY WAS NOTHING LIKE BLACK. THE SILHOUETTES OF THE OVERARCHING TREES WERE BLACK. BLACK AGAINST THE PALE GRAY OF THE SKY.

AND, SHE THOUGHT, AS SHE SCRATCHED THE BOTTOMS OF HER FEET, THIS MUST BE TRUE EVERYWHERE. SHE WAS CURLED CRESCENT UNDER THE COVERS, LOOKING UP THRO___ ___ ___ ROOM WINDOW. THE ANGLE WAS ___ ___OMFORTABLE ___ BUT NOT IMPOSSIBLE. DEEP S___ ___IS NO VOID, ___ VACUUM, NO UNFATHOMABLE VA___. THERE IS L___ ___ EVERYWHERE, ALL THE ___, TOUCHING EV___ ___THING. CREATING THE FINEST, ___ST IMPOSSIB___ ___INTRICATE COBWEB OF RAYS, SO DENSE AS ___ ___BE SOLID, SO LIGHT AS TO BE NOTHING.

SH___ TURNED HER HEAD AND LOOKED AT THE ___IVERSAL GLOW HALOING FINE STRANDS OF HIS HAIR. SHE KNEW HE WAS AWAKE. AND SHE ___ED TO ___

___EYES SILENTLY ___ ___IGHT BACK ___STARS, TINY ___ ___RATING USE___ ___IN

Silas

Back in the garage, still sitting in the wet, black Jag, Silas opened the sack of drugs the punk kid had gotten for him.

The stuff was gross. It looked like weed, but it was damp and smelled of lemons. Silas had no idea how to consume it, so he just put a pinch of it under his lip, as though it were chewing tobacco. He sucked on it, the acidic taste filling his mouth and nose, making his eyes water.

When he woke up later, he had no idea how much time had passed, but it was still dark outside. He had a massive, painful erection. He lurched out of the car, the rest of the drug spilling out of his lap, and all over the cement floor of the garage.

He had never felt so horny. He was like a deranged cat in yowling heat. The only organ he could feel was his dick. He felt like he was inside it. Like it was a log flume, and he had no control. He was sweating, his eyes were bugging out, teeth gnashing.

He tumbled inside, tearing off his jacket to cool down. In his room he opened the bottom drawer of his dresser and started going through the collection of porno tapes he had filmed, but he quickly abandoned this endeavor and started flipping through the back of his JailBiscuits magazines, looking for a sex line, an idea that gave way to the phonebook, under the heading 'escort services,' and no sooner had he reached that page than he dropped the phone book in favor of his little black book, which had the numbers of prostitutes that he had employed to fuck his friends in the past, when an authentic victim couldn't be found for an episode of the VirginVan. The VirginVan. Dolores.

He fell down the stairs, and slammed into the front doorway in his mad scramble to get to the back of the van as fast as possible.

THE PAST

They were in the SNOOTY FOX one night, shortly after they had met. They were young, unformed. Ollister had received, earlier that day, from a friend, a small tattoo on the inside of his left wrist. It was white, a small heraldic griffin. To this day, his only tattoo. She liked the size or maybe the placement of it. She didn't know him that well, would probably never see him again. She asked if he would mind if she copied him, or rather, copied the tattoo. He said sure. He didn't think she was serious.

191

DOLORES

"Do you think you could untie my hands now?" Dolores. Gasping for breath.

"Oh, yeah, sorry." Silas. Tugging at the knot. He had only untied her ankles to complete the deed that the drug had compelled him to do. It had continued to compel him for the better part of four hours, and he had performed a litany of unspeakable acts with Dolores, that rivaled any previous episode of the VirginVan. His housemates, inside, huddled around the computer, astonished.

"That was amazing." Dolores. Staring at the ceiling, exhausted and ecstatic.

"I feel amazing. Yeah. Yeah. I mean, I've never really done all that before."

"Really? It was like you were a pro, like, I don't know, the king of some harem."

"Yeah, earlier today I couldn't even..." Silas. Pausing.

"Oh Silas." Dolores put her head on his chest and threw her arms around him. "That was with Miriam, but you see, you're meant to be with me."

"I feel so good."

"Would Miriam ever let you do those things to her?"

"God. I've never been this high." His chest expanded. "I feel... god... I don't know..."

"No. Is the answer. No way."

"I fucking love everything."

"Does that include me?" He looked at her now, for the first time, pupils dilated, eyes spinning, post-coital sweat seeping from his skin.

"Yeah, I totally love you."

"Oh Silas, I love you, too!"

Adelaide

She walked with her head down, *leveled* against the **cold**. The wet leaves piled up to her nose. She *shuffled* through them, *sniffling*.

"I want him back." She thought. And to **punctuate**, swung her galosh out in a splash of limp leaves. The disturbance *startled* a sparrow, who **ejected** from the warm and dry spot where it had, a moment ago, been still.

This, in turn, *startled* ⟨Adelaide. The surprise and the sparrow triggered nostalgia. The sparrows. He had some way, **some trick.** She remembered clearly the first time it happened. They were outside, in the park, where they had brought along *wine* and *bread* and a *pair of peaches*. It was warm, and it felt the way a picnic should.

A small group of sparrows had discovered their afternoon tryst and were hopping about demurely, a few feet from the wooden bench, *feigning casual*. Ωllister threw bread crusts in their direction, and their masks of disinterest were **dropped** as they rushed to peck them up, *wallflower friends* joining them from the *vibrating branches above*.

He tossed the next offer nearer, and the next nearer still. There were two or three that didn't seem to mind being a foot or so from him.

Then he did something she **did not expect**. Moving *more slowly* than she had ever seen anyone move he slid off the bench and crouched toward the feeding birds. All of the others flew off when he came too close, but a *small speckled one* stood petrified. Moving even more slowly, he bent down and gently **closed his hand around it**.

She **gasped**, involuntarily, anachronistically, femininely, against usual inclination. It wasn't so much delight either, she thought for a moment that he meant to crush it.

But he did not. He returned, just as slowly, to his place beside her on the bench. She **stared** at the hyperventilating sparrow encased in the long, bony fingers.

He gave her a sly smile, one of her favorites, and opened his hand. The bird stood on his palm for *half a moment*, as if it too could not really comprehend what had just happened. Then it **flew off.**

The thing that struck ⟨Adelaide was that this minor miracle was *entirely repeatable*. Indeed the next few times he repeated it, she was **incredulous**. She was sure it was a parlor trick, an illusion. He must be *surreptitiously* planting drugged sparrows in likely locations around the city. But, eventually, the repeated evidence softened her objection to this particular absurdity. One time, bird in hand, he slid his open palm next to hers, and, *as if for a circus crowd*, the sparrow of that day performed the intended hop from his palm to hers. It was much lighter than she expected. And **ticklish**.

But today she could only think of **the first time**, the picnic. He was wearing that red sweater she loved, inside out. It was *soft*, and the only one he owned that was too big rather than too small. She remembered when he threw it away.

As she turned the corner onto the busier street she *startled*. A bum, his hand **exploding upward** and fluttering, not unlike a bird, cried 'Hey!' He was the usual bum on this corner, and, lost in reflection she had trudged past him, forgetting the usual quarter or two that had become their ritual.

"Sorry." She mumbled, and fished the change from her coat pocket.

"Hey," Calmer now. Serious. "Did you hear what happened downtown today?" His **sober tone** held her against an inclination to keep walking.

"No. What?"

"Some guy dropped a beer bottle out of a window. It landed on a baby."

"What?"

"Yeah, from like three stories. Just some drunk guy."

"That's terrible."

"But the baby was fine. Perfectly OK." He followed this statement with a *toothless grin* and her mind raced. Was he absolving himself to her? Was he '**some drunk guy?**'

"It was a light beer." The grin again.

Oh. It was a joke. She looked at the ground again. She felt suddenly *separated* from herself. "You know, I give you change every day. Why do you have to act so prickish?"

"What did you call me?" The bum's face turned **red**, and he pressed his hands to the ground, as if to **stand up**. *Adelaide* became frightened.

"Nothing, I mean, I didn't mean 'prick' as an insult. I was just using it as, you know... as an adjective."

"Oh." The bum abandoned his attempt at the vertical but his eyes remained confused, suspicious **slits**. "God bless." He grumbled.

She walked home quickly. The **invitation** was on her doorstep. THE WHITE BALL.

She shouldn't go. She shouldn't go because she didn't have anything to wear. Or any money to buy something new, and nice. Selling some art would **not** be worth it. Because she knew that Euphrates would be there, and he was **suing her**. Because she knew that Pete and Vance would be there, doing their Art Terrorism, which she could only assume meant **trouble**. Because 𝕿𝖍𝖊 𝕻latypus was just luring her into some other sort of *trap*, because he thought Ωllister would be there.

As soon as this occurred to her, she realized that 𝕿𝖍𝖊 𝕻latypus might be right. If Ωllister came back, if he ever showed his face again, THE WHITE BALL would be an obvious choice. **He would be there.** She didn't know how she knew, but she did. He wouldn't miss this party. He would be there, lurking, and she could find him. And give him the **gray papers**. And they could go on picnics again. Sparrow hunting.

The Platypus

Barely potable, it tasted of rainwater, bear vomit, and ancient urine. Bits of **something** kept getting stuck in his teeth. Franc had brewed it in his friend's basement. He said he followed the instructions almost exactly, just a bit of *improvisation* here and there, a few substitutions. Of course, Franc had **fangs tattooed on his face.** The beer was successful in one regard; it was highly **alcoholic.** There was lots in the cooler at his feet. Puɴk kept drinking it.

They were at a show. Behind the *Pizza Pit*, where Franc *pretended* to work. The amps set up in the alley. Extension cords and beer bottles. A **dangerous idea** in the rain. The band was enacting some *contrived writhing* for a handful of lazy on-lookers, or beer-drinkers, more accurately. The guy who **screamed along** to the music was climbing the chain-link fence that partitioned the wide alley from an idyllic baseball field just beyond. He was screeching in the lowest baritone Puɴk had ever heard. And dripping with a mixture of blood and feces. But vomit was often that color too. Puɴk swallowed hard.

The drummer pounded *furiously* with a live chicken in each fist. At least, they **were** alive when they started ten minutes ago. One guy moshed with himself. Feathers traced peaceful spirals over the lethargic and sparse crowd.

It was a **disappointing night.** Flyers used to work well for bringing the kids out. If they were passed out at the **SNOOTY FOX**, on a few key corners, given to the meth dealer, an audience would show. But the cops somehow were getting a hold of them now. They could just be picking them up off the ground, but everyone suspected favorite enemies as *leaks*. So it had to be word of mouth. Not too many mouths had been talking about tonight. The ones that had were now *flexing* and *yawning*, lapping up warm beer, tongues loose with **hateful speech.**

Puɴk was too **bored** to even talk. He gazed druggedly at Franc and then followed his sight line to some skater girl who had passed out, slumped against the back door. Some guy was *lazily urinating* on her. Puɴk was staring when his torso was gripped from behind, and he was **hoisted** off his feet by strong arms, an elevation which caused him to pour most of Franc's homebrew in his right front pocket.

He was set down and spun around:

"Puuuuunk! My best brother. My truest confidant. My darling little minion." Ωllister. Unbelievably *buoyant.*

"Where the fuck have you been?" Puɴk. Pulling soggy lint from his pocket.

"I know everything..."

"Are you..."

"Fhuuuucchhhking everything Puɴk. And don't you fhucking forget it."

"Are you drunk?"

Ωllister. Girlish delight. "Hold the phone. We've got a prodigy on our hands. Oh Punk, we must get your darling precocious ass back in a school desk…"

"Shut up, man. I'm serious. This show…"

"Punk." His voice dropped three octaves. Streetlights dimmed. The band's clatter faded. Ωllister's eyes darted *desperately* from under his eyebrows. "Punk. It's too late. Everything is coming apahrt. It's all…"

"What is? What's going on?" Punk. Genuinely **disconcerted**.

Ωllister gripped him violently, scarily, by the shoulders. "We have to get out of here. Now. White Suits."

He lurched off down the dark alley. Punk started after him, but couldn't reach him before Ωllister's 45-degree walk had sent him *careening* into the concrete.

"Come on, man." Punk pulled him up, wrapped a drunken scarf of an arm around his neck and started to help Ωllister toward the baseball field.

"Thank… thank you, Punk… you're my bhest friend… I never tell you… oh god…" Ωllister. *Actually gushing.*

"Shut up, man. Come on. Right foot. Left foot… you must be on some good shit. Did *you* take that drug I gave you?"

Ωllister concentrated his crossed eyes on the ground below him. It was a million miles away. The grass *felt nice* on his left foot.

"What the fuck happened to you anyway?" Punk. Pissy and out of breath from dragging his limp friend toward the dark. All this crap was **sobering him up.**

The secretive hush again. "They know about me. Found me. Found me out…"

"Who man? Who are you talking about?"

Ωllister's face crinkled in confusion. As they traipsed across the outfield he was silent for many minutes.

"It would make… I could…"

"What? Who?" It was hard to hear the choked whispers. They passed second base.

"You don't know." Despair. "You don't know." Turning to *smoldering* resentment. "You don't know shit. Fhucking idiot." Ωllister pushed Punk away with **sloppy force** and stumbled over the pitcher's mound. The pitch of his squeal crescendoed with the pace of his feet and he took a diving slide for home plate. The late evening drizzle had moistened the ground. The **fresh mud** gladly obliged his momentum.

He was laughing *buffoonishly.* Wrapping his arms around his sopping heaving torso. The shirt would be ruined. Punk did not think about this as he picked him back up.

"Come on man, we gotta get you home."

"PuNK. You shitface. Take me home… please take me…" Ωllister. Meaning it.

"OK man. We're going home. Where's your house?"

"You can't come to my house." Indignant again. He **stomped off** into the tangle of *trees* and *undergrowth* that sprawled out behind the bleachers.

"Fucking hell." PuNK. Muttering to himself as he obligingly followed. He parted a curtain of shrubbery and started a slow crawl through the **dark, dripping foliage.** Looking only down, for snakes or possible sinkholes, he *very nearly* crawled between Ωllister's frozen legs.

He was standing ten feet into the brambles staring at a dagger-sized **thorn** that was letting a preposterous amount of blood drip from the center of his palm. Ωllister stared at his injury quizzically, gently swaying in the *alcohol breeze.*

"Dude." PuNK. Wide-eyed. "Are you OK?"

"You know…" Ωllister. Thoughtful now, reflective. "They don't make band-aids for black people." He grasped the thorn gingerly between his teeth, tugged his hand away **violently**, and spat the *offending spike* back into the brush. "They only come in pink."

"I never…"

"That's sort of racist, don't you think?"

PuNK paused to consider this, his eyes rolling up toward the canopy. By the time his brain came back around, he found himself **alone** once again. He *sighed* and trampled off again in the direction Ωllister must've gone.

The brambles suddenly gave way to a manicured lawn. It was strewn with weathered tombstones that looked as though they had rained down from **outer space** and lodged themselves firmly, if slightly off-kilter, over the heads of those whose *stars had set.* He scanned the graveyard for signs of his friend. Suddenly, from behind one of the larger markers a clear stream of piss *glinted* in the moonlight. PuNK remembered that he'd had to piss since the alleyway.

He loped over to the offending site. Ωllister was on his back, his head resting on a fresh bouquet. With his **bloodied hand** he aimed his urine straight into the air. Taken by gravity at a *rather impressive* height much of it returned to slap at his already wet legs and thighs.

PuNK undid himself and, standing, *rather politely* began to make his toilet on the next headstone over. He took care to trace all of the letters of the person the stone claimed to remember.

"The stars are so beautiful." Ωllister. Sticky wistfulness bubbling from between his lips. "Dead pharaohs and…"

PuNk didn't even need to glance upward. "We're in the city. Can't see any stars." Punctuated with a **zip**.

He looked down at Ωllister's face, full of *sharp, wet pain*. He thought it might be piss, but now, unmistakably he saw **tears** tracing new paths down Ωllister's finely formed temples. This was a first.

"Uh…" PuNk was flabbergasted. If someone had told him Ωllister even had the *ability* to cry, not only would he not have believed it, but he probably would've **punched** them.

"She's gone." Ωllister mumbled though throaty sobs. "She's not coming back."

Then a scream. "She's gone." His limbs fiercely alive, he flipped over, *skull-duggery* flashing in his eyes. On his hands and knees he began to **claw** at the sodden soil. "Let me in. Let me in…" He muttered madly, *cartoonishly*, as he dug into the sodden grave.

PuNk's flapping jaw snapped shut. He leapt on Ωllister's back and started to **pry** his stiffening arms from their task. The gravedigger squirmed around to attack this new demon. The tussle was muddy, but hardly epic. PuNk had always *assumed* that Ωllister was stronger than he was, and maybe it was the **alcohol**, but he was quickly subdued. Once his wrists were pinned, his hands stopped grasping and he went limp and weepy again.

PuNk ungracefully scooped him up, like a sleeping child too old to still be brought in from the car, and headed back across the field.

"Take me home." A tired voice from the *limp silhouette*.

"You won't tell me where your house is, Ωllister." Flatly.

"Your house…"

"I don't have a house, man. You know that."

"You can't come to… my house…"

"You already said that, man. Listen, Matilda. She'll let us crash at her pad. She's cool…"

"She can't know… tell…"

"Nah, she's no one important. Just a lonely chick, like, she won't tell anyone. She's safe."

"PuNk?"

"Yeah, man?"

"Thank… thank you…"

This was embarrassing. "OK, man."

The **black cut-out** of a skinny kid, with legs sticking out from one side of his torso, and a bobbing head from the other, *slowly sunk* into the drizzle.

Miriam & Graham

The next morning, she couldn't escape the guilt. Miriam lay on her bed. Her stomach was in knots. Already she had polished off a six-pack of diet shakes between crying jags and scalding showers. She couldn't get what had happened with Silas out of her head. Betraying Graham in that way made her skin crawl. She wished she could take it all back.

A frantic honking rocketed her to the window. There was the van, parked crookedly in front of her dorm, horn blaring. Her blood boiled. She ran outside, through the rain, intending to bash the window in. She lifted her fist to strike, and stopped. Peering meekly from behind the wet glass was not Silas, but Graham. He rolled down the window a crack. "Get inside." Graham. Shouting through the crack. She did.

"Why are you driving the Virg... Why are you in this van?" Miriam. Nervous.

"No, it's not the actual VirginVan. I rented it."

"You know about the VirginVan?" She felt ashamed, sitting there dripping.

"It was on your laptop. And all over the Internet, I guess..."

Miriam looked down at her hands.

"I was mad at first. But then I wanted to win you back. I thought that was what you wanted. So I got this van, thinking..."

She started to cry.

"No baby, don't cry. I just want to be with you. I want to prove that I'm good enough for you. I can do it in a van better than Silas. I mean, this van doesn't have carpeting, or a ..."

"That's the sweetest thing... ever." Miriam. Between sniffles. "You're like my white knight in a shining van." He took her hand, and led her to the backseat. They had short, uncomfortable intercourse, Miriam crying intermittently.

When it was over, they lay in each other's arms, clothing half undone, relieved.

"I love you Graham." Miriam. Whispering.

"I love you too, babe."

punk

Someone *sighed* next to him and the room snapped back into focus. Matilda. Her down comforter soft and dirty, sticking **guiltily** to his skin. Her attempts at décor **glaring fishily** from neat little corners.

Punk had awoken early. Being **bored**, with no thoughts of his own, he had picked a book off the stack on her nightstand. It was *mesmerizing*. It was too bad he didn't like to read because **here** was a book he could get into. He had only read page 199, but when the narrative voice was female he could *feel a tunnel gaping between his legs*. When the character was male he got *erections that curled backwards*. He tried to put one of these to **use** by gently probing Matilda's familiar behind with it. When he received no response he **poked harder**, but the answering groan spoke of *unconsciousness* rather than *pleasure*. Not that the difference was drastic.

Something had to be done, so he threw the clinging bedclothes from his nudity and vaulted outwards and upwards in search of a **cool glass of water**. To drink or to stick his cock in he didn't know.

The kitchen windows stung of *early dawn*. Dust floated through the air, atoms **strung out** in the hallway. He was padding out of the kitchen, his cock bouncing in time with the slap of his feet, when he *suddenly remembered* Ollister. He spun around quickly, 180 degrees. The momentum transferred to his brain and it rotated in his skull, a few seconds delayed.

The sofa was **empty**. The blanket folded innocently on the armrest. *He was gone again*.

"Shit."

SHE STOOD OUT ON THE WINDSWEPT PLAIN. IT WAS LONG AND LOW, AND BULGED UPWARD AT THE MIDDLE, WHICH MADE HER FEEL AS THOUGH THE PLAIN WAS WIDE ENOUGH TO SHOW SOME CURVATURE OF THE EARTH'S SURFACE. IT WAS RINGED BY TREES AND ARABESQUE VINES WRITHING ACROSS THE SHAPES OF SHRUBBERY. HEAVY INSECTS PUSHED THROUGH THE AIR, DRONING LIKE THE CLOUDS.

SHE COULD SEE THE CABIN FROM THE PLAIN, THE CABIN ON THE HILL, JUST HALF OF IT, BUT ITS STARK BROWN SQUARE STOOD OUT FROM THE LUSH GREEN THAT SURROUNDED IT.

SHE SQUINTED. THE SUN WAS BRILLIANT BEHIND HER, ITS LIGHT OBSCURING EVEN THE DISC OF ITSELF, SO THAT IT WAS JUST A BLINDING SPLOTCH, FILLING UP THE WESTERN SKY. IT CAUGHT STRANDS OF HER HAIR AND LIT THEM UP, CURLING IN THE WIND.

SHE FELT WARM AND SLEEPY. THE EASY BREEZE OCCASIONALLY PROVIDED A COOLER TOUCH. HER CLOTHES WERE OLD AND THREADBARE. THEY FELT SMOOTH AGAINST HER KNEES AND ELBOWS.

SHE HAD THE FEELING OF MOVING, OF BEING LOST IN THOUGHT. AS SHE SAT IN THE TALL GRASS, SHE FELT HERSELF TRAVELING ACROSS GREAT DISTANCES, LOOKING OUT TRAIN WINDOWS, TRYING TO LOCATE HERSELF, HER TRAVELING PARTNER. HER THINGS STILL

HE WAS IN THE CABIN. ITS ROOMS DUSTY, FLOORS FULL OF SPLINTERS. HE WAS IN HIS LONG UNDERWEAR.

HE HAD CHOPPED THE WOOD AND STACKED IT. CLEARED THE PATH IN FRONT OF THE CABIN OF DEBRIS, SET OUT A NEW SALT LICK FOR THE SPRING DOE, FIXED A LEAKING PLANK IN THE ROOF, AND FOUND A ~~POSSUM~~ PLATYPUS SKELETON UNDER A SHRUB DOWN BY THE RIVER, ON HIS MORNING HIKE. HIS DOG, PUCK, HAD BARKED AND BARKED, CIRCLING IT AS THOUGH IT WERE A STILL-LIVING THING HE SQUATTED DOWN AND LOOKED AT IT FOR A LONG TIME, RUBBING THE BACK OF THE DOG'S BLACK HEAD WITH HIS HAND.

BACK IN THE CABIN, EVENING HAD COME. HE FELT HE HAD EVERYTHING THAT COULD BE SEEN IN HIM ON THE OUTSIDE OF HIM. HE FELT ENTIRELY ACCESSIBLE, INVULNERABLE, AND ALONE. HIS HANDS FELT ROUGH AND DELIBERATE. ALL AROUND THE SOUNDS OF THE NIGHT CRUNCHED AND FLIPPED ABOUT IN THE DRYING LEAVES. THEY WERE INHUMAN AND UNRECOGNIZABLE, BUT NOT OMINOUS. HE LAY DOWN ON THE MATTRESS.

HIS HEAD WAS CLEAR, FRESH. HE THOUGHT OF HER, HOLDING HIM, AGAINST THE NIGHT, LIKE A TALISMAN, A SEASTONE, A FEATHER

PART 3

THE WHITE BALL

ART TERRORISTS

VANCE: Thanks, all, for coming. I am here to do what Ollister could not. Today we...

PAUL: Everyone followed my protocols when coming here tonight, right?

FRANC: What proto-what?

SEB: Oh, please.

PAUL: Seriously, anyone could have followed any one of you here if you weren't careful and took a few necessary precautions.

VANCE: Seriously, Paul, we don't even know what we're doing yet. How could anyone be on to us?

NICK: Vance, please.

VANCE: Nick and I have the perfect place to stage our first... uh... incident.

SEB: Performance.

PAUL: Strike.

PETE: Are we sure this is such a good idea?

FRANC: Better be worth it.

NICK: Quiet, please. We are going to infiltrate The Platypus's White Ball. Tonight.

VANCE: Yes, that's the plan, and so...

PAUL: Oh. You don't know who you're fucking with there. These are some very warm waters gentlemen. The Platypus has ties...

NICK: Oh sure Paul, next thing you'll tell us is that he's an alien.

PAUL: Well, actually...

PETE: Who is this The Platypus?

SEB: Peter, darling, he is only the most famous philanthropist, tastemaker and most generous patron of the arts in the city. The man is a giant...

FRANC: Does he have expensive shit?

SEB: Rest assured my friend, his demands are top shelf. Vance, Nick, you two are darlings, libschions, for taking over. This will make us famous beyond our wildest dreams. It will be a performance for the ages. Art beyond art...

PAUL: Are you faking a German accent, Sebastian?

SEB: Faking nothing, Paul, I'm just back from Berlin.

NICK: You were there for a week. You were born in Utah. Anyways...

PAUL: Anyways we don't want to get famous here. We need to keep a low profile. These are not people to cross. I'm not having my name on the hit list of The White Sodality...

SEB: Please, next thing it'll be the fucking Freemasons.

PAUL: Not far off, my friend, in fact…

VANCE: The goal is Art Terrorism.

NICK: Indeed, let me recite the new mission statement, as realized perfectly by myself. Art Terrorism is not…

PAUL: Look, we could still act. But under the cloak of anonymity. Move in a black cloud, like ninjas, strike from a distance.

FRANC: I say we just smash in and grab this guy's fucking stuff.

VANCE: Franc, I'm sure there will be something worth filching, however the goal is…

PAUL: How about we wire the toilet to the power grid—so when he goes in for a whiz—zap. Pete—you can do something like that, yes?

PETE: Well… I, uh… I know how to install a hidden webcam in a bathroom.

SEB: Oh god, a webcam? I've got a story about that…

PETE: Or, do they have a mainframe, a network? I could hack into that and…

PAUL: Or, how about we mail him a snake, like a… like a fucking… asp or cobra or something? Something to bite his ass, and then slither away, leaving no trail of evidence, no link to us.

NICK: What does that have to do with art?

SEB: Exactly. So Nick, Vance, who will be there? Redcote, Van Clone, Sorenson, I assume. This is the fucking party of the year. Such big names. I can't wait to rip down all that art and just piss all over it.

FRANC: Wait, aren't we gonna sell it or whatever?

VANCE: Well, that presents some logistical problems, Franc, the thing is…

FRANC: No problems—my brother, he knows the black market in Paris. He'll fence it.

SEB: Shut up, darling frog. There will be a bloody bracelet, or something to swipe.

PETE: This doesn't sound very safe. Can I just uh… run the command center?

NICK: A command center—you could build one.

PETE: Well…

NICK: That'd be brilliant. Naturally, I would run it. But how will I lead the team inside at the same time?

PAUL: Yeah, I think I'd prefer to stay in the background, too. If it's all the same.

VANCE: No we're all doing it together.

PAUL: Fuck that, these people are in deep, you understand? You ever hear of the underground prisons? That's right, all those people that supposedly go missing every year. Where do you think Mackerel is? Where do you think fucking Elvis is? I'll be damned if…

VANCE: Franc?

FRANC: We are in together.

SEB: Yes, yes. We need a name. No, a logo! A color scheme, a complete identity! What are we wearing? Black, yes? Please?

PETE: I, uh, could build a website.

VANCE: We don't need a website, we need to decide on…

NICK: Black is fine with me. Always been flattering to my features.

SEB: A smashed cat. That could be our insignia! How divine. Imagine: we could smash a cat, Franc here could smash a cat at every performance. It'd be fabulous. People would be crazy for it.

FRANC: I'm not smashing no cat.

PAUL: Cats, you know, came on the same UFO with the Egyptians. That's why they were worshiped, as opposed to, say eaten, or whatever.

PETE: Really?

PAUL: Oh definitely, why do you think they're so strange?

VANCE: That's absurd.

PAUL: Huh, it's practically a fact. I'm talking about mountains of evidence. A fucking pyramid of evidence, if you will. Water erosion on the sphinx (a cat, originally) that makes it at least 10,000 years old, way before 'Egyptians.' The unmarked, undecorated great pyramid aligned to the cardinal directions and the exact proportions of the northern hemisphere to a degree of precision unknown until the 20th century…

NICK: Can you stop now?

PAUL: You can't make this shit up, man. Anyways, I'm out before anyone unexpected shows up to this little meeting.

SEB: Oh, you wish…

VANCE: Well, fine, I guess it's getting late.

NICK: We still haven't decided on the perfect role for me.

VANCE: OK, it's on then. You are all on your own to infiltrate the party. We'll meet in the basement supply room at 8 PM, sharp. Take these photocopies, I made them from the blueprints.

FRANC: Whole thing is a big waste of time, man.

OLLISTER & PUNK

They stood in the shadows of the trees, Ollister and Punk. They smoked, the umbrella of leaves sheltering them from a light drizzle. Ollister stood stock-still and stared at the glowing entrance to The Platypus's mansion. Punk picked his nose, or dug a steel toe in the wet ground. They had been standing here, doing nothing, for at least an hour and a half.

They couldn't just enter through the main gate, with the butlers and valets. For whatever crazy reason in Ollister's head, they had to sneak onto the estate from a back road, and trample though the heavily wooded areas between what seemed to be horse fields. And now they weren't even going inside. Punk sighed and glanced furtively at the silhouette of Ollister, married to a tree. He was afraid that if he interrupted whatever gargantuan thought Ollister was having, he would leave him in the woods, outside of the city, with no idea how to get back.

The fear was not irrational. Ollister's brain was chugging ahead full steam. Coal was being furiously shoveled into the great engine and steam was coalescing to form a grand vision in the sky. It was a prophetic thought, no mere daydream. This happened to Ollister often enough. He would act out some scenario in his head. Rehearse his lines. Go through a chess-players assessment of possible outcomes, make ultra-logical conjuncture, and then, later, in the moment, everything would occur exactly as he had foreseen it. He could guess the most absurd, unlikely things were going to happen and even though he knew, it was always surprising to take part in a self-made, self-fulfilling prophecy. He never once thought of this as a supernatural or psychic ability. He just happened to always be right.

"New plot. Tonight is a resolution." Finally speaking, though still not looking at Punk. "We must be merciless."

"Um… OK." Punk. Mumbling.

"We need the gray papers back and we need them tonight."

Punk looked around cautiously for the rest of "we." He wondered what had happened to the others.

"It's a shame that that which we love stands in the way of that which we love, and thus requires itself to be destroyed leaving us neither obstacle nor reward."

"Uh… yeah."

"Punk." Ollister's eyes refocused back on the present. "Did you bring the drug?"

"Yeah. Course I did. Are we gonna…"

"No. Let me see it."

Punk pulled the baggie out of his hoodie pocket and began to open it. There wasn't much left.

"OK." Ollister waved it away. "Tonight, Punk, is very important for us. We must follow the plan exactly."

"What fucking plan? You said the terrorism thing was off. Man, you are confusing the shit out of…"

"Just do as I say, understand?"

Punk nodded sheepishly. He always said yes. There was a tightness in his stomach. He was tired of being dragged around, pushed around. Hanging out with Ollister used to be rad. Ollister would have him destroy other people's lives or art. But in fun ways, without all this moody shit. Ollister took care of whatever he needed, sure. But even when he was gone, he lorded over Punk's life. When was his time going to be his own? He could be huffing model airplane glue, or trying to scam out with some preteen girls, and instead he was out here in some rich dude's fucking forest.

"I know about you and Zella." Ollister. Calmly, evenly. "And, of course, Matilda."

Punk tensed up.

"Don't worry. I have nothing to say about it. I only bring it up because they'll be here tonight. They'll be here with Adelaide."

"Listen man, it was the drug. I took some and got all fucking horny and she was on the roof… She did it to me, man…"

"Seriously Punk, I don't care. Please focus on tonight. Adelaide will be there, with Zella, Matilda, and all her other friends. I don't want you to be seen by any of them, understand? Stick to the shadows. I think you know how to move about undetected, right?"

"Yeah, but…"

"Tonight is important. It is a resolution; I will take back what is mine. And I will see that justice is served. And you will help me do it."

"Seriously man. I don't know about these stunts anymore, I mean…"

Ollister turned and looked Punk in the eye for the first time that evening. He reached out and grasped him just above the elbow in a way that made the hair on Punk's neck stand up. "Just one more, Punk. Only tonight."

The way he said it softly, and full of weight, it made Punk suddenly sad, and afraid. He was struck by the idea of losing Ollister again, of being without anyone to look after him or care if he was alive or dead.

"I'll do anything for you, man. Just point the way." Punk tried to sound brave, meeting Ollister's steely gaze. Ollister let his arm go and without a word turned to walk across the grand and sparkling lawn. Toward the mansion, lit up like some haunted acropolis. Punk followed.

MIRIAM & GRAHAM

Miriam and Graham arrived together. She was wearing a black strapless dress that she kept pinching and pulling up around her bosom. Graham looked a little awkward in his baggy suit and over-combed hair. Being damp from rain didn't help either, but they certainly belonged at this party.

"Daddy has been talking about this party forever, it's the most important. Ever." Miriam. Scanning for familiar faces. "There's supposed to be loads of famous artists here."

"Yeah." Graham. Tugging at his tie.

"Yeah. He's going to introduce me. I'm going to be famous someday, too, you know."

"I've never seen you make any art."

"That's not how you get famous silly. You come to things like this and meet people. Daddy says we'll get the art when we need it, but the schmooze is more important."

"The schmooze?"

"Yeah." Tugging on her dress and flipping her hair.

"Is that like booze? Is there booze here?" Miriam rolled her heavily made-up eyes.

"There was supposed to be an open bar. Let's check the kitchen." She retightened his tie, grabbed his hand, and pulled him through the chattering crowd.

ADELAIDE

"Good evening Adelaide." Isadora. Knowingly.

"Good evening." She replied softly, looking downwards, as she shuffled behind her friends into the party, invitation in hand.

The foyer was large with an impressive candelabra. They were helped out of their coats, and Adelaide shivered slightly in her evening costume.

Matilda, Zella, and all the other girls were excited about the party. They wanted to meet boys. Flirt with young, dweeby trust-fund babies or even suckle up to old perfumed society cunts, whose patronage could pay their way. There was something in the air. And Adelaide wanted no part of it. She only had things to lose.

She wasn't going to meet any boys. But she was also sure that that wouldn't stop them from meeting her. Pete had already told her his plan to sneak in by disarming the alarm system or something. She was counting on her premonition that Ollister was going to be here. Because of his feelings about The Platypus, or rather, The Platypus's feelings about him, there was a good chance he wouldn't come within ten miles of this mansion. She didn't know if she could make it through the night with her chest feeling squeezed like the bellows of an accordion. She had brought the gray papers.

Thankfully, there were other things to keep her mind occupied. She glanced around nervously as Matilda and Zella picked over the lavishly displayed hors d'oeuvres. She knew that Euphrates would most definitely be at this party and his lawsuit was still pending. The lawyers were getting nastier by the day. Like squirrels caged too long. If it came to a court battle she had planned to dip into the secret savings accounts her mom was keeping in her name. It would be difficult now that they were frozen. Anyway, she knew that her mother's wrath would be far more difficult to endure than any kind of poverty. But there would be no other way. She had to avoid seeing him at all costs tonight. By all accounts he was dumbfounded with rage at his school's inclusion in her 'nasty little expose' of the art school admittance procedure. Zella handed her a hard chocolate martini glass filled with vermouth gin mousse. She quickly set the disgusting thing back on its tri-tiered display rack.

The Platypus made her nervous too. Isadora was very kind on her way in. It was impossible to tell what kind of kind. This whole party was her black web and she certainly didn't want to get caught up in it. Adelaide felt like she should leave or hide.

Zella grabbed her wrist and she grabbed Matilda's and their little train wreck made its way to the open bar set up in the grand sitting room. Zella ordered elaborate drinks and forced them into the limp hands around her. She was clearly determined to make a party out of it.

Adelaide couldn't hide, or leave. Her gallery reps were here. And a few of her pieces were up. The Platypus must have done that. The Velveteen Gallery people were thrilled. They were schmoozing on her behalf, and she was at their beck and call to go meet whatever old perv, and smile, and play the pretty young artist with big ideas. It was bullshit, but she was broke, and if she sold a piece or two then risking her neck at this pompous put-on would be worth it, she supposed.

She left the girls and moved into the library, where quite a few of the younger partygoers were dancing. She figured since it was darker in there it might be a good place to lie low. Adelaide felt if she could just make it through the night without undue attention called upon her, she would be all right. She leaned against a bookcase and sipped her drink lethargically. Then, suddenly, she noticed the only other person in the room not dancing. It was Punk. Why was he here? And what did that mean? She stared at him. He seemed lost in some dystopian daydream. He certainly could not have been invited. This was a bad sign.

DOLORES & SILAS

Dolores arrived with Silas. She wore her now too-short prom dress and some furry underwear he had picked out for her. He was in his usual tailored pinstripe, shoes shining, hair gel sparkling, eyes twinkling. They were damp from the rain.

They were together now, by most accounts. He no longer screwed anyone in the VirginVan (except her, sometimes) and though she could still tell it was him filming the videos, she didn't let that bother her so much. He bought her things and fucked her often and viciously.

"Let's find the drinks." Silas. Glancing around.

"No kidding." Dolores's nails felt weird. She had recieved a French manicure for the party that afternoon.

"But we've got to make sure to pay our respects to Euphrates before getting sloshed. You'll have to pretend to be my sister. He still wants me to be dating his daughter."

"Your sister?"

"Oh, come on. Later we'll find a closet and I'll show you what I used to do to my real sister when we were kids."

"Well… fine then, deal." Dolores. Smiling.

ART TERRORISTS

Vance arrived at the party as the guest of his friend Margo, an editrix with webbed toes and a penchant for vaginal brooches. They walked through the front doors, a little damp from the rain.

Franc slowly walked up to the service entrance, at the rear of the property, already wearing the proscribed black outfit and facemask, very damp from the rain. When the guard started to ask him his business, he simply punched the man in the throat, crumpling him to the floor.

Sebastian was actually on the guest list. He arrived with painted eyebrows and a gender-ambiguous entourage, his invitation pinned garishly to his crotch. He was not damp, thanks to a sequined parasol.

Pete had spent weeks studying alarm systems and hacking into the mainframe network of the home security company employed by The Platypus to secure his premises. He disabled the entire system and opened all automatic door and window locks between 8:05 and 8:07 PM. His satellite-linked watch told him when it was time to slip through the unobserved lower kitchen door. He watched the panel on the inside wall show the system quietly coming back online. He was soaked from waiting in the bushes.

Nick just walked through the front door in a tuxedo, acting as though he belonged there. No one stopped him.

Paul had snuck in, seizing his opportunity during a shift change that afternoon. He had spent ten hours sweating in the basement and twitching at every creak of floorboard. Damp with sweat, he was the most relieved at 8:34 that night, when they all met.

The Art Terrorist group assembled in the basement supply room of The Platypus's mansion. Vance verified that all 6 members were present by flashlight and began to solemnly hand out the black overshirts and face masks, all a little damp… the bag had been exposed to the rain.

PUNK

Punk stood in the library, watching people dance. He had come in with an erection. It was all but gone now.

He thought about thumbs, his own monkey thumbs, evolution. An irrational yet familiar scenario played itself out in his mind. An angry dog, one of the wolf-looking sort, broke free of its chain after significant taunting and Punk, trying to shield himself from carnal retribution stuck his hands, palm-outwards, in the dog's direction as if to signal '10 point dive' or 'you've pulled the pick-up too far forward' or 'stop.' At which point the dog promptly bit off both his thumbs. The sequence was always scary. And the thoughts that followed were always sad. Eating a hamburger with no thumbs, using a queer-ass rolling machine to roll his joints, staring wistfully at video game controllers, cell phones and fountain pens, all technology beyond the reach of his invisible thumbs.

Sometimes he could feel pain in his phantom thumbs, even though they weren't there, even though, in fact, the thumbs were there, the accident never having actually occurred.

He felt it now, holding his drink. He felt restlessness, exhaustion, and disdain for having to do Ollister's bidding. For having to be in the library of some rich fuck's party listening to some half-ugly socialite with a plentiful inheritance, and a plentiful bosom, bang on about diphthongs, fricatives, and the human tongue as muscle.

He would like to challenge Ollister to a thumb-wrestling contest. While he still had them, of course. He would like to win. No, he would win. And that would mean something. It would be important. It would change how Ollister treated him.

Ollister would never agree to a thumb-wrestling contest.

ADELAIDE

Adelaide left the library. She had spotted Punk, but certainly didn't need him noticing her, or worse, approaching her.

She moved back into the foyer, where Euphrates was talking frenetically to a number of jewel-encrusted old biddies. Wrong room. She spun on the heel of her shoe, and skirted briefly through the library, her face down and turned away from the sleep-dancing crowd.

The parlor was no good, either. She walked in too quickly, and nearly fell into The Platypus's lap. He had joined the party, and was seated in a grand purple armchair, lazily lecturing on art, politics, philosophy, whatever came to his well-lubricated mind. A half-dozen people, young and old, sat rapt at his rumination, wheedling. They all turned to look at her as she skidded through the door. The Platypus certainly must have marked her presence, but he would not look at her.

She mouthed the words, "Excuse me," and mouse-stepped quickly to the other side of the room, and out through the open doors. She could hear The Platypus beginning his rant again.

She found herself in the kitchen, where a cursory examination of the crowd revealed no one that she knew, or at least no one she had to avoid. Disconcerting, that there was more and more overlap between these categories.

The kitchen had an open bar set up and she ordered a stiff drink from the prim and pressed girl behind the counter. Past the breakfast nook she could see a door leading out, cracking slightly in the breeze. She made for it.

Outside the air was damp. She was on a small balcony overlooking the gardens of the estate. It had an awning that the drizzle banged noisily against. The dusk had almost succeeded in pushing out the light of the previous day. Bits of it were clinging to the horizon and the edges of clouds.

She softly shut the door and sat down. The cool of the day felt nice. After the chaos inside, it was like coming up for air.

She remembered times she'd had to leave Ollister at a party and go outside to be alone. He would say something cruel in some round-about or condescending way. And she would grow sad and exasperated. He had a tendency to ignore her. At parties, at shows, in front of other people. She always felt like he was embarrassed. When she confronted him about it once, he said that he went out to put on a face, speak to the masses, show off his tongue. Everything that he wanted to say to her was best said in private. And she had nodded along to this. After parties, when it was just the two of them, he did rip everyone they had just seen to shreds. But that wasn't what she had really meant. When they first went out together he ignored everyone else in the room. Then he just ignored her.

Like when he would roll over in bed, and leave his hunched back as a goodnight to her. Or when he would feign insomnia, and exit their chambers altogether, and go and take his rest with the phantoms of late-night novels. It felt like the dinners during which he would say nothing, not a single word, masticating and staring at some speck on the floor. It felt like weeks without phone calls, toilet seats left up. Questions unanswered, midnight goodbyes, and tardy airport pick-ups.

None of these ever felt like problems, though. She was cruel, too, in her own little ways. And his quirks, his selfishness, his foisting or floundering, she would never complain about. To herself or her friends. They weren't like problems. They were more like… facts.

Suddenly there were voices from the now darkened garden below. She sat stock-still and watched Isadora glide into view with a few guests. Her expansive hand motions and expressive head tilts made clear that she was touring the gardens, showing around, showing off, despite the creeping dark.

Adelaide realized they might climb these back stairs. She should go back inside. She stood up quickly, forgetting her drink, resting neatly beside her on the ledge. It tipped over, crashing, and sent liquid and glass spilling over the edge. The touring party looked up at her. The tightness in Adelaide's chest returned. She turned quickly and walked back inside, leaving the upturned glass and faces behind her.

DOLORES, MIRIAM, SILAS, & GRAHAM

Dolores, Miriam, Silas and Graham all arrived in the kitchen at precisely the same moment. There was nothing to do but join the line for drinks. Alcohol was the only thing that might relieve this tension.

"Hey." Silas to Miriam.

"Hey." Dolores to Graham.

The guys nodded solemnly to each other.

"I like your shoes, Dolores." Miriam.

"Thanks. They don't make my feet bleed, only bruise. They're good. I like your dress."

"Thanks!" She pulled it up around her cleavage in response. Both boys stared. The party grew louder around them.

"So…" Graham. Trying to fill the air. "Some party… eh?"

"Listen, Silas. I'm sorry I lied to you about Miriam, I didn't…"

"No, Dolores, I'm sorry." Miriam. "When I slept with Silas it wasn't to get back at you, I was just…"

"No, no, I know, and I'm not mad. I mean I was. It was me that ruined all your photographs. I'm really, really sorry…"

"Oh, don't worry about it…"

"Hey, dude." Graham to Silas. "Sorry for… uh… shaking you up that one time."

"Listen." Silas. Holding out his hands. "Can we all just not talk about what happened? Put the past behind us? OK? Everybody cool?"

Three heads nodded in grateful agreement.

"Cool. Fine. Let's do what we came here to do." Silas.

"Get sloshed?" Graham. Guessing.

"Precisely."

ART TERRORISTS

PAUL: Guys, they are on to us.

NICK: If they were on to us don't you think someone would have come down here by now?

PAUL: I'm serious, I know it. There's probably a camera in this supply room.

PETE: Actually the nearest camera is above the basement stairs, and they aren't live-monitored tonight, just recording.

PAUL: Shows what you know.

FRANC: No cameras, eh?

VANCE: All right, enough chatter, can we stick to the plan?

PAUL: Ow! Could you not shine that fucking flashlight in my eyes? I'll remind you that I've been in the dark for ten hours.

SEB: That's your own stupid fault.

NICK: Here shine it on me. Now, first I would like to thank you for gathering here at the appointed place, at the appointed time. Our day has come, my disciples, and I…

SEB: Your disciples?

FRANC: Yeah, I ain't nobody's nothing.

NICK: Well, I don't know, what else should a leader say? 'Team' sounded too… corporate or something, and 'friends' sounds unorganized…

PAUL: We are unorganized. Who is supposed to knock off the big guy? Franc?

FRANC: Big guy?

VANCE: Nobody is killing anybody. 'The difference between an artist and a murderer is that the murderer knows when to stop.'

PETE: I, uh, think you've quoted it backwards.

VANCE: I know. It's truer that way.

SEB: Oh, come on. We should at least capture The Platypus or something. We could tie him up, and cover him in paint and piss and set him on the buffet table as the centerpiece of his own party.

PETE: Can't we just… shut down their Internet service or something? I don't want to get in trouble for…

SEB: What good would that do? We're here for glory.

NICK: Agreed.

VANCE: No, our glory will come tomorrow, in the newspapers. Tonight we must be stealthy. We must strike and disappear.

PAUL: Yeah, like ninjas. We could take out the Sodality one by one…

FRANC: I bet they have some nice-ass silverware in this joint.

VANCE: No, no. This is the plan, I have these stamps, bearing our insignia, one for each of you. We will crawl through the air ducts and the spaces between the walls, here's blueprint maps, pass them around, and each of us will go into our designated gallery rooms and deface all the art we can find.

SEB: And bring it out for the whole party to see.

VANCE: No…

FRANC: Which room is the jewelry in?

PETE: Oh, it's that one, but careful, there are motion sensors here, here, and uh… here. I think.

VANCE: No one is stealing anything.

SEB: Except for the hearts and minds of our audience.

NICK: I'm clearly the best one to stay here at HQ and oversee the entire operation.

VANCE: This isn't HQ. There's nothing to do here. This is a supply closet.

PAUL: Well, I'm not leaving it…

PETE: I can show you where the mainframe is…

PAUL: …until someone brings me the severed hand of The Platypus.

NICK: What?

PAUL: For proof, I need proof.

PETE: …or the water mains.

PAUL: That's it, let's just poison the party. Does anyone have any…

SEB: Poison? Fantastic idea. You are a brilliant genius.

NICK: Sarcasm is a crutch, Sebastian.

SEB: And your face is a broken foot.

VANCE: Can we please discuss the plan, gentleman?

NICK: My face? My face is perfect.

PETE: If there's no plan maybe we should all just go home.

PAUL: Hey, I wasted ten hours in a closet for this.

SEB: This is our moment to shine. Our first step onto the grand stage of the art
world.

FRANC: If I go home, I'm taking something with me.

NICK: I'm not afraid. I'll go first. Whoever so dares may follow me.

VANCE: Wait, Nick. You need a map.

FRANC: I'll take one of those. I'm outta here.

VANCE: Shit, Pete?

PETE: Um, how 'bout I just steal the surveillance videotapes? We need documentation,
right? I think I'll go do that… now.

SEB: Before it starts?

VANCE: I guess it's starting now.

SEB: This is a yawn. I'm going back to the party. There's got to be a better conversation
than this going on.

PAUL: Fuck, don't you guys leave me in the closet again. Guys! Fuck!

P U N K

The lounge was crowded. But Punk could always pick out Zella in a crowd. And there she
was, seated at the built-in bar, talking to Matilda.

He pushed toward them, determined to finally settle the score with them both, to come
clean, to admit his dalliances. No more waiting for scabby little punk girls to come to him,
with their chunky insecurities. No more leaning on Ollister to fish him drunk teens out of a
crowd. He was going to take things into his own hands.

He walked up behind them, their backs presenting two impenetrable walls. Their coats
were hung from the backs of the bar chairs. As was a brown purse. Instinctually, or without
thinking, or as though guided by an outside force, or, really, because it just happened that
way; instead of talking to the girls, or tapping Zella on the shoulder, he lifted the purse off
the chair, and turned around to push back through the crowd.

Now he had to go somewhere, he couldn't be seen walking around with a purse. His
mission might've been abandoned, but he wasn't looking for attention, necessarily. The
girls' bathroom. He always felt comfortable in there.

Two blondes shot him a look as he swished in, but carrying a purse while pursing his lips provided an adequate disguise: just another art queer who preferred to use the ladies' room. They pushed out past him, white powder flaking off their noses.

Once inside he locked the door, sat on the toilet and began emptying the contents of the purse onto his lap. Lipstick, tampon. Cigarettes, lighter, he took those. Wallet, credit cards, he didn't mess with, but he took the cash, 24 dollars.

There was a small gray book in the side pocket. It looked identical to the one The White Suits had stolen from him. He opened it up, and it wasn't blank. He began to read the handwritten, splattered black ink.

WE LIVE IN A CABIN. THE RAIN POUNDS HARD AND NEAT...

Boring boring. He closed it and resumed rifling. Eyeliner, some random business cards. Chapstick. He applied a bit.

Someone banged on the door, hard. He stood up, the contents of the purse spilling onto the floor. He quickly opened the cabinet door under the sink, and began throwing the evidence of his thievery into its dark recesses. In it all went. Except the thin gray book. He slid that into his back pocket.

When he opened the door, Isadora's massive frame filled the doorway, looking at him.

"Hello." Isadora. Smiling.

"Uh… hey."

"Why don't you tell your boss to come see me sometime?" Seductively. Making her intentions crystal clear.

"Uh… OK."

"You know where my room is?"

"Uh… yeah. I think."

"Good." She closed the door behind her with a gentle click.

ART TERRORISTS

"Could you be any louder?" Paul. Still sweating, despite being removed from the hot basement closet.

"No." Franc. Also sweating. But not due to paranoia. He was just a big guy and sweat a lot. He didn't seem to wear deodorant either. Paul chalked it up to his being French.

They were creeping through a darkened wing of the house. Or rather, Paul was creeping around behind Franc, who was striding around, touching expensive things and frowning at them.

"Seriously Franc, you have no idea what would happen to us if we got caught." Franc lifted an eyebrow in mock-interest. "We're, like, in the center of the snakepit. The White Sodality, man, they can make you disappear."

"I don't disappear."

"No man, like you were never born. They erase all record of you, birth certificate, social security, school records, hospital records, fingerprints, criminal records..."

"They can erase criminal records?"

"Yeah, man, they control every..."

"Where do I meet them?"

"That's not funny Franc, it's not a service, they don't do it without erasing you first. My friend, he told me about this one guy who..."

"Hey."

"What?"

Franc froze. Paul got nervous. "What? What, what is it?"

"You hear that?" Whispering.

"No..." Paul's eyes frantically searched the dark recess of the long hall.

"That's cause you're not talking." A smirk spread across Franc's unshaven mug. "You want quiet? Shut up."

Paul glowered. And they moved on in silence. The house was a maze, rooms and halls connecting and inter-connecting in ways that made it impossible for them to tell where they were, where they had been, and which direction they might be facing. The dark didn't help, but they did not dare to turn on lights. Even in the murkiness they could see all the walls covered with artworks, statues interspersed with antique furniture. The place felt abandoned, but it was not dusty, everything was perfectly clean and ordered. It felt like a haunted museum, ominous and omniscient.

They were supposed to be scouting for The Platypus's location. Apparently he had been seen around the party a few times, talking to select people, but he still had not made his official entrance. None of the other Art Terrorists could determine where he came from or where he went bracketing these sightings. So Vance had sent Franc and Paul, a bad pairing really, to locate him, for what purpose remained unclear.

Franc had no intention of carrying out this mission. In fact he hadn't even listened to the post-basement 'debriefing.' He was blatantly casing the joint. Looking closely at the art, and the locks on various windows and doors. This was making Paul's heart thud wildly in his chest. But, he figured, running around checking things out for a later robbery was a lot better than trying to find The Platypus. There was no possible way that they could scope him out without being detected. Especially with Franc, the least subtle of the entire group. And if they did find him, Paul knew there would be hell to pay. Wandering around in the empty wings of the house was the best of all possible options right now.

Franc stood by a large, ancient-looking painting in a gold frame. It was a naked Greek woman, surrounded by satyrs, who were rubbing her feet, braiding her hair, one seemed to be masturbating over her shoulder.

"Ah, here's our lady." Franc. Loudly, to the woman's face.

"Yeah, I actually happen to know that painting, I think it's a…"

"OK, let's go."

And with that, Franc hoisted the gigantic painting from the wall, tearing out the brackets that it was mounted on. A loud, duck-like alarm in the opposite corner of the room sounded.

ADELAIDE

Adelaide, back inside, and having caught her breath, wanted to find another drink. But she couldn't go downstairs just yet.

She found a long hallway without doors, that connected one part of the upper story with another part. She felt as if the floor below her was all that was between her and the earth, but she had no way of verifying that. The hallway had large windows, scattered randomly along the walls. Some were too high to even look through, and others interrupted the baseboards. She stopped and peered out of a lower one. It seemed to frame a particularly bright star, alone in the night sky.

Also along the walls, neatly lined up, were some photographs she recognized.

A while ago, for her final project, Adelaide had dissected her friends' desks. She gained entry to Zella's house, Matilda's, and Ollister's and hired movers to steal their desks, contents and all. She knew that no one would report the thefts. Matilda would be too scared, Zella too lazy, and Ollister too busy.

She set them each up in her studio, and removed the contents of the drawers, one by one. She made label placards for all the objects, arrayed them around and on top of the desk, and photographed the resulting dioramas. She reassembled the desks afterwards and had the movers put them back.

She looked at Ollister's things, unused plain notebooks, unsharpened pencils, a handful of old photos. The gray papers. It was like looking into a dark face. There was nothing of him there. The objects were devoid of personality.

Suddenly she heard the faint sound of an alarm going off at the end of the hall. She walked quickly back in the other direction. What was The Platypus doing with these photos? The gallery told her that a young businessman bought them. It was quite some time ago, and she hardly remembered these early experiments, and it wasn't that she was embarrassed to see them here, she just felt creeped out.

She walked down the stairs, pressing her sharp heels angrily into the carpet. She thought to go to the open bar in the kitchen, but then Zella appeared in front of her, pressing a drink into her hand.

"This party is over."

OLLISTER & PUNK

Ollister wandered back down the stairs, his jaw set. He knew what to do now. Send Punk after Adelaide.

Punk and Adelaide had always regarded each other with a kind of contempt, born of reverse jealousy and the natural conflict of vying for Ollister's time and attentions.

Ollister rather enjoyed it. He would revel in Punk's dismissals of her. His doubts could find a place there. His bitterness could easily be brewed into spite, and they would pick her apart, laughing. He would feel terrible and cruel afterwards, being untrue to his heart, but destruction felt good sometimes, and the weight was such that he had to throw it off now and again, to run around under the sky, screaming drunk laughter. And really, the conversations weren't malicious, at least from Ollister's side. He considered her flaws and idiosyncrasies with true affection. He tried to think of it as a healthy laughter.

Adelaide was never much concerned with, or threatened, by Punk. Which agitated the situation, certainly.

Punk saw Adelaide as too serious about herself. And he couldn't take seriously people who took themselves too seriously. Although it was true that she was less inclined to make an ass of herself than say, Punk, it wasn't true that she was unable to laugh at herself.

There was something in her that lacked a self-assuredness. It was at times balanced by a confidence, a purpose, and a shining intellect. The self-doubt she had, that was the thing Ollister had a hard time taking seriously. Her potential was so clear. But he had to put that out of his mind. Now was a time to act.

Punk was easily found at the center of a handful of giggling girls in cocktail dresses. The rich always loved Punk. He was thrusting his hips violently back and forth, clearly in the middle of a story in which he screwed someone's brain wide open. The girls inhaled as a group with each thrust.

Ollister burst into the circle, pushing past all the jeweled wrists and perfectly tanned shoulders.

"Punk. I need you to…"

"Excuse me. He's telling a… oh! Ollister!" This girl was clearly captain of the society club. Her earrings flashed. "Ollister, Darling Maebeth Whorls." She extended a hand. "We met at…"

"Oh yes, I remember." Ollister. Speaking very loudly now. "We slept together." Her jaw dropped. "Oh, you were probably so drunk you don't recall." All of her friends' jaws dropped. "But it was fantastic. Anyways, how are you?" Mouth snapping shut, she spun on a heel and walked away, chin held high. The social club followed. Ollister and Punk were alone.

"Um… this one fancy lady told me to tell you…" Punk. Stammering.

"I want you to drug her."

"The fancy lady?"

"Adelaide."

THE PLATYPUS

The Platypus lay upstairs on his leather sofa, in his study. He had only the dim desk lamp on, but even that light bothered his eyes. Consequently he had a pillow over his face. He could still hear one of his alarms going off somewhere. He casually wondered if it was possible to smother oneself.

Not really his style. He could pay someone to do it, maybe. Although lately the people that he paid didn't seem to be worth their checks. He told Euphrates that he wanted every camera on, and a man watching every screen, and if Ollister was spotted, the standing order was to bring him directly to The Platypus's office.

He had been downstairs a few times, but the pressure was too much. He could hear the party below him rumbling like a thunderhead, the occasional electrical charge of a dropped wine glass or a shrill woman laughing.

He had been thinking of his various problems. The complexities of the present situation quickly multiplied, spinning out into future possibilities, likely and unlikely, each hypothetical action on his part creating a new branch, off which further options grew like little twigs. Until the entire thing was an entangled, unfathomable mess. He had been a chess champion as a child, and sincerely wished that his parents had not put him through all that. Viola lessons or horseback riding would have been preferable to chess. Now his brain was hardwired for exhausting logic, thinking in terms of probability, thinking three moves out.

Instead of thinking about the minutiae of each single problem, he was thinking in general, about all of the problems at once. Their sheer number. This was, surprisingly, a more comforting line of thought.

There was this hot-shot gallery owner, in town from big bad New York, who was clearly looking for star treatment, and who, admittedly, The Platypus was desperate to impress. The local community, which he had controlled for so long, could be brought into the national spotlight, showering them all with fame and fortune. Unless he lost control of it. There was Ollister, chief among his concerns. The boy had surreptitiously wormed his way into almost everything having to do with anything in this town. He was gaining control, but not by any public obvious means that The Platypus could easily deflect. He was coming in the back door, and stopping him was of the utmost concern. The White Sodality was also concerned about this. The last meeting had not gone well. Members were upset. They were calling for heads to roll. They were calling for the blood of Ollister. His power was more clear, his gestures more blatant. There were pieces, in galleries now, that were quite clearly slaps in the face to the Sodality. Also, he suspected, Ollister had had some sort of relation with his wife. Isadora was fiercely loyal. She was calculating, calm, and one of his favorite instruments of his will. She was like a hidden pistol, a thing of beauty. And she had always had a sexual appetite that had little to do with The Platypus. When they were younger, yes. But, she had particular tastes, which she appeased at will. This had never bothered him in the slightest. He had his own appetites as well, appetites that a wife would just not do for. But he heard the way she talked about the boy. Saw her eyes shift when his name came up. And something was different. Her desire went beyond the sexual. And this he could not abide. He had tried a mild sort of revenge, by making himself known to Adelaide. But things had not progressed much beyond that. Euphrates's lawsuit did not help matters much, he thought. Euphrates did not help matters much. The man was grossly incompetent, needing his hand held at every little step of the way. This, also, was a problem. Currently he was dispatched, along with all of the white-suited groundsmen, who had been called for duty whether they were scheduled or not, to watch the premises and provide security during The White Ball. This was important, because of the persistent rumors of a terrorism organization, headed by Ollister, that planned to assassinate him. Even though it seemed preposterous, and he doubted the boy was ambitious in that particular way, one could never be too safe. He had underestimated before. There were standing orders to look for suspicious youths, and to keep a vigilant eye out for their chief, Ollister.

To think, these parties used to be fun.

ART TERRORISTS

Franc stood with the giant painting in his arms, alarm blaring. Paul was frozen in fear.

"Putain!" He set it down, with great effort, and leaned it against the wall. He strode over to the nearest window, and smashed it with an expensive-looking Chinese vase. Paul thought this was a particularly inane thing to do, as the window was barely large enough for a cat to go through, much less Franc with a seven-foot naked lady and her attending satyrs. Additionally, the window breaking caused another, different, higher-pitched whining alarm to go off.

The lights came on.

"Putain!"

Two White Suits slid into view, brandishing actual, shining automatic pistols.

ZELLA, MATILDA, & PUNK

"Why do you want to call him over?"

"I don't know, Mattie, maybe I'm bored. Hey, Punk!" Zella shouted across the few folks still browsing the buffet tables. Punk was talking to himself while collecting squares of cheese impaled with toothpicks in his left hand. He was palming about twenty-five. He looked up, surprised to be called, surprised at the caller, and shuffled over, looking nervous.

"Hey dudes, you, uh… want some cheese?" Did they know about the purse? He tried to act casual.

"No, thanks." Matilda. Theatrically glowering.

"I don't know, Punk, are they gonna give me the shits?" Zella. Laughing hard at her own joke. Matilda smirked in spite of herself. Punk looked down. They didn't know.

"You know, fuck you man, I ate some really bad barbeque chicken enchiladas and then drank like six or seven…"

"Don't get your dick in a knot, I'm just teasing you." She took a cheese cube from his pile, and pulled it off its spike slowly, using her teeth. "That kid right there, you see him?" She pointed out a toddler gripping his grandmother's hand, red eyes and cheeks still flushed. "Well I heard that his mom, this rich collector's daughter, just like totally threw up on his head. She was all woozy, and like aiming for the trash bin, but just ended up coating her kid instead, isn't that hilarious? She passed out right after that, and I think they moved her somewhere else." Punk was just kind of staring at her face, mouth hanging open a little. "What are you doing?" Zella. Finally asking.

"I'm… uh… at a party? What does it look like? Jeez."

"Yeah, you're all dressed up. I don't think I've ever seen you out of your costume."

"Costume?" Punk. Indignant.

"You always wear the same thing, babe." She pulled on his lapel. She was flirting. "I mean, not that I don't like it. I'm just saying. You clean up nice."

"I'm not clean."

"Omigod." Matilda.

"And why would I care about that?" Zella. Putting on a seductive smile, which was not unlike Isadora's, now that Punk was looking at it. Strange.

"Omigod! Addy's purse!" Matilda. Swiveling her head back and forth frantically, scanning her immediate vicinity. Punk could feel his pits moisten.

"You lost Addy's purse?" Zella. Her eyes widening.

"She gave it to you!"

"Whatever, you had it, you lost it. She's gonna be pissed." Zella crossed her arms.

"You, uh… maybe you left it in the… uh… man, that sucks." Punk. All he could offer.

"Yeah, you'd better go find it." Zella. An edge of reproach in her voice.

Matilda looked back and forth at each of their faces, with no small amount of panic. "OK." She smoothed her dress nervously. "I'll be right back."

Zella turned back to Punk with a roll of her eyes. "Some people. So, where were we?"

"Uh… I dunno."

"I think we were discussing your, uh…" She looked at his crotch, with marked deliberateness. "…bathing habits."

THE PLATYPUS

The White Suits were rough, holding them by their shirt collars, pulling up so they had to walk on their tiptoes, dangling like kittens. Something metal was pressed into their backs, whether it was a gun or a baton, its intention was clear.

The alarms had been turned off, but the silence that replaced them was scarier.

They were hauled up staircases, and down long hallways, through heavy doors, some that required the guards to swipe cards, or give finger prints, another required one of the huge ancient keys that was pulled from the hidden jacket pocket of the guard. The feeling that they were truly and deeply in trouble mounted.

They were finally brought into some sort of office room, old, and cluttered with papers. Euphrates was there, with two other suited men.

"These them?" Euphrates. Looking down his nose.

"Uh… Yeah." One of the guards.

"They don't look so smart." His smiled at himself. "All right. Fine. Leave them."

The guards that had escorted them turned and left. Euphrates came from behind his desk, a finger pointed in each of their faces. "Your jig is up." He pinched his eyes into slits of menace, trying to add weight to the weak line.

"Come on, let's visit The Platypus." He motioned to the suits in the corners, and they gripped the boys, more formally than the guards, but with no less force. Euphrates led them all out of his office and through another twisting round of tunnels, halls, and stairs.

Finally, a pair of heavy doors swung open revealing a long low office. It was smoky, and the rectangle of a giant oak desk could barely be made out at the other end of the room. Bookshelves, mahogany and musty, lined either wall, and the place had a very specific smell, of age, of thought, of the jungle. Ancient wood furniture littered the floor, threadbare and disused. Lamps gave off little glowing fairy lights, which flickered pleadingly in the fog. There was the faint sound of a raven crowing. One of the suits coughed a little.

The boys were dragged forward, a wake of disturbed smoke curling out behind them.

"Sir. Here they are. We caught them. They were actually trying to…" The Platypus looked up. Euphrates stopped talking. Some wiry white hairs were loose, caught by the soft lamplight. His eyes were ringed with red, and underscored by dark semi-circles. He looked drunk, or half-asleep.

"Euphrates." His voice was low, but surprisingly even and calm, given his appearance.

"Yes? Yes, sir?" Euphrates. Proud. A soldier to be commended.

"That's not Ollister."

"Hmm?" They all swiveled and looked at Franc, who lifted his right eyebrow. Paul wiggled frantically in his own skin.

"That. Person. Is not Ollister."

There was silence. Euphrates hid his hands.

"Remove them." The Platypus. His voice was softer, but somehow more menacing.

"But, sir, he was stealing your painting, we caught them as…"

"I don't give a good goddamn what they were doing. They're likely part of his entourage. Put them away."

At this Paul gave a decidedly feminine whimper, and a dark wet spot began to spread across the front of his pants and down his legs, twisted together. The Platypus lifted his hand, and the guards hauled them back through the wooden doors at the far end of the room.

"I'm terribly sorry, sir, I didn't know." Euphrates.

"Asking a simple question of your prisoner can often clear up these little matters of identity."

"Yes, sir."

"He won't be stealing anything. And he won't be with anyone. Unless he is with that filthy lieutenant of his. Or the girl, Adelaide, your special friend."

"I think we should…"

"I know very well your grievances with that child, dear Euphrates. But if she is here, the better to have a… conversation with her. You understand?"

"Yes… sir. Absolutely. I'll inform all my men to be on the look out for her as well. And for Ollister."

"Possibly together."

"Possibly together."

"Yes, I think that would be wise." The Platypus slammed down on his cigar cutter, sending the end of his finely rolled Cuban flying off, onto the floor, to rest with the others.

PUNK & SILAS

Punk sat on a footrest in the shadows of the upstairs drawing room, partially concealed by a curtain. There were only a few people milling around. He sat still so no one would notice him. The room was expansive, and drizzled in velvet, chandelier, and gaudy opulence. People seemed to be smoking.

He had one eye on a man in a white suit, just in case. But the real object of his surveillance was, in the far corner, Zella talking to Silas. He hadn't been aware that she and Silas were acquainted, or maybe they weren't. Silas was a real slime factory. He remembered that night in his sickly, smelly black Jag, what a complete cunt the guy was. He felt not a little twinge of jealousy at his obvious flirtation, inexplicably.

Then, as if out of nowhere, Punk had an idea. His own idea. He wasn't going to drug Adelaide, he had no reason to, nothing against her. It was clearly some sick sexual or revenge fantasy of Ollister's, and he was tired of living his life according to Ollister's dictum. He didn't have to be this lackey, this sad gopher. He could be in control, he could be a mastermind.

Especially now that he had an idea.

The idea was to drug Zella instead of Adelaide. Zella, who he had it bad for. Zella who had humiliated him that night on the roof. Zella, who he was way more interested in seeing all bugged out by the sex drug. He would drug Zella, and then have his way with her.

Just then, Adelaide entered the drawing room and joined the party. Punk watched Silas try what must have been a lame line out on her, from the withering look she shot him. She turned a shoulder to him and began to engage her friend in heated discussion. He slowly backed away, and came toward the exit, toward Punk.

When he was close enough to bite, Punk slid out of the shadows.

"Whoa, what the… ?" Silas. Gelled hair coming out of place.

"Sorry, I, uh.. didn't mean to, uh…"

"Scare me? Well you did. You are one weird dude."

"Yeah, I guess…"

"All right, well, man, I have to get back to my friends downstairs, so later…"

"No, wait." Punk. Sliding in front of him again.

"What?"

"I have some more of that drug. You know, the good stuff?"

"Oh, no way, man… last time…"

"Not for you. I want you to give it to that girl."

"What? Who?"

"That one. The crazy one." Punk. Pointing at the girls whispering to each other across the shoddy Oriental rug.

"You hate her or something?"

"No, dude, it's to make her horny."

And then, suddenly Silas had an idea. It was the same idea that Punk had had just a few minutes before. Why had he never thought of using the drug in reverse? That spunky one, Zella, she would be on fire with some of this stuff.

"I'll do it." Silas. Keen.

Punk grabbed him by the front of his suit and quickly pulled him into the shadow of the curtain. He stuffed the dirty baggy of wet stuff into Silas's pants pocket, in not an unsexual way.

"Thanks, man." Punk. Grinning right into Silas's desperate face. "Watch out for The White Suits."

MATILDA

With increasing panic, Matilda had scoured the rooms of the mansion, for both the missing purse and its missing owner, Adelaide. Able to locate neither, she found herself on the verge of tears.

That's when she had noticed a man in a white suit, with an earpiece in.

"Do you, um... work here?" Matilda. In a mouse voice. She approached the White Suit with trepidation.

"Mm." His grunted response.

"Cause... I... uh... lost my purse around here somewhere. I don't know if you have a lost and found. I mean, you wouldn't, I know this is someone's house, but maybe, someone turned it in or...?"

"Name?" His voice was gruff, but not unhelpful.

"W... What?"

"Your name. What's your name?"

"Uh... Adelaide. Adelaide. My driver's license should be in there."

"You're Adelaide?" His eyebrows lifted.

"Un-huh."

"I think you'd better come with me."

Matilda followed, hopeful that they had already recovered her friend's purse.

ADELAIDE

The armchaired reading room of the second floor library had cleared out, inexplicably. It was now dark and quiet. Adelaide and Zella stood talking.

"I think I just saw Ollister." Adelaide. Clutching her hands nervously to her chest.

"Here? Adelaide, really, at The Platypus's house?" Zella. Drunk now. "He wouldn't be caught dead being here or if he got caught here he would be dead. Here. Or whatever."

"I don't know… I mean… I think, I'm pretty sure it was him."

"You're paranoid." Zella. Pointing at Adelaide's face. "You need to calm down. You need a drink."

"I've had plenty of drinks. But, yeah, I guess they aren't taking the edge off. Fuck. I mean. I knew he would be here."

"The Platypus has like, security."

"Hello ladies, trouble?" As if from some forgotten wardrobe, Silas slid back into the room like a well-oiled drawer. The girls shuffled backwards. "If you got a problem, yo, I'll solve it." Addressing them both, but starting intently at Zella.

She planted a disbelieving hand on her hip. "All right. Looks like we do have a problem. How you gonna 'solve it?'"

Silas reached into his inside blazer pocket and presented the drug as though it were some golden goose egg.

"What's that?" Adelaide.

"Just pot." Silas said, overly causal.

"It doesn't look like 'just pot.'" Zella squinting.

"Trust me." Already pinching a wet wad into a rolling paper. He gazed at Zella from under his brow as he massaged the joint back and forth in his knuckly fingers.

She hooked her arm in Adelaide's. "I don't know if I want drugs." Glancing furtively at her friend.

"I do." Adelaide. Resigned more than enthused. Silas stuck the joint in his face and lit it.

Then, suddenly, Graham, Miriam and Dolores were there. Dolores thrust her hand at Zella. "Hi, I'm Dolores. Silas's girlfriend." Zella shook her hand meekly. The girl was marking her territory. Adelaide watched Silas blow out his hit and roll his eyes in annoyance.

"Who is Silas?" Zella. "Come on Addy. Let's go get another drink." But Adelaide was sucking hard on the joint, and shaking her head slightly. Zella gave her friend a drunken look of defiance, and stomped away.

"She don't look like the type that'd be all uptight about drugs." Graham, pulling on the joint he lifted from Silas's hand. "Oh well." He passed it back to Adelaide, now moistened.

Silas stared at the door Zella had just exited by. Dolores stared icily at him.

"Unh!" Adelaide was holding her hit in, but pointing frantically to the opposite corner of the sitting room, where one of the large wooden wall panels had begun to creakily rock back and forth.

"Fucking ghosts, man." Graham. Flatly.

Miriam screamed a ridiculous, horror movie scream.

The panel fell forward, making a loud enough thwack to make everyone jump. Vance, and then Sebastian, emerged covered in white dust. The two couples stared. As did Adelaide, joint burning slowly in her hand. Vance and Sebastian stared back, frozen in their crouching poses. They had not expected to see people in this room.

Silas started to say something when Sebastian snickered loudly. "Gras! Vance! Willst du Kiffen?" He dusted himself off with a limp wrist and walked over to the surprised circle. Vance followed.

"Who are you dudes?" Graham. An obvious question, but the entrance seemed to warrant it.

Sebastian pinched Silas's butt, hard. "Hey, can I fuck with that?" Silas looked consternated. "I mean the joint." Sebastian pointed to his hand. "Though I do like your hair, very… um… how do you put it… not refined. Refinery. Oil refinery. There's a huge one in Karlsruhe."

"Adelaide." Vance.

"What?" Adelaide was annoyed, Vance staring at her longingly.

"We're here on an Art Terrorism mission. You have to join us."

The whole group laughed as though they were on a sitcom. Adelaide shrugged, and Sebastian and Vance easily assimilated themselves into the group and heartily assisted with the smoking of joints, seven more of which were rolled and consumed.

Adelaide noticed that Silas was pulling his hits, not really inhaling, but that was no business of hers, and he was being plenty generous with his strange sack of wet lemony weed, and that was good, because it was helping. She was feeling better. She liked these people. She even thought she might like Vance. He wasn't so bad. She was feeling great. She liked them all a lot.

Were her last thoughts before blacking out.

OLLISTER

Ollister waited behind a planter. A large ficus tree with a spiraling trunk. He leaned casually against a vestibule window and peered out into the party. He slowly monitored the drinking, talking, laughing crowd. He watched for people who might be watching for him. If he was seen, fine. As long as he wasn't noticed.

Occasionally one of the guards, easy to spot in blinding white, would stiffly stroll by. Ollister would turn around, and pretend to look out the window, or examine the ice cubes in his long-ago-drained drink. He had been a guest at this house once. His right temple was starting to throb, in a far-off way, a warning beacon that heralded headache.

Punk was supposed to meet him by this particular pot of indoor foliage well over half an hour ago. He had stood on all sides of it, but if he had to hang out there much longer it would surely become apparent that he was talking to no one at the party besides the plant.

He shifted his weight. He found himself smiling sheepishly in response to some old bird that had smiled at him, clearly mistaking him for a 'nice young man.' She had her sagging arm hooked through her husband's, a white-haired, tomato-faced fat cat. They were the archetypical guests of this party: rich, dull, and desperate to appear cultured.

He had often thought of himself and Adelaide at that stage in life. Old, comfortable, bonded together permanently by a long life spent in each other's company. Imagining the way he would look, the way she would look, the weight of their knowing glances compounded by time. It made him sad, nostalgic, for something that never would be. It made him mad, at her, at himself, for tampering with fate, for sidestepping something that was clearly supposed to be, for marring perfect biographies with sordid blemishes, and pitfalls.

There he was. Punk. Standing, talking to Zella. In high spirits, one drink in each hand, pants sagging to reveal the crack of his ass. Had he forgotten? What did he think they were here for, schmoozing?

He was clearly engrossed, putting every effort into wild flirting, his arms gesticulating frantically. Zella looked bored, her eyes roaming around the room sleepily. Suddenly they fixed on him. Her mouth opened a little.

There was no point in holding back now. He strode across the room, and confronted the two of them directly.

"Come with me." Fast. Serious. Neither brain, pickled as they were in alcohol, thought to question the forceful order. They followed him. Out of the main room, through the library, into a back hall, down some dark stairs, through two more twisting halls, with faux-torches lining the dusty walls, into something like a wine cellar. Which is what it was, technically, but it felt more like a secret lab. There were no dirt floors, or ancient stained barrels, no wooden racks housing dusty bottles. The wine was kept in giant, climate-controlled glass-doored cells. The floor was burnished steel. He led them to a leather settee outside one of the giant wine refrigerators.

"Whoa…" Zella. Head tilted all the way back, to take in the height of the stacked bottles. "We could get so drunk. It's like a supermarket of wine."

"Indeed." Ollister. "Let's do just that." He handed her a glass of white, glowing in the fluorescent light. Neither had seen him open a bottle, get out glasses, or pour the wine. It had just appeared in his hand.

Without looking at him she reached out for the glass, and took it, unsteadily.

"Where's mine at?" Punk. Ollister raised a finger to his face to quiet him, his own eyes fixed on Zella's face, all hunger.

She took a long swig, eyes closed. When she finished, Ollister took the glass gingerly from her hand. She barely noticed, as she looked around, unseeing. Ollister gripped her shoulders and steered her backwards, till she was above the leather-cushioned furniture, and then dropped them. She slumped over onto the settee.

"Dude!" Punk. His hands palms up, imploring. "What the fuck did you do? She was already drugged. I got that slimy guy to give her the drug! She was almost fucked up enough, I mean, I was, like, right on the verge of talking her into…"

Ollister grabbed Punk's jaw with one hand, with no small measure of violence. "You listen to me." Punk stopped mid-sentence. "You are not here to flirt or fuck or fool around. We are here on a mission. You have an objective. Is that objective complete?"

Punk lowered his eyes.

"Is that objective complete?"

He never should have disobeyed. Ollister had done so much for him. Ollister was counting on him. He felt guilty and vulnerable. Ollister squeezed his face harder.

"Punk?"

His eyes started to tear up. Finally, from between squeezed lips: "No. I gave it to her instead of Adelaide."

Ollister let the face go, gently. "Goddamn it." Under his breath.

He opened one of the doors to the giant wine coolers. A sickly sweet smell curled outwards. Ollister grabbed two bottles of ancient looking wine, gripping each by the neck, his arms outstretched and stiff. Then, in some bizarre approximation of a jumping jack, he leapt into the air, his straight arms smashing the bottles together above his head, into an explosion of wine and glass and noise.

Punk jumped back, shielding his face too late, it was already covered in wine.

Ollister started pulling wine bottles out at random, flinging them behind him to crash to the ground, leaving splatters of red on the steel floor. An alarm started going off, a machine screaming.

Punk cowered on the floor, hands over his head, ass in the air, the bottles increasingly aimed in his direction.

Then it stopped. The alarm echoed around them, everything was still.

"Punk. What's that?" Ollister. Quietly.

He walked over, wet shoes crunching glass. He reached down to Punk's quivering ass and pulled something out of his back pocket. The gray papers.

"Oh, Punk." Ollister sat down, in a purple puddle. "Oh."

"Oh yeah… I just, like, found it… it's kinda boring boring…"

Ollister pressed the book against his face. His smile was far away.

"Punk, you've done better than I could've hoped." He was barely audible above the shrill alarm. "You've won me back my prize. This is so much... thank you. And Adelaide... she's not drugged?"

"Uh... no."

"Wonderful Punk. You couldn't have done better. I have to find her. Let's go..."

Three white guards thundered down the stairs. Ollister leapt to his feet, grabbed Punk's hand, and ran for a large wooden door at the other end of the metal cellar.

ART TERRORISTS

After Adelaide passed out, Vance and Graham carried her over to the chaise lounge and laid her out. There were some mild attempts at waking her – face-slapping, shaking, gentle screaming. These proved ineffectual, and it was judged that she was best left to sleep, mostly because there was nothing else to do. Alerting anyone to this scene was a bad idea, not only because of the renegade presence of the two terrorists, but also for the fact that they had all just consumed a very large amount of very sticky weed. The room reeked of lemons.

Another alarm sounded. There was frantic discussion of what to do next. The couples, in their rumpled evening-wear looked on as Vance and Sebastian bickered cattily. Sebastian wanted to bury her in a coat closet. Vance was of the mind that she was useful, and hot, and she could join them, or at least be used as some sort of hostage or bargaining chip. They all jumped when Nick crawled through the same hole made by Vance and Sebastian upon their grand arrival. He was quickly apprised of the situation and came down, opinion-wise, on Vance's side.

It was decided that Vance would try to procure smelling salts, a defibrillator, or at the very least water, from some sort of first-aid stash that must be in the house somewhere. He wanted to wake her. So she could see the whole thing go down. He had passed on the drug, but he had his own desires, in no need of enhancement. Sebastian would escort the witnessing party guests to a secure location. Nick would stay by the shallowly breathing body, as bodyguard. He was cool with this. Very, very cool.

In fact, once the idea of leaving the room had come up, everyone was quite in favor. Sebastian flipped a hand up into the air, and declared "Onwards!" And the two couples followed him, confused, excited, apprehensive. His four charges would certainly have reported the entire operation, had they been in a right frame of mind. Drug-addled as they were, and after listening to plans and counterplans of a clearly organized terrorist squad, they were no longer sure quite who they were or what their roles should be.

Sebastian would define it for them.

"We need to get out of here before the knights in white satin come round. Let's trash the fanciest room in this fascist hotel!" He made that sound like fun. Miriam and Graham locked arms, as did Silas and Dolores, and they followed their new ringmaster all over a house they had each been to many times. This time was markedly different though, and not just due to an altered state of mind. They had never seen the back rooms, the little nooks and crannies, the rooms where the truly expensive things were kept, the servants' quarters, the private lounges. Also Sebastian made things up as he gave them this faux tour, telling them about the heritage of this, or the expense in transporting that. It was amusing. They shuffled from doorway to doorway, mouths flapping with laughter.

Finally they came to a large, opulent bedroom. At the sight of this, even Sebastian was rendered wordless. It was a king's bedchamber, luscious and overwrought. It could have been a museum replica of a 17th century monarch's private quarters. Ornately carved furniture, gilt-and-mirror walls. Historic ideas blown up to monstrous proportion, dripping with rococo and baroque flourishes. Embroidered settees, in royal colors, rich tapestries depicting scenes of rabbit hunting and sexual conquest. Fauteuils as thrones, ivy-festooned bedpans, delicately carved ermines on their haunches, supporting the armrests of a prie-dieu. The entire pathological over-indulgence was barely lit by an actively dripping candle chandelier.

Dolores walked over to the bed, an elaborately canopied four-poster, pulled tight with ropes. Everyone, mouths still agape from the blinding room watched her underwater dream-walk. She lay down on the gold lamé peacock quilt and spread her limbs out as far as they would go. The orgy started almost immediately after that.

The entire thing was a blur to its drug-addled participants, but there was the sense that even on the security cameras later, this riot of depravity would still have only appeared as a blur. Most of the time, Sebastian acted as ringleader, pushing faces into crotches, tying stray hands when they needed it, whipping unidentified ass with one of the giant golden tassels hung all over the room. There was double penetration, an oral daisy chain, asphyxiation, some urine drinking, fisting, and plenty of anal. Graham and Silas were surprisingly attentive to each other, being tenderly shown the ropes by the obliging Sebastian. At one point Dolores had a toe in every single one of her orifices. Everyone did everyone, without prejudice or exception. It might have lasted hours, or perhaps just a few minutes, it was difficult to tell. When the end came, it was messy, and there was considerable loss of blood. No one remembered passing out.

When they awoke, Miriam was in Graham's arms, and Dolores was in Silas's, they were perfectly clean, fully dressed, and neatly tucked into the overstuffed bed. Silas would never tell any of them that he had been pulling his hits, and was relatively sober during the entire orgy. Sebastian was nowhere to be seen.

THE PLATYPUS

"You're sure it's her?" Euphrates. Standing, fixed on his walkie-talkie.

"Uh, yeah, I mean, I guess." One of his White Suits.

"No guessing. We need to be sure. This is Adelaide?"

"Yes."

"How do you know."

"She said so."

"You got her to admit it?" Euphrates. Wringing his hands in excitement.

"Well, I mean, yeah, she just told me…"

"Freely admits it, eh? Good."

"Yeah, but, she said she lost her…"

"Bring her directly to The Platypus's office. I'll meet you there."

He made his way into the office, a spring in his step. The Platypus stood at the mini-bar pouring himself a neat Scotch.

"I've got her."

"Who's that, Euphrates?" The Platypus.

"Adelaide."

"Fantastic. Would you like a Scotch?"

"Um… Yes. Please. Thank you."

The Platypus poured a good measure of foul-looking liquid into another tumbler. The fumes warped the air above the glass.

"Sir, may I ask you? After you're done with her, or, I mean, I'd like to tell her a thing or two, because…"

"Yes, yes, Euphrates, I'm aware of your ax. You'll get to grind it."

Euphrates's walkie-talkie squawked. He instructed them to let her in.

And through the smoke they came, the guard with his hand gripping her elbow lightly, Matilda, scared and confused.

Another alarm could be heard outside the doors.

"Gross incompetence." The Platypus. To the air.

Euphrates began wringing his hands again. Matilda's knees shook.

"Put her away, I suppose."

ART TERRORISTS

There were wide marble stairs that flowed waterfallesque from the top of the mezzanine down into the great ballroom where most of the party was gathered. Vance took them down two at a time. He felt a little conspicuous, coming down the main stairs like this, the gaggles of guests clucking around its foot. But this was an art party, and someone dressed in all black, running around like a maniac, just didn't stick out.

He pushed past all of the perfumed old partygoers, keeping an eye out for White Suits. He couldn't believe that Adelaide was at the party. If he could convince her finally to be his girlfriend, or convert her to their cause, that could be the start of something big. She was a semi-celebrity in this town. In the art scene at least. And she would probably bring a lot of folks over with her. They would start to get press. They would be taken seriously by the world. It had to be. It was fate. If she wasn't amicable, he would just kidnap her for a while. Stockholm Syndrome would do the rest, or he could hold her hostage. The first order of business was to wake her up, make sure she was alive.

He thought of getting some alcohol from the kitchen, a glass of water, maybe. But she was out cold, she might need something stronger. He made his way to the basement. Maybe a first-aid kit with some smelling salts, maybe just some random chemicals, which he could use to concoct his own pick-me-up. He was trying to think of what chemicals he knew and which might do the trick as he made his way though the back halls, and down the dank basement stairs.

He rooted through the laundry room, finding nothing stronger than soap. Finally he opened the door to the supply room where the terrorists had had their debriefing. Something twitched in the corner, barely illuminated by a white square screen.

"Pete!"

"Oh Vance, thank god, I thought it was…"

"Pete, what the fuck are you doing in here?"

"Well, I was monitoring the alarm systems on my laptop, here. I'm tapped into the mainframe. Did you know that three have gone off in the past half-hour? What the fuck are you guys doing up there?"

"I don't know. I haven't tripped any alarms."

"Well, there's also some awful poetry on an upstairs computer. I almost erased that hard drive just to, you know, spare us all."

"That's great. Uh, didn't you have a mission?"

"Yeah, it was the smoke bombs."

"Smoke bombs?"

"Yeah, Nick didn't tell you about that? It was his idea. Hey, have you seen him?"

"Yeah, he found me and Sebastian upstairs. Look, change of plan. We found Adelaide passed out upstairs, she could really be a boon to our, uh, organization. So I say we get her and get out."

"She wants to join us? She always seemed so weird about the whole thing. She's come around? You talked her into it?"

"Uh, yeah. Pretty much."

"OK. Well, then I will hack back into the mainframe, and see if I can take remote control of the alarm system, which will allow us to…"

"Actually Pete, do you have those smoke bombs?"

"Uh, yeah, they're right here."

"That would probably work a little better. Let's just plant those, blast 'em, and that will create enough confusion for us to get out of here."

"OK, well, there are eight remotes here, and I've got the detonator in my bag…"

Just then Ollister and Punk came bursting through the large wooden door, looking panicked and reeking of wine. They both pushed the heavy old thing closed, and started to move boxes and other things in front of it, as if to barricade themselves in.

"What the fuck are you guys doing here?" Vance. Eyes wide.

"I could ask the same of you." Ollister. Without turning around. He had already marked them upon breathless entry. "Except by the look of your costumes, I would assume that's something you'd rather not answer."

Punk finished pushing a large, if empty, filing cabinet against the door. Some heavy banging from the other side began. Fists.

"That door is trip-wired." Pete. Staring dumbly.

"That hardly matters when there are already White Suits outside it, now does it?"

"You can hide in these closets." Vance. Quickly. He was no friend to Ollister, but that was better than being found out by the Sodality.

Ollister turned around, entered the closet door directly behind him, and slammed it closed, leaving Punk lurching. The wooden door shook, and the filing cabinet began to teeter on its edge. Vance motioned for Punk to come into their closet, which he did, as quickly as he could manage, his feet nearly slipping out from under him, wet with wine.

Vance just closed the door behind Punk when the expected crash came, the two White Suits bursting into the supply basement, one ordering the other to check all the doors. The first one they opened was immediately on their right. The one containing Ollister.

Vance listened, along with Punk and Pete, to the brief struggle across the basement.

"Where'd your friend go, eh?" White Suit.

"He ran." Ollister. Calm. Simple.

"No matter, you're the one we want."

He could hear them both laughing and pushing Ollister around as they dragged him away up the stairs.

"Well, that was close." Vance. "Are you gonna go after him?" Addressed to a tired Punk, sitting on the floor of the storeroom.

"Yeah, man, I guess I should." He didn't move.

"Well, we could help you. I guess. I mean, he sort of started this whole thing. Or named it anyway."

"He named you?" Punk's eyebrows lifted in surprise.

"Well, named our organization. We're Art Terrorists. But we've grown a lot from what he started, so we would certainly help spring him. We're fully equipped. That's what we are doing here. You know, Art Terrorism."

"Yeah, I never could understand what that was about. Is that like a type of artist?"

"Kind of. It's more like a type of terrorist."

"I guess that sounds fun."

"It is." Vance. Broadly grinning first at Pete, then at Punk.

"So… uh… what do you do?"

"Well…" Vance. Sensing the sort of thing that Punk meant by the word fun. "We were gonna go plant some smoke bombs in the main hall right now. Wanna come?"

"Uh… sure, man."

"What about Ollister?" Pete. Looking concerned.

"Nah, fuck him, man, I'm done with all that shit. Let's have fun."

Vance debriefed his new recruit on the plan: smoke bombs in the tree planters that lined the grand staircase, and encircled the ballroom. One per planter, angled up and toward the stairs, which would provide a good cover for their escape. It was decided that Punk was wearing enough black, and therefore did not need to be issued a uniform. Pete loaded up the bag with the bombs and the detonator. And they left the supply closet, in pursuit of their fun.

ADELAIDE

Adelaide woke up in a closet. A large one. A woman's one. She could tell that by smell alone, but the dresses were also a giveaway, their soft hems forming a canopy above her head.

To think why she was there, how she got there, never crossed her mind. She felt high. Her senses heightened, the softness, the quietness of the closet consumed her entire consciousness. She wriggled and kicked in a cozy ecstasy. Where was her lover, where had he been?

She felt like she had been dreaming, but couldn't remember. Like she had no hands until she checked they were there. Like she never wanted to move from this spot. Like she was born here.

"Hey…" A voice came through the louvered door. "Are you awake in there?" It sounded husky, honeyed, like a summer zephyr. Was it him?

She slowly pushed the door open from the bottom and the light flooded her vision, she thought the silhouette it framed could be none other than her perfect, clever love.

"Vance told me to guard you. You're important to our cause."

She gazed up from the floor, mouth agape, at her guard, her champion as the lines of his face came into detail.

He had buck teeth, that could be said with certainty. He was not shaven, and splotchy brown patches mottled his neck. There was considerable hair between his eyebrows. The closely-set eyes must have belonged to his mother before they belonged to him, darkly lashed as they were.

"Lemme help you up." He thrust meaty fingers forward. "You're not gonna run or anything, right?"

"No." She mouthed, not quite audible, feeling herself blush as she took his offered paw. Nick had never looked like this before, she had always been repulsed by him. She couldn't place what it was now, but she felt nervous and itchy. Like he was looking at her, like she wanted to look at him. She stood, rubbing her legs together like a cricket.

"Good, yeah, I'm running the central command from up here while my operatives… uh… execute objectives, you know, downstairs."

"Operatives?" Adelaide. Gazing fixedly.

"Yeah, I'm their leader. Pretty much."

"Leader?"

"Yeah, of the Art Terrorists."

"Oh. Wow, Nick. I've heard of that. That's really so fascinating." Adelaide. Gushing.

"Well, I came up with it myself."

"Oh, yeah?"

"Yeah, you know how there hasn't been a new art movement, in like, decades? Well I'm it. I mean, I'm outside the whole art world commercial thing, but also inside it, you know, penetrating it? If you think about terrorism in an art historical context…" He droned like a talk box stuck on. She squeezed her thigh muscles.

"Yeah, it's like turning the creative process on its head, making it into a 'destructive process,' you know? Like anti-creative, anti-art, but not against it, just making some new creative stuff out of it. It's the next logical step."

"That's genius." Adelaide. She felt dizzy and queasy, and like she was hearing pure truth for the first time ever, echo and bang around inside her head.

"Yeah, I know. The goal would be, I mean imagine if I could recruit enough, if like, we could destroy all the art? Do you know how frickin' famous I'd be? The master who had outdone all the other masters. Who conquered all art that came before him."

"Woooow…" Slurring.

"Vance thinks you could help. You're over him, right?"

"What… me?"

"Yeah, you know, we need someone on the inside, someone respected, we need a platform."

"Um, OK, we could do it now. At The White Ball." She felt desperate for his approval, his attention.

"Huh?"

"I'll help you. I can help you. I'll do anything—we'll use this party. It would be the perfect launch."

"Well… that's what we were thinking…"

"I know what to do." She grabbed his hand, thrilling at the touch. She felt really high, really really good. "Come on."

"Uh, don't forget who the leader is, though…"

OLLISTER

The two White Suits dragged Ollister through the halls, gripping his upper arms. He tried to walk at a slower pace than they did, and drag his feet a bit, but when he did that they just squeezed harder, so he was mostly compliant and walked along with them. He felt sure they had guns.

Ollister would know what to do if it were just him. He wasn't particularly scared of The Platypus. Even though he knew what the man was capable of. Maybe he would lock him up in the mansion or try to cut some deal with him. Ollister wasn't above reneging, and he wasn't above lying. The Platypus wasn't going to torture him, he didn't have anything, physical or informational, that The Platypus really wanted. The man just didn't like him. And that was hardly grounds for torture. He might not mind being locked up. They would have to feed him.

He had occasionally fantasized about jail. There was something about the forced nothingness that appealed to him. The time would have to be spent in his own mind, which was a place he rather enjoyed being. It would be boring boring, that was sure. But with no way out. A place where he could fully embrace the boring boring, where he could really get to know it. It might encourage him to do sit-ups more regularly.

So, if it were just him, he would be fine. But he knew they wanted Adelaide, too. And he didn't know where she was. And for that reason, he had to be free. He couldn't be caught.

They stood in front of the large door to The Platypus's office. One of The White Suits opened it just a crack. The other White Suit shoved him through.

It was smoky in the room. The glowing tip of the cigar was all he could see from behind The Platypus's enormous armchair, which was facing away from the door, toward the window.

"You're a fool. And a fuck." Ollister. To the back of the chair.

Slowly it spun around. Isadora. She eyed him steadily, her nails dug in the armrests.

"Oh Christ." Ollister. Muttering. More at the cliché of the tableau, than the fact of her presence. He was going to have to be careful. She was a coiled serpent.

"So nice to run into you." Isadora. Her voice dripping.

"The pleasure is mine." Ollister. Holding position by the door.

"I have a proposition for you, my young prince."

"I had a feeling." Again under his breath.

"I want you to do my portrait. In the nude."

"Well, I don't really paint much these…"

"I'm *sure* you'll be fantastic."

"Sounds…" Ollister. Clearing his throat. "Splendid." A small cough. "I'll have my assistant call you and we can make…"

"Now." Isadora. Standing.

"Oh… uh… OK."

She slipped behind a Chinese paper partition, conveniently back-lit, and began some kind of gangly strip tease, rocking back and forth like a giant stork.

Ollister took the opportunity to open the large office door and slink out, shutting it gingerly behind him. "I've been dismissed." He told the guards before striding purposefully and quickly away. They looked at each other, and rushed into the office to confirm this order. The last thing Ollister heard as he padded down the stairs was a shriek of surprise turn to embarrassment, turn to rage.

N O T **A D E L A I D E**

"Excellent. Bring her up." Euphrates set his walkie-talkie down on his desk. Finally. Adelaide. Now, here, he would have her. Perhaps she would lead The Platypus to Ollister, whether she did or not he didn't really care. He wanted her for his own, he wanted to scare her. That was the entire purpose of the lawsuit anyway, to exact some revenge. Put her in her place. He was still scathing at the public embarrassment her little art stunt had caused him, not to mention, many other fine institutions of art education.

The Platypus's men found her passed out in the wine cellar, she had drunk quite a bit, and smashed quite a bit more. The destructive urges of the young appalled him. But this didn't matter much, she would have to answer to more than just some minor vandalism.

When the guard dragged her in, he didn't know whom to slap. The girl for not being Adelaide, or the White Suit for incompetence.

"That. Is not her." He squeezed his hands together and looked at the limp body, covered in red wine. "Put her with the other vandals."

EVERYBODY

Adelaide was leading Nick through the Grand Hall, where chandelier light splashed over gaudy busts of long-dead French kings, and sparked in both their eyes. She gripped his hand tightly, and pulled him forward. He felt warm and important.

Punk crouched behind a bush, smoke bomb detonator in his hand. He suddenly wondered what he was doing. Who were all these people? Who was he? It was time to leave Ollister. It was time to leave Punk behind, too, and become someone different.

Isadora, looked up as she wrapped herself in a robe. She was truly ashamed. Unused to rejection her heart ached for a real connection. Just then Sebastian stumbled into The Platypus's office, completely by accident, coming down off the worst drug and sex experience of his life. They were the closest of friends from that moment onward.

Pete and Vance stood stock-still behind a curtain in the main gallery. They were both sweating profusely. Vance felt a creeping suicidal madness grip his brain.

Matilda and Zella found themselves locked in the downstairs billiards room with Franc and Paul, the other captives of mistaken identity. Zella, naturally, had begun to immediately flirt with Franc, who had an accent, and muscles besides. They had quickly moved into a side room, filled with beer kegs, and started loud, inappropriate noisemaking. To cover this embarrassment, as well as their own, Matilda and Paul were forced to keep up conversation. They found they rather liked each other, and both secretly resolved to ask the other on a date, upon escape.

The Platypus had made the decision to decamp from his office of command, and head out into the party, to scout for Ollister himself. If the threat could not be put down, he would have to call off the party early. There was just too much at stake. Euphrates fluttered behind him nervously, eager for resolution.

Dolores and Miriam walked out in front, down the drive, away from the party. Their matched stride was silent and purposeful. Silas and Graham laughed and joked a few paces behind, out of earshot. The evening's homosexuality would go unspoken of. They were ardently discussing the best means of proposing marriage to their respective girls.

ADELAIDE

And suddenly her voice could be heard. Barely audible above the ballroom din at first, but shouts of 'Quiet, quiet!' were quickly heeded, and the crowd hushed and turned to see what the frenzy was about.

Adelaide stood at the top of the grand stair, her hair kinked and wild. There seemed to be a breeze emanating from her and her eyes rolled around madly. She held her hands out to the crowd, palms outward, in a gesture of control or supplication or rejection. Nick stood just to the left of her, grinning around the room like a friendly idiot.

"Quiet, all, I have an announcement to make." The entire party turned toward her, and looked up, as if at some newfangled firecracker in the sky. The Platypus and Euphrates had entered, thirty feet behind her in the doorway onto the mezzanine. The White Suits pressed their ear buds deeper, waiting for commands. Euphrates's face flushed, a thermometer nearing bursting point. The Platypus restrained him with a limply raised hand. The room waited, all nerves standing on end, dead with anticipation.

"This is art manifest. He will save you all." The silence did not abate. "He is our next great artist. The savior of all art kind. He is the best artist I have ever…" She stared off at some infinite point in the distance, squinting with her prophetic words.

Punk, emerging from behind a bush, looked up at the stair-become-stage, saw the wild temple priestess, mad with divination, saw the ill-fated fool next to her, and began to laugh. At the kid's stupid face, mostly.

Then they all began to laugh. The murmur of jovial asides rose. Maybe it was a joke, maybe the open bar hadn't been such a good idea after all, maybe the guy was a robot; animatronic art was gaining in popularity. But mostly they laughed at wild, desperate Adelaide, and the goofy, grinning thing she was hysterically championing.

Euphrates seized the opportunity. "Grab him!" he shouted into his walkie-talkie. Immediately and from all directions, White Suits sprang on Nick, tackling him to the floor. They flipped him over, making a great show of subduing him, even though the only resistance he provided was covering his face with his hands and squealing girlishly. "I knew they would finally slip up." Euphrates. Knowingly to The Platypus. "Now we've got him."

"That's not Ollister, you fool." The Platypus. Calm in the storm. "That is." He pointed to the bottom of the staircase where Ollister had emerged and had quickly quieted the room with his composed and authoritative air.

Ollister blinked, and saw Adelaide as he had always seen her, as she had always been. He felt his surroundings, and his own self, peel away in layers. The ballroom and the guests and the art and the terrorists began to dissolve in the rain. It was like they were back in the cabin. In a chapter of the gray papers. It was like he was alone, and she was alone, and they were alone, simultaneously, together. Later it would feel like a scene observed, a static diorama, or a bullshit story three friends removed. He was not in this moment. He would have no recollection of it.

He stepped forward. His clear voice commanded the attention of all present.

"Wait. She speaks the truth." Ollister. His steadiness held the crowd silent. It was a direct contrast to Adelaide's histrionics. "I'm here, this is my doing. This man, this... He is my last work, my last gift to the art world. I will never pick up a brush again, the torch now belongs to him."

The crowd began to murmur. "Silence." Ollister. A demand met. "Art is his now. His art, not mine filtered through him. I have made you all. Paul, I sculpted your entire collection. Jolene, I got you a show, and told you what to put in it. Mr. Phrates, I told you exactly whom to buy and when, and probably made you, oh, about a million and a half in the last three years? That sound about right? Paolo, July, and Vivica, I wrote your artist statements. Virginia, I got you that grant. Zero, I procured your rather expensive materials." He paused, drawing breath into his chest. Loudly now: "I created you all! And you are all boring boring!"

The silence was more tense than ever. Ollister recomposed himself. Euphrates and his men started to walk cautiously toward the stairs, as if they were approaching a wounded animal. "Stop." Ollister. Raising his palm to them but directing his comment toward The Platypus. They obeyed. "My quarrel with you is finished. I'm done. I'm no good, our contest is finished. This world is yours." The Platypus peered down at him sadly, and flipped his wrist, causing The White Suits to let go of Nick and start to pound down the stairs aggressively. Ollister held his ground. Nick made a break for it, off the other side of the mezzanine. Suddenly Vance popped out from a potted plant and yelled, "Traitor!" pointing at Ollister, and also the escaping Nick. He held a detonator high in his right hand.

There was a loud explosion, and smoke enveloped the room, obscuring the scattered screaming of the panicked party gone bad.

OLLISTER & ADELAIDE

Later, on the lawn, in the rain, the gray papers in hand.

"Sorry, but I think I've changed my mind."

"What do you mean?"

"Physicality wouldn't serve it."

"…"

"It wouldn't do."

"I don't think I understand."

"I think you do. You would, if you thought about it."

"Stop. Stop this, Ollister. Don't do this."

"You were the one I made art for. About."

"It's not funny, Ollister. I don't like this one."

"You were the beheld. You'll go down in history as such. Graduate conference papers will begin 'Although Ollister later married multiple times, the only one who ever caught his full and rapacious imagination was Adelaide. And thus, I put forth the argument that whenever he was pressed to create, at whatever stage in his life, it was she who moved behind him…'"

"That isn't… supposed… I don't know. Don't be so dramatic. You have always been a thinker. So take time here, and think about it…"

"Thinking is not a thing that can undo itself. It can never be its own solution."

"This could be perfect."

"That's the problem. It has already been made so."

"It's not…"

"Stubborn. That's one of your many epithets that I find myself strangely fond of now."

"Don't be cruel."

"I'm not. I'm being bitter."

"You're being boring…"

THE END.

Appendices.

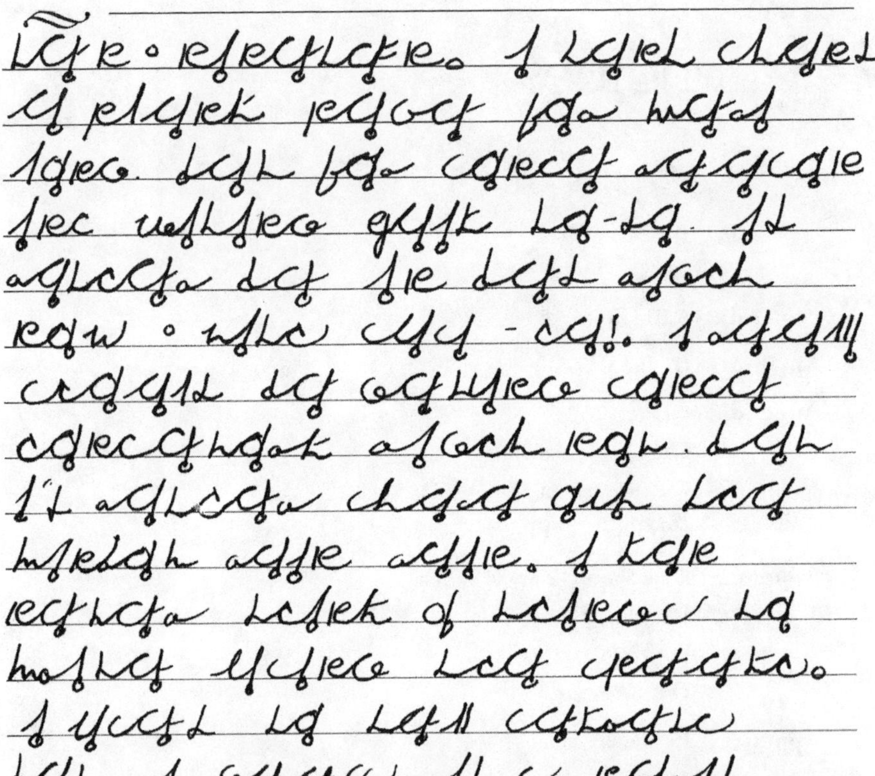

Appendix A. *The Town*

The town was small, or rather the city was small. Small for a city, large for a town. It felt bigger than it was, because of bungalow-sprawl and softly twisting hills that constantly obscured vantage points, changing the backdrop.

There was ample foliage, an arboretum, as some would call it. Simple homes, laid down in rows. There were stores, movie theaters, places to eat, a highway; it was, in almost every way, American. Unremarkable.

One of its few defining characteristics was its sense of its own character. The town thought something special of itself, infrastructure with ego. To be fair, it might've had slightly more artists than your average city of comparable size, or more people who thought of themselves as artists, at least. There was the school, The University of Fine Arts and Academia. There was an excessive numbers of galleries, studios for rent, painting classes, public sculpture, nude figure models, et cetera, in much the same way a roadside town that declares itself "Hot Dog Capital of the U.S.A." might have proportionally more postcards, magnets and T-shirts bearing the insignia of the hot dog. A civic had to take pride in something. Some people knew how this city felt, a few artsy scenesters in New York, or LA, or Miami were aware that this was a 'location,' something mentioned offhandedly, the next little art mecca maybe, and this only exacerbated the local over-inflated sense of place.

The denizens of this city said its name with their noses in the air. They said the name with a despicable lilt. They said the name and waited for the listener to ask "Really?" Or "Are you an artist?" or "Do you know so and so?"

It was insular, inward-looking, a big fish here was a big fish. The pond did not drain into the sea. This city had a strange pull over its inhabitants. A gravity. Even for those who escaped it, it always remained the first point of reference, the axis mundi. Kids went away to college, on years-old momentum, bottled up, talking about leaving, only to drop out and return a few months later. People traveled, took jobs or lovers in other cities, but always returned after a short absence. People died and they were talked about, for years afterwards, their ghosts kept fresh in the local watering holes.

This miniature art kingdom, isolated, and fenced in by a great wall of pretension was lorded over by another name. One that no one said much out loud. But one that everyone knew. This town belonged to The White Sodality. To 𝕿𝖍𝖊 𝕻𝖑𝖆𝖙𝖞𝖕𝖚𝖘.

Appendix B. *The School*

The University of Fine Arts and Academia, was its proper name. UNI-ARTS, everyone called it.

The school was set, as if by the hand of the god of railroad miniatures, on the highest hill on the edge of the West Side. It lorded over the town. It was sometimes hidden, obscured by lesser hills or trees. It was other times in full and picturesque view. All the buildings were brick, three stories, thin and useless windows, every side iced with sparkling green ivy. It was the Platonic ideal of itself. The way it looked down its nose, from its 100-year-old perch, a human couldn't help but feel inferior, petty, and fleeting.

UNI-ARTS owned the large swath of land that girded the hill. It was gated, black iron on all sides, the moat of grass was immense. Standing at the gates afforded a view of specks of people drifting from door to door, or out under the trees, eating lunch. This distance existed to confirm the school's reputation.

The building was designed to be nostalgia-inducing. Alumni felt it, certainly, but this aura was so convincing that parents who had never before visited the campus suddenly believed their precious goslings must attend the old alma mater. The dew sparkling on the surface of the green lake of grass and clinging to the trees gave the grounds an added dimension of mysticism, like a postmodern Avalon, hung in jewels.

The estate was of considerable size, and the winding road from the gates to the main building left plenty of time for anticipation. The parking lot was usually full of cars that were inadvisably expensive for teenage use. It was surrounded by sports fields: lacrosse, polo, an archery range. Not that any of the students played sports, or even pretended to. They were just there for show.

The dorm buildings were lower, but of the same brick, all turned toward the main in supplication. Most of the student body lived on campus, in these crumbling structures, which reeked of age and overcrowding. East Slope was the most nefarious of the dorms. Goldenplate Girls was the most expensive.

The main building itself was a work of art. Red brick. Black tile sloping roofs, long dirty windows, ancient oak doors. Its guts were smelly, and poorly lit. The common room was stocked with old torn leather sofas. Bookshelves with centuries of dust netting them. Various hideous artworks by supposed alumni. All of the walls and ceilings were intricately carved mahogany, the carpets so threadbare it was impossible to tell what color they were originally. There was a large fireplace, with small benches under its casing, long unused.

Most kids stuck to the low-ceilinged halls. Even if they weren't necessarily less musty and creepy than the bigger rooms, there were at least other kids in them. Thick doors with opaque little panes of glass led to various classrooms or studios, covered in paint and graffiti from years of messy, bored students. There were two larger lecture halls, with proper seats and fold-out desks, and a little stage with a podium from which various professors could bang on while languidly clicking through slides.

The administrative wing was nicer, or rather, better kept. All of the offices adjoined a large mosaic-tiled rotunda with a domed ceiling. In an architectural drawing there would be people milling about in the large open space, casually chatting, gesturing about nothing. But in reality no one lingered in the round hall. It was decidedly creepy, and paranoia and suspicion were not rare amongst the administrators, most being failed artists, or rich, or occasionally both. The secretaries disliked children, the janitors were monosyllabic, even the librarian, with a tight bun and glasses, fit the ideal.

New students could practically see the secret doors, smell the hidden tunnels. The place was crawling with them. The ones in the student wings had long ago been discovered by bored kids, who were in turn discovered by observant teachers, and then the passages were boarded up. Others were unused, completely forgotten.

The building was a living entity, an old sponge which had assimilated so many petty triumphs, bad ideas, boring boring students, wasted time and money, secret conversations, and smoke into its bricks that it had a Frankenstein life, artificially engendered, but palpable nonetheless.

When one heard the name UNI-ARTS, it was invariably the building itself that would first rise in the mind, before the students, before the town, before any experience had there. The building stood above them all.

Appendix C. *Pre-19*

CI. Ωllister, *at 16*

Ωllister was too cool to have parents. But he hadn't learned it all on his own. Most of it, sure. But just like anybody, Ωllister, too, had a teacher.

He had two, in fact. Both informal in their occurrence, but equally rigid in method, manners, and category of instruction.

The first was The Platypus. He was an intellectual in the ways that mattered. He had been expelled from academia for mysterious reasons and he landed as the Director of Academics at UNI-ARTS, a position he held while Ωllister attended the school. He was published in various books, journals, and languages all over the world. His mind was staunch and difficult. It tended to get in the way of his life, and if one wasn't careful, one's own life, as well. He was well-versed in mythology, geometry, the history of astronomy, philosophy, literature, theology, ancient history, exobiology, plate tectonics, meteorology, oenology, cartography, calligraphy, cryptozoology, symbology, astrology, astrobiology, mysticism, teratology, alchemy, and quantum physics. There were plenty of other fields that he was learned in, but so diametrically opposed to, that he would never want his name associated with them. Psychology chief amongst them.

Ωllister's other mentor was the Book Bum. The Book Bum's real name was Joe Biloxi but everyone called him the Book Bum, except for Ωllister, who called him Joe. He lived, or hung out, behind the huge used bookstore on the East Side. The store where people took their books to be sold, or traded in for others. More often than not, when someone brought a box of books in, the store would buy a number of them and refuse the rest. Most people didn't want to carry a box of unwanted books home and would leave them at the store, at which point the employees would just throw them in the dumpster. Actually, they didn't do that anymore, because the Book Bum would just fish them out again, and by now he was friendly with most of the younger employees, so they would leave them on his picnic table. One that he had dragged back there a few years ago. He would keep what he wanted and bury the rest in cardboard boxes. The reading available to the Book Bum was completely random. The only common thread between these books was that someone else didn't want them. Books from estate sales or closed library branches were the best. He could always tell when he got

252

a box of those. One time the posthumous bookshelves of a translator and scholar of ancient Chinese texts kept him going for six months. He learned to read Chinese from them. There were also dry spells. For a while all he had was an old encyclopedia set, except for volumes *Bundesstaat to (Lord) Chamberlain, Kinshasa to lime (chemistry), paranoia to Photorealism,* and *St Joseph of Arimathea to Technicolor.* He had the index volume. When the store closed for a month one winter, all he had was half of the romance section, cut during a remodeling. Most of these seemed to be written by the same idealistic yet bitter author. He got to know her extremely well that season.

The Book Bum had previously pushed around a cart with the books he intended to read. But no one had messed with his space of late. So now a basket on his old bike was all that was needed to contain those volumes that he found to be invaluable. There were very few of these, even though the Book Bum had read tens of thousands of books. More than 𝕿𝖍𝖊 𝕻latypus even. But he had more time. Ωllister often caught him napping behind the store, but the Book Bum went somewhere else to sleep at night. Ωllister had no idea where.

Between these two men, Ωllister learned an incredible amount. At sixteen, he was a voracious student, and with these expert guides through the world of knowledge, he quickly became very well read, and well rounded. Which was good, because he had dropped out of Uni-Arts not long after the incident with *Adelaide* at East Slope. Which also sundered him from 𝕿𝖍𝖊 𝕻latypus.

C2. *Adelaide, at 14*

She was a month 14 and discovering she had attractive wrists. How eyes would follow the trail of her hair. How promise and permission were a breadth apart.

She was a month 14 and a practiced smoker. Often when her mother was out of town her father would bum a smoke and try to cheer her up with jokes on the porch. He didn't smoke. And she wasn't sad. Her grades were good. Her friends were rich. She charmed older ladies with an eager brand of bright-eyed politeness. Their husbands squirmed in shiny shoes. She was destined to softly glide into a well-kept life.

She was a month 14 and her first parties revolved around heroin and blowjobs. She was in control. And good at it.

She was a month 14 and giving clothes and jewelry away to her friends. To make friends. Her mom would always take her on another shopping spree, where she would dispense endless business advice, and endless cash. *Adelaide* liked those pills when her mother took them, even more than she liked them when *she* took them.

She was a month 14 and her art was winning school prizes, recognition. Her photographs exposing the svelte underbelly of the Dean's Office politics. Already her parents would smirk bemusedly and affectionately at her creations. For seconds at a time.

She was a month 14 with bright green eyes stinging in the cold. Her cat dead in the wet street. No car in sight.

Constant perusal of teen fashion magazines meant not only that she was in style at school, but often set the style. All of the girls loved her, all of the girls hated her. She felt so desirable that she couldn't imagine ever desiring anyone herself.

She was a month 14 and in driver's education. An insipid class replete with gory videos, utterly lacking in humor. But they were necessary if she were to take possession of the glistening pink chariot that she had picked out two years ago. It waited, just as eagerly as she, under a dust cover, in her parents' second garage. Riding, piano, Latin, ballet, fencing, cross-stitch and voice lessons all had to be rescheduled.

She was a month 14 when a girlfriend told her what a dildo was.

She was a month 14 and had eaten only creamsicles and her mother's diet bars.

She was a month 14 and angry that her mother said she had to go to a finishing school. She was angry that her father insisted the public high school was the only socially conscientious thing to do. Angry because she would prefer to go to France. Her mother's dictum was the one followed.

She was a month 14 when she convinced the boy she was currently letting pose as her boyfriend to get a tattoo of her name, inside a ring of thorns, around his arm. When he returned to show his scabby boon, she dumped him and, along with all of her friends, laughed mercilessly at him for months. Five years later she would not have to convince another stand-in to get the same name tattooed, this time on a tombstone, on his forearm. It was almost as funny.

She was a month 14 and casually ordering subordinates around her mother's office. Water that plant. Take this stapler over there. Do that homework assignment.

She was a month 14 and sitting in a car with her best friend near the nature preserve, in the rain. They had been smoking pot and giggling for three hours. Now the car wouldn't start, and she felt trapped.

She was a month 14 and the princess of the local business cooperative Annual Good Cheer Parade.

She was a month 14 and she already knew that the end would come soon.

C3. PuNk, at 12

The years are much longer when less of them have accumulated. PuNk's twelfth year was not his worst but it was long. It hung around his body like a summer heat, reluctant to dissipate.

Shearwater County Day School, for Christian boys and girls, for wealthy boys and girls, did an altogether inaccurate job of disciplining and educating the young man. Many of his teachers had no idea there was supposed to be a twenty-fourth pupil in social studies class, or someone in the back row of seventh-grade algebra. Those that were aware he was missing sighed with relief and neglected to mark the absence down. They didn't want the administration to find him and drag him back to school.

Meanwhile, PuNk was wherever he felt like being...

He was riding his bike much faster than necessary along the asphalt catenaries of his upper class suburbia-hood. Throwing rocks through well-chosen windows along the way.

He was sitting in the plaza downtown under a tree with two derelict homeless men of Jamaican origin who were more than happy to buy him 6-packs of beer at $20 a pop, and who were thus also generous with their endless supply of marijuana.

He was getting his right hand put in a cast.

He was ranting and roaming at three in the morning outside of the house owned by the parents of his schoolgirl crush, picking the leaves off of every one of their bushes and piling them neatly on the doorstep.

He was beating up that red-haired kid in the park, squirting sunscreen in his eyes and testing the effects of a large rock to the skull.

He was up late masturbating timidly to a single coveted porno tape, procured from his best friend's father's extensive library. The girl that aroused the most fury in his hot new fist was not the screamer, nor the moaner, nor the writher, but the black-haired girl, with the dead eyes, who just sort of lay there and didn't do anything.

He was at the public pool, face covered in Fudgebomb, urinating in strategic underwater locations, snapping bikini bras, dunking toddlers.

He was getting stitches in his forehead.

He was sitting in his parents' three-story, mock-Tudor-château-ranch estate-home sneering at its clean white lines, and blindingly color-coordinated floral and botanical reproductions. Dragging his toes across the pristine carpets, using every bit of his strength to keep from spray-painting the empty walls.

He was waiting outside of a frat party, his bike stashed in the bushes, until the frat boys got to the point in their drunkenness where they would welcome him in with jeers, and chant strange initials in a masculine crescendo as he was hoisted to his first keg stand.

He was talking to a real-life, actual prostitute.

He was slowly backing his dad's car out of the garage, about to find out what it meant to really drive.

He was perfecting a double flip, with twist, off of the high dive.

He was backing terrified, yet thrilled, 12-year-old girls into corners at the point of his pocket knife and making them lift their shirts, whether they had any or not.

He was pressing his hands against his newly shaved head as his mother launched into one of her stock hysterias, fringe and diamonds flying everywhere. Ever since PuNk had become tall and gangly, and not small and cute, his mother's equivocating affections had been directed solely at the toy dogs. They had run of the house. They lounged in bubble baths, answered the phones, did their fussy business on gold toilet seat covers. The fits were now reserved for PuNk.

He was trying to get from his house to that of the girl he liked, solely by leaping from rooftop to rooftop, crawling across tree branches when necessary. He had made it halfway there and was staring at a canyonesque distance to the next awning.

He decided to change his name. To PuNk.

He was sitting on the curb in front of his best friend's house, their shaggy heads propped on bored elbows as they waited for the steaming stack of feces PuNk had recently deposited in the road to be run over. By a large truck, they hoped.

He was kicking ass at video games.

He was bounding through a moonless night, joyfully tearing down every strand of Christmas lights he could find.

He was wondering what it would like to be thirteen.

He was beating up his best friend. Because the kid was a pussy.

He was crying and crying face down on his bed because he wanted his fire to burn stuff down, but not half of the nature preserve. It was too big and scary.

He was shoving yet another pair of crapped-in skivvies into the back corner of his closet. He didn't know why that only ever happened to him.

He was flying down the biggest hill in his neighborhood, belly down on his skateboard, eyes stinging with wind and wonder.

He was looking at his father's face registering disinterest at his shivering figure on the doorstep flanked by two policemen. The groundskeeper of a local apartment building had caught him sleeping out on the pool deck at 4 AM. He was in the apartment office being interrogated by humorless cops when he decided to make a break for the door. He got up and ran right into a corner, stopped, turned around with eyes widened, and this time ran for the real door but was quickly tackled by the larger of the cops, the element of surprise no longer on his side.

He was stealing records from his best friend's older brother. The Clobbers, Fist and Tooth, The Spangers, Dirty McGee.

He was smashing the new guitar he got for Christmas because he couldn't play his favorite punk song. Smashing was more punk anyways.

He was thought responsible for every toilet-papering of medium quality or above in a five-mile radius, whether he was the responsible artist or not.

He was sick of using crutches.

He was doted on by a certain over-the-hill, coked-up biker barmaid who was happy to trade screwdrivers for large tips from an underager. Among the soft old lushes at the dank little dive he was a popular personality.

He was stealing more of his dad's argyle socks. He knew the old doctor objected, but he was much too busy, distracted, and besides a little afraid, to really say anything about it. He only had the child at his wife's request, and she could go to hell.

He was trying to eat the world alive. His grades suffered.

Appendix D. *A Short History of Terror*

D1. *Franc*

Franc grew up in the Parisian suburbs. His parents were well-to-do intellectuals. His father was a telescope engineer and his mother was a small-time celebrity in political theory circles. Her surreal, nihilistic approach to economics was made popular by her 1978 treatise on bartering in African prisons. This blazing comet proved to have a long tail indeed. She had more or less rested on its laurels since.

It was then, a curiosity, how their only child Franc, had turned out so utterly dull and clumsy. His cheeks were ruddy, his fingers were fat, and the word *déshonneur* did not begin to sum up his existence.

His mother's exorbitant fees for speaking engagements had sent him to the finest Parisian schools, and no small number of them. He was taunted and humiliated by the clever, richer, more poised boys, achieved very poor marks and was subsequently flunked, then expelled, again and again.

His parents decided, after many arguments during which his mother would noiselessly cry and his father would go out and study stars all night, to finally remit him to the public schooling system. Really, they were the only ones who would take him.

This proved a mistake. In public school, his size provided easy entry into the rougher crowd. He joined a gang, which was nationalist, if not political, in nature. Its main purpose was to combat the immigrant gangs that held sway over certain suburbs: Arab, Muslim, Pakistani, Hindu, African, Indian, other. He was white, a Gaul, and so were his brothers, and France rightfully belonged to the French, unpolluted. This was a point, unbeknownst to either party, on which he and his parents agreed.

He quickly rose to the top of this teenage organization via a reputation built on petty thievery, lynching, pranking, brutal initiation ritual, drug procurement, alleged rape, and police-car egging. Eventually, he was caught, implicated in a lawn-art and multi-car-garage arson by two fellow gang members who were nothing more than kids really, and scared shitless by an all night police slap-around session. He served 18 months in a Paris correctional institution. This was also a place he found success. His mother's near constant prattle about the finer points of cigarette- and sodomy-bargaining served him well.

He made particular friends with a French intellectual, of the same age and constitution as his dear old *mère* and *pepere*, who was in for white collar stuff; fraud, forgery, antique and fine art fakery. It was from this smelly old French man that he learned about the value of art.

Upon his release, a government work-assistance program landed him a job as a vintage scooter mechanic in Paris proper. He worked on scooters by day, and went out for trouble at night. But not the old sort, just boozing, carousing, bar fights and strip clubs.

When the little scooters suddenly became *le mode* in America, he was dragged to the states by a friend who had opened a shop there. Again, Franc found success, importing beaters from the old world, spraying them with high-gloss paint, and selling them at a disgusting mark-up to unwitting American fad-addled yuppies.

He became enamored of '70s era British punk rock. Picked up English, albeit with slightly outdated slang, rolled (French) cigarettes into his plain white T-shirts and cuffed his tight black pants, and stopped bathing.

Although the business went well, Franc found that another old world pastime was also easier in the new world: theft. The care that he needed in France to evade authority was unnecessary in this small, trusting, American town. He pulled off a few easy burglaries, and then he met PuNk.

D2. *Paul*

Paul had a penchant for things Mediterranean. He had spent seven years there as a boy. His father had been trying to breed a new species of grape that would produce a wine so delicate that it would not register on the taste buds at all. Invisible, odorless. As crop after crop failed to produce the grape that would turn wine into water, he increasingly turned to lesser, more tasteful wines to drown his defeat.

Meanwhile, Paul was busy drowning himself. On weekends, at various tourist beaches. He discovered that a floundering American too far out in the cresting waves would often be swept up in the bronzed arms of some curly-haired Poseidon masquerading as a lifeguard.

His sexual predilections eternally written in those soft sands, Paul had a more difficult time when shipped back to the States, to attend UNI-ARTS, where sand and sun were no longer his co-conspirators in seduction. Ωllißer was a friend made in a Classics class:

From Paganism to Christianity. The young instructor that taught the course was so passionate about his subject matter that he couldn't resist acting out entire scenes from *The Iliad*, complete with different lilting voices for each Greek or Trojan hero. He took advantage of his captive audience, none more captivated than a thin tan boy especially susceptible to the cult of the hero.

Paul was completely smitten. And rather desirable himself, even without taking into account his seemingly endless supply of ecstasy. No one could quite figure out where it all came from. But much of it clearly went to the instructor.

The affair was a predictably passionate one. They spoke Greek to each other. Latin during lovemaking. Trojan condoms, seemingly appropriate, were dismissed as unnecessary. The disease, after all, was love.

They were both obsessed with fine art, and it was during this time that Paul made a brief splash on the local art scene. Ωllister set it all up. He provided everything: the ideas, the materials, the money, the contacts, the gallery openings, the patrons. But the work, the work itself was perfection. Had Ωllister been bothered to lift a finger he could have scarcely produced such quality.

Giant marble busts. Acrolith cult statues, wood bodies with marble hands and heads. The first showing featured the heads of most of Paul's punk friends. The arching mohawks down to the painstaking piercings, mellowed by those empty statue eyes. They were widely regarded as actual works of art. They all sold. Save for the bust of Punk, bought for him by Ωllister, which ended up in a dumpster under a stream of its muse's urine.

His next show sold out, as well. Busts again, this time of famous socialite suicides, expressions captured at the moment of death. This led to a lucrative series of commissions, many from members of The White Sodality. Ωllister managed to secure a handsome cut of the profits.

After those trickled out, Ωllister and Paul didn't have much contact. Paul's beloved Greek instructor, studying late one night at the museum archives, accidentally impaled himself on a 2nd century spear he was "examining" and, unable to move, bled to death. The Platypus, under the direction of The White Sodality, had covered up the whole thing. Paul disappeared completely after that.

D3. *Sebastian*

Sebastian was a born ringleader, a ringmaster, a cabaret barker. He knew the true nature of fun; decadent, subversive, and perverse. Those who were around him couldn't help feeling like they were being led through a funhouse, a house of coke mirrors, by some mad hatter, a piper not pied, but clad in black.

He pretended to come from Karlsruhe, a small town in Germany. It was located near the French-German border, in the south. Nothing much happened there. It was cold a lot of the time. Kids would gather in sweaty underground warehouse basements. To listen to hardcore industrial music, and splash beer all over each other. He spoke of it fondly and often. He was actually from Utah.

His preteen years were spent fucking older rich men, taking their money, acquiring their tastes. He had an elaborate system of alibis and witnesses that allowed him to escape most of his schooling while he tooled around on four-wheelers wearing cowboy boots, ass naked to the world.

When he was about 14 he moved to Berlin, where he quickly became a popular figure on many fronts. In the club scene, for his superb and eclectic DJing. With the gay crowd, for his poise, dignity, and unrelenting promiscuity. On the fashion scene, he was always in all black, which was not new, but the different colored paperclips pinned on his collar had become wildly popular, some sort of occultish fad.

He was always well received by the art crowd, though the reason was never certain. He went around to other people's shows and loudly made fun of whatever they happened to hang on the walls. If he came to a show without doing this, it was the high watermark of critical praise. Better than any review any art critic could give. Everyone talked about it for months afterwards, in no small part because it almost never happened.

He was also known for elaborate stunts. Organizing a gaggle of prostitutes for a day trip to the retirement home. Slicking down miles of sidewalk with petroleum jelly. Urinating from high-rise windows. Faking his death, faking his friends' deaths, faking his pets' deaths. Purchasing every hamburger in an American-owned fast-food chain in Germany and mailing them all individually back to the States. Renting a dump truck to dump a full load of ice into a local public pool. Initiating a monthly pub crawl for him and twenty-five select friends, on horseback. These sorts of things.

He published a scathing memoir-cum-absurdist philosophy-critique-self-help book entitled "Bohemian Body, Bourgeois Mind." It made a modest splash.

He converted to Judaism, and used that to rub against his fake German heritage in ways that made most people very uncomfortable.

He often appeared in the German press, in *Nouveau* magazine, or others devoted to celebrities or society. There would be a picture of him, all in black, soaked by the rain, his hand flipped up in some ridiculous gesture. "Berlin's Black Cat, Sebastian Schlingensief, was seen hailing an ambulance on Oranienburger Str. late last Friday night." All of the newspapers latched on when he offered a free boiled egg to anyone who appeared naked on the corner of Oranienburger and Friedrichstraße at 7:24 AM one morning. 2,400 people came. He had enough eggs.

Just when he could do no wrong, the tide of public and private opinion turned against him. He was caught in bed with a pop starlet of the female gender, and of the naïve sort. This fact was widely disseminated. And while many of his more ridiculous exploits had been talked about endlessly, this one didn't sit well with the gossip circles. He thought it was funny. No one else seemed to. Maybe it was the heterosexual thing. Or the stooping to the pop culture level. People were disappointed. For them, his persona had fallen apart. He was disgraced, embarrassed, and unable to handle his new status as topic of malicious gossip, rather than mirthful gossip.

One night, on a particularly brutal cocaine and crying binge, not sure if he had imagined the whole thing, he packed all of his bags, and bought a one-way ticket back to the U.S. A friend there went to an interesting art school called UNI-ARTS.

Appendix E. *The Beeramid*

A Beeramid is a pyramid made from empty beer cans. The word is a portmanteau of *beer* and *pyramid*. Calling it a 'beer can pyramid,' or 'beer tower' is not nearly as clever.

As a party wears on past the point of true fun, a Beeramid can be constructed from empty beer cans. Bottles or plastic cups are a poor substitute. The true Beeramid is made of cans.

The best way to dispose of a Beeramid is accidental destruction. If this hasn't occured, leaping through the Beeramid, or shooting it piecemeal with a BB gun is also acceptable.

Appendix Z. *Zella*

Z1. *Zella*'s most successful piece to date was a harebrained idea she stole off some friend. Something about carrying a bowling ball around everywhere she went and her friend taking all of these pictures of her. With the bowling ball. In random places. It was uninspired.

Uninspiring was the theme of all of *Zella*'s art. *Adelaide* had met her their first year of Uni-Arts. *Zella* liked art because it was the subject that made school most like kindergarten. Cutting. Pasting. Mom and Dad footing the bill.

Zella came up with her art by asking everyone who stepped within range for ideas. She would then take these ideas and ask everyone else if they were any good. Majority won.

Random, but usually amusing, *Zella* seemingly had infinite reserves of energy, and although she aspired to art, this interest was more of an excuse for hanging out, scamming out and getting fucked up with the in-crowd. An explosion of personality and other things besides, none of her spunk could be harnessed into ventures that were truly productive. She would bang on for hours about the fame and money that would surely soon be hers. Waiting around to be discovered. Dressing like The Fashion Network cameras were around the corner.

Adelaide could never quite figure out if *Zella* really knew that it didn't work that way or if the ignorant bliss was more conducive to her fun-making. She was good at fun. Drinking, smoking, cussing, spitting. She was forthright and aggressive in opinion, yet had a way of making people feel in her confidence immediately. She had many friends, and many of those loved her, *Adelaide* not least among them.

Z2. *Zella* was wearing a neon orange plastic tube skirt with an over-sized red and blue lumberjack flannel, wooden beads, Christmas earrings, and a tiara.

Or a mesh tank top over two bras: one black, one white, shiny parachute pants, sequined high heels, a rainbow scarf with clown faces knitted on it, hoop earrings, a black plastic headband, and a giant candy ring.

Or a vintage kimono, orange plastic waterwings, a black tube top, elbow-length gloves, a flowered scrunchie, large fake ruby earrings, fishnets, camouflage cargo shorts, a necklace with a tea saucer hanging from it, thigh-high leopard-print wrestling boots, a fedora with a peacock feather over a baseball cap on backwards over a do-rag, designer men's sunglasses with no lenses, four watches, headphones, and crotchless panties.

Appendix F. *A Midsummer Night's Longueur*

Miriam's dream, in her own words: "It was like, almost another planet. I was at this resort place, like an island, with a beach, but indoors. There was like this huge glass dome over us and there were all of these guys on jet skis, jumping off ramps that were, like, built for that... purpose, or whatever, and I was in there with my dad and like there was this bulge in the back of his Hawaiian shirt, like a lump, you know? I was touching it and telling him he needed to have it removed, it was like soft and distended, and a weird color, like an old soft peach, and then, like I don't know how I got in there, but it was like this sauna sort of room, it was big and circular, and all of the walls were made of aquariums, or rather they were aquariums, but you know, like all around, but they were dirty, and it was hard to see inside them, and they had a little sign up, like those signs at zoos that tell you what the heck sort of animal is supposed to be inside the little cage or whatever? But the sign was for a mountain lion, and like six different species of birds, and the sign had a name, for like, a grouping of those particular kinds of birds, it was like Raahh-something, began with an R, but there was nothing in the tanks yet, the fish tanks, isn't that weird? The rest of the room had all of these people in it, like tourists, and they were sitting on these things in a circle around the edge of the room, like almost against the fish tanks. They were like little thrones, or toilets, they were more like toilets, and everyone who was on one was naked, and these seats had like rubber rims, that created a seal with your tushy, like a suction, and everyone on them was really enjoying themselves, like it was a spa treatment or something, a suction enema, like a pleasure ride, they were all oohhhing and aahhhing, and there was this weird voice-over, like over a P.A. system, being pumped into the room and it was the voice that's on like television commercials for chocolate, you know those ones where there is chocolate drizzling everywhere, and almonds dropping from the sky, and a voice going 'Induuhlge,' and nougat stretching and stuff, and I got on one of the thingies, because, you know, that's what you were supposed to do, and when I was on it, I mean, I don't remember it doing anything in particular to my tushy, but I noticed that my chair was right next to this vat in the ground, like the size of a whirlpool, like the ones the Klines have, you know? And I was staring at it, the surface of the water was all, like, covered in white foam, but it was active, I mean it was moving, like gurgling, or bubbling or whatever, like a hot tub, and so the foam that was on the surface kept breaking up, or cracking, and under the foam I could see this... this... poo-water, that was basically like all of the poo, from all of the people in the room, there were all of these tubes connected to it, along the ceiling, and it was like a big soupy vat of poo, and I kept seeing the color of it through the breaks in the white foam, which I somehow knew that they had just placed there to cover up the poop pool, and it was making me sick, like vomitrocious, but then my dad came in, and I was still talking to him, naked, and it wasn't weird or anything, but it kind of was, isn't that weird? Anyways, he had those things they removed from his back wrapped in a paper towel, and he gave them to me, and they were so weird, at first it looked like a tailbone or a part of a spine or something, and then they uncurled right there in the paper towel, and then there were lots of them, and they were flying all around, they were like a cross between a bird, and a mouse, and, you know how in drawings for children or whatever, they draw those really fat little airplanes, and they were flying all over the room, glowing kind of menacingly, real weird, and I was getting scared and so were a lot of other people on those… poo-thingies, and then one bit my arm, and it really hurt, it had like seven little triangle teeth in a round mouth, it had a round mouth, I can remember exactly what the bite looked like, it was right here on my arm, but then like some zoo official-type caught it and put it back in this little cage shoebox thing, and I was at a zoo then, and we moved over to the dolphins, you and me, or it was supposed to be the seal pen, you know where they all splash up on that rock in the middle? The seals, I mean, because the dolphins wouldn't come out, there was some cave, or cove, or whatever thing at the bottom of the pool, and we could see them in there, but they wouldn't come out, so we moved on to the next pen, which was more like a desert setting, and in it there were these snakes, but like, with bobcat heads, they were almost like Chinese dragons, but good, not evil, you know? And in their pen they were hunting miniature foxes, and I watched one catch a fox and eat it, and you thought it was cool, and I was pretending to be grossed out and burying my face in your shoulder, your shirt was this really light billowy material, like a pirate shirt, I remember, but really I thought it was cool, too, the bobcat-snake eating the fox, and the whole time that song, that oldie that goes 'you got to change your evil ways… baby…' you know the one I mean? Anyways, it was playing in the background like the whole time, isn't that weird to have a song in a dream? And then I wanted to go because we were like, aware that the snake was going to poop the miniature fox right back out real soon, and I really didn't want to see that part, but to get out I had to crawl through this system of tunnels, like really long, curvy, organic type tunnels, and it was kind of dark in there, but not really, the walls were like pink and soft, almost as like, a protection, you know, like in a rubber room? And there were all these bums strewn around through the tunnel, wrapped in brown rags, just like sleeping on the ground or whatever, and I couldn't see their faces, but I was scared that they were watching me, still, it didn't feel safe in there and I didn't know how long it was till the end, and it was getting smaller, but brighter, and I was crawling on my hands and knees, till I came to this like open room, that had a tree in it, and there was my dad, but not my dad, you know? And it was a kitchen, not unlike my dad's kitchen, and there was a huge, I mean, like trunk-sized, box of plastic forks, and some people and I were standing around idly commenting on it. It cost fifty dollars. A lot of forks. And then someone was like 'the girls are here!' and this parade of girls came through the door, it was all the Cheerbleaters from UNI-ARTS. Anyways, at the end of the line were you and Dolores, and we went into the adjoining breakfast room, and I hugged you both, and Dolores said that the two of you had just smoked a joint in the back of the van, and I could tell you were stoned. Silas was there, sitting on the floor. He was black, and balding, and he wasn't really talking but mumbled when he did speak. We all got plates of food, and then I had to go to another Fourth of July party. I set out walking across these fields at night, eating ribs leftover from my plate of food. I wanted to bring you up to my roof for the fireworks but it seemed like it would make Silas jealous. I passed an animal shelter that was closed for the holiday, which I thought was inadvisable, cause dogs always get spooked on the Fourth. I came up on the side of your aunt's house. And Dolores was using a mechanical buffer to clean some black gunk off the front of her Goldtoothwa DVD. I'm sure she doesn't even like Goldtoothwa that much. But she, like, nodded me inside, and I went inside, and my dad was there, and he was English, and some sort of butcher or shopkeeper, but still the Dean, and I was aware of all these like, cow-like animals moving around in the room behind him, doing disgusting things, and I asked him for my pea-coat, you know the crimson one? Like, to buy, but he only had one, and it's black and an extra large, and it folded out into an umbrella with a handle, so I didn't want that one, and he said I'll have to wait while he goes out to his car to get one that fits, so he left, but I followed him and we were in this car lot, like a car sales place, what is that called? Oh yeah, a car dealership. And we were looking for a new car for me, and there was this one with the dash all covered in different lights and buttons, like the inside of a UFO or something, and I liked that one, but we also had to go look at this neighbor's jeep, some black guy that Dolores was in love with for a while, I drove that one around, and he was like, in there with me, and was trying to ask me to come to some kind of fetish party, but his dog-cat-thing in the backseat was making too much noise and we were like, on the freeway? And so I was pretending that I couldn't hear him, and turned around real quick and went back to my house, and my dad was outside and he was wearing this really cool Hawaiian shirt, it, like, extended into this diaper part at the bottom, he was talking about putting a pool in our front yard, we were out there because some truck had been there to deliver me all these like packaged Chinese toys, you know, the really cheap ones? Anyways the truck had made this huge hole in the yard with one of its wheels and my dad was thinking, like, why not dig it out and put in a pool in the front and screw the neighborhood association and stuff, but the shirt thing, it was amazing, I know it sounds retarded, but the diaper part was so cool. I want to open my own fashion boutique. Wouldn't that be so cool?"

Appendix G. *A Particular night, well advanced.*

12:24 AM. A particular night, well advanced, slipping from grasps.

Nick was practicing spray painting again. His debut would have to be spectacular and he was still at the nascent blob stage. The last five hours, in his sealed-off room had been spent with reds, blacks, silvers. He was incredibly high on paint fumes, and just beginning to penetrate the centuries-old mysteries of the high art of graffiti.

Ωllister was sitting at a strange girl's dressing table. Smoking, or not. The mirror in front of him balanced his darkened face and her disheveled heap in the bed behind him, trepidations within its frame.

"I love you." He said softly, looking deep into the silvered back of the glass.

"I know we just met, but I feel the same…" The girl. Gushing.

"I wasn't talking to you." Came the reply.

Isadora, sleep having eluded her, floated angrily from room to room to gather all of the silver in the house. To send to the polisher. Or to throw away.

Silas was carefully inspecting his genitals. He had manipulated himself to the point of blister. Whether or not this fact should stop his current encounter with himself was up for internal debate.

Sebastian was in attendance at some smoky artist's reception for a friend of a friend who was displaying 'Gay Business Art.' He had snuck into the coatroom and was urinating on every single coat. Most were damp from the rain anyway, but he knew he could count on the smell.

Franc was down to half a bottle of Scotch and horizontal on the couch. Imagining his geometry teacher naked.

The Platypus was sleeping like a great bear. Dreaming of a great bear mounting another great bear. By a tepid river. Against a smattering of stars, spinning into galaxies.

Miriam was crying.

Dolores was crying. But louder.

PuNk was once again in the swankiest club in town. In the V.I.P. room. Where he was well liked, and well received. All of these rich fucks clearly thought his dress and manner was an affectation, and a terribly clever one at that. The bouncer always waved him past the bored and freezing lines to gingerly unclip the velvet rope for his passing. He and Glen, a pool-table tycoon from Sweden with a communal attitude toward coke, were telling Jim, a bespectacled space-weather forecaster specializing in radiation storms and asteroid warnings, about some dumb fashionista blonde that had caught them doing mega-bumps in the lady's lavender washroom. She was young, clearly new on this scene, and bent on reporting what she had witnessed to the club owners. This wouldn't have mattered. But they knocked her out on principle, PuNk ripping the soap dispenser off the wall, and proceeded to shove her in a stall and toilet-paper her. Like a tree. Like a mummy. Like a childhood enemies' parents' house. They laughed as loudly as they could, so that the gods might hear. Jim was eager to see this sight himself and the three rose in unison, prepared to laugh again.

Pete was drawing up plans on his circuitry software for a robot child. It was as simple as that, he thought, as he wiped mud from his desk.

Adelaide lay in bed with her novel. Page 253 and she still couldn't tell if all of the women "friends" in it were sapphic or just sappy.

Paul was in the bunker again, waiting. He turned all of the cans of tomato paste so their labels faced north.

12:24 AM. The rain started again.

appearing at

Concordance.

zach plague

THANK YOU:

Ryan, *Andrea,* SETH, Sam, Jonny Mess, *Mary,* Pete

AND THANKS:

Ambrose, Cokie Ferrelli, *Mom and Pop,* Molly,
Jason, David, SLEIGHT-WEIGHT DWAYNE, *Kate,*
Mark, JONATHAN M., Stefan, Samia, **Todd,** John,
Bobby, **JAY,** JESSE, James, *Nathan & ANNA,* Steve

AND LOVE

Allison

BIG PHOTO by ANNA
LITTLE PHOTO by LAUREN
POSTER by DIRK

featherproof BOOKSTORE

this is a CATALOG

featherproof books is an indie publisher based in Chicago, dedicated to the small-press ideals of finding fresh, urban voices. Our catalog features two categories of work: full-length, perfect-bound books like the one you hold in your hands, and downloadable mini-books available through **featherproof.com**. Our mini-books are individually designed short stories that can be downloaded for free and printed and assembled with ease. You can also order our books through our site at a friendly discount.

featherproof
light reading series

Life Sentence
by Ambrose Austin

December 26th, 2004
by Brian Costello

Max and Emily
by Kate Axelrod

Donovan's Closet
by Elizabeth Crane

So Little Impression
by Kyle Beachy

My Father's Hands
by Mary Cross

Every Night is Bluegrass Night
by Tobias Carroll

Grandpa's Brag Book
by Todd Dills

The Feast of Saint Eichatadt
by Pete Coco

All My Homes
by Paul Fattaruso

Shooting Music
by Jeb Gleason-Allured

 Slave-making Ants
by Anne Elizabeth Moore

 M is for
My Hair
by Abby Glowgower

 A Fourth of
July Party
by Kerri Mullen

 Anniversary
by Laura Bramon Good

 Sunday Morning
by Susan Petrone

 Women/Girls
by Amelia Gray

 In the Dream,
by Jay Ponteri

 Flash
Flicker Fire
by Mary Hamilton

 The Camp
Psychic
by Kevin Sampsell

 This Is
by Andrea Johnson

 And if I Kiss You
in the Garden...
by Fred Sasaki

 Witch of
the Bayou
by Rana Kelly

 The Lovers
of Vertigo
by Timothy Schaffert

 Our Pilgrimage
to Dollywood
by Heidi Laus

 Flat Mindy
by Patrick Somerville

 101 Reasons
Not to Have
Children
by Ryan Markel

 The Nightman
by Zach Stage

 Eight Permutations
of the Binoculars
of Power
by Jonathan Messinger

 Letter from
the Seaway
by Scott Stealey

featherproof BOOKSTORE

the ENCHANTERS VS. Sprawlburg Springs

a novel by
Brian Costello

The Enchanters vs. Sprawlburg Springs is a satirical, riotous story of a band trapped in suburbia and bent on changing the world. A frenzied "scene" whips up around them as they gain popularity, and the band members begin thinking big. It's a hilarious, crazy send-up of self-destructive musicians written in a prose filled with more music than anything on the radio today.

SONS OF THE RAPTURE

a novel by
TODD DILLS

Billy Jones and his dad have a score to settle. Up in Chicago, Billy drowns his past in booze. In South Carolina, his father saddles up for a drive to reclaim him. Caught in this perfect storm is a ragged assortment of savants: shape-shifting doctor, despairingly bisexual bombshell, tiara-crowned trumpeter, zombie senator.

degrees of separation

Edited by Samia Saleem

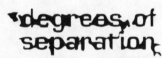

Degrees of Separation features 33 detachable postcards from graphic designers with ties to New Orleans. Each one articulates their experiences and reflections upon Hurricane Katrina. This limited edition volume comes wrapped in a gorgeous customized sleeve.

HIDING OUT

decoys by jonathan messinger

Nothing is as it seems: A jilted lover dons robot armor to win back the heart of an ex-girlfriend; an angel loots the home of a single father; a teenager finds the key to everlasting life in a video game. In this much-anticipated debut, one of Chicago's most exciting young writers has crafted playful and empathic tales of misguided lonely hearts. Sparkling with humor and showcasing an array of styles, *Hiding Out* features characters dodging consequences while trying desperately to connect.

by Susannah Felts

At the beginning of a lonely summer, 16-year-old Vaughn Vance meets Sophie Birch, and the two forge an instant and volatile alliance at Nashville's neglected Dragon Park. But when Vaughn takes up photography, she trains her lens on Sophie, and their bond dissolves as quickly as it came into focus. Felts keenly illuminates the pitfalls of coming of age as an artist, the slippery nature of identity, and the clash of class in the New South. *This Will Go Down on Your Permanent Record* is a sparkling and probing debut novel from a rising literary star.

featherproof BOOKSTORE

boring boring boring boring boring boring boring is a mulit-platform, multi-modal, cross-bred work of art. That's art school-talk for "available in different formats." We guarantee that if you are bored by one version of the book, you'll be equally bored by any of the following:

1 *THE PERFECT-BOUND VERSION* (which you are ostensibly holding right now): 288 pages to be read straight-through, just like a novel. *boring boring boring boring boring boring boring* is a hybrid typo/graphic novel, where font, format, and design converge to create new layers of meaning beyond the text. And what's all that stuff poking in on the pages? Well, to understand its larger architecture, jump to **5. The Poster Version.**

2 *THE E-BOOK*: Downloadable at *featherproof.com* as a pdf file. Read the book on your newfangled contraption. We're not sure we understand it, but it is free. And everyone likes free.

3 *THE AUDIO VERSION:* This won't be the full boring book, read to you long and slow. Instead, it's packed with only the most explosive bits of the book read by the strangest voices we could find. Digital or CD format, from **Flameshovel Records**.

4 *THE WEBSITE:* A dynamic, serialized version of the book, including a downloadable mini-version, all for free at *zachplague.com*. Because we just didn't think there was enough stuff on the Internet.

5 ***THE POSTER VERSION:*** Nine double-sided, over-sized posters, containing the entire text of the story. ***boring boring boring boring boring boring boring*** was printed on large sheets called signatures, which contain 32 pages before they're trimmed to fit between the covers. So this book is designed at signature size, creating posters for the wallpapering of your bathroom or street corner. The graphic elements in the book coalesce on the posters to create nine cohesive works of art.

g *boring* boring b

ng boring *boring* bor

ring boring boring borir